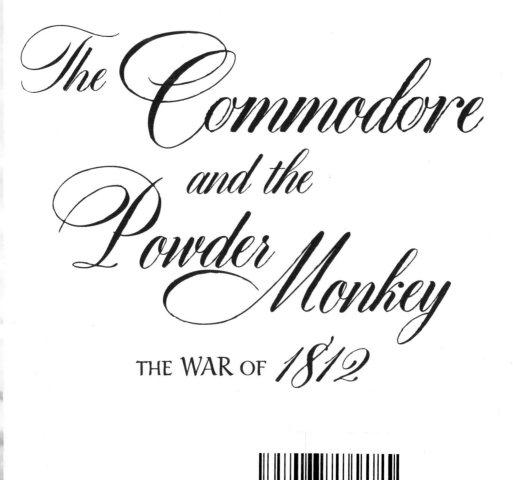

The Commodore and the Powder Monkey

THE WAR OF 1812

D1104137

A NOVEL BY MARK BARIE

Barringer Publishing, Naples, Florida
www.barringerpublishing.com
Cover, graphics, layout design by Linda S. Duider

ISBN: 978-1-954396-18-0

Library of Congress Cataloging-in-Publication Data
The Commodore and the Powder Monkey / Mark Barie
Printed in U.S.A.

This is a work of fiction. All characters, organizations, and events portrayed in this novel are either products of the author's imagination or are used fictitiously.

Other Books by the Author

Other novels by Mark Barie,
available at Amazon.com include:

"War Calls, Love Cries"

"Sister Marguerite and the Captain"

Barie has also authored or co-authored several local
(upstate New York) history books, all available at
Amazon.com. They include:

"Crossing the Line"

"The President of Plattsburg"

"The Boat People of Champlain"

The author can be reached at:
authormarkbarie@gmail.com.

DEDICATION

To my mom, whose passion for reading I inherited.

ACKNOWLEDGMENTS

This missive, on the War of 1812, is very special for a number of reasons. The action takes place in Plattsburgh, New York, the place of my birth and area in which I was raised.

But for my wife, Christine, this book might not have been written at all. It was she, who discovered and documented the active role of my fourth great grandfather, during the War of 1812. Julian Belonge, a private in the New York Militia, fought at the Battle of Plattsburgh.

And finally, I thank and acknowledge my family plus the countless friends, readers, and cheerleaders, who celebrate with me, this, the final installment, in my trilogy on love and war.

No author has been as fortunate, or more grateful, than yours truly.

TABLE OF CONTENTS

Historical Notes. 1

Chapter One 3
Charlie's Birthday

Chapter Two 17
The Widow Wheeler

Chapter Three. 41
One More Run

Chapter Four 55
Reuben Quimby

Chapter Five 75
On Her Own

Chapter Six 93
War

Chapter Seven. 110
The *Vermont*

Chapter Eight 126
The United States Navy

Chapter Nine 158
   Tensions

Chapter Ten 190
   The Trial

Chapter Eleven 220
   On the Run

Chapter Twelve 246
   Preparations

Chapter Thirteen 274
   Surprise Moves

Chapter Fourteen 304
   The Battle of Plattsburgh

HISTORICAL NOTES

- Commodore McDonough utilized more than 800 sailors during the Battle of Plattsburgh. It is certain that he employed "powder monkeys." The ideal candidates for this job were boys between the ages of 14 and 18, small of stature, and fleet of foot. The idea that a girl, pretending to be a boy, would be approved for service in the Navy as a powder monkey, is not only possible, it is quite likely. McDonough's hand written reports listed two boys as having been killed and one, wounded, in the Battle of Plattsburgh. In addition, the commodore, desperate for all the sailors he could recruit, proselytized from the Army, the local jail, and as far south as Albany. He also had two women on board the *Saratoga*–the wife of the ship's cook and a lady named Phoebe Joe. Little is known about either woman except that they did not ask for McDonough's permission to serve on the ship. They simply informed the commodore and he did not object. Some would say, wisely.

- The *Vermont* steamship was launched in June of 1809. In the book, I have the *Vermont,* on the lake, in the spring of 1809.

- In 1802, the name of Isle LaMotte was changed to Vineyard. In 1830, the name was changed to Isle LaMotte, once again.

- Constable William Blanchard is not a made-up character, having served as Isle LaMotte's first constable.

- I have collapsed the date of McDonough's arrival in Plattsburgh with the departure date of the Army troops leaving for Sacket's Harbor.

- McDonough's requirement for a surgeon's mate, was reduced to writing in May, 1813. In the book, it is described as having occurred in March 1813.

- Kai's character is based loosely on the character, Aze, in Charles G. Muller's book, *The Proudest Day*.

- The execution of the three soldiers in Plattsburgh in early May, 1814 is shown in the book as having occurred at the end of May.

Chapter One

CHARLIE'S BIRTHDAY

The scream of a newborn infant catapulted Benjamin Wheeler to his feet.

Mrs. Wheeler's painful labor, lasting for most of the night, came to a sudden end. He thanked God for sending Doctor Roebach, in Elizabeth's time of need. Ben rushed forward when the doctor emerged from the couple's bed chamber. Roebach held a tiny bundle wrapped in a cocoon of blue-checkered cotton. He spoke in a terse and businesslike manner.

"Benjamin, hold her please. We're not finished."

Ben gawked at the pink face in his arms.

"A girl?"

The doctor ignored Ben's query and returned to his patient. The baby squirmed and fidgeted. Benjamin chuckled when the child reached for her father's little finger and squeezed. He told his daughter their first secret.

"Your momma insists on calling you Charlotte Elizabeth Wheeler. But, as far as I'm concerned, your name is "Charlie."

An ear-splitting scream filled the room. The infant jerked in her father's arms and started crying. Ben ran to his wife's bedside. His knees buckled. The bed covers, beneath Elizabeth's writhing body, oozed crimson-red blood. Her face twisted in agony. Dr. Roebach, beads of sweat on his forehead, used both hands to push on a bloody rag, positioned between the woman's legs. Her face, void of color, dripped with perspiration. Her eyes, blood shot and swollen, revealed the pain of her hours-long labor. Ben yelled over the infant's cries.

"Dr. Roebach, what's wrong?"

"She has yet to expel the afterbirth."

Benjamin knew enough about cows and sheep to understand the gravity of Roebach's pronouncement.

"I'll be back as soon as I can," said Wheeler.

He wrapped the infant girl in two more blankets and ran to the barn. While Charlie cried, Ben saddled the mare. A boarding house, less than a mile down the road, leased rooms to several women. The infant would stay with one of them, for at least the day.

Several minutes of banging prompted the proprietor to open the door. Ben, with a screaming baby in his hands, and arriving there in the middle of the night, did not have to explain. In minutes, with the mare at a full gallop, Benjamin returned to his ailing wife.

Dr. Roebach opened the door. He motioned to the table and collapsed in a chair. Ben followed the doctor but remained standing. His eyes darted to the burlap curtain that served as a wall, in their one room cabin.

"Is she sleeping?" Ben asked.

But he knew the answer to his question.

The doctor closed his eyes and murmured his response.

"I'm sorry, Ben. There was nothing more I could do."

Benjamin stepped back, as if Roebach suffered from a highly

contagious disease. With the closed door to his back, he slid to a seated position on the wooden floor. For a moment, his blank stare and unblinking eyes camouflaged the man's reaction. He caught his drooping head with two large and calloused hands. Ben's chest heaved. He struggled to breath. His head jerked up. The man's tear-filled eyes focused on the curtain-turned-shroud, which hid his dead wife.

And then he wept.

Today marked Charlie's twelfth birthday.

She woke to the sound of her stepmother's scratchy voice.

"You've got chores to do. Get moving."

Charlie lingered in her bed, surveying familiar surroundings. Her loft-bedroom afforded a measure of privacy, if there could be such a thing, in a sixteen by sixteen, one room, log cabin. Moss and dried clay filled the cracks between each log. The natural caulking, designed to keep the rain and bugs at bay, did not always work. Down below, a curtain made from a dozen burlap sacks, created a small chamber where a husband and wife could spend their nights. A fireplace for cooking and heating plus the requisite hand-made rocker, made the home livable. A few wooden chairs and a crude table, made smooth by years of use, occupied the remaining space. Charlie enjoyed her modest existence. She did not enjoy Harriet.

The girl required seconds to cover her night shirt with a well-worn, second garment. In less than a moment, she slid into her trousers. Charlie hesitated as she stepped on the top rung of the short ladder which accessed her loft. She flashed a smirk in the direction of Harriet's back and then jumped. Her leap to the rough-hewn, wooden floor below, irritated Charlie's stepmother.

But then, everything the girl did irritated that woman. Harriet growled.

"I told you not to do that anymore."

"Sorry ma'am," said Charlie, reaching for a slice of freshly baked bread.

Harriet slapped Charlie's outstretched hand.

"Go feed the chickens. And if you break another egg, like you did yesterday, I will instruct your father to whoop you good."

Charlie scurried out the door, unperturbed by Harriet's cold-hearted behavior. As far back as the girl could remember, the bitter woman despised Charlie. She wondered if Harriet's sour disposition derived from the woman's inability to have children. It didn't matter. Benjamin Wheeler would never lay a hand on his only daughter. The girl happily clucked at the chickens as she tossed handfuls of dried corn and retrieved a half dozen eggs. A voice behind her, interrupted Charlie's stream of thoughts.

"You forgot one."

Charlie swiveled in the direction of her father's voice.

"Harriet said if I break one more egg, you're gonna give me a whoopin."

Her voice, more of a taunt then a complaint, achieved its desired effect.

Her father's eyes narrowed, and a devilish grin crossed his face. He retrieved an egg laying in the hay and tossed it high in the air. Charlie considered this a direct challenge to her athletic prowess. She focused on the brown spot against a sky of blue, and made a spectacular diving catch, using both hands. But the egg did not survive the impact of her fall and Charlie's fingers dripped with yellow goo and pieces of brown eggshell.

"Prepare yourself for a whoopin," Benjamin yelled.

Charlie squealed and scampered into the barn, her father in hot pursuit. He searched the dark interior of the shed for his "victim" and noticed a rustling of loose hay in the far corner. Benjamin leapt in the direction of the movement. Soon father and daughter rollicked in the hay. Charlie screamed. Her father laughed. When they came up for air, he clasped his daughter's innocent face with both hands and spoke softly.

"Happy birthday, Charlie."

"Are we still going?" she asked, catching her breath.

Benjamin nodded his assent.

"A promise is a promise. We take the raft north of the line, stay overnight in Canada, and come back tomorrow."

Charlie wrapped her arms around the man's neck.

"Thank you, Papa."

"Those barrels are heavy, I'll need your help."

"I will," she replied, an acknowledgment that one barrel of pot ash could weigh as much as one hundred pounds.

Pot ash resulted from the mixture of boiling hot water and the ash from burnt wood. The dried powder commanded a high price, north of the international boundary line. This particular trip, just one of Benjamin's many sojourns over the years, could prove risky. Just a few months ago, in March of 1808, President Jefferson enacted a land embargo. The new regulation prohibited the export of such goods to English Canada. But Benjamin sold the six barrels of pot ash to his Canadian customer, well before the embargo. And he had received the money, weeks in advance. He saw no choice but to deliver the goods.

"How about your friend, Hank? Any chance he can come along and help?" asked Benjamin.

"I'll talk him into it, but I get to steer the raft," she said, bartering with her papa.

Benjamin wagged a finger.

"Only to the line."

"Deal, she replied, vigorously shaking her papa's hand.

Harriet, slammed Benjamin's cup of coffee on the table.

"A raft is no place for a young lady."

A portion of the hot liquid splashed on Ben's lap. He slapped at his pants with the back of both hands.

"You're being unreasonable, woman. Besides, I need the help."

Charlie wolfed down a slice of bread, covered with strawberry preserves. Harriet's lips formed a straight line. She retreated to the fireplace. Benjamin took a deep breath, extinguishing his urge to argue with the woman. He forced himself to recall the reasons he married her.

When Charlie's mother died, word spread quickly in the small town of Isle LaMotte, Vermont. Harriet, living in a room above the town tavern, was the first to offer assistance. She tended to the infant when Benjamin worked the lake on his raft. A more pleasant lady, he could not imagine. He was twenty-three; she was twenty-two. Love did not enter into his decision to marry the woman. It was the practical and sensible thing to do. Love would come later, he thought. Only after their modest wedding, did Benjamin discover that Harriet was bereft of funds and about to be evicted. She seemed happy, however, and prattled on about 'children of their own.' Her choice of words troubled Benjamin. He viewed Charlie as her child too. After a few years and still no children, Harriet's demeanor changed. She refused to believe she was barren and blamed her husband. She complained that Benjamin was never home, that Charlie was 'a handful,' and that he needed to 'find a real job.' One that paid better. Benjamin wondered what she did with the money he did earn.

"One is enough," Harriet announced, slapping Charlie's hand once again, as the still-hungry girl reached for a second slice of bread.

When the unsmiling child got up from the table, Harriet turned her back. Benjamin donated his bread to the girl. Charlie disappeared. Harriet resumed her rant.

"That girl of yours acts like a boy. She refuses to wear a dress, wears her hair short and is always hanging around with that Hank kid."

Benjamin could feel a pang of guilt in his gut. As Charlie got older, she looked more and more like her late mother. He liked her better as a "boy" and did nothing to discourage her masculine ways. Short hair, freckles, a deep, husky voice and baggy clothes, didn't bother him in the least. A boy, even a tomboy, made Benjamin's heartbreaking loss of long ago, less painful.

"And you don't help matters any, when you wrestle with the girl, take her hunting or go rafting. She should be here with me. I'll teach her what she needs to know. Cooking, cleaning, sewing, and woman stuff."

When Harriet turned to get his reaction, she discovered Benjamin's empty chair.

Charlie scarfed down her father's slice of bread as she walked the mile and a half to Hank's house.

She overheard Harriet's harangue about her acting like a boy. Charlie pretended that the old woman's opinion didn't matter. But it did. She descended the embankment to Hank's favorite fishing spot. He wasn't there. The quiet waters of Lake Champlain shown like a mirror that morning. For a moment, she stared at the surface, inexorably drawn to the boyish image that stared back. Charlie snarled at the face in the water. When the reflection snarled back, she pounded the water with her fist. Being a girl is a curse from God, she concluded. She despised girls, their prissy ways, their frilly dresses and their constant giggling. Catching a fish, navigating a raft or hitting your target with a long rifle, those are useful skills. And she was darn good at all three. Before the girl in the water could argue the point, Charlie punched her in the face, once more. Harriet be damned.

As she trudged down the dusty lane to the Wells' place, Charlie spotted the boy's flaming- red hair from a hundred yards away. The clumsy adolescent bobbed up and down, as he chased a chicken in the barnyard. Hank threw his hands in the air when his mother's Sunday dinner escaped, once again.

Charlie's friend was a year older and a head taller, but the girl could out-run, out wrestle, and out swim the kid, with ease. And she could also beat him in a "who can spit the furthest" contest. The boy lived alone with his mother. Hank never knew his father, and no one ever offered an explanation as to where and when he left. The local gossips insisted that Hank's father worked as a wealthy trader in Hartford, Connecticut. He made enough money to build Mrs. Wells the only two-story, brick home in Isle LaMotte. It had windows made of glass, a novelty at the time. But the rich merchant abandoned the house, the boy, and Mrs. Wells. She struggled to pay the bills, taking in laundry and sewing projects. She also sold eggs, baked goods and rented out rooms to boarders. Hank did the outside chores, which included fishing, his favorite past time and his favorite meal.

"It's gonna be a right-skinny chicken by the time you catch it," said Charlie, flashing a big grin.

"I suppose you can do better?" said Hank, a frown on his sweaty face and breathing heavily.

"Watch me," she said.

Charlie waited until the animal stopped running. As the chicken pecked away at some dried corn, the girl approached from behind and squawked like a rooster. Her size and, possibly her strange performance, startled the animal into thinking a rooster approached. When the chicken assumed a submissive position, Charlie reached down with both hands and retrieved the bird before it could flap a wing.

"One of these days, I'm gonna beat you at something," said Hank, as he yanked the chicken from her hands.

Charlie watched, as the boy used his left hand to grab the animal by its legs and hold it upside down. With his other hand, he reached for the chicken's head and yanked–fast, hard, and away. The animal, killed instantly, twitched and convulsed as Hank and Charlie walked to the front porch.

"My father is taking the raft over the line. We're staying the night. Six barrels of pot ash. They're heavy. Can you help?" Charlie asked.

"You're not leaving until you clean that thing," said Hank's mother.

Mrs. Wells stood in the doorway, a smile on her face for Charlie, the girl she never had.

"Yes ma'am" said Hank, his adolescent voice cracking, in response.

"Be at the dock by sundown," said Charlie. "And thank you, Mrs. Wells. My father and I are much obliged."

As she ran from the yard, Mrs. Wells yelled.

"You be careful out there, Charlie."

"I promise."

When Harriet realized that her words fell on absent ears, she stopped cleaning and hurried to the door.

After scanning the horizon, she pushed the small, square kitchen table to one side. She dropped to her knees and, with a butcher knife, pried up a two-foot section of the floorboards. The nervous woman twisted and swiveled in every direction. She looked for prying eyes. Harriet reached under the floorboards and located the object of her search. The leather pouch contained a handful of notes and dozens of silver and gold coins. She reached into her apron pocket and deposited another coin, smiling and arching her eyebrows in glee. As she returned the table to its original position, she mumbled.

"I may not love you, Mr. Wheeler, but I love your money."

Ben Wheeler spent most of his life on Lake Champlain.

He started as a boy, under the tutelage of his father. Despite his relative youth, thirty-four years, Ben enjoyed seniority over most of the other rafters. Moving people and goods up and down the lake became his life's work. Charlie might even follow in his footsteps, he thought. There would always be a demand for the products he transported to Canada. Wheat, corn, cheese, butter, honey, salt pork and potash, brought a good price in British-controlled Canada. And there would always be a demand for Canadian products, like glass, leather goods, cloth, furs and hardware.

Still, Benjamin's stomach churned. The government's recent crackdown against smuggling grew more onerous. Initial efforts to enforce the federal legislation and stop all trade across the line failed miserably. Local militia men, sent to Windmill Point, hesitated when called upon to seize goods belonging to friends and neighbors. The majority walked off the job, sacrificing the dollar a day they received in payment for such distasteful work.

Soon, the government in Washington would dispatch federal troops to replace the local militiamen. These heavily armed Regulars would be on the lookout for people like Ben. They would not show leniency and the rumor mill reported that the Regulars now possessed small cannon, both on shore and in their cutters. (Government owned boats).

Ben checked the canvas sail, situated in the middle of his raft, confident that the evening's wind and the south-north current of the lake, would send him flying past the customs checkpoint.

"Where are the barrels?" asked Charlie.

Ben pointed to a patch of tall grass and small trees, a few dozen yards from the shoreline.

"Where's Hank?"

"Should be here in a bit. We gonna roll 'em on board?"

"Yes, but I'm in no hurry to leave. I don't want to be going past Windmill Point until after dark," said Ben. "The revenue agents are less likely to notice us, especially if they're eating their dinner."

The father-daughter team rolled two barrels on-board and finished the job when Hank arrived.

"Mr. Wheeler, is it true you got the fastest raft on the lake?" asked Hank.

Ben frowned.

"When you're on this lake, son, thinking fast is just as important as moving fast."

Ben watched, as his two young helpers stowed foodstuffs, blankets and supplies under the small lean-to, at the center of the raft. Ben flinched when Harriet's words rung in his ears. Moving goods on the lake used to be a way of life. Now they called it smuggling. Ignore the law and feed your family. Obey the law and starve to death.

"Some choice," he muttered.

Ben built his raft, smaller than most, with a medium-sized sail and a small lean-to for shelter during rough weather or cool nights.

He transported small goods, and, on occasion, a few head of livestock. He could steer the raft by himself, if necessary, using the natural flow of the lake and a strong wind.

A hundred-weight of pot ash, used in the production of soap, glass and fertilizer, sold for eight dollars, north of the line. And tea, doubled in price, once it arrived in Canada. Ben made a decent living. Until the embargo, he encountered no resistance, while conducting his business. As the sun sank into the western sky, and the threesome approached Windmill Point, the hair on the back of Ben's neck rose in protest. The goosebumps on his arms were not caused by the cool night air.

"Mr. Wheeler, are we close to the line?"

Ben interrupted Hank's inquiry with a desperate whisper.

"Quiet, boy," said Ben, leaning forward and bringing an index finger to his lips.

Charlie scanned the darkening horizon. She rarely saw her father in a nervous state, much less scared.

"There," Ben whispered, pointing to the east.

The dark water kissed the gray sky in a long, even line. A patch of dirty-white sail, spoiled nature's canvas and warned Benjamin. The slow-moving scene told Wheeler that he and his raft-mates, were not alone.

A flashing tongue of orange flame suddenly illuminated the night sky. The loud boom of an artillery piece echoed across the water. The low-pitched groan of a two-pound cannon ball, confirmed the obvious. Ben's raft was under attack. When the projectile splashed harmlessly into the lake, a dozen yards ahead of their craft, Benjamin made a split-second decision.

"Cease your fire. We go no further," he screamed.

He motioned to his young helpers and grabbed a paddle. The threesome slapped at the water until their efforts redirected the raft to the Vermont shoreline. Several men, exposed by a sliver of moon, pulled alongside. As Ben and his two helpers reached shallow water, they struggled to catch their breath.

"You're all under arrest for smuggling," said a voice in the dark.

"Now just a minute," said Ben. "These are my children. The pot ash was ordered and paid for, long before the embargo took effect," said Ben. "I have the papers to prove it."

"Save it for the magistrate," said a third voice, hopping onto Ben's raft with a tow rope in hand.

"Bring her in," he ordered, pointing to the customs dock at Windmill Point.

When the prisoners reached land, Ben confronted his captors.

"Firing that cannon was a right fool thing to do. We could've been killed."

"Then you're lucky we missed," said the youngest of the three men, none of them in uniform, all of them, members of the local militia.

Ben studied the youngest one, in particular.

"I've seen you before," said Ben. "At the tavern, mostly. Name's Delaney. You're the town drunk,"

"You've got a big mouth, mister," said the man, stepping forward, winding up, and then attempting a large right hook.

Ben easily blocked the blow and delivered a powerful punch that sent the man crashing to the ground.

"That's enough," said the older of the three.

As Ben turned to the senior man, Delaney reached for his right boot. He pulled a hunting knife from its sheath. A muffled thump sent Ben to his knees. Charlie saw the handle of a large blade, protruding from her father s back. She screamed.

"Papa," she said, rushing to his side.

"Get outta here, Delaney, before I shoot you myself," said the senior man.

Ben, now face down on the ground, lay motionless, as the red stain on his back grew to the size of a large dinner plate.

Chapter Two

THE WIDOW WHEELER

They loaded Ben onto a horse-drawn buckboard, for the ride back to Isle LaMotte.

Charlie never left her father's side. Hank, white with fear, watched as the wounded man slipped in and out of consciousness. The rough, dusty road made Ben groan in agony with each wheel rut. The senior militia man abandoned the seized raft and drove the government wagon to Ben's place. He offered no explanation for his kindness nor an apology for the unjustified stabbing of Benjamin Wheeler.

"What happened?" Harriet shrieked, as the unconscious body of her husband, came into full view.

The militia man, speaking in hushed tones, explained the circumstances of their encounter with Ben.

"I told him not to go. But he's always thinking about the money," Harriet said.

Her lie caused Charlie's head to jerk up in protest. The senior man spoke again.

"He needs a doctor, ma'am, right quick."

"No, he doesn't," said Charlie, her voice just above a whisper.

She gently rested her father's head on a blanket roll. The image of her hero's face, now ashen gray, would forever haunt the young girl. Her father's smile, his bronze complexion, and the blue eyes he gifted to Charlie, no longer existed. It didn't matter if she closed her eyes or opened them wide. She saw nothing but the man's death mask. She leaned over and kissed him on the forehead. Harriet aimed an accusatory finger at Charlie.

"This is all your doing, Charlie Wheeler. You might as well have stabbed him yourself."

Charlie stepped off the wagon. For a moment, she appeared lost and uncertain of her destination.

"Papa is dead," she said, walking mechanically, as if in a trance.

Harriet's eyes darted from the body of her husband to the militia man and then to Hank.

The boy, cowering in a corner of the buckboard, fixated on Benjamin's face. Harriet, as if on cue, began to wail. The boy jumped to the ground and ran after Charlie.

The militia man removed his hat and studied his dirty boots.

"Charlie?"

Hearing no response, Hank searched the barn and then the horizon. A small speck sent him scurrying down the road. He caught up to Charlie as she turned down the path to his favorite fishing spot. For some time, they sat in silence, surrounded by the sound of hungry birds. Hank spoke softly, unwilling to interrupt the gentle whisper of tiny waves as they caressed an endless bed of pebbles.

"I'm sorry about your papa," he said.

Charlie looked away. Hank swallowed hard. His throat tightened and he licked his dry lips.

"Charlie?"

She faced her best friend, a tear rolling down each cheek. Her grief, at least for a moment, made his adolescent awkwardness, disappear. He reached for the girl and pulled her close. Hank squeezed, as if the strength of his hug could stop her heaving chest. It didn't. He wanted to comfort the girl with more than his arms, but the words did not come. The fatherless boy could not fathom the pain that Charlie must be feeling.

Hank knew instinctively that the absence of a father left him at a disadvantage. He envied Charlie's confidence and blamed many of his shortcomings on the lack of a man in his own house. Hank also wondered if the death of Charlie's father would change things. He wanted his best friend to treat him like the young man he was becoming. He also wanted to be more than just her friend. Perhaps her broken heart would encourage the girl to look at Hank in a different way. Perhaps not. Right now, her sobs blanketed the waters of Lake Champlain, like a morning fog.

The tomboy cried like a girl.

Charlie slept very little in the immediate aftermath of her father's death.

In the midst of her agony, a well-attended service for her popular father, took place. Dozens of friends and neighbors came to the graveyard and paid their respects. Charlie fixated on the pine box and the freshly dug grave. When she did look up, Charlie noticed the huge man on whose arm, Harriet leaned. Everyone in town knew Otis Skinner. And yet, he looked out of place, with his unshaven face and unruly head of black hair. His blood shot eyes, dark and beady, darted in every direction and made the oversized man look naturally suspicious. Charlie could not remember how and when she first laid eyes on the bear-like man, but clearly, he knew Harriet and Harriet knew him.

When the minister signaled an end to his brief remarks, the pine box slowly disappeared into the gaping hole. Harriet, with great drama, reached for a handful of dirt and tossed it onto the crude coffin. When Otis mimicked Harriet, Charlie glared at the couple, spit on the ground, and stormed off.

As she exited the cemetery, two men approached.

"Go ahead, Nathan, you've got to learn sooner or later," said the senior man.

The younger fellow cleared his throat. He used both hands to brush back a head full of dark, brown hair, neatly tied into a proper-looking ponytail. His light blue eyes grew wide as Charlie got closer.

"Excuse me, young man, my name is Nathan Coldwell and I am a student at the medical college in Burlington. This is one of my instructors, Mr. Cornwall."

Charlie, accustomed to being mistaken for a boy and angry at the world, chose not to correct the medical student. She took note of his impeccably clean suit, his unsoiled hands, and clean-shaven face.

"What do you want?" she asked.

"Well sir, are you related to the deceased?" Coldwell asked.

"His name is Benjamin Wheeler and he is, was, my papa."

"My sincere condolences, Master Wheeler. We are in desperate need of cadavers at the medical school, and we pay the family a handsome amount. And this is how we study the human . . ."

Charlie cut the medical student off.

"What in tarnation is a *cad*aver?" she asked, mispronouncing the word.

The older doctor turned to Nathan.

"Explain yourself, Mr. Coldwell."

Coldwell took a deep breath and rolled his eyes.

"A cadaver, young man, is a dead body. As I started to say, before you interrupted me, we use them for medical research."

Charlie took a step forward and swung hard. Her small fist missed Nathan's chiseled features, by inches. She snarled when she saw the young man's face turn crimson red.

"Next time, I won't miss."

Nathan Coldwell, still smarting from his encounter with "Master Wheeler", sulked in his room at the Burlington boarding house.

The eighteen-year-old Boston native led a sheltered life. He grew up as the only child of a successful New England banker. Confrontations, of any type, rarely occurred in his highly civilized society. Nathan fumed for a while and then reached for a writing quill. The medical student vented his frustrations in a letter to his mother.

He reminded the woman that the Burlington medical school was not his first choice. And while he enjoyed his studies, under the very reputable Dr. John Pomeroy, taking instruction in the doctor's Battery Street home, seemed awkward and unprofessional. Making matters worse was the scarcity of cadavers upon which he could master the required surgical skills. A respectable university in Boston, would not have him soliciting commoners for the bodies of their loved ones, he argued. Nathan also noted that Burlington housed an inordinate number of taverns. Alcohol consumption, prohibited in his strict Methodist household, appeared to be rampant.

As he finished his letter, an image of the angry young boy at the cemetery flashed in his mind. Nathan's face grew pink as he recalled the details of the confrontation. His request for the cadaver, perhaps ill-timed, did not justify the boy's reaction. An acute shortage of specimens meant that Nathan's experience with the human form would be severely limited. *The boy, obviously ignorant of the opportunity to perform a public service, reacted in a most inappropriate manner,* thought Nathan. Nathan declared victory in the unspoken argument with his conscious and decided to reward himself.

He donned his best suit of clothes and struck out for one of Burlington's finer dining establishments.

Otis opened the cabin door for Harriet.

"Where's the girl?" he asked.

They both assumed that Charlie returned to the house, after the graveside ceremony.

Harriet scanned the room, and stood on her toes, to inspect Charlie's loft bedroom.

"She's not here."

Otis arched his eyebrows and grinned.

"Then we are alone."

He pulled Harriet close and kissed her passionately on the lips. Harriet pushed on his chest, but not enough to drive the man away.

"Why, Otis Skinner, I just buried my husband. I'm in mourning," she said, looking stern but ruining her serious demeanor with a broad smile.

"And I'm drunk," said Otis.

Skinner lunged for the woman's neck, kissing her cheek and nibbling on her ear, as he tugged on the bodice of her dress.

"Otis. The little monster is likely to return," she whispered, tilting her head to one side, but obviously enjoying his amorous intentions.

He reached for the short, flat board used to barricade the door.

"Business first," she announced, pointing to a chair and assembling the fixings for tea.

Otis grimaced his disappointment, dropped the board, and adjusted the lump in his trousers. He fell into a chair.

"I know, he said. "We have to get that raft back."

A smirk crossed Harriet's face.

"I think the sergeant in charge of the local militia is feeling guilty right about now. Just tell him that the widow Wheeler intends to sell the thing. I need the money for food and firewood."

"You're a right smart woman," said Otis.

"I got more ideas where that one came from. Just you watch and see," she said, pouring the tea and pulling up a chair.

"You got anything to put in the tea?" asked Otis.

"Not a drop in the house," she said.

Harriet paused and then rose to her feet.

"Something wrong?" he asked.

Harriet retrieved the board and barricaded the door.

Their tea grew cold.

"I've got to go," said Charlie, her eyes red and swollen, but dry.

She pushed away from Hank and paused for a second. Charlie didn't want to be rude.

"Thanks," she said, as if someone had just passed the bread at dinner.

"See ya," said Hank, his tanned face, a slight shade of pink.

Charlie rose to her feet and studied the boy as if noticing him for the first time.

"You're my best friend, Hank."

"Yeah. I know."

Charlie climbed the embankment and walked home.

"You've got chores to do. And you can forget about supper. A little late for that," Harriet barked.

Charlie's head drooped as she turned around in the doorway. She wanted to scream, and she wanted to cry. She even thought about running away. But a yelling match with her stepmother would be fruitless and there were no more tears to shed. She tended to the barn animals in silence and spent the night in the hay mound.

At sunrise, Charlie woke to the sound of a horse's hooves.

She peeked out the barn door and saw Otis Skinner, standing on the front porch of her home. He knocked softly and only twice. When the door opened, Charlie stepped back into the barn, still able to hear and witness the conversation.

"Did you get the raft?" Harriet asked.

"Delaney's gonna deliver it tomorrow," said Otis.

"I ain't paying him for it," she announced.

"No, but you may want to pay him for some help, down the road."

"What do you mean?"

"Delaney's gonna let me know when he's on duty, at Windmill Point. That means I got clear sailing all the way to the line."

"And if he double-crosses us?"

"He's worried about you going to the judge. He stabbed your husband in the back, you know."

"He did me a favor. But don't tell him I said that."

They both grinned.

"Where's Charlie?" he asked.

"Slept in the barn last night. Should be up pretty soon. You'd best go, now."

Otis leaned forward. Charlie watched as they kissed on the lips. She hurried to a corner of the barn, bent over, and wretched.

The fall season in Vermont, normally a months-long extravaganza of spectacular beauty, appeared and disappeared in record time.

The bitter-cold winter which followed, mirrored the harsh conditions in Charlie's world. She missed her father terribly and continued to mourn his loss. On some days, she blamed him for their risky trip to the line. On other days, she blamed herself. Most of the time, she blamed her greedy stepmother. Charlie's ugly thoughts always concluded the same way. She would never see her handsome and loving father, again.

Harriet didn't wait for Otis to propose. She manipulated the normally inebriated brute into a hastily arranged marriage. He never thought to object. They made an odd couple. She stood no more than five feet in length, prided herself on a two-dress wardrobe and spent most of her days calculating how much money she possessed. Otis towered over his new bride, weighed at least 350 pounds, rarely shaved, and struggled to read and write. He spent his days drinking. His new wife, the first woman whose company he did not pay for, used her modest charms with great effect. Otis lusted after Harriet. Harriet lusted after money and Otis knew how to earn money.

A more perfect couple did not exist.

Charlie did not attend their wedding. The girl's obvious disdain for her stepparents prompted Harriet to leave Charlie at home.

Charlie's stomach churned when she realized that her new family consisted of Harriet and Otis. In the evenings, Charlie covered her ears when the sound of giggles and moans from below, prevented her sleep. The long stares from Otis, especially when Harriet was otherwise occupied, left the nape of Charlie's neck covered in goosebumps.

Harriet regularly reminded the grief-stricken girl, that her father might still be alive today, were it not for Charlie's selfish demands. Her stepmother's steady drumbeat of disparaging remarks, combined with an endless list of chores and the woman's refusal to feed the girl more than one meal a day, left Charlie, desperate, discouraged, hungry and alone.

Harriet stood in the middle of the room, waving her arms and pointing her fingers.

"I want the porch cleared of snow. And when you're finished with that, you can clear a path to the barn. And then I want this house cleaned and dusted from top to bottom."

Charlie braved the cold without a wrap because the old one no longer fit. Harriet refused to purchase or make a new one. A one-hour struggle with the falling snow, left Charlie cold and shivering. She rejected the warm fireplace in her own home and ran down the road to Hank's place. The quick jaunt would keep her warm and Hank's mother always had something to eat, she thought.

"Lord Almighty," said Mrs. Wells, as she reached for Charlie's red cheeks and pulled the girl into the toasty-warm house.

Charlie trembled violently, as Mrs. Wells brushed the snow and ice from the girl's hair. Hank rushed to the girl's side with a blanket.

Charlie stood just inches from the roaring fire.

"Ssssorry, ma'am. I didn't think it was that bbbbad, out there."

"I've got leftover chicken soup. All I have to do is warm it up," said Mrs. Wells, scurrying to the cupboard for a bowl.

"Did you run away?" asked Hank, knowing the details of Charlie's wretched existence.

"I'm not sure," she said. "I was cold and hungry and I ended up here."

Hank grinned.

"I'm glad," he said.

When Charlie caught the boy's gleaming eyes, Hank blushed.

"I mean, it's so boring here. Nothin' to do," he said, clearing his throat.

Charlie devoured two bowls of the soup. She fell asleep in front of the fire, curled up in a large quilt.

Hank accomplished his morning chores, in record time, because Charlie helped.

The sound of approaching hooves, crunching muck-covered snow and ice, brought their work to a halt.

"Your mother sent me," said Otis, perched on his horse, but surveying the scene around him.

"She's not my mother," said Charlie, hurling a large clump of hay high into the air.

"Who's he?" Otis asked, staring at the boy.

"My friend, Hank Wells."

"He can do his own chores. Harriet ain't too happy," said Otis.

Charlie glared at Otis, scanning the barn for an excuse to stay longer. Otis yanked hard on his fidgety horse and leaned forward.

"You don't want me to get off this horse, little girl."

Charlie tossed her pitchfork in Hank's direction. He reached for the handle but missed it, distracted by the bear-like demeanor of Otis Skinner. She hopped on his horse, choosing not to put her arms around the man's waist. Charlie glanced back and Hank watched, as horse and riders disappeared over the line that separated snow-covered ground from bright, blue sky. Otis burped, long and hard. The expulsion of stomach gas brought him relief and triggered an attempt at conversation.

"You sweet on that boy?" Otis asked.

Charlie snarled at the man's back.

"He's my friend. I reckon he's my only friend," she said, looking back one more time.

"You must like him an awful lot, seeing as how you do his chores, for him."

Charlie refused to respond. She pulled her wrap tight and wondered what Harriet would say. The hand-me-down coat, given to her by Mrs. Wells, kept the girl warm.

Otis hiccupped for most of the way home.

Harriet took notice of the coat as soon as Charlie walked through the cabin door.

She grilled the child for details and Charlie's innocent responses enraged the woman.

"We don't need no charity from strangers," she barked.

"Well, I was freezing. And you didn't seem to care," Charlie snapped, slamming the door behind her, as Harriet yelled about cleaning the barn.

"You should put that girl to work," Harriet said, glaring at her new husband.

'She works like a man, I'll give her that," said Otis. "I'm sure she'd like the money," he said.

"Who said anything about money?" Harriet replied. "She's got a roof over her head, and a bed to sleep in. That's her pay."

"I'll talk to her."

Charlie spent much of her time in the barn.

The cow, the pig and the chickens never yelled at her. And Harriet, stingy with the firewood, often kept her home colder than the hay loft. Otis made a noisy entrance, breathing heavy and stomping the snow and muck from his boots.

"The ice is coming off the lake. I'm hoping you'll help me out on the raft," he said.

She leaned on the rake, thought for a moment, and spoke while she raked.

"You're not my papa. Ain't gonna happen."

"No. I'm not your papa. You'd be my hired hand," said Otis.

Charlie stopped raking. She frowned her confusion and looked up.

"Hired hand?" she asked.

Otis swiveled in place, looking for earwitnesses.

"I'll pay you," reaching in his jacket for a flask.

"Your wife won't part with a half-cent. You're lying to me," she said, and resumed her raking.

"It'll be our secret," said Otis, taking a long swig.

Charlie, although excited by the prospect of earning money, did not kid herself. If she refused, Otis and Harriet would force her to work.

"I work best, with Hank," she said, not wanting to be alone with Otis.

Otis grinned.

"I knew you was sweet on him."

Charlie groaned and attacked another pile of hay.

Nathan, unwilling to tolerate the bitter cold of a Vermont Spring, spent most of his time poring through an endless series of medical texts and taking copious notes.

An unexpected visitor interrupted his studies.

"I would like you to read with me," said Dr. Pomeroy.

Nathan's eyes grew wide. In his haste, he missed the inkwell and ruined the tip of his writing quill. In time, he stuttered a response.

"You mean like an apprentice. I would be your apprentice?"

"Not immediately, but yes. You will read on various subjects and, depending on your progress, you will become my assistant," said Pomeroy.

Nathan swooned. Pomeroy recently became the Chair of the University's Medical Department. *Pomeroy chose Nathan for his academic prowess,* thought Nathan.

"Thank you, sir. I am honored that you would give me such an opportunity."

"Don't be honored, Coldwell. You will work harder than you have ever worked before."

"Thank you, nevertheless."

"Tomorrow, we go to Champlain. Dr. Moore has utilized a similar program for his students. I wish to compare curriculums and seek his advice. You are able to join me?"

"Yes, of course," said Nathan.

Pomeroy instructed the boy to be at the Burlington dock by eight in the morning. They would travel to Rouse's point, (historically correct spelling), on the newly launched *Vermont.* The steam-powered boat, although plagued by frequent breakdowns, would allow the doctor and his student to make their journey to the boundary line, in several hours. Dr. Moore would meet them dockside.

"Dress warmly. The lake air is very cold this time of the year," said Pomeroy.

Hank visited his favorite fishing spot, as soon as the ice went out on the lake.

"You gonna fish all year or you wanna make some money?" asked Charlie.

"Who's hiring?"

"My stepfather."

"He gives me goosebumps," said Hank.

"Me too," she said.

Hank twisted in the girl's direction, in search of her eyes. Charlie focused on an imaginary boat.

"He wants help on the raft," she said. Charlie refused to admit that she needed and wanted Hank's company.

Hank jiggled his fishing pole and waited for a fish to bite.

"My mom says they're really cracking down on the smuggling," said Hank, letting his worm sink to the bottom.

"Otis says we'll stay south of the boundary line," said Charlie.

"Will we stay away from the revenuers? Them's the ones that killed your pa," he said.

"Yeah. It's not like I forgot, you know."

"Sorry."

"I miss him, Hank," said Charlie, close to tears.

Hank looked up and rested the pole on his lap.

"I never knew my papa," he said.

Charlie ignored the boy's observation.

"And his ole lady is driving me crazy," she added.

"I don't like her either," said Hank.

Charlie noticed Hank's pole twitching in his lap.

"You got one, silly," she said.

Hank jumped to his feet, holding the pole high in the air. He used the other hand to reel in as much line as he could.

"Don't lose it, Hank. I'm hungry," she said, grinning for the first time, in months.

Hank couldn't take his eyes off the churning water, but he managed to respond.

"My mom says you're always hungry."

He pulled fast and hard on the fishing line. The body of a large pike broke through the water.

Both of them squealed with joy.

Nathan queried Dr. Pomeroy when the steam engine on the *Vermont* suddenly went silent.

"What happened?"

"Another breakdown," said the Doctor, frowning as he looked around the lake to get his bearings.

"We're still way north of Burlington," he said. "That looks like Isle LaMotte over there. We may not get home tonight," said the doctor.

As the boat drifted closer to the island, Nathan noticed two kids fishing off the white rocks that lined the shoreline.

"Drop the anchor," someone yelled, the steamer now just a few dozen yards from shore.

Nathan could hear the excited voices of the two young fishermen. They pointed to the crippled craft and talked, non-stop. One of the boys held a large fish, hanging from a line, still wriggling in protest. The youngsters, mesmerized by the large boat, gawked in Nathan's direction. Nathan smiled, guessing that a newly minted steamboat on the waters of Lake Champlain fascinated the kids.

As the western sun focused its setting rays on the eastern shoreline, Nathan stepped to the railing and leaned forward. Nathan recoiled. He recognized that short hair, pug nose and cherubic face. It was the young man at the cemetery. Nathan's face reddened. He saw the boy shade his eyes for a better look. The boy stepped forward and looked again. Nathan could not hear their conversation. The two fishermen scrambled up the embankment. The boy from the cemetery stopped for one last look.

Nathan turned his back.

Otis Skinner used a single, large oar to steer his raft north to the boundary line.

The lake's current and a slight breeze, billowing in the raft's lone sail, moved the vessel four to five miles each hour. Hank and Charlie stood at the forward corners of the raft, each with an oar in their hands, but with nothing to do. Their labor would not be necessary until the return trip, when rowing south against the lake's current, required extra effort.

"Why don't we have any cargo," asked Charlie.

"It's against the law," Otis grumbled.

The absence of liquor since noon, Harriet's idea, put the man in a bad mood.

"I don't understand," said Hank.

"Just do as you're told," said Skinner.

"We got company," yelled Charlie, pointing towards Windmill Point.

A revenue cutter, with six men aboard and rowing hard, approached the raft.

"What are you hauling," asked one of the uniformed officers.

"Look for yourself," said Skinner, as he dropped sail and slowed his raft to a near stop. "We're fishin'," he added.

"Where you headed?"

"Our fishing hole, near the line. Is that a problem?"

"Let's go," said the officer, disappointed that his dream of catching a smuggler, would not be realized.

Skinner growled under his breath.

"Damn fool."

He hoisted the small sail and guided the raft down the middle of the channel. As he approached the line, Skinner yelled to his raftmates.

"Slow her down. We're pulling up here."

He pointed to the Vermont side of the lake.

"Here," he barked, using a rope to secure the raft to a small clump of bushes.

"Ain't nothing here," said Charlie.

"You stay with the raft, Charlie. And throw out your fishing line. The boy comes with me," Skinner said.

As they waded through four feet of frigid water, the object of their trip to the line came into view. A smaller raft, with a few barrels and a dozen wooden crates, lay secreted in the bushes. Otis and Hank removed the camouflage, undid its tether, and pushed the vessel toward the open lake.

"Hang onto that rope," said Skinner. "We've got to make sure it gets to the channel," he added.

Hank and Otis made their way back to Charlie. When they re-boarded, Skinner yelled at Charlie.

"Start rowing,"

The hidden raft, laden with contraband, floated west to the channel. Eventually, the two rafts lined up. Otis turned to Hank.

"Let her go," said Skinner. "And grab an oar."

Hank released the tether and watched as the small raft floated due north and crossed the line into British Canada.

"Keep rowing," Skinner yelled.

Hank rowed. Charlie rowed and watched at the same time. She noticed a small boat, with several occupants, emerge from the brush, just north of the line. The men boarded the drifting vessel and directed its voyage further north into Canada. Otis interrupted her observations.

"We're gonna get stopped on the way back. You keep your mouths shut. Understand?"

"Yes sir," said Hank.

Charlie nodded and wondered if Otis would pay them for the day's work.

By mid-August, the warm waters of Lake Champlain welcomed children and adults of all ages.

Charlie and Hank, disappointed that two hours of fishing in the hot sun produced no results, decided to cool off.

Modesty required that Charlie wear her night shirt. Hank abandoned his undergarment when the clear, blue waters reached waist level.

"We still ain't been paid," said Hank, coming up for air after yards of swimming underwater.

"Otis told me this morning he didn't have any coins," said Charlie, floating on her back, and soaking up the sun.

"Do you believe him?"

"Nope. And it would have been nice to have that money in

time for my birthday," she said."

Hank stared at Charlie's chest, two tiny bumps, now visible under the wet cotton that clung to her torso.

"Mama says I'm too old to be swimming buck naked, with a thirteen-year-old girl."

Charlie smiled when Hank's voice cracked, yet again. She stood in the water and stepped closer. Hank caught the girl's eyes and then looked away.

"Look at me," she said.

He turned in her direction, his eyes downcast. She leaned in and kissed him on the cheek. A flush of pink covered the boy's face. He took a deep breath, trembling when he exhaled.

"It's getting a might cold, out here," said Hank, checking to ensure that the water kept his private parts from view.

"Lemme guess," she said. "Your first kiss?"

"No," said Hank, squatting in the water.

"Your momma don't count," she argued.

Hank sprang to his feet. The boy's eyes flashed, and he gnawed on his lower lip.

"And I suppose you've kissed lots of boys," he yelled.

Charlie looked up, studying a cloud as it floated by. She turned back to Hank and whispered her response.

"Only one," she said.

"Who?" he asked, an indignant look covering his face.

Charlie smiled.

"You."

Hank grinned. The tension drained from his body.

"I'll race you," he yelled, leaping toward the shoreline, his white buttocks bobbing in the foam.

Charlie rolled her eyes. She walked to the shore, giving Hank time to reach the rocky beach and get dressed. When she reached the pebble-covered beach, Charlie rested on a large rock. She faced the boundary line, her back to the boy. Hank threw pebbles in the water. A slight wind, whispering through the trees, dried Charlie's hair and Hank's bare feet. Hank stopped and spoke to Charlie's back.

"Charlie, did I do something wrong?" asked Hank.

"No, Hank. You didn't do anything wrong," she said.

"Are you missing your papa?"

Charlie nodded her head.

Hank took a seat on the rock and reached for her hand. When she did not resist, Hank leaned in and delivered a fast peck on her cheek. Charlie, a surprised look on her face, leaned away. Her objections melted away when she noticed Hank's crimson-red face. She spoke in a whisper.

"That's enough kissing for one day, Mr. Wells."

Otis handed Charlie and Hank his flask.

"Drink this."

The two of them sat in the back of Skinner's buckboard, packed with wooden crates and two large barrels, all of it covered by a sheet of canvas. Charlie assumed that Otis intended to cross the line.

"We ain't thirsty," she complained, guessing that the smelly liquid was alcohol.

"It's gonna be a might chilly, by the time we reach the line," said Otis.

Hank took a big sip, gagged, squeezed his eyes shut, and shook his head.

"What is that stuff?" he said as he handed it to Charlie.

"No thanks," she mumbled, examining the French-made container, which Otis claimed to have won in a fight.

Otis twisted in his seat and flashed a vicious glare in the girl's direction.

"I said drink it. And I'm not gonna tell you again."

The adolescents giggled and babbled until the whiskey disappeared. Darkness approached as they got closer to the line. The children grew quiet. Overcome with nausea and dizziness, Hank threw up. The splashing vomit, speckled with the chicken and dumplings he ate for supper, triggered a similar reaction from Charlie. Otis pulled the canvas over their heads.

"What are you hauling," asked the border official.

"Two sick kids," said Skinner, raising the canvas tarp just enough for the inspector to hear the gagging and moans of pain.

"I think they picked up the yellow fever when they were in Burlington. I'm moving them to their aunt's place in Saint Johns," said Skinner.

The inspector jumped back. His eyes grew wide,

"Get 'em outta here. Now," he shouted, backing away even further.

Skinner snapped the reins and both horses took off at a fast trot.

He turned to his passengers.

"How you doin' back there?"

Neither child answered, both of them, passed out from exhaustion and alcohol.

Skinner grinned.

"Why are you still sleeping? You've got chores to do," said Harriet.

She pulled on Charlie's hair until the girl's torso hung over the side of the bed. Charlie mumbled, her head pounding and stomach, still queasy.

"I'm up, I'm up."

Charlie rose with great effort. She gave Otis a dirty look when she walked by the kitchen table. Otis studied his cup of coffee, avoiding the girl's angry eyes.

When Charlie entered the barn, she spotted Hank, sleeping in a mound of hay. He stirred but his eyes remained closed.

"Hank? You been here all night? Your momma's gonna have a fit."

Hank struggled to his feet, holding his head with both hands and squeezing his eyes shut.

"I don't even know how I got here," he complained, brushing the hay from his clothes as he stumbled to the door.

"We're not doing that again," she said.

Hank shook his head and left. Minutes later, Charlie stopped feeding the chickens when she heard a rustling noise behind her.

"I'm sorry about last night," said Otis.

He repeatedly turned in the direction of the cabin, as if Harriet spied on him.

"Can't spend an apology. Where's my money?"

Once again, Otis looked over his shoulder. He pulled two half-pennies from his pocket.

"That's all I got."

Charlie scowled her disapproval but grabbed the coins She shoved then into her trousers as Otis checked the house again. Charlie finished feeding the chickens.

"Charlie. I don't want any hard feelings between us," he said.

"Too late for that."

"Fall's in the air. I got just a few more runs and that's it," he said.

"I want my money in advance. And no more whiskey," she snapped.

"Agreed."

Otis walked to where the girl was standing. He reached out to put his arms around her. Charlie pushed him away and stepped back.

"I got chores to do."

Chapter Three

ONE MORE RUN

Charlie could hear the urgent whispers that emanated from her step-parents' bed chamber.

She concluded they were arguing. Otis did not want to make another run across the line. Harriet insisted.

The winter of 1809-1810, now well underway, reduced the lake to a frozen tundra. The back roads to Canada were not much better. A series of chest-high snow drifts blocked most of the roads. Later that day, Otis found Charlie in the barn.

"We gotta make one more run to the line," said Otis.

Charlie shivered and looked for eggs.

"The lake's frozen over," she said.

"I got a sled."

"Most of the roads are plugged. Your sled won't do us any good," she said.

"We'd be on the lake," he replied.

Charlie whipped around. She stared at Otis, her eyes wide open.

"We'd be *in* the lake, you fool. My father always said you can't

41

trust the lake when it's frozen. Six inches of ice where you're standing and open water just a few yards away."

Charlie tried to explain.

"Something about the warm currents. It's too dangerous. Count me out."

"That's why I need you and Hank. Someone's got to keep an eye out."

"Not interested."

"I'll pay you. In advance."

"Heard that before," she snapped.

Charlie's egg basket, half-empty, forced her to keep searching.

"Two dollars each," he announced.

The girl's head jerked in Skinner's direction. That kind of money would allow her to leave home. For good. Maybe stay at Hank's place and pay room and board. Charlie found two more eggs.

Her stepfather stared in silence.

"I'll think about it," said Charlie.

Otis stepped in her direction. Charlie grimaced. The big brute, unusually nice to her during the last month, seemed almost affectionate. He actually tried to hug her a few times.

"Here," she said, handing the basket to her stepfather and avoiding an embrace.

"I gotta go," she said.

Charlie and Hank were talking in hushed whispers.

They did not want Mrs. Wells, busy in the kitchen, to hear their conversation.

"I don't trust him, Hank. And the lake, even when it's frozen over, is dangerous after dark," said Charlie.

Hank's jaw dropped.

"But two dollars, Charlie. That's a lot of money," Hank argued.

"Not if we get killed earning it. I'm gonna tell him no," said Charlie.

"He's gonna force you to go whether you want to or not," said Hank.

"I don't care," she answered. "I'm telling him no. We're not going."

Hank jumped to his feet. He shook an index finger in the girl's direction. His voice didn't crack anymore. He sounded more like a man.

"You don't speak for me, Charlie Wheeler. I'm going."

"I can't let you do that, Hank."

"You're not my mother, Charlie."

Charlie's eyes turned into slits.

"No, but I can *tell* your mother."

Hank's lower lip curled. His face reddened and he growled through clenched teeth.

"I thought we was friends. Good friends. You gonna tattle on your best friend?"

Charlie sensed she crossed some sort of line with Hank. She turned away from his angry face.

"Yes," she whispered.

Hank's eyes flashed. He reached for the girl with both hands and yanked Charlie to her feet, using her shirt for leverage. Charlie, too stunned to fight back, stood in silence, as Hank pulled her close. He whispered through clenched teeth.

"If you tattle on me, like a girl, you will have no friends at all," said Hank.

Charlie couldn't recall a time when Hank looked so angry. His comment about girls, stung like a mad hornet. She did not want to be one of those girls. Never. Charlie stared at her best friend, and then blinked. Hank didn't blink. He stared back, his scowl, etched in stone. Charlie wanted to save face. She rolled her eyes and grimaced.

"Well, I can't let you go by yourself. You'll drown for sure," she said, trying hard to appear irritated. But she wasn't irritated.

She was scared.

The frigid night air transformed each breath from the horse's nostrils into a white puff of steam.

Otis Wheeler checked the reins, the harness and the sleigh, for the third time. He scanned the road for signs of his two helpers. Charlie promised to bring Hank. Both children would play a critical role in the sleigh ride to the boundary line. Lake Champlain froze over, weeks ago, but its eddies and currents, left patches of thin ice, even no ice, in the deepest parts of the lake. Otis planned to stay as close to the shore as possible. His helpers would have to keep a sharp eye out and scream their warnings. If all went well, the threesome would be returning before dawn, their sleigh empty, and their pockets full.

"Where's our money?"

Otis jumped and twisted in the direction of Charlie's voice.

"Charlie. You scared the dickens out of me," he barked.

Hank, standing at Charlie's side, put his right hand out, palm up, and focused on the man's scraggly face.

"I'll pay you when I get paid. When the job's done," said Otis.

"That wasn't the deal. Good luck," said Charlie, as she grabbed Hank's empty hand and started walking.

"Half now, half when we get home," Otis countered.

Hank stopped and stole a look at Charlie. The boy looked like he just snagged a large pike. Charlie shook her head in disgust.

"Fine," she said, reaching for the coins in Skinner's outstretched hand.

In minutes, Skinner's sleigh glided effortlessly over the snow-covered ice.

With plenty of moonlight to guide them, the trip to the line proved uneventful. Charlie fell into a fitful slumber. The sights, sounds, and smells of that evening triggered a series of bittersweet memories; the moon playing hide and seek with the clouds, the musty smell of woolen horse blankets, and the muffled sound of a horse's hooves as they hit a thick layer of snow. She thought she heard sleigh bells and the sound of her father laughing. She could even feel the squeeze of his hands on her knee, after which he would always say, 'I love you.'

"We're here, kid," said Otis, his oversized paw squeezing Charlie's leg.

Charlie's dream disappeared like a wisp of smoke on a windy day.

"We drop the stuff off here," said Otis, pointing to a lone dock with a small torch to light the way.

Charlie and Hank moved the smaller crates. Otis rolled the barrels. She could see the dark outlines of several men at the shore-end of the dock. Delivery and payment required only a few whispered words. Otis jumped back on the raft, wearing a huge grin.

The return trip to Isle LaMotte did not go as planned. Otis leaned forward and squinted.

"I ain't seeing my tracks," he complained.

"Too much cloud cover and it's starting to snow," said Charlie, as she too, leaned forward.

Otis pulled the horse to a stop and motioned to Hank.

"You. On the horse."

Hank didn't hesitate. He jumped the distance from the sleigh onto the horse's unsaddled back.

"If the snow gets dark, you yell and pull up on the reins. Hard. Do you understand me, boy?"

"Yes sir," Hank said.

Otis kept the horse at a slow trot. A dozen yards later, Hank bellowed.

"Stop!"

Otis and Hank leaned back, each of them, using their weight to pull on the reins. The horse reared up. A front hoof splashed into a pool of frigid water. The animal twisted sharply to the left. Hank didn't anticipate the animal's gyration. He lost his grip and flew into the dark spot with a loud splash. The horse recovered and moved further left. Otis pulled hard on the reins, forcing the animal away from the danger. Charlie jumped from the sleigh. The clouds obscured the moonlight. She could hear the desperate splashing of her friend but she couldn't see him. She fell to the ground and crawled on her belly to the dark spot. Hank, choking and sputtering, managed two words.

"Help me."

"I'm over here," Charlie yelled.

The splashing noises continued as Hank tried to climb back onto the ice. Charlie inched her tiny frame dangerously close to the edge and stretched her arm as far as she could. Water. Nothing but icy cold water. The splashing slowed and then stopped. The moon peaked from behind a drifting cloud. Otis saw the glimmer of Hank's wet face.

"There. To your left."

Charlie scrambled to her left. She reached over the edge. Her hand made contact with hair. Hair laced with frozen ice. She grabbed a fistful and pulled. The boy's motionless body drifted closer. She struggled to lift him from the water, straining every muscle and yelling at the same time.

"Help me, Otis."

Otis jumped from the sleigh and pulled hard on Charlie's legs. Charlie plunged her arms in the water and wrapped them around her friend. She screamed,

"Pull, Otis. Pull."

Otis leaned back, digging his heels into the snow and ice. It worked. After a minute of struggling, Hank lay on the surface. His long eyelashes, covered with ice, sealed the boy's eyes. He didn't move. He didn't even shiver. Charlie pressed her ear to his chest and then the boy's mouth.

"I think he's still breathing."

"Let's get him in the sleigh," said Otis.

They each took an end of the water-soaked body and heaved the boy onto the sleigh. Charlie climbed in after Hank. She did her best to warm her friend using woolen blankets and the heat from her body. Hank started to shiver again. Charlie thought it was a good sign. Otis guided the horse around the dark spot. With the help of a now partially exposed moon, he rediscovered their original tracks.

Charlie hugged her best friend, sobbing and praying, all the way home.

Nathan stood in the middle of Dr. Jacob Roebach's eerily, quiet parlor, unsure of what he should do next.

Two days earlier, Roebach, collapsed and died. The

sixty-nine-year-old, born in Prussia, was the epitome of good health—muscular, an avid horseman and skilled with the sword. His premature death shocked the small community. Nathan's teacher and mentor, Dr. Pomeroy, dispatched Nathan to stand in, until a more suitable replacement could be found.

At the funeral that morning, Nathan repeatedly expressed his condolences to the family. Secretly, he welcomed the opportunity afforded him by the doctor's untimely demise. A country practice, with occasional surgical duties, appealed to Nathan. Most of all, he looked forward to the prospect of being on his own, independent and unsupervised. A loud banging on the office door reminded Nathan that his duties as the local doctor began immediately.

"I'm looking for the doc," said the man, big, surly, and smelly.

"Dr. Nathan Coldwell, I'm standing in for the late Dr. Roebach."

"I got a young boy. He's in real bad shape," said the visitor.

"And your name?"

"Skinner. Otis Skinner. I've got a sleigh. Can you come, right now?"

Nathan threw on a wrap, grabbed his medical bag, and left with Otis. While in route, Skinner explained the boy's near drowning, omitting the reason for their trip to the line.

"How long has he been unconscious?" asked Nathan.

"A day and a half. And he's burning up."

"Pneumonia, no doubt," said Nathan.

The scene at Hank Wells' home grew more desperate by the moment.

Hank's mother, hysterical when Charlie and Skinner first arrived, screamed for the doctor.

"Where is that doctor?" she yelled.

Charlie could only say that Otis would soon return. Hank's labored breathing grew shallow and the boy's high fever persisted. His mother used cold compresses on Hank's forehead. The fourteen-year-old adolescent did not respond. His ashen face scared Charlie. Her father looked that way. She stared and prayed. And prayed some more.

"Why were you on the lake, in the middle of the night?" said Mrs. Wells, increasingly frustrated with her failed ministrations.

Charlie's head drooped. She murmured her response.

"Mr. Skinner offered us two dollars apiece if we went with him to the line."

The girl reached into her pocket.

"Here. It's yours."

Mrs. Wells stared at the money with unblinking eyes.

"My only son. For two dollars? What in God Almighty's name were you thinking?"

Charlie, tears in her eyes, tried to defend herself.

"I said no. But Hank insisted."

"Why didn't you tell me?" she demanded.

A long, slow, rattle from Hank's congested lungs interrupted the woman's interrogation. Mrs. Wells turned to the boy. His face transformed into a motionless gray mask.

"Hank. Please, Hank. Don't leave me. You can't leave me. Please," she cried.

Mrs. Wells sat upright. Her eyes fixated on Hank's lifeless form. She used her fingers to brush his hair into place, as if preparing him for Sunday services. Charlie noticed a complete change in Mrs. Wells' appearance. The woman's face, as if etched in stone, betrayed no emotion.

"Good bye, son," she said, her voice strong and steady.

She rose, walked to the fireplace, and stoked the flame.

"Please tell the doctor we don't need him anymore."

Charlie, stunned by the woman's reaction, decided to leave. She too, refused to cry. When she opened the door, Skinner and Nathan blocked her exit, the two of them about to enter the home. For a moment, the girl and the medical student locked eyes. Nathan shoved his nose into the air, refusing to make further eye contact. Charlie's sorrow, her guilt, and her anger, drained into a closed fist. The blow to Nathan's jaw catapulted the young doctor down the porch steps. A loud grunt announced the man's painful landing. He lay there, sprawled on the snow-covered ground, rubbing his jaw. Otis stared, bug-eyed and shocked.

Charlie, her face now stained with tears, ran into the deep woods.

Harriet Skinner slammed her rolling pin on the table, sending a white cloud of flour dust into the air.

"Four dollars? You gave those brats four whole dollars?"

Otis sat nearby, running his fingers through a head full of dirty hair.

"One of those kids is dead, Harriet. And it's my fault. It's all my fault," he repeated, shaking his head in disbelief.

"You're a fool, Otis Skinner. I should never have married you." she said, untying her apron and throwing it in his direction.

Otis jumped to his feet. Using both hands, he grabbed the wooden chair and flung it across the room. The handmade furniture splintered into pieces. Harriet screamed and scurried to the door. She stopped in the opening, stealing furtive glances at the floorboards under the kitchen table. Otis followed her darting eyes.

"I know where you keep the money, you stupid woman. And I

know where you sleep," he said.

Otis pushed her to one side as he stormed out of the cabin.

Charlie, unable to view Hank on his deathbed, refused to go back to Mrs. Wells' place.

Going home to Harriet appealed to her even less. She walked the main road, to the southern tip of Isle LaMotte. A bright sun exposed the naked trees and blinded the girl when she stared at the snowdrifts which covered the landscape. She blamed the sun and the wind for her moist eyes and wiped the tiny icicles which formed on her red cheeks. Charlie perched herself on the rocky shore that used to be Hank's fishing hole. She squeezed her eyes shut to block out the image of the boy's face. A loud crunch of feet in the snow and ice brought the young girl to her feet.

"I followed your tracks," said Otis.

"Go away," she snapped.

"I'm sorry about Hank"

"So am I."

"Harriet's pissed cuz I paid you guys."

"That's your problem. I'm moving out."

"Where you gonna go?"

"Mrs. Wells place, if she'll have me. She'll need someone to do the chores. And I can pay her too."

"Why'd you punch the doctor? He wouldn't tell me. Left almost as soon as he came. Embarrassed I guess."

"He's a bloodsucking bottom feeder. Now leave me alone."

"I will leave. But first I wanna say something."

Charlie's head swiveled in the man's direction. Otis did not sound like himself. His head drooped and he brushed his hat with the back of his hand. The brute wet his dried lips and looked up.

"There's nothing I can say that'll bring the boy back. I should have listened to my gut and told the ole lady, 'no'. But let's face it. Half the time, I'm drunk. And I ain't thinking straight. I don't want nothing to do with her, no more," said Otis, his eyes, glassy. "And I'm sorry, Charlie. I'm really sorry."

Charlie turned back to the frozen lake, speechless. Otis appeared to be sober, and he sounded sincere.

"That's all I got to say," said Otis.

Charlie heard the snow and ice crunch under his boots as he climbed the embankment.

"I expected to see you at the service," said Mrs. Wells.

Charlie, sitting and waiting on the front porch of the Wells' house, jerked to her feet. She gulped and looked away.

"I did the chores, Mrs. Wells."

"And I thank you for that. But you should have paid your respects to my son," she said.

Charlie's head drooped. Mrs. Wells climbed the steps and disappeared into the kitchen. Charlie hesitated and followed the woman. The woman stood at the kitchen table, her back to the girl, folding and refolding one of Hank's nightshirts. Charlie mumbled her request, fear in her voice.

"I need a place to stay, Mrs. Wells. I can pay you. And I'll do all the chores, just like Hank did," said Charlie, biting her quivering lips.

Hank's mother turned, her face set in stone. She spoke, as if in a trance.

"I could use another boarder. If you do the chores the rent will be reduced by half," the woman said.

Charlie gave the woman a dollar.

"I'll pay in advance," said the girl.

The spring of 1810 did not begin well.

Charlie stumbled down the stairs in Mrs. Wells' boarding house, wearing nothing but her night shirt. Mrs. Wells turned to see which boarder rose so early in the morning. Her eyes fell to the red stain, just below Charlie's waist. Blood streaked down the adolescent's leg.

"I'm bleeding," said Charlie, "And I don't feel so well."

"Come with me," said the woman, brushing past the girl and climbing the stairs to her bedroom.

They sat on the edge of Charlie's bed. Mrs. Wells explained the monthly phenomenon in a brusque and unemotional manner. Charlie, who would turn fourteen in August, objected.

"Every month?"

"Yes. Every month," said Mrs. Wells. "It means you are a grown woman now."

"Well, I don't like it," said Charlie.

Mrs. Wells jumped to her feet. She folded her arms and glared her disapproval.

"How much longer are you going to pretend that you're a boy?" asked Mrs. Wells.

Charlie refused to answer the question, changing the subject, instead.

"I think I got a job."

"I think I *have* a job," said Mrs. Wells, correcting the girl's English.

"His name is Reuben Quimby. Runs a raft off Windmill Point. Mostly cargo, some animals and a few people. That sort of stuff. No smuggling. Just like papa used to do but nothing north of the line. But if he finds out I'm a girl, I won't get the job." said Charlie.

"And your schooling?"

"I done learnt all I'm gonna learn," said Charlie.

"Your English leaves a lot to be desired," said the woman. "My Hank did his schooling. Why can't you?"

"I'm gonna earn fifty cents a week. That's more than enough for room and board," said Charlie.

"I'm not your mother. Do as you please," the woman said, leaving the room and slamming the door behind her.

Charlie winced from yet another cramp. She lay on her bed in a fetal position and whispered to the wallpaper.

"She misses Hank. So do I."

Chapter Four

REUBEN QUIMBY

Reuben Quimby didn't walk. He waddled.

The old man looked more like an aging grizzly bear than he did a seasoned businessman. But the bear could no longer accomplish the physical portions of his work on the lake. He suffered from a persistent cough. His knees could not support the old man's massive weight, without excruciating pain. And the swollen fingers on each hand made the simplest of tasks impossible. Reuben needed Charlie.

Always in a gruff mood, the man never married. "Too ornery," he would say. Quimby made a nice living. He moved people, animals and cargo, up and down Lake Champlain. His rough countenance, bulbous nose and a face covered in long, gray whiskers, didn't frighten Charlie. That fact alone prompted Quimby to give the kid a chance.

"Well, you're on time, at least," he barked, as Charlie reached the end of the dock where Quimby's raft was tied.

"Yes sir. My dad always said, showing up for work on time, is half the job."

"I knew your father," said Quimby. "Hard worker. It's a shame how he died."

Charlie acknowledged the compliment with a quick jerk of her head. She cleared the emotion from her throat.

"Thank you, Mr. Quimby."

"Didn't know he had a boy," Quimby added, catching Charlie's eyes and holding her gaze for a suspiciously long moment.

Charlie stiffened. She could feel the heat covering her face.

"Well don't just stand there, boy. Slip the cable. We've got a load in Champlain."

Charlie worked hard at her new job. Her days began at dawn and didn't end until the sun disappeared behind the western shore of Lake Champlain. Moving cargo and animals required constant attention and lots of rope. A choppy lake sent costly merchandize overboard. Neither Quimby nor his customers tolerated such losses.

Charlie sensed that Reuben liked her. He paid her, at times, for no more than the pleasure of her company. Always respectful and a good listener, the girl learned a great deal more about rafting on the oft-times, treacherous waters of Lake Champlain. Quimby made it a habit to introduce the new helper to each of his clients. The business duo became well-known and welcomed, on both sides of the lake.

One of their customers, a store owner near Plattsburgh Bay, reminded Charlie that being a girl could be a serious handicap. The man's grown daughter, he had three of them and no sons, dropped a jar of honey, on the loading dock. As the sticky liquid drained through the cracks into Lake Champlain, the man cursed his daughter. When he struck her on the face with the back of his hand, Charlie recoiled. The man's blow sent the girl into knee-deep water. She sobbed and slogged to the shore, her face red with shame.

"God has cursed me with three daughters and ain't one of them, worth a lick," he growled.

Reuben's brown eyes drilled into the bully's back. Charlie could say or do nothing to right the wrong she witnessed.

"Slip the cable, Charlie. And let's get out of here," said Quimby.

Barely out of ear shot, Quimby informed Charlie they would no longer be calling on that particular customer.

Quimby, by contrast, treated Charlie as if she were his only child. When Reuben inquired about her schooling, and discovered it lacking, he insisted on helping her. Although he never received a formal education, the old man, raised mostly by his grandmother, read voraciously. He demonstrated great skill in math, history, and the English language. He often brought books on board, for Charlie to study. While he navigated, propelled by the current, she sat on the deck, textbook and paper in hand. Charlie practiced her reading, writing, and arithmetic. Her spoken English improved considerably.

"You're smarter than most boys," said Quimby, the two of them on a long ride home from Plattsburgh.

Charlie glanced at her chest to confirm the tightness of the cloth wrap, she now wore on a regular basis.

"Thank you, Mr. Quimby."

Quimby smiled. He rarely smiled. She wondered if he knew about her secret. It didn't matter. Quimby became one of the few men in Charlie's life that she trusted. He treated her with respect and dignity. He could teach without being arrogant. He could mentor and not be condescending. He could be an adult, without treating her like a child.

Charlie, the girl, would be ecstatic in a world filled with Reuben Quimbys.

After his apology to Charlie, Otis returned to an empty cabin.

He noticed that Harriet's modest wardrobe no longer hung on the wall hooks in their bedroom. More importantly, the floorboard under the kitchen table, remained askew. Otis concluded that Harriet absconded with their stash of cash. As he sat at the table, an empty, pewter flask in one hand, the anger in his heart grew into a full-blown frenzy.

"The witch took all of the money," he grumbled to himself.

As if in response, he heard the sound of a horse-drawn wagon, rolling into the barnyard. He marched to the door and flung it open.

"That's him," said Harriet, pointing to Otis, as he stood in the doorway.

She and another man, who Otis did not recognize, sat together on a buckboard. The man introduced himself.

"Mr. Skinner, my name is William Blanchard. I am the new constable here in Isle LaMotte."

"Constable you say? Well, maybe you can get the money she stole from me," said Otis, spitting on the ground in the woman's direction.

"I don't know anything about no money, Mr. Skinner. I'm here to give you notice. This property belongs to Mrs. Skinner," said the constable. "You have twenty-four hours to vacate the premises."

"You got papers?" asked Otis.

"Mrs. Skinner is Mr. Wheeler's widow. She's the rightful owner."

Otis threw the flask, hitting the horse instead of his intended victim.

"Come back when you got some papers, Mr. Constable. Otherwise, you can go to the devil."

Harriet poked the constable's chest with a long, bony finger,

"I thought you was the law. What am I paying you for? I want him off my property. Now," she yelled.

"She's paying you with my money, you crooked bastard," said Otis.

He reached just inside the open doorway and retrieved a shotgun. He raised the weapon to eye level and pointed.

"Now git," said Otis.

Charlie and Reuben Quimby grew close.

On her fourteenth birthday, Reuben surprised the girl with a used musket. The flintlock weapon, known as a *Brown Bess*, originally served as the standard infantry weapon, for British soldiers. Over the years, it became the weapon of choice for civilians in the United States.

"I figure a boy your age should have a gun. Can't understand why you don't," said Reuben.

Charlie explained that her father's musket disappeared shortly after he died. She confessed her suspicion that Harriet sold it for the money.

"No matter," said Quimby. "You got one now. Can you shoot?"

"Yes sir. My papa taught me, years ago," said Charlie, as she pointed the ten plus-pound long gun at a slow-moving cloud.

"Well good, cause . . ."

Quimby's voice disappeared into a deep-throated rattle. The old man started coughing. The coughing fit continued for minutes. Quimby used a handkerchief to trap the expectorant. Charlie noticed a streak of blood on the man's lower lip.

"Mr. Quimby, you've been coughing a lot. And now, you're spitting up blood. That's not good," said Charlie.

Quimby stopped hacking long enough to catch his breath. He inspected a lumber raft, as it drifted by. Reuben's eyes glazed over.

He looked so lonely, Charlie thought. Another cough stirred deep in Reuben's chest.

"You're just a kid, Charlie. And I'm an old man. Can't be rafting on the lake, forever," he said.

The hacking cough grew worse. The old man's face turned deep red. Charlie raised her voice, to be heard over the noise.

"Mrs. Wells makes a mean chicken and dumplings," said Charlie, calculating that Hank's mom would be willing to nurse Quimby.

Reuben jerked his head in the direction of the Isle LaMotte dock.

"Let's bring her in," said Quimby, in between gasps for air.

Charlie rowed with vigor until they reached the Vermont shoreline. Mr. Quimby, beads of sweat dripping from his face, did not stop coughing. He leaned on Charlie, as they approached the Wells' boarding house.

Hank's mom agreed to take Quimby in, even though he was sick. The crusty merchant offered to pay extra for the nursing. Mrs. Wells agreed. They laid him in the downstairs bedroom. Charlie remembered the tiny room as the place where Hank died. Mrs. Wells made Quimby comfortable, fed him some beef broth, and then left the room. He grew somber.

"Charlie, please take care of things until I get better," he said.

"Yes sir."

Quimby closed his eyes and settled into a restless sleep.

Otis paced the floor in the cabin, stopping at one point to kick a chair.

The chair hit the wall and flew into pieces. One of the legs came to a rest on the floorboards, just beneath the kitchen table.

Otis sat on the edge of his bed, glaring at the door. His alcohol-induced rage grew worse by the minute. His eyes drifted to the floorboard which once hid the couple's money. He imagined that she may have accidentally left a few coins behind, in her haste to leave. Desperate for a drink and without funds, he pried the loose board from its place. Otis lay on his belly and reached into the hole with one hand. Using his fingers to sift the loose dirt, Otis systematically covered the entire area that lay within his reach. He cursed, as his dream of finding something, evaporated. But in the far reaches of the damp and dirty hiding spot, his fingers rested on a smooth surface. Paper or perhaps well-worn leather. He drew a sharp breath and lay there, motionless. Clutching his discovery, Skinner pulled his hand from beneath the floorboards and rolled to a sitting position. The man trembled as he pulled at the red ribbon which tied the document into a neat rectangle. Wrapped in oil paper, the missive appeared to have been undisturbed for years. Fourteen years, to be precise.

Otis struggled to read the hand-written document, but he recognized the most important words.

**_Bequest, all my possessions, my personal property,_ and
to my daughter, Charlotte "Charlie" Wheeler".**

Otis folded the legal document and re-wrapped it in the oil skin. He didn't bother with the red ribbon. He sat on the last unbroken chair and studied the document, once more. He slapped the table and smirked.

"Maybe I don't own this place. But that witch ain't gonna get it neither."

Otis didn't have the money for a lawyer, but he knew the local justice of the peace.

A previous brush with the law made for an awkward encounter.

Otis didn't care. The judge wasted no time. He read the document and announced his opinion, without reservation.

"If this case were in my court, the girl would get everything. And, if she wasn't old enough, I would appoint the adult of her choice as a guardian, assuming she had no blood relatives in the area."

Otis knew where to find Charlie.

"You shouldn't be here. What do you want?" Charlie demanded, glaring at Otis through the open door of Mrs. Wells' boarding house.

Otis stood on the front porch. He started to speak, thought better of it, and thrust the document into the girl's hands.

"What is this?"

"It's from your father. You best read it."

Charlie checked for Mrs. Wells' whereabouts and motioned to the wraparound porch. She sat on the steps. Otis sat with her, but not too close. Their heads swiveled for fear that Hank's mother might appear. Charlie's eyes grew wide as she scanned the document. Her jaw dropped and she turned to Skinner.

"Does your wife know about this?"

"No. Not yet. And she's not my wife anymore," said Otis, looking away to hide the pink glow on his face.

"Papa never told me. I had no idea."

Otis shrugged and grinned.

"Why are you doing this?" she asked.

Otis grew serious. He focused on his shoes and wrung the hat in his hands. He mumbled.

"The boy died because of me. It's my way of making it up to you."

Charlie studied the handwriting.

"Nobody treated me better than papa."

"You may end up in front of a judge, if the old lady puts up a fight," said Otis.

"She doesn't scare me."

"You're just a young'un. You may need a guardian. I'm guessing Mrs. Wells can help you."

Otis rose to his feet and walked to his waiting horse.

"What are you going to do?" she asked.

"Don't really know," he said.

Skinner nodded his good bye, mounted the horse, and squeezed the animal into a slow trot. Charlie jumped to her feet and yelled.

"Wait."

She ran to his side and extended a hand.

"Good luck, Otis"

Skinner flashed an uncertain smile.

Despite Mrs. Wells' hot tea laced with honey and a series of other homemade remedies, Reuben Quimby's condition worsened.

"I need you to fetch the doctor," said Mrs. Wells.

Charlie recalled the last time a doctor visited the Wells' homestead. Hank died and she decked that Coldwell fellow. She agonized over her conflicting feelings. A genuine concern for Quimby versus her bitter disdain for the young doctor. In the end, Quimby won. She rode to the eastern shore, jawboned the ferryboat owner out of his usual fee and crossed the lake. She stood on the porch at Coldwell's Alburgh residence for minutes. She thought about what she would say and rehearsed it in a series of silent whispers. She knocked on the door.

The girl's stomach churned when Coldwell opened the door. The young man immediately flinched, stepped back and slammed the door shut. Charlie could feel the anger rising in her chest. She wanted to punch the fool, again. But Mr. Quimby came first. He needed a doctor. She banged on the wood with her fist. When the doctor did not respond, she tried again, with a long series of loud and rapid knocks. Coldwell relented and the door swung open.

"What is it you want?" he asked.

"Mr. Quimby is very sick. He's got a fever and he's coughing up blood. And he won't stop coughing," she said.

"Who is this Mr. Quimby to you?" asked Nathan, keeping a safe distance.

"I work for him on his raft."

Coldwell and Charlie locked eyes but neither of them budged. Charlie blinked first, somewhat embarrassed but concerned with the welfare of her friend.

"I'm sorry I hit you, Dr. Coldwell. I was angry and frustrated. Hank is . . . was . . . my best friend. And you've got a right to be angry with me. But not with Mr. Quimby. He needs your help," she said.

Nathan snorted, pivoted in the doorway, and retrieved his medical bag.

"We'll take the wagon," he announced.

Otis, his conscious clear, decided to pay a call on Harriet.

She now occupied a room at the boarding house down the road from Charlie's cabin. He looked forward to telling her about the will. And he intended to recover his half of the money. The black servant girl pointed to the door at the top of the stairs.

"Miss Harriet be up there, Mister Otis."

She did not know that Harriet Skinner's visitor might be an unwanted guest.

Otis moved as quietly as he could. He knocked gently so as not to warn his ex-wife. When the door opened, Harriet gulped a scream and stepped back. Otis stepped into the room and shut the door.

"What do you want?" she asked, retreating until her back touched the wall.

"I got something to tell you. And you know what I want," he said.

"You fool. I've got the law on my side. You ain't got a chance. Now, get out of here before I have you arrested."

Otis recounted how he found Mr. Wheeler's last will and testament and brought it to the judge.

"The cabin belongs to Charlie, right and proper," he said.

Harriet got strangely quiet. She ambled over to the pitcher and vase which served as her bath. As she gazed into the mirror, Otis could see her face grow red with rage. He chuckled.

"What's wrong, Harriet? You ain't angry, are you?"

The taunt sent the miserly, old lady into a frenzied rage. She grabbed the ceramic pitcher and flung it across the room. Otis ducked. The projectile missed, well wide of its oversized target. It crashed into a far wall. Bits and pieces of white ceramic, decorated with pink roses, flew in every direction. She rushed Otis, scratching at his eyes and face. He grabbed her arms and shoved her onto the bed.

"Now where's my half of the money," he growled.

She lay there for a while, catching her breath. A strange smile. crossed her face.

"Otis, my love," she said, her voice a soft and sensuous purr. "Think about what you are doing."

"Miss Harriet? Mr. Otis? I dun heard a terrible crash. Is you hurt?"

It was the servant girl from downstairs. Otis watched as Harriet sprung from the bed. She signaled to Otis, to say nothing.

"We are fine. Just a little accident. Now you best get back to work," said Harriet.

"Yessum," said the servant.

Otis studied the woman he married.

"You would do anything for money, wouldn't you?"

Harriet approached Otis.

"Otis, listen to me."

She stood within an arm's length. Harriet pretended to rearrange her hair. She simultaneously retrieved a long, hat pin. Otis noticed the glimmer of the needle, but too late to react. She stabbed him in the face. He screamed in pain and reached for his cheek. The pin fell to the floor. She grabbed for his hand and bit hard. When her teeth struck bone, Otis used his free hand and punched his attacker in the face. She fell to the floor, hitting her head on the wooden bed post. The injured woman lay still. A small circle of blood, behind her head, grew larger.

The woman's color changed to a ghastly gray. Otis nursed his mangled finger and used a sleeve to swipe his bloody cheek. He sat on the edge of the bed and forced himself to think clearly. The lack of alcohol in his system, made it easier. He had no choice but to run. No one would believe it was self-defense. His sparring partner stood a foot shorter and weighed half as much as he did.

But first, the money. It must be in this room, thought Otis. Her fixed and dilated pupils seemed to follow him as he rifled through the woman's meager possessions. Nothing. He moved the small dresser, lifted the braided-area rug, and with no remaining places to search, returned to the bed, catching his breath. He stripped the mattress of its covers. Nothing. His head swiveled and he twisted and turned, looking for a hiding place he may have missed. And then, above the sound of a creaking bed, the slight tinkle of metal against metal. Coins. He groped the mattress and found a lump that wasn't straw. One slice of his knife revealed the familiar leather pouch which Harriet often fondled.

He looked again at the body, saw no signs of life, and then tiptoed out of the room. The servant girl, busy in the kitchen but hearing footsteps, leaned to one side for a better view of the hallway. Her face and hands, although dusted with flour, did not prevent the required amenities.

"Come again, Mr. Otis."

Otis smiled his goodbye and departed.

Nathan Coldwell broke the silence during the awkward ride to Mrs. Wells' farmhouse.

"How old are you, young man?"

"Fifteen," said Charlie, working hard to make her husky voice a bit more guttural.

Coldwell's eyebrows arched.

"You're fifteen years old?"

"Well, almost," Charlie lied, thinking about Quimby's present, just a week ago.

Charlie thought it necessary to counter Coldwell's air of superiority.

"Are you still digging up the *cad*avers?" asked Charlie, deliberately mispronouncing the word.

"It's ca*dav*ers," said Coldwell, "And we use them for anatomical research."

"Still ain't right." said Charlie, forgetting Mr. Quimby's admonitions about the English language.

"Still *isn*'t right," said Coldwell, rolling his eyes.

"Glad we agree," said Charlie, mimicking his reaction with an exaggerated roll of her eyes.

"You are impossible," said Coldwell, snapping the reins in frustration.

"And you are an arrogant ass," she replied.

"You are clearly intimidated by someone more learned than yourself, Master Wheeler."

"My papa used to say that the most important things in life cannot be learned in a classroom."

Nathan frowned.

"I do not spend all of my time in a classroom."

"Really? Can you shoot a gun? Can you steer a raft? Can you clean a fish? Ever been hunting? How do you track a bear without getting killed?"

Nathan gnawed on the inside of his cheek and pouted in silence. Charlie flashed a triumphant smile.

Mrs. Wells greeted Charlie and the doctor, on the porch.

"He's still coughing up blood."

Charlie handed Coldwell his medical bag and the twosome quick-stepped into the home. Mrs. Wells led the way. Quimby, traces of dried blood on his lips, lay unconscious in Hank's death bed. Charlie refused to approach her boss, observing Nathan instead. He listened to Quimby's heart and chest, examined Reuben's hands, and placed an ear very close to Quimby's open mouth. When finished, Coldwell pulled the bed covers to Quimby's chin, returned his medical instruments to the bag, and motioned to the kitchen table. Charlie took a few tentative steps forward, anxious to hear Coldwell's report.

"I'll make some tea," said Mrs. Wells.

Coldwell turned to Charlie.

"He has the consumption," said Coldwell.

The girl's furrowed eyebrows and puzzled look prompted Mrs. Wells to explain.

"My uncle had the consumption. He suffered for almost six months and then he passed," said the woman.

Nathan explained.

"Reuben's lungs are slowly filling with blood and mucous. His coughing will get worse. He'll suffer from high fevers and night sweats. He will lose much of his weight," Nathan reported.

"What can we do to help him?" asked Charlie.

"Some patients respond to warmer climates. Absent that, there's nothing we can do."

"Nothing?" she asked.

"He is unlikely to survive the onset of winter," said Nathan.

Charlie blamed Nathan. The man brought death, wherever he went. Her face grew red. She took a step in his direction. Her fingers clenched into fists. The doctor leaned back and cocked his head to one side. Charlie stopped. Her lips quivered as she blinked back the tears. Her eyes squeezed shut.

"Not again. Please. Not again."

Charlie backed away from the kitchen table and ran out the door.

"I don't understand, Mrs. Wells. Were they close?" asked Coldwell.

"Mr. Quimby has become like a father-figure to Charlie."

"The boy has certainly seen his share of death," said Coldwell.

Mrs. Wells did not correct the doctor's misidentification. Her head filled with memories of her dead son.

"Yes. We all have all seen our share of death," she whispered.

She turned her back to the doctor, her eyes darting everywhere as she poked at unlit wood in the fireplace.

Charlie didn't return to Mrs. Well's boarding house, until after dark.

Mrs. Wells looked up from the kitchen table. Charlie could see Quimby's bed from the doorway. The old man was sleeping. For a few moments, the woman and the girl sat together in silence. Mrs. Wells broke the silence.

"After you left, Mr. Quimby woke up. He asked me for some help."

"What kind of help?"

"He asked me to write this. It's for you," she said, and handed a meticulously folded piece of paper to Charlie.

Charlie locked eyes with Mrs. Wells and carefully unfolded the note. Mrs. Wells stared into space. Charlie read the note.

Charlie-

> *I won't be able to join you on the lake again.*
> *I knew this cough would get me sooner or later.*
> *The business, the raft, the sled, and the rest of my possessions are yours. You know my customers and they know you.*
> *Just wanted to say thanks. You have been like a daughter to me.*
> *I guess I've known your secret for a while, now.*
> *Boys aren't that pretty.*
>
> *Your friend,*
> *Reuben*

Charlie squeezed her eyes shut, desperate to stop the tears from flowing. It didn't work.

"Sorry, Mrs. Wells. I'm blubbering like a little girl."

"You're not a little girl, Charlie. You are a young lady. And it's quite acceptable to cry when you have to say goodbye to someone you love."

"But I haven't seen you cry. Not even when Hank died," said Charlie.

Mrs. Wells jerked in her chair. Her eyes blazed. She pushed her teacup and saucer to the center of the table.

"How dare you?" she hissed.

She jumped to her feet. Her chest heaved with every breath.

"Mrs. Wells, I'm sorry. I didn't mean . . ."

The woman's open hand hit Charlie square on the cheek. The unexpected blow came close to knocking Charlie off her chair. She grabbed the table, for balance. Mrs. Wells wasn't finished.

"I think it's high time you found some other place to live, Charlie Wheeler."

Charlie, still stinging from the vicious slap, stared up at the woman. She rubbed the tears from her eyes with one swipe of her shirt sleeve, and cautiously rose to her feet. The girl stood face to face with her attacker and spoke with a clear voice.

"You had no cause to hit me, Mrs. Wells."

Mrs. Wells stabbed the girl in the chest with her index finger.

"You killed my Hank, Charlie Wheeler. If it wasn't for you, I'd be living with a real boy, and not some spoiled little brat who thinks she's a boy."

Charlie took several deep breaths.

"Hank had his mind made up. He desperately wanted the money. A team of horses could not have stopped him. He intended to go with or without me. What was I supposed to do?"

"You're lying," said Mrs. Wells, as she fidgeted with her hair and smoothed the surface of her apron.

Charlie's face grew soft. She reached for the woman.

"Please Mrs. Wells. I'm telling you the truth."

The woman stepped back, refusing the girl's touch. The grieving mother trembled, and her eyes twitched out of control.

"No. You're lying. Now get out of my house. You hear me? Get out of my house."

Mrs. Wells repeated her demand as Charlie climbed the stairs to her room. The girl shoved a few possessions into a burlap bag and left.

Mrs. Wells said it over and over again.

"Get out of my house."

Otis paced the floor of the barn, jerking his head in the direction of the closed door each time he heard a noise.

Although his horse remained hidden behind the building, Skinner worried. The Wheeler place would be the first place that Constable Blanchard visited, once they found Harriet's body. He replayed the struggle in Harriet's room. The witch attacked him. He tried to stop her, that's all. He didn't intend to kill her. He reached for the large lump of coins and currency in his pocket. The money slowed his pounding heart but did nothing to assuage his paranoia. Something or somebody lurked outside.

His rifle, still in the house, would be of no use. A pitchfork, resting on the floor near the haystack, became his weapon of choice. His eyes darted wildly as he tiptoed to the door. He could hear footsteps. They grew louder and closer. He raised the pitchfork to eye level and tightened his grip on the wooden handle. As the door opened, he leaned back, poised to pounce.

"Otis, you scared me half to death," said Charlie.

She threw her empty egg basket at the man. He swatted it away and released a long, slow breath.

"You scared *me* half to death," he said.

Charlie pushed Otis to one side, retrieved the basket, and sat on a milking stool.

"You and I have to talk," she said.

Otis reached for the barn door. He checked the barnyard before shutting it. He used the wooden pole to bar it shut.

"What's the matter with you?" she asked. "You look like you saw a ghost."

Otis Skinner's chest heaved. He leaned against the closed door, as if another intruder would appear. Charlie ignored his antics.

"I'm planning to move back to the cabin. And I won't have the time to do chores. Got myself a business to run," she said. "I could use a hired hand. I'll pay you well," she added.

"I'm going away," Otis mumbled.

"What did you say?"

Otis took a step forward.

"I'm going away."

"Where? How long? And why now?"

"I don't know yet."

"You're acting awful strange, Otis. What's going on?"

"Nothing. Why are you asking? I don't answer to you. You're not my wife. I gotta go," he said, turning to the door.

"Are you walking? I didn't see your horse out there."

Otis checked the landscape and made a quick escape. Charlie followed. After Otis disappeared behind the building, he reappeared, riding at a full gallop.

Charlie watched the cloud of dust as the man and his horse flew down the dirt road.

"I knowz sumpin wuz wrong when she dun miss her suppah. Miss Harriet ain't never missed her suppah," said the servant girl.

Constable Blanchard nodded.

"Did Miss Harriet have any visitors?"

"Yassir. Mistah Otis cum by, yesterday mornin. Was right nice like."

"And you found her this morning?"

"Yasser. I figger the ole woman fell and hit her head."

Blanchard hesitated to inform the young black girl, but she had to know in case Otis returned.

"There was a struggle. The room was searched, top to bottom. She was murdered," said the Constable.

The servant girl fell against the wall and smothered a scream.

"Oh lawd. O lawd. Miss Harriet dun been killed. Oh Lawd."

The constable turned to the owner of the boarding house.

"You can move the body. I'm gonna pay Mr. Skinner a visit."

Chapter Five

ON HER OWN

Charlie finished the chores and rode her horse to the water's edge.

Reuben Quimby's raft lay in the water, tied to the dock, where she and the owner left it. She stepped on to the vessel and sat with her back against the large, storage chest. A soft breeze on Lake Champlain gently rocked the vessel, cradling Charlie until she drifted into a daydream of childhood memories. Summer days, jam-packed with rafting, swimming and fishing, filled Charlie's head to overflowing.

She longed for those lazy days, but a voice in her head said it was time to move on. Reuben Quimby thought the girl was old enough and smart enough to own a gun and operate a rafting business. His confidence in the girl gave Charlie the confidence that she needed. On that morning, she said goodbye to her youth and the people of her youth. The adult world could be scary and nerve-racking. But Quimby and Charlie's papa, prepared her well for the journey. She stood ready, willing and able to make her living on the water. And she would do it as a young man.

"Are you all alone, boy?"

Charlie's head jerked up. She jumped to her feet and faced the man behind her.

"Why do you want to know? And who are you?"

"My name is Blanchard. I'm the new constable in town."

Charlie stood on her raft and watched the man tether his horse to a nearby tree. When he descended the embankment, she moved nearer to her long rifle. Blanchard stopped at the end of the dock.

"I'm Charlie Wheeler. And the raft is mine, if that's what you're wondering about."

"Nope. I'm looking for Otis Skinner's raft," said the constable. He scanned the horizon and scratched the back of his head.

"It was my papa's raft," said Charlie. "He took it. Never returned it."

The constable ignored her complaint.

"I just left your place. No sign of Skinner."

"He may have gone to see Harriet, but I doubt she'd let him in."

"She let somebody in. She's dead."

Charlie steadied herself on the large chest.

"Dead? Are you sure?"

"Took a bad hit to the head after a struggle."

"Otis, you damned fool," said Charlie, to herself.

"If you know something, you best tell me, boy. Tell me now or you're gonna spend the night in my jail," he said, waving his hat in her direction.

Charlie did not anticipate that her debut in the world of adults would occur so soon. She stepped forward with her chin in the air. She glared at the man with one eye closed.

"Around these parts, you'd get a lot more flies with honey, Mr. Constable."

Blanchard, intent on boarding the raft, took a big step forward.

"We'll see about that."

A sudden chop on the water raised and lowered the dock, by several feet in each direction. Too angry to watch his step, Blanchard planted one foot on the raft and left the other one on the dock. Charlie smirked as the constable struggled to keep his balance. He shot Charlie a panicked look. The girl waited for a second and then yanked the Constable aboard. The constable frustrated and angry, blushed pink with embarrassment.

"You're welcome," said Charlie.

The constable stared at the deck.

"I'm just doing my job, you know," he mumbled.

"I know," she said. But there's no reason to be disrespectful. Even if I am a kid." she said.

The constable turned to leave.

"Wait," she said.

The constable pivoted in place.

"Otis was at the cabin this morning. Acting very strange. Said he was going away but wouldn't tell me why or where."

Blanchard told her what he knew.

"Otis and Harriet argued a few weeks back. They was arguing over who owned the place and Otis said she stole his money."

Charlie shook her head in disagreement.

"The cabin and everything on the spread, belongs to me. My father said so in his will. But I can tell you she was never going to part with that money, even though Otis earned most of it."

"If you see him, will you let me know?" asked Blanchard.

"Yes. I will."

The constable hesitated when he reached the edge of the raft.

"Want some help?" asked Charlie.

"No, I got it," said the man.

Charlie watched the constable climb the small hill that led to the main road. The sun warmed her back, but a cluster of goose-bumps made a sudden appearance on her arms. Charlie's head swiveled as she searched the landscape. She saw nothing but the dark blue line that separated green trees from blue water. No movement and no sign of life. And yet, she felt certain that someone watched her every move. The memory of her father's favorite admonition flashed in her mind.

"*Trust your gut.*"

The next morning, Charlie busied herself, preparing the raft for her first solo trip on Lake Champlain. She darted from the dock to the raft and back again, duplicating Reuben Quimby's ritualistic routines and her late father's strict protocols. She repeated Benjamin Wheeler's words, out loud.

"You must prepare for the unexpected."

"I agree."

The unexpected response yanked Charlie in the direction of the voice. Her eyes searched for the hunting rifle.

"You left it on the raft," said Otis.

Charlie twitched.

Otis stepped forward, brandishing a large hunting knife.

"Stay where you are, Charlie."

"I thought you were leaving town," she said.

Skinner struggled to speak clearly. His eyes glistened and he reeked of alcohol.

"I need a ride to Canada."

"You still have papa's raft. Use it."

"I had to throw off the constable. I figure it's somewhere north of the line right about now," said Otis, shrugging his shoulders.

"You killed Harriet," Charlie said.

Otis glared at Charlie through eyes that narrowed to slits.

"It was an accident. She attacked me. I had to defend myself,"

Otis growled, thrusting his mangled finger in her face.

Charlie studied the man, unsure if she should believe him or not.

Otis bit his lip and studied the girl.

"I can pay you."

"I don't want your blood money," said Charlie.

"You can drop me off at the line. Tonight, right after dark," he said.

"No."

"You owe me, Charlie."

"How do you figure that?"

"I found your father's will. If it wasn't for me, you would've lost the farm."

Charlie shook her head.

"You've got a lot of nerve."

Otis asked again.

"Please?"

Charlie paused and then reacted.

"No. I won't do it," she said.

"They can't hang me twice," said Otis, carefully examining the sharp edge of his hunting knife.

"I'm not afraid of you, Otis Skinner."

"No. I don't suppose you are, Charlie. But I noticed that Mrs. Wells is pretty much alone for most of the day. It would be too bad if something happened to that nice lady."

Otis focused his blood shot eyes on the girl. He ran his thumb across the blade. A sudden hiccup made him wince. He shoved the injured thumb in his mouth and sucked on the cut.

"I may be drunk, Charlie. But I'm serious. I got no choice."

Charlie took a deep breath and blew the hair off her forehead. She and Mrs. Wells rarely spoke, but Charlie wished her no harm.

The woman suffered enough.

"You're not giving me much of a choice," she said.

Otis staggered backwards and grinned.

"I'll be here at the dock. Sundown. Don't be late." said Otis.

Otis shuffled into the thick underbrush and disappeared from view.

"You're early."

Otis Skinner's voice sent a chill through Charlie's slender frame.

"I want this over with. And I never want to see you again," she said, untying her raft from the short dock on Isle LaMotte's west shore.

Otis hopped on board and used the large trunk as his chair. Charlie calculated that the eight-mile trip to the international boundary line would require less than an hour. The lake's current would push the small vessel northward. But the half-moon, now rising in the eastern sky, worried the girl most. The memory of government revenuers firing their cannon and then murdering her father, flashed in her mind.

"If anyone should ask, we're night fishin," Otis announced.

Charlie rolled her eyes and shook her head in disgust.

"I snapped my fishing pole and lost my line, last week."

"Well, let's hope we don't get no visitors," said Otis, feeling for the hunting knife, secreted in a boot.

"*Any* visitors," said Charlie, remembering Reuben Quimby's never ending effort to educate the girl.

She took pleasure correcting the blackmailer's English.

"When did you get so high and mighty?" asked Otis, reaching into his wrap for his flask.

Charlie ignored him and focused on the extra-long paddle she used to steer the raft. Otis took a long swig and burped his satisfaction.

"That's for your trouble," he said, tossing a few coins in Charlie's direction.

Charlie yanked her long paddle from the water and slammed it on the deck. She scooped up the money and flung it at Otis. He lunged but failed to grasp a single coin. Otis twisted in his seat, and watched, as Lake Champlain swallowed a portion of his blood money. He yanked his hunting knife in anger and shoved the blade deep into the large chest that served as his chair.

"You stupid girl. I should whip your ass," Otis yelled.

"Who goes there?"

The strange voice came from the direction of Windmill Point. They both turned their back to the voice. They did not want the moon's reflection on their face.

"Start rowing," whispered Otis, as he retrieved a spare oar and quietly plunged it into the water.

The voice at Windmill Point went silent. Charlie guided the raft to the lake's eastern shoreline. When it lurched to a stop, she snapped at Otis.

"Get off my raft."

Otis smiled.

"Hope to see you again."

"Not likely," said Charlie.

She pushed away from the shore as Otis stepped off the vessel.

Charlie worked the lake through the fall of 1810 and into the cold winter of 1811.

When the lake froze over, she dusted off Reuben Quimby's sled. She made her runs on the ice-covered lake, careful to avoid open areas on the frozen surface. She visited Reuben Quimby several times a week, saying little or nothing to Mrs. Wells. Charlie told Quimby about her travels, their customers, and the latest gossip. She would spend hours at his bedside. The sickly man found it difficult to speak. Charlie repeated the compliments of happy customers. They referred to her as 'the boy who worked like a man.' Quimby flashed a rare smile.

Charlie retired each evening, exhausted. In addition to her trips on the lake, there were daily chores at her cabin and the barn. She also helped Mrs. Wells with the outside chores. The woman never acknowledged the girl's kindness but Charlie did it anyway. She also paid Mrs. Wells for tending to Reuben Quimby, disciplining herself to save as much money as possible. The funds, more than Charlie ever possessed, would go to Mr. Quimby when he got better, she thought.

The spring of 1811 brought with it, endless signs of new life. Straw-colored fields laced with wide swaths of green dotted the landscape. Swollen streams raced to the lake. Fruit trees, clothed in green buds, housed hundreds of birds singing the arrival of warm weather and bright sunny days.

Unlike the winter snow, Reuben Quimby's symptoms did not disappear. He regained consciousness less and less. The old man coughed continually and struggled to breathe, using a long series of quick, shallow breaths, to survive. On many occasions, the dying man and his young helper said nothing, content to hold hands and speak with their eyes. Charlie strongly suspected that Reuben knew he would soon breathe his last.

"Mrs. Wells. Come quick," said Charlie, springing from her chair, but remaining at Reuben's bedside.

The old man stopped breathing for seconds at a time. Charlie thought her long vigil ended. But then, he took another breath.

This pattern repeated itself for an hour. Finally, the old man exhaled loudly and at length. His last breath ended with a rattle of fluids, deep in the man's lungs.

"It's over. He's gone," Mrs. Wells announced.

The woman left the room. For an instant, the girl did not budge, her eyes fixated on the body of her best friend and mentor. And then, as if awakened from a deep slumber, Charlie quietly resumed her post on the chair at Reuben's bedside. She reached for his hand, brought it to her lips and, with great care, kissed the cooling flesh.

Reuben Quimby's hand caught each and every tear.

When Nathan responded to the knock on his door, he saw Charlie Wheeler standing on the front porch.

He opened the door and offered his condolences.

"Charlie. I heard that Mr. Quimby passed, yesterday. My deepest sympathies."

The young doctor didn't flinch this time. The boy with the nasty punch, no longer posed a threat. He hoped. He watched as Charlie shifted her weight from one foot to the other and used her tongue to wet her lips. She said nothing and the awkward silence made him uncomfortable.

"I'm making a pot of tea. Would you like some?"

Nathan immediately regretted the offer. What sensible doctor would invite a fourteen-year-old boy to join him for tea. But Charlie affected Nathan that way. The kid's very presence confused Nathan. And the doctor's ordinarily logical thought process went awry.

"No sir. I don't drink tea, unless I'm sick."

Nathan bit his lip. His frustration bubbled to the surface. He folded his arms and stepped forward.

"Why are you here, Charlie?"

Charlie took a deep breath.

"Do you want the body or not?" she asked.

Nathan's eyes widened. He absentmindedly checked that his hair remained in a neatly tied ponytail.

"I guess I. I mean. I wasn't going to ask you."

Charlie stared. Nathan paused.

"Well, he must have family," said Nathan.

Charlie corrected him.

"No, I'm his family."

Coldwell rubbed his jaw. The pain from Charlie's punch disappeared but not the memory.

"The University does have a fund."

"I don't need your money," she said.

Nathan grimaced. His head drooped and he spoke in a murmur.

"Of course not. I apologize. I didn't mean to insult you."

Charlie posed with a hand on each hip.

"Well. What do you want to do?"

"I can be there this afternoon."

Charlie turned away. Nathan watched as she rubbed her eyes. She sniffed and cleared her throat.

"Thank you, Nathan."

Nathan noticed the relief on Charlie's face. He saw a vulnerability and sadness in the boy's face, that he failed to notice in the past. And Charlie called him by his first name. A good sign, he thought. Nathan resisted an urge to hug the adolescent. That too, would be inappropriate.

"I thank you," said Nathan, emphasizing the "you" as he studied Charlie's glistening, blue eyes.

Her lips quivered. She turned and left.

Charlie could not recall a season when she worked as hard or as long as she did during the summer and fall of 1811.

Ruben Quimby's customers became her customers. The location and destination of her clients' cargo placed her on the lake, almost daily. Docks at Alburgh, Chazy and the customs house at Windmill Point became regular stops. She rarely traveled after dark unless a full moon lit her way. She enjoyed those windy days when the crude sail made her journey easier and speedier. She avoided those days when a storm appeared on the horizon. Lake Champlain could produce four and five-foot breakers. A raft loaded with cargo could not survive that kind of weather. Dozens of vessels now dotted the watery landscape. Not all of them were as cautious as Charlie. Some of them posed a threat.

"What's in the barrels, kid?"

The man's voice came from a timber raft that Charlie first noticed a mile back. The raft, three times larger than her own, featured four sails. It could easily overtake her smaller vessel. As the visitors approached, Charlie counted a five-man crew. She secretly admired its on-board shelter. The A-frame cabin, about five feet high, could be used for storage or shelter in bad weather. And this one had a small fire pit, for heating and cooking.

"They're empty," Charlie lied.

"Where're you headed?" asked the same voice.

Charlie lied again.

"Back to Champlain."

She slowed her vessel and studied the large raft as it sailed past. One of the men on deck, scurried to the small A-frame shelter. The large man turned his back, dropped to his knees, and hid from her view. Charlie could feel the goosebumps rise on her arms. She gnawed on her lower lip and grimaced when the pot ash kettle, on the deck of her raft, came into view. The large, cast-iron kettle stood more than two feet high, measured forty inches in diameter, and weighed five hundred pounds. Such kettles, used almost exclusively for the production of pot ash, might well have been a full-page ad in the local paper. Anyone carrying the kettles would very likely be carrying pot ash. The nosy crew, almost certainly, did not believe her lies.

In fact, she carried two barrels of the black powdery substance. Since the embargo went into effect, the price of pot ash in Montreal rose to $15 per hundred-weight. A farm hand didn't earn that much money after three months of hard labor. Charlie lied for a reason.

Some men would kill for less.

When Otis thought it safe, he backed out of the on-board shelter and explained the situation to his boss.

"That kid ain't going to Champlain," said Skinner, jerking his head in the direction of Charlie's raft.

Otis, anxious to curry favor with his new boss, filled in the details.

"The kid lives in Isle LaMotte. Took over Reuben Quimby's business, when the ole man got sick," said Otis.

The boss, a seasoned smuggler, beamed with joy.

"And that scrawny, little kid ain't gonna move those barrels by herself, he said.

Otis grinned and nodded his head in agreement.

"Nope. My guess is that it stays on the raft tonight. Gets picked up in the morning," said Otis.

"Do you know where he docks?" asked the boss.

"Yup," said Otis, smiling like a satiated barn cat.

The boss chuckled.

"We'll go tonight."

Charlie docked the raft, checked the canvas which covered her cargo and climbed the embankment which led to the main road.

She walked a short distance, stopped abruptly, and scratched her head. In less than an hour, darkness would envelop the dock. A half-moon meant that her precious cargo lay in full view of passersby. She thought of those men on the lumber raft. The nosy one with all the questions and the shy one, who seemed to be hiding from Charlie. The girl's stomach growled with hunger. Her "gut feeling," to which papa so often referred, pulled rank. Charlie forgot about eating and turned back to the dock. Her nightly chores, like supper, would wait.

She retrieved her musket from its hiding place and spread an old quilt near the large chest. Charlie closed her eyes but couldn't sleep. Hunger, exhaustion, a hard bed, and the noises of the night made sleeping impossible.

A man's voice, carried in by a slight breeze, got her attention. The sound of boots on wood, and a noisy splash, forced Charlie to her feet. Visitors. Charlie crouched behind the storage chest, her Brown Bess primed and loaded. In the dim light, she could see the outline of a tiny A-frame cabin. The men on the lumber raft decided to pay their respects, she thought. She recognized the size and gait of the man who walked half the length of the raft. The oversized shadow carried a rope, intent on securing the large vessel to Charlie's dock.

Charlie pointed her musket at the man. She tried to sound calm.

"Welcome back, Otis," she said.

Skinner didn't break his stride and tied the large vessel to one of the dock's wooden uprights. When he stepped onto the dock, Charlie pulled the hammer back on her musket. The distinctive click brought Otis to an abrupt halt.

"You wouldn't shoot a man in cold blood, would you Charlie?" Charlie yelled.

"Get back on your raft. Now."

Skinner's crewmates stepped forward. The thieves stood shoulder to shoulder.

"There's five of us Charlie. Them two barrels ain't worth dying for," said Otis.

He took a step forward. Charlie raised her musket to eye level. Otis didn't flinch. She tightened her grip and retreated, but just one step. Otis walked ahead until the barrel of her gun pressed against his chest. She fingered the trigger.

"I'll shoot, Otis. I swear, I'll shoot you."

"Don't be stupid, Charlie," he growled.

Otis used his right arm and brushed the weapon to one side. The gun went off. The musket ball tore through the sleeve of Skinner's shirt. The projectile creased the man's skin, surprising the victim more than hurting him. Otis noticed a small amount of blood. His face turned a crimson red.

"You snotty little brat."

The brute's temper triggered a shot of adrenalin. He backhanded the girl with enough force to spin her around. The gun fell out of her hands. She landed on her face, striking her head against the pot ash kettle. Dark-red blood oozed from the gash on her scalp. Charlie lay motionless.

"Load the barrels and let's get out of here. Now," said Otis.

Charlie missed the spectacular sunrise which occurred the next morning.

While she lay unconscious, a brilliant sun transformed the blue waters of Lake Champlain into a shimmering blanket of undulant diamonds.

When her lifeless form came into view, Charlie's customers scurried to her rescue. The wagon, required for transporting the pot ash, became a temporary ambulance. They delivered her to Dr. Coldwell's office in Alburgh.

"We think he's been laying there half the night," said one of the men.

Nathan Coldwell wiped the victim's blood-covered face. He drew a sharp breath when Charlie's face, came into view.

"Let's get him inside," he ordered.

A half dozen sutures and a whiff of smelling salts brought Charlie back to consciousness. She struggled as she focused on Nathan and, without thinking, inspected her chest. The wrap remained in place with her shirt still buttoned. When Charlie's clients gathered round, she recalled the events of that evening.

"The pot ash?" she asked.

"Gone," came the response.

Nathan interrupted.

"You're lucky to be alive," he said.

Charlie scowled.

"It was Otis Skinner. He's running with a bunch of smugglers on a lumber raft. From across the line, I think. I've got to get . . ."

Charlie's voice trailed off when she tried to sit up. The pain and the dizziness made it impossible. Her head fell back on to the bed. Nathan intervened.

"Thank you, gentlemen. I'll see to it that he gets home."

As her clients exited the doctor's home, Charlie spoke to the ceiling.

"Can you bring me home, doc? Please?" she asked.

"Perhaps later. I would like to keep you here for a while. You were unconscious for hours. I'm worried about a bleed in the brain."

As Charlie's eyes fluttered closed, she murmured her thoughts. "Thank you, Nathan."

Nathan came to his patient's bedside, a tender smile on his face. "You're welcome, Charlie."

Charlie recovered from her run-in with Otis Skinner.

She visited Constable Blanchard's office to report the incident. She also decided against the transport of pot ash, anytime in the future. The precious commodity posed too much of a risk. Weeks later, an unexpected visitor came calling. Charlie heard the knock on her kitchen door while she raked hay in the barn. When Charlie turned the corner, she saw Nathan Coldwell on the front porch.

"Doctor Coldwell, over here," she yelled.

Nathan swiveled in the girl's direction, clearly startled. As he approached Charlie, she noticed beads of sweat on his forehead. She wore a wide grin as she greeted her visitor.

"I don't wish to disappoint you, Nathan, but I'm not sick and I'm fresh out of dead bodies," she said.

Nathan faked a weak smile.

"I just came to say good bye."

Charlie's eyebrows arched.

"Where ae you going?"

"I'm leaving the area."

Charlie confessed her disappointment.

"I'm very sorry to hear that," she said, a solemn look covering her face.

"I'll be in Burlington and Plattsburgh," he announced.

"Studying or practicing?"

"Both," he said, his head swiveling as if someone might be watching.

"Nathan. You're acting like a nervous cat."

Nathan stopped fidgeting. He sighed heavily and bowed his head.

"I shouldn't be bothering you."

Charlie scolded her visitor.

"You're not bothering me. But something's bothering you."

Nathan murmured a response.

"No. Not really. I've got to go."

Charlie extended her hand.

"Good luck, my friend."

Nathan thrust a sweaty palm in her direction.

"Thank you, Charlie. I hope we see each other, again. I mean, I don't want you to get sick, or anything like that. I just mean that . . ."

"I know what you meant Nathan. I feel the same way," she said.

Nathan went stiff.

"You do?" he asked, a look of surprise crossing his face.

"Yes, of course," she answered.

"Very well then."

Nathan turned to leave, stopped, and pivoted abruptly.

"And good luck to you too," he added.

Charlie grinned as Nathan jogged to his horse and galloped off.

Nathan cursed himself, for most of the trip back to his office.

Why did he go out of his way to say good bye to a teenage boy? It made no sense. As he packed the remainder of his things, Nathan considered the reasons for his behavior. One particular conclusion triggered his anger. He reached for a bed roll and flung it across the room.

"I am not attracted to him," he argued, the voice in the back of his head, suggesting otherwise.

Surprised by the sound of his own voice and shocked by the angry denial, Nathan fell into a nearby chair. He closed his eyes and massaged his aching head. Sodomy was illegal. The mere thought of such a thing gave Nathan the cold sweats. He enjoyed woman, although most of his female acquaintances were either unsightly or dimwitted or both. Thus far, he experienced no interest, emotionally or physically, in a relationship with a woman. His medical studies came first. But now, thanks to an adolescent boy, Nathan couldn't think straight. He couldn't concentrate, and he couldn't get the kid out of his mind. What in God's name, was the matter with him?

After an hour of wrestling with his thoughts, Nathan seized on his imminent departure as a solution. If he never saw the boy again, he would never experience those feelings again. His life would return to normal.

Or so he hoped.

Chapter Six

WAR

In 1811, Charlie celebrated her fifteenth birthday. The country inched its way to war.

The government in Washington did not want to be accused of aiding and abetting the British, in its war against France. But the residents of upstate New York and Vermont did just that. Their livelihood depended on trade with British Canada. Not surprisingly, Lake Champlain continued to be a hotbed of smuggling activity and violence. Border guards seized a significant number of boats and huge amounts of cargo. Even Charlie, moving cargo among and between New York and Vermont, found herself stopped and harassed.

As the summer and fall of 1811 morphed into the winter of 1811 and 1812, skirmishes occurred with greater frequency on Lake Champlain. The English, the Americans. and the smugglers, grew more and more violent. In November, a revenue agent shot and killed a Vermont man, for "smuggling" no more than a few bags of salt, intended for his family's consumption. When the government refused to arrest the border guard, tempers flared even more. In January of 1812, Customs collector Peter Sailly, of Plattsburgh, used pistols to ward off a handful of home invaders. The interlopers, intent on retrieving previously seized contraband, escaped to Canada.

Abroad and on the high seas, the Brits repeatedly seized American merchant ships and forced American crews to serve on British ships. America, despite its efforts to stay out of the European war, could not avoid its inevitability. The country declared war against Britain on June 18, 1812.

The sixteen-year-old girl, who everyone considered a boy, now lived and worked in a war zone.

When the United States declared war against Great Britain, Nathan's life took a sharp turn.

Although enthusiastic about his studies and medical practices in Burlington and Plattsburgh, the onset of war sent Nathan in an unexpected direction. His desire to become an experienced surgeon, prompted him to volunteer with the U.S. Army. Construction of a large cantonment, including a general hospital, began in Burlington, on the bluff overlooking Lake Champlain. The two-story hospital, which included beds for 300 soldiers, required army surgeons and surgeon's mates. Nathan Coldwell did not yet qualify as a surgeon but he easily qualified as a surgeon's mate. And that, he hoped, might one day lead to his promotion to full surgeon.

The site in Burlington began as a camp for the 11th US Infantry. Although the grounds initially consisted of tents and huts, it soon became a permanent facility for the U.S. Army. Nathan would serve with Colonel Pike's 15th regiment.

"I'm Coldwell. Nathan Coldwell. Surgeon's mate."

"You're the third surgeon's mate in this camp. And there's nothing to do."

The cold welcome came from Nathan's tent-mate, a medical orderly, himself.

Nathan extended a hand. The roommate did not rise from his cot. He rolled his eyes, and offered a limp wrist, in response.

"Tom Sackett."

"Where are you from, Tom?" asked Nathan.

"Not here," said Sacket, rolling on his side and facing the canvas wall.

"You must be tired," said Nathan. "I'll leave you alone."

Nathan stored his belongings underneath the remaining cot and stepped to the opening.

His new roommate dismissed Nathan with a loud snore.

Charlie agonized about her rafting business.

The mere prospect of war sent prices soaring. Foodstuffs, staples, and lumber that could be smuggled into British Canada generated huge profits, payable in gold or silver. A good number of Charlie's customers requested that she sell their items, north of the line. Some of them took their business elsewhere because she refused.

A customer in Chazy, pointed at two barrels of tea sitting on his dock.

"I can double my money, Charlie, if you bring it across the line. It came up from Boston. I paid a dollar a pound. You can get at least two dollars a pound, north of the line. I'll give you 25 percent of the profit," he said.

"But I could lose the whole thing, Mr. Saxe. The Revenuers are everywhere," said Charlie.

"I trust you boy. Been doing business with you for more than a year now. I assume you'll cross the line at night," he said.

Charlie grimaced and scratched her head.

"And if I say no?" she asked.

"If you refuse, I have no choice but to take my business elsewhere. All of it," said the man.

"I'm sorry, sir," she said, extending her hand in friendship.

Charlie continued to lose clients because she refused to cross the line with their goods. The inflationary impact of the war also affected her domestic shipments. Anything that could fetch a good price in English Canada became an easy target for smugglers-turned-pirates. Charlie's small sailing raft and her skill, especially in the evening hours, made it easier to avoid trouble. For a while, she enjoyed a string of good luck, by staying far away from the line and keeping a watchful eye out for unfriendly interlopers.

On one evening, just a few miles short of her home, Charlie's luck ran out.

"What are you carrying?"

The voice came from behind. Charlie carried a single, knee-high barrel of rum. A customer in Plattsburgh sold it to a Vermont tavern owner. The alcohol sold for three dollars a gallon in Plattsburgh. In Canada, it would be worth nine dollars a gallon.

"Who wants to know?" asked Charlie, as she reached for her musket.

The vessel behind her, also traveling north, carried at least one man holding a lantern aloft. The light grew closer, and the voice persisted.

"Whatever it is, it's gonna get seized. Your raft, too, if you give us a hard time," said the voice.

"I'm not even next to the line. How can I be smuggling?" she asked.

"You're headed north. We're pulling alongside."

Charlie saw no point in resisting. She rested her musket on the storage trunk. The loss of the raft and a long walk back to Isle LaMotte, bothered her more than the loss of her customer's rum. The man with the lantern stood on the edge of a large raft. He held a rope in the other hand and jumped onto Charlie's vessel. Charlie got a closer look and barked her objection.

"You're not customs."

The man tethered his raft to hers.

"No, we're not," said a second voice, stepping to the edge of the large raft and into the light.

"Otis Skinner, you murdering thief," Charlie growled, reaching for the long rifle.

The man with the lantern stepped between Charlie and the trunk.

"Sorry, kid. If you touch that thing off, we'll have every revenuer in the county, on our back."

Otis jumped on board and sliced the ropes that held the barrel of rum in place.

"Rum or cider?" he asked, hoisting the barrel onto his shoulder.

Charlie glared at the oversized brute.

"Lake water, you fool."

Otis chuckled.

"Now is that anyway for a young lady to talk?"

The lantern man retrieved his rope and followed Skinner. In the moonlight, Charlie could see Otis, using the barrel as a chair. Her eyes closed to slits as she grabbed her Brown Bess off the trunk. She squatted behind the chest, primed the weapon, and rested the barrel on the trunk. She pulled the hammer back. Papa's voice rang in her ears.

"Don't hold your breath. Let the air out and then squeeze."

The Adirondack Mountains of New York partnered with the Green Mountains of Vermont and repeatedly echoed the explosion from Charlie's musket, from shore to shore. The noise resembled a cannon more than it did a long rifle. Otis Skinner jumped from his perch, forced to step away, as the knee-high barrel, sprayed rum in two different directions. Charlie's musket ball flew clean through the wooden barrel.

"Don't let her get away. After her," Otis screamed, yanking a large hunting knife from his boot.

"Who goes there? Stop or we will fire."

Several lanterns approached from the north. The small cutter, a single-masted affair with several men and a small cannon on board, could easily overtake the lumber raft. Border officials designed their cutters for just that purpose.

The lantern on the large raft disappeared from view. Extinguished. From the splashing of oars in the water, Charlie concluded that Skinner and his friends raced to the line. She rode east, giggling when the government vessel turned north in hot pursuit of Otis and his smuggler friends.

"I hope they catch the bastards," she muttered.

After no more than a few weeks, Nathan questioned his hasty decision.

Life at the Burlington Cantonment, except for the occasional injury and common place sicknesses, proved tedious and boring. He performed no surgeries and learned of no opportunities to even assist with one. A voice, just outside the canvas tent, revealed what would happen next.

"We have new orders," announced the corporal, standing in the tent's opening.

Nathan's tent mate, jumped from his cot. He could not recall seeing Sackett in such an animated state.

"Pike's regiment is being moved to Plattsburgh," said the officer.

Sackett snarled, grabbed his haversack, and flung it at the corporal's head. The young officer ducked, and the projectile landed harmlessly on the ground, just outside the opening.

"I could have you court-martialed for that, Sackett," said the officer.

"The stockade would be an improvement over Plattsburgh. I heard that the men don't even have tents," Sackett complained.

The corporal ignored Sackett's protest and turned to Nathan.

"They'll be a warm welcome for you, Coldwell."

"Why is that?" asked Nathan.

"Not enough doctors and too many sick soldiers," said the corporal.

"The yellow fever?" Nathan asked.

"Nope. The measles."

Nathan did not have the opportunity to ask more questions. The corporal pivoted in place and exited the tent.

The 15th regiment would be transported across Lake Champlain in bateaux.

The flat-bottom boats, as much as thirty-five feet long and eight feet wide, could each carry up to forty men. Some featured a single mast and often took advantage of the occasional winds which buffeted the lake. A handful of the boats included a 3-pound cannon, installed in the bow of the vessel. But most of the boats did no more than carry cargo and passengers. Depending on the size of the bateaux, at least four men accomplished the rowing. Another man used his oar as a tiller and steered the vessel. The

Army utilized more than 200 bateaux, their popularity leading to occasional collisions. Strong currents and reckless rowing were the most frequently cited causes.

Nathan bowed his head to avoid the bitter wind that buffeted his bateaux, during that first week of September 1812.

"Did you say you was a doctor?" asked one of the men, breathing heavy as he pulled on two oars.

"Yes. A surgeon's mate," said Nathan.

"You must be the replacement," said the soldier.

"I'm sorry. I'm not sure what you mean."

"Well, we lost a doctor just last week."

The soldier went on to explain that a Dr. Brewster, with the 11th Regiment, somehow fell overboard.

"They tried to save him but he drowned," said the oarsman.

Nathan's eyes grew large but the oarsman, now busy with the approaching shoreline at Cumberland Head, said nothing more.

Camp Plattsburgh did not impress Nathan Coldwell.

A scarcity of tents forced most of the soldiers to sleep on the ground. They survived with nothing more than blankets and pine boughs. Even the blankets, Army issue and only one per man, came up short. Literally. They measured three feet by four feet.

The men, each tasked with the construction of his own hut, spent their days in the forest, harvesting wood. Sanitary facilities, less than ideal, consisted of trenches. The foul-smelling latrines, located adjacent to the camp, lay very near the graves of dozens of soldiers. Ironically, most of the dead succumbed to the brutal living conditions rather than the wounds of battle. Rations, also in short supply, did not satisfy the appetite of men who worked, daily, in the forest. The lack of food, shelter, and cleanliness, spread sickness and disease throughout the camp.

Nathan, because he served as a doctor and surgeon's mate, enjoyed a modest hut. His shelter also served as an infirmary. Within weeks of his arrival, he treated dozens of men for intermittent fever, diarrhea, dysentery, jaundice and rheumatism. Coldwell's most devastating diagnosis occurred with an increasing frequency. Measles. Although not always fatal, the disease kept the burial detail very busy. On average, three to four men were buried each day, in a series of unmarked graves.

Nathan, organizing his medical supplies and equipment did not bother to look up, when he heard a rustle behind him.

"What's the problem?"

"I have the fever," said the voice.

Nathan's head snapped up and he turned.

"Sackett. You look terrible. How long have you been this way?"

Sackett, who said less than a few dozen words to Nathan the whole time they shared a tent in Burlington, recited his symptoms, *ad nauseum.* He ended his soliloquy in the same way that all of Nathan's patients ended theirs.

"Can you give me something, doc?"

Nathan's medicine chest included opium, ipecac, (used to induce vomiting), calomel and preparations of certain tree barks. Men with dysentery usually ran a fever. Coldwell's customary response, a bleeding of at least eight ounces, often preceded a cathartic. The remedy achieved modest results.

"What you really need, Sackett, is warmer conditions. Is your hut completed"

"No sir."

Sackett's voice and the fact that he addressed Nathan as "sir," betrayed the man's desperation.

"You may sit over there," said Nathan, pointing to the only

chair in the wood and canvas shelter.

Nathan explained the bleeding process and the purgative effects of a cathartic.

"You can spend the night in here if you'd like," Nathan added.

"Thank you, sir. Thank you very much."

Sackett's high fever continued, at one point causing the man to convulse. Nathan did what he could. When the exhausted man's eyes closed, Coldwell too, collapsed onto his cot.

"How are you feeling, this morning?" asked Nathan, rubbing the sleep from his eyes.

He searched for a scrap of wood to resuscitate the small fire, just outside the tent's opening. Nathan called again.

"Sackett?"

Sackett did not respond. Nathan approached his patient and saw no signs of breathing. He dropped to his knees for a closer examination. When he rolled Sackett over, Nathan moaned. The man's pupils, fixed and dilated, indicated that Sackett died sometime during the night.

He closed the dead man's eyes and whispered a prayer.

Charlie, exhausted and shivering in the frigid night air, tied her raft, bereft of cargo, to its dock.

She calculated that it would be several hours before sunup. As she approached the cabin, the girl thought of nothing but sleep. A full day of sleep. The smell of smoke from her cabin's chimney and the soft glow of candlelight in the kitchen, forced the girl to an abrupt halt. Someone occupied her cabin. The musket she lugged up the hill, would be of no use. She carried no powder and no musket balls on her person.

Charlie tiptoed off the beaten path, hoping for a better view of the trespasser. The shadow of several large pine trees reduced her visibility to near zero. She tripped over a swollen tree root. As she struggled to her feet, the cabin door opened.

"Hank, is that you?"

The voice belonged to Mrs. Wells. Charlie, relieved and terrified at the same time, approached the woman.

"It's me, Mrs. Wells. Charlie Wheeler."

The woman ignored Charlie's mild correction.

"You must be hungry. I'm warming up some soup."

"Thank you," said Charlie, her voice barely above a whisper. "Why are you here?" she asked.

Mrs. Wells responded with a series of non-sequiturs.

"It's been such a busy day. I did your chores this morning, Hank, but you mustn't forget to do them tomorrow. Tomorrow is laundry day. Oh, and I forgot to tell you. I visited the general store yesterday. Loaded up on supplies," said the woman.

Charlie stood in the kitchen doorway, trembling and yawning at the same time. The girl wanted to believe that Mrs. Wells simply misspoke. The woman wore a distant look in her eyes and appeared as if in a trance.

"Have a seat, Hank. Your soup's almost ready."

Charlie pulled a chair close to the table. She squirmed in her seat. Her mind raced. Mrs. Wells prattled on.

"I heard all the latest news, yesterday," said the woman.

She placed a bowl of soup in front of the girl and returned to the fireplace, her back to Charlie. The bowl contained nothing but cold water. Charlie sat upright afraid to say or do anything.

"Lieutenant McDonough and Colonel Clark are desperate for new recruits. There are advertisements in the local papers," said Mrs. Wells.

Charlie pretended to swallow a spoonful of the "soup".

"And they're cracking down on smuggling, too," Mrs. Wells added.

Charlie swallowed another spoonful of water. That's when she noticed that Mrs. Wells wore no shoes. Mrs. Wells continued:

"Anyone caught going over the line has to pay a $1000 fine and they go to prison for seven years. And to make sure the new law is enforced, the governor sent more troops to all of the border towns in Vermont."

Charlie avoided her gaze.

Mrs. Wells turned, a hand on each hip.

"Hank Wells. Did you understand what I said?"

Charlie murmured.

"Yes, Mrs. Wells."

"And don't you dare call me Mrs. Wells. I am your mother. You will call me 'mother' or 'momma'. Is that understood?"

Before Charlie could respond, the woman grabbed Charlie's bowl of water with both hands and dropped it in to the large pot of water, bowl and all.

"Now I'm going to bed and I do not wish to be disturbed."

She removed her apron and threw that too into the pot. Her bare feet slammed into the wooden floor as she marched onto the porch. Charlie, glued to her chair, did not understand the woman's bizarre behavior. After several moments of silence, the girl rose and went to the door. A hint of morning sun shone in the eastern sky.

The barefoot lady disappeared.

Charlie slept for most of the next day.

She lay in bed, giving the sleep in her brain, a chance to escape. Since inheriting Reuben Quimby's business, the girl slept with ease. Not even a dream. Last night was an exception, she thought. And it was her silliest dream, ever. A tiny voice in the back of her head objected. Her gaze drifted to the fireplace. She squeezed her eyes shut, unwilling to believe the picture in her mind. The pot of water remained in place. She rose and tiptoed to the large container. She hesitated, as if a wild animal might spring from the pot and attack her. When she saw the bowl and the apron, Charlie shuddered.

Perhaps she should tell someone. The constable or a neighbor. But what would she tell them? Mrs. Wells is going insane? Mrs. Wells misses her dead son? Mrs. Wells is trespassing on my property? None of the alternatives seemed reasonable or even necessary, thought Charlie.

As the chickens pecked at their corn, Charlie arrived at a solution. Of sorts. She would take the raft out. With no cargo to deliver, the trip promised to be a pleasant one. She might even throw her fishing line in the water. The prospect of perch for dinner made her stomach growl. Charlie slipped the rope on her raft just as the November sun made its early-morning appearance. For the first time in weeks, Charlie's sojourn on the lake would be sunny, scenic and peaceful.

As she approached the south end of Isle La Motte, Charlie heard a number of men, yelling and cursing. A slight breeze from the north, brought her to the chaotic scene. She saw two bateaux, one of them sinking fast, portions of its cargo floating on the surface. At least a half-dozen men, soldiers she concluded, thrashed violently in the frigid water. Several of them clutched barrels and screamed at the remaining bateaux for assistance. The first bateaux carried a full load of men and cargo. Its occupants could do nothing.

Charlie, using her extra-long oar as a tiller, maneuvered her raft into their midst. She did not have to invite the freezing men to climb on board. They scrambled on to the deck and several of them managed to rescue a portion of the cargo. Charlie's raft, although smaller than many of its counterparts, easily accommodated her new-found friends.

"Thank you, boy. You showed up at the right time," said one of the men.

Charlie, her raft now drifting north, smiled and skipped the amenities.

"Unless you want to cross the line, I suggest you grab an oar and get to work."

Two of the men, anxious to warm up, rowed with great enthusiasm.

"Sargant Joshua Burnham," said the older soldier, extending a hand.

Charlie squeezed hard. The beneficiary of her quick action stood a head taller than her. His hair, soaking wet and dripping, shone bright red. But the man's eyes fascinated her. One was green, the other blue.

"The name's Charlie Wheeler. Where are you boys headed?"

"The bay at Plattsburgh," he said.

"That's going to take most of the day," she said. "I don't usually go much past Chazy landing."

"I'm sure my lieutenant will take good care of you, seeing as how you saved our lives," he said. "And those barrels of pork," said the sergeant, gesturing toward the cargo.

Charlie stammered.

"But I'd have to."

The sergeant interrupted.

"We'll put you up for the night and pay you for your trouble, I promise."

Charlie sped through her mental checklist. She did not look forward to another visit from Mrs. Wells. The evening chores could wait.

"Deal," she said, extending her hand, once again.

The trip south to Plattsburgh, made easier by a number of shivering oarsmen, triggered Charlie's anticipation and excitement.

The village of Plattsburg, if Charlie could travel all of its streets, dwarfed the girl's hometown. A cluster of more than 100 dwellings, four hotels, a handful of taverns, thirteen stores and a dozen shops, made the village both crowded and busy. There were carpenters, wheelwrights, a forge, several sawmills, two tanneries and a gristmill. Plattsburgh also included a recently constructed academy for schooling, a large courthouse, (the village also served as the county seat), two newspapers and a bustling trade in lumber.

"This is a busy place," said Charlie, her head swiveling in every direction as several of the soldiers docked her raft at one of the smaller slips, in Plattsburgh Bay.

"We should report in. Lieutenant Edgerton's hut is this way," said Sergeant Burnham, pointing to a well-worn path, leading up the embankment.

After listening to Burnham's story, the lieutenant leaned forward and glared.

"It is a very large lake, Sergeant. How exactly did your bateaux collide with the other one?"

Burnham's face now matched his red hair. He took a deep breath.

"We were in a competition sir, anxious to arrive at our destination," said Burnham.

The lieutenant closed his eyes and let his head droop. He used several fingers on each hand to massage his temples. When he looked up, he forced a smile in Charlie's direction.

"We owe you a debt of gratitude, young man. Thank you for your assistance," he said.

"You're welcome, sir," said Charlie, hesitant to smile at the frustrated lieutenant.

"We could use someone like you in my regiment. What's the last name, again?"

"Wheeler, sir. Charlie Wheeler. But I've been rafting the lake since I was little, sir."

The lieutenant scowled. His voice rose.

"Do you go north of the line?"

Charlie shook her head, vigorously.

"No sir. I am not a smuggler."

"Good. That's what I wanted to hear," said the lieutenant.

He sat in his chair and reached for a quill and paper. After a few scratches, he folded the document, and handed it to Charlie.

"We have a navy here. You should check in with them. Hang onto this. You may need it someday," said the lieutenant.

Charlie, puzzled by the lieutenant's actions, flashed a big smile and thanked the man with a quick nod.

"Sergeant, see to it that Mr. Wheeler is compensated for the use of his raft. Get him a decent meal and a bed for the night."

"Yes sir," said the sergeant.

The lieutenant looked at Charlie once more.

"I've got a little surprise for you, Mr. Wheeler."

Charlie cocked her head.

"Sir?"

Tomorrow, you can hitch a ride on a steamer. The *Vermont* is coming through here midmorning. Headed to Alburgh to pick up more troops."

Charlie beamed.

"Thank you, sir."

"You're very welcome," said the lieutenant.

Charlie's smiling face turned into a question mark.

"But my raft . . ."

Her voice faded into an awkward silence.

"The owners of the *Vermont,* work for us now. They'll tow it. Enjoy your trip, young man."

He then turned to his reckless sergeant.

"You are dismissed," he barked.

The sergeant and Charlie scrambled to the exit.

"What's in the note?" asked the sergeant.

Charlie read it aloud.

Nov 7, 1812

I happily vouch for the character and bravery of Charlie Wheeler, who on this day rescued six of my men from certain death.

Yours,
Cpt. B. S. Edgerton
11th Rgmt.

"Very nice, Charlie. Very nice." said the sergeant.

Chapter Seven

THE VERMONT

When Nathan volunteered with the army, he expected and anticipated the life of a surgeon.

Camp Plattsburg offered nothing of the sort. A seemingly never-ending parade of soldiers with the measles, a fever, diarrhea, dysentery, pneumonia and a long list of other ailments, prompted him to protest.

"I volunteered as a surgeon's mate and thus far I have accomplished not a single surgery," said Nathan.

Nathan assumed that a firm but polite conversation with his company lieutenant would make a difference. The officer avoided Nathan's gaze, the man's eyes darting in every direction. When Nathan finished his diatribe, the lieutenant responded.

"I understand," he said.

Nathan jumped to his feet and leaned on the lieutenant's desk with both hands. He thrust his jaw to within inches of the officer's face.

"I don't care if you understand my predicament, Lieutenant. I would like to know what you intend to do about it," Nathan snapped, slamming a fist on the man's desk, for emphasis.

A quill bounced from its inkwell and landed on the lieutenant's papers, leaving a black puddle in its wake. The lieutenant clenched his teeth, reached for the quill and returned the feather pen to its original location.

"Dr. Coldwell, please accept my apologies if your assignment here at Camp Plattsburgh is not to your liking. There is a steamer leaving for the line in two hours. Bring your instruments and medicines. They will be required," he said.

"What should I expect, when I get to the boundary line?" asked Nathan.

"About 5000 American soldiers and they won't be there for long," said the lieutenant.

"Our Army is going north of the line to attack the British?" asked Nathan.

"You're going to miss your boat, Mr. Coldwell."

Charlie stood on the dock and watched the *Vermont* as it grew closer.

The large clouds of black smoke, spewing from its single stack, dispersed in the wind. Until recently, the 120-foot-long vessel made regular trips from St. John's in Canada to Whitehall in New York. Although suffering from frequent breakdowns, the steamer now moved troops and cargo to and from both sides of the lake. The boat, plain if not ugly in its appearance, had no pilot house or bridge. It used a tiller for steerage. Its twenty-horsepower engine could propel the vessel at an average rate of five- to-eight miles per hour. As Charlie waited dockside, her raft nearby, the girl's excitement grew.

A steam-powered ride back to Isle LaMotte, would be the

adventure of a lifetime, she thought.

While dozens of soldiers boarded the vessel, Charlie worked with pilot, Hiram Ferris, to secure her raft.

They used a long length of rope so as to avoid an unexpected collision. With their work on the dock completed, Charlie ventured below deck. The large room, more than 400 square feet, included berths for sleeping and tables for dining. Most of the cabin's features could not be seen, however. Dozens of soldiers packed into the chamber, leaving standing room, only.

"Charlie, over here."

The girl instantly recognized Sergeant Burnham. She elbowed her way through the crowd to acknowledge her new-found, but grateful friend.

"Hey everyone, this is Charlie. I'd be at the bottom of the lake if it wasn't for him," said Burnham, slapping Charlie on the back.

"You should have let the rat, drown," yelled a voice from the back of the room.

A noisy round of hearty laughter put Charlie at ease. She enjoyed a series of congratulatory shouts, words of praise and countless handshakes. From the scrum, she heard a voice that made her stomach do an unexpected flip flop.

"Congratulations, Charlie."

Charlie spun around, her eyes wide and mouth half-open. Nathan Coldwell held his hand aloft, waiting for Charlie to return the wave. She pushed through the crowd, reached out, and squeezed with both hands.

"What are you doing here?" she asked, unsure as to why she was so happy to see the doctor.

"I have the same question for you, young man," said Nathan,

an uncertain look on his face.

"Headed back to Isle LaMotte. They offered me a free ride," said Charlie, nodding in the direction of the soldiers behind her.

"The war has only just begun, and already you are a hero," said Nathan, unsmiling and visibly ill-at-ease.

"I didn't do nothing,"

Nathan twitched. Charlie caught herself.

"I mean anything. I didn't do anything," she blurted.

Charlie could feel the heat on her pink face. She recovered with an inquiry of her own.

"I don't see a musket. Do you intend to attack the British with a bone saw?"

Charlie's ridiculous question made Nathan grin. Charlie did the same. For a brief moment, the two were old friends. Nathan grew solemn.

"Soldiers need doctors. Measles and musket balls. Bad for your health, you know."

"I understand. And I heard the army is desperate for men. They even asked me, to sign up," she said.

Nathan frowned.

"And your answer?" he asked.

"I told them I prefer the water," she said.

"Do we even have a Navy?" Nathan asked, the concern draining from his face.

"Yes, a small one," she said.

The couple, now at a loss for words, avoided each other's eyes. The awkward silence prompted a manufactured excuse from Charlie.

"I really should check on my raft. It's being towed behind the steamer," she said.

Nathan nodded.

"Enjoy the ride."

"Be careful, Nathan," she said.

"You too, Charlie Wheeler."

The girl disappeared into a sea of soldiers.

Nathan rifled through his supplies and medical equipment.

He verified that several tourniquets and a number of clean bandages, would be on hand, when the battle commenced. He anticipated an immediate need for his surgeon's kit, which included bone saws, amputation knives, scalpels and sharpening stones. The instruments lay on a bed of red velvet in a hinged, mahogany box, next to needles, thread, bullet probes, and sponges. The entire collection, a gift from his parents, did not require cleaning. They were, as yet, unused.

As he waited for the boat to dock, Nathan thought again about his chance meeting with Charlie Wheeler. After their last goodbye, Nathan took solace from the fact that he would never see the boy again. And yet, he did. Was it fate or coincidence? It didn't matter. Nathan justified his butterflies with logic. Obviously, the tragedies in Charlie's young life, exaggerated Nathan's concern and empathy for the boy. *Sympathy and compassion are very appropriate reactions,* thought Nathan. The idea that he might be attracted to Charlie, either physically or emotionally, did not comport with the facts. Nathan forced himself to put his mind at ease.

His heart was another matter.

When the steamer arrived at its destination in Rouse's point, the soldiers shuffled their way to the exit. Nathan did not complain about the four-mile hike to Champlain. Half of the troops traveled on foot from Plattsburgh, some twenty miles away. Nathan considered himself, lucky. Because doctors and surgeons were often treated like officers, Nathan bunked with a number of them, at a large farmhouse in the village. Pliny Moore, its owner, complained that his place now resembled a hotel more than a home. But he enjoyed the attention given to his piano, one of the first to be seen in the area.

After several probes across the boundary line and a careful review of local intelligence, the officer in charge, Colonel Pike, commenced the attack. He ordered hundreds of regulars and dozens of militia men, across the border. Whether Pike's troops knew it or not, they enjoyed protection from the American Navy. Although modest in size, the fleet patrolled the north end of the lake, to prevent a surprise enemy attack. Unfortunately, the presence of thousands of troops in the tiny village of Champlain, became widespread knowledge. On both sides of the line. British troops wasted no time and retreated to safer locations, considerably north of the line.

Colonel Pike decided to split his forces in two columns. Within hours, one half of the troops encountered the other half, at an abandoned enemy encampment. They mistook each other for the enemy. Several volleys took place before the error could be corrected. A number of men lay wounded and dying. After witnessing the deadly mistake, local militia men suddenly recalled a proviso in their agreement with the federal government. Fighting outside of the continental United States violated the terms of their accord with the Army. They were not required to serve in foreign countries. The militia men, many from Vermont, decided to abandon their federal counterparts. When they left, Pike lost his ardor for the invasion. He ordered the balance of his forces back to Champlain.

Nathan received a dozen or so casualties plus two soldiers, dead on arrival.

His makeshift hospital, a corner of Pliny Moore's large barn, included planks and barrels for an operating table. He pressed two men into service as medical orderlies. They surrounded Nathan's workspace with a dozen litters, each carrying a wounded soldier.

His first patient, perhaps the most seriously wounded, suffered musket wounds to an arm and a leg. Nathan witnessed several amputations during his training but had not yet performed one. The soldier, with several shots of rum to his credit, did as instructed. He bit down on a cigar-shaped piece of wood. When Nathan's scalpel sliced into the man's skin, just above the knee, the patient lost consciousness. One of the temporary nurses, blanched white and fell to the ground. When Nathan cut into the man's legbone, another soldier ordered by Nathan to stand in, watched in awe. Nathan cut the man's femur in less than one minute. The two flaps of skin, which the novice surgeon thoughtfully left intact, folded neatly over the gaping wound. Nathan quickly sutured them in place. He executed a similar procedure on the man's arm. After bandaging the wounds, Nathan's patient disappeared, and another wounded soldier took his place.

Because the damage caused by musket balls almost always shattered a man's limb, amputations became routine. Hours later, and with a nearby pig trough filled with severed limbs, Nathan collapsed onto a milking stool, covered in blood and exhausted.

The doctor required no more than one day to become an experienced surgeon.

Nathan traveled back to Plattsburgh by bateaux.

Some of the troops marched to Rouse's point and hitched a ride with the American fleet. Most of the army returned to Camp Plattsburgh on foot. The troops, forced to abandon their food supplies in Champlain, left behind more than one hundred thirty barrels of flour and fifty-five barrels of bread. Local residents pilfered the valuable foodstuffs as soon as the army marched out of sight. After several days, the entire five-thousand-man army arrived in Plattsburgh. Nathan, pleased with his experience in battle, returned to his hut, where a not-so-pleasant surprise, awaited him.

"I'm the replacement for Doctor Davis," said the man in Nathan's tent, now crowded with two cots.

Nathan knew that Doctor Davis, surgeon for the sixteenth regiment, might soon resign because of difficulties at home. Apparently, the surgeon's decision became final while Nathan was absent.

"I'm Nathan Coldwell, surgeon's mate, for the 16th."

"Doctor William Beaumont. I've heard of you, Nathan. I studied in Saint Albans while you practiced in Alburgh," said Beaumont.

Nathan struggled to hide his surprise and disappointment. Beaumont appeared even younger than Nathan.

"You are friends with Doctor Davis?" asked Nathan, a discreet attempt to ascertain how Beaumont got the job that Nathan wanted.

"No, I didn't know the man. General Bloomfield recommended me for this position."

Beaumont also announced that the forces stationed at Camp Plattsburgh would soon be divided in two regiments. Colonel Pike's men, including Nathan, would remain at Camp Saranac, just west of the village. The remaining regiments would move to Burlington, Vermont and Pittsfield, Massachusetts.

"I'm looking forward to working with you, Doctor Coldwell," said Beaumont.

Nathan flashed a phony smile.

"Thank you, sir."

Days after her ride on the *Vermont,* Charlie stood on the dock in Isle LaMotte.

Her raft, safely obscured inside the nearby tree line, would remain there until spring. She noticed a series of military sloops, scows, and bateaux, as they sailed south on the lake. Her grateful friend, Sergeant Burnham, previously hinted about a planned march into Canada. She concluded as much from her ride on the steamboat, jam packed with soldiers in route to the line. But now, just two days later, the Army traveled south-bound back to Plattsburgh. The planned invasion of Canada did not go as planned, she concluded. A closer look confirmed her suspicions. Many of the navy vessels contained dozens of army soldiers. Troops, in sudden retreat, could not be a good sign, Charlie thought.

"You shouldn't be out here by yourself."

Charlie snapped to attention when she heard the man's voice. Constable Blanchard, still on his mount, stood roadside, at the at the top of the embankment.

"Constable Blanchard, you scared me," said Charlie.

"You should be scared. I believe that Otis Skinner is looking for you," said Blanchard.

"He's north of the line. I'm not worried," said Charlie.

"He paid a visit to the servant girl, where Harriet was murdered," Blanchard announced.

Charlie's eyes opened wide.

"Is she alright?"

"She got away with a few bruises and a black eye. Skinner told her to keep her mouth shut or he'd be back."

"She didn't see him do it. Why did he threaten her?"

"We got wanted posters up everywhere. Skinner's getting nervous. But it's you he wants. Ain't nobody in these parts gonna believe a nigger girl. But a jury will believe you. And Skinner as much as admitted it, that night you brought him to the line."

Charlie looked out over the lake.

"I'll be careful," said Charlie.

"Why don't you stay at the Wells' place?"

"That's not going to happen," said Charlie, unwilling to recount the details of her last encounter with Mrs. Wells.

"Suit yourself," said Blanchard, squeezing his mare into a trot.

Charlie lit the lantern in her kitchen, figuring it would be dark when she finished her chores in the barn.

She stepped onto the porch, stopped, reopened the door and reached inside for her musket.

"No need to be careless," she muttered.

When Charlie pulled on the barn door, she did not receive the usual greeting. Her always hungry chickens did not approach. The candle in her punched-tin holder, could not illuminate the entire shed. She searched the darkness, walking slowly. She stumbled. A chicken, his neck broken, lay at her feet. She found the balance of her brood, all of them dead.

Charlie's eyes darted everywhere. Whoever did this, might still be in the barn, she thought. She heard nothing except the winter wind whistling through the rafters. With gun in hand, she checked on the cow and her pig. They did not appear injured, only hungry. Charlie sat on the floor at the far end of the structure, her back against the wall, facing the door. She shook with anger.

"You can go to blazes, Otis Skinner."

The first month of 1813 included weeks of gloomy days, bitter cold and constant snow.

As the weather worsened, so also did Nathan Coldwell's disposition. The novice surgeon, unable to improve the living conditions of the men around him, floundered in a sea of diseased and dying soldiers. By year's end, more than 200 men in the camp had succumbed to a variety of ailments. Typhus, pneumonia, consumption, (tuberculosis) and severe dysentery ravaged the troops. The first of the soldiers' huts, not completed until Christmas of 1812, made no more than a slight difference. Many of the men continued to sleep on the frozen ground.

Lieutenant Thomas McDonough, Commandant of the U.S. Navy on Lake Champlain, used these tragic circumstances to his advantage. Frantic to staff his ships, he personally recruited a number of army men. Soldiers, desperate for an improvement in their living conditions, readily agreed. They ignored the Navy's strict training requirements and the serious risks associated with service on a ship of war. McDonough also dispatched his officers throughout the region, in an all-out effort to recruit more men.

Nathan Coldwell responded to the call.

"I understand you require the services of a surgeon's mate," said Nathan.

He stood just feet from the lieutenant, a tall-slender man of no more than thirty years. The naval commander wore an impeccably clean, square-cut, blue coat, decorated with a single row of brass buttons. The tint of red in McDonough's full, but somewhat unruly, head of hair, did not comport with the man's solemn and deliberate manner.

McDonough's smile welcomed the young doctor, but the experienced naval officer rarely acted in haste. The lieutenant's father, a physician and military man, died when McDonough was eleven years old. The lieutenant understood responsibility, hard work, and the field of medicine.

"Tell me, Dr. Coldwell, precisely what experience do you bring to this very important assignment?"

Nathan rubbed his sweaty palms together. He licked his dry lips and fixed his eyes on McDonough.

"I accompanied Colonel Pike and received the wounded in Champlain," said Nathan.

"Forgive me, Dr. Coldwell, but we suffered only a handful of casualties at Lacolle."

Nathan chose not to embellish his limited experience.

"Two of the men died from their wounds before they reached Champlain. Five went missing. I operated on a total of thirteen soldiers. Eight of them required one or more amputations."

Nathan's head drooped. He studied the rough-hewn wood floor in McDonough's office chamber. His experience as a surgeon seemed insignificant. McDonough, his face unsmiling, focused on the young doctor.

"Very well then. You will assist Dr. Briggs. And the enemy will provide you with the experience you lack," said McDonough, rising from his chair. He extended a hand to Nathan.

"Thank you, sir. I will do my very best," said Nathan.

"And I will expect nothing less," said McDonough.

Charlie rarely left her home.

Bitter cold and military decrees made commercial travel by sleigh unworthy of the risk. In an effort to staunch the flow of smuggled goods, military commanders on both sides of Lake Champlain issued new orders. Travel across the line now required written permission. Violators would be executed. Military patrols dotted the international boundary line. Only an empty sleigh would guarantee unfettered access to the lake.

Charlie stayed close to home for yet another reason. The slaughter of her brood of hens, served as a constant reminder that the intruder might return. Otis Skinner, her chief suspect in the matter, could easily lurk on either side of the line and remain undetected. Vermont, in particular, featured a series of waterways, back roads, and pathways that led directly to the line.

All of this weighed heavily on Charlie's mind, as she stood on the dock. She suffered from cabin fever and gazed longingly at the frozen surface of Lake Champlain. Although hidden by a thick blanket of February snow, an ice cap measuring between one and three feet thick, covered the entire surface. The brilliant, white scenery triggered a vigorous debate in the girl's sixteen-year-old mind. Remain at the cabin, guarding against intruders, or harness the horse to an empty sleigh. She could bask in the sunlight and slide effortlessly through the snow, just as she did so many times in the past. It required only a few moments for her most cherished memories to win the debate in her mind.

The muted sound of a horse's hooves in the snow and the whisper of metal runners on ice, brought tears to Charlie's eyes. She and her papa used to ride the frozen lake for hours. They conducted business, of course, but those times became the happiest times of Charlie's young life. The morning flew by. The constant jets of white steam, flaring from her mare's nostrils, prompted Charlie to take a break. The girl and her horse needed a respite.

Chazy Landing would be ideal for resting her horse. A cup of hot cider for its master, made the stop an easy decision. Her visit to the lakeside village also introduced Charlie to an unexpected opportunity. Large broadsides, (printed sheets), announced Lieutenant

McDonough's need for volunteers. They decorated the walls and windows of several business establishments in Chazy. Boys and men between the ages of sixteen and forty could earn between eight and fifteen dollars per month. In return, the enlistees would make a two-year commitment to the Navy.

After a profitable year, conducting business on behalf of the late Reuben Quimby, Charlie did not require an immediate infusion of cash. She owned a house, a raft, a sleigh, a horse and some livestock. In fact, the young girl, although frugal, never worried about money. But the prospect of continued success, moving cargo over and around Lake Champlain, seemed unlikely in time of war. Serving on a navy sloop, would keep her where she most wanted to be, on the water. How difficult could it be, serving in the Navy, she wondered. Certainly, better than being a grunt in the Army, thought Charlie. She recalled the Army soldiers, packed like a bag of cotton, on the *Vermont*.

The remainder of her farm animals would have to be sold. The cabin and barn could be rented. As she glided across the frozen lake, Charlie's thinking grew more and more optimistic. The only reason she did not make an immediate inquiry, related to her name.

Charlotte Elizabeth Wheeler might not be welcomed in the Navy.

As the girl's horse-drawn sleigh approached the north end of the lake, billowing clouds of black smoke could be seen in the eastern sky.

When Charlie calculated that the fire could be very near her cabin, she snapped the reins and urged the horse to quicken its pace.

"Stay where you are Charlie, there's nothing you can do."

Constable Blanchard, standing in the barnyard, deliberately blocked Charlie's path to the large shed. The structure, fully engulfed in flames, could not be saved. A worn horse blanket, laying on the snow-covered ground, hid what appeared to be a body.

"What's under the blanket?" asked Charlie.

Blanchard explained that a few of the neighbors failed in their attempt to rescue the animals.

"That's when they discovered the body," said Blanchard.

"Let me guess. Otis Skinner," said Charlie.

"No. The body appears to be that of a woman. I want you to take a closer look," said Blanchard, motioning Charlie to the blanket.

When he tugged on the woolen material, Charlie recognized the blackened face and the soot-covered, blue-checkered dress. When she saw the woman's bare feet, a hand flew to her mouth, smothering a loud gasp. Charlie looked away. She choked her conclusion.

"Mrs. Wells."

"We think she set fire to the place. And then she hung herself. We found this in her apron."

Blanchard handed Charlie a handwritten note:

Dear Charlie,

>*I want to be with Hank.*
>*It wasn't your fault. I know that now.*
>*And I'm sorry about the chickens.*

>>>*Mrs. Wells.*

The constable spoke softly.

"What's this about, Charlie?"

Charlie, struggling to hold back the tears, recounted Hank's death. She related the story of Mrs. Wells' increasing hostility, the incident with the soup, and the dead chickens. She confessed her guilt and took full responsibility.

"I thought it was Otis Skinner, trying to shut me up," she explained. "This is all my fault," she said, gawking at the covered body. "This is all my fault."

Blanchard corrected the girl.

"The woman lost her son, Charlie. That would make any mother crazy. There was nothing you could do."

Charlie's head ached. She walked deliberately to the cabin and shut the door behind her. She collapsed onto a kitchen chair and used the table to rest her head on folded arms. Behind closed eyes, she watched as her father stood tall on their raft, smiling, and unafraid. His face disappeared and Hank's frozen-blue face, bobbing in the frigid water, suddenly came into view. He screamed for help but slowly sank beneath the surface. The picture in her mind changed again. This time, Reuben Quimby's smiling image greeted her. The old man called Charlie by her real name, but when she ran to him, he disappeared. Mrs. Wells blank stare came next. An image of the woman's charred dress and bare feet flashed in Charlie's mind. And finally, Charlie saw herself. Laying in a pool of blood, her eyes closed, and all alone.

She woke from her exhausted stupor with a scream. She jumped to her feet and stood trembling in the middle of her kitchen.

"I can't do this anymore," she whispered to herself. "I can't do this anymore."

Chapter Eight

THE UNITED STATES NAVY

Wanted posters, with a crude sketch of Otis Skinner's unshaven face and a general description of his appearance, dotted the Northern Tier of New York and Vermont.

Otis learned of his new-found popularity the same week he learned that British officials offered gold and silver for military intelligence. British officials knew nothing about his sordid past. Otis saw an opportunity. He knew the pathways from the international boundary line into northern Vermont better than most. He could slip, undetected, into the United States, collect the intelligence his British friends required and return safely to Canada.

He would be wise to alter his appearance. Otis chuckled, as he viewed himself in the mirror. The tiny room he occupied, above a tavern in the Quebec farming settlement of Noyan, would be the scene of his physical transformation. His head, now bald, matched the clean-shaven face. A well-placed scarf, not uncommon at this time of the year, hid much of his head. He could do nothing about his massive frame, and practiced a studied slouch, instead.

For a small advance, British officers authorized Skinner's first trek to Vermont. Despite the bitter cold, Skinner's travels, made easier by snowshoes given to him by the British, went smoothly. Within hours, he memorized the location of military stores, the number of bateaux dry docked for the winter months, and the extent of the government's massive dragnet, designed to catch smugglers. He also took note of the preparations by local militia.

While in Northern Vermont near the shoreline, he hoped to visit Charlie Wheeler's cabin. He and Charlie needed to talk. He rested on a fallen tree and munched on a piece of hard tack. Otis used a mouthful of snow to wash it down. Using trees for cover, he resumed his journey. Otis reached the shoreline at Windmill point, without incident. His view included the customs facility, a number of crude-wooden huts and a large building he knew to be a warehouse for seized goods. He waited patiently for the revenuers, about twenty in all, to complete their morning rituals. Otis would report nothing unusual to his superiors, regarding government personnel.

He changed his mind when he glanced at the lake, looking south. Otis saw sails, mastheads, and a number of smaller boats, gliding north through the as yet, unfrozen channel. More vessels rounded the tip of Windmill Point, coming from the east and headed west towards Champlain. Each vessel carried as many men as it could hold. Otis Skinner's heart beat a little faster. It would appear that a large-scale movement of American troops, was underway.

The British government would pay handsomely for this information, thought Skinner.

Nathan, after observing a steady stream of men exiting the camp, accosted one of the soldiers.

"Where's everybody going?" he asked.

The enlisted man couldn't say for sure.

"The rumor is Canada, by way of Sackets Harbor. But who knows, I'm just a grunt in the army," he grumbled.

Nathan returned to his shelter and continued to pack his personal possessions and medical equipment. His initial assignment with McDonough's navy would be on the *President*, the lieutenant's flagship. The Growler and the Eagle would soon arrive, fresh from refurbishments and refitting, while at Vergennes, Vermont.

"You're leaving us?"

Nathan turned to face the inquiring Dr. Beaumont.

"Yes sir. I've accepted an offer from Lieutenant McDonough to serve on his flagship, as a surgeon's mate," said Nathan, now wearing a flush of pink. He didn't intend to surprise his supervisor.

"I understand, Dr. Coldwell. Have you served aboard a navy ship, in the past?" asked Beaumont.

"No sir."

"You may not live long enough to regret your decision, my friend."

Nathan's eyes grew wide.

"And I suppose that you have such experience?" Nathan asked.

"No. I relate only what I have been told by surgeons who have experienced similar assignments."

"It has been my personal ambition, for some time now, to become a surgeon," said Nathan.

Beaumont reached for Nathan's hand.

"Good luck, Doctor Coldwell. And may God be with you."

Nathan's stomach churned as Beaumont left the tent.

Charlie scoured the lake from her dock in Isle LaMotte.

She noted several wagon-sized flows of ice, glistening in the early morning sun. Most of the water, ice cold and with a harmless chop, posed no hazard to her raft. She filled her lungs with the cold brisk air of spring, and searched her mind for an excuse to launch the raft. It didn't take the lake lonely girl, very long. She decided on a quick run to Windmill Point. The soldiers, accustomed to ill-tempered travelers looking to cross the line, would welcome a friendly face. It would be a fun but easy trip. The untrained, overzealous, militia men, of the type that killed her father, all but disappeared after war was declared. The regular soldiers, overworked, underpaid, but mostly friendly, often asked Charlie to move cargo. The trips, usually across the lake to Champlain, paid very little but Charlie didn't mind. She loved being on the lake. The money was extra. Charlie recalled that several of the officers urged her to enlist. Their appeal, both flattered and amused Charlie. Her disguise as a capable young man, fooled everyone.

The snow-covered bank simplified her effort to move the raft from the woods to the water. Already on its edge, the log vessel slid down the slight embankment and, once on its flat side, glided easily into the water. She barely reached the channel, when she noticed a number of bateaux, following her raft, north. A familiar voice hailed the girl, as the man's bateau approached.

"Charlie, I don't need rescuing today, but it's nice to see you," said the man.

Charlie easily recognized Sergeant Burnham, one of the men she pulled from the lake, months ago.

"Where're you headed, Sergeant?" asked Charlie.

"Champlain and after that, I can't really say," said Burnham.

"I understand. Just stay out of the water and you'll be fine," said Charlie, flashing a big smile.

Burnham rose to his feet, taking advantage of the flat-bottomed boat. He doffed his hat and executed an exaggerated bow, in Charlie's direction.

Charlie stood at attention and returned the compliment with a crisp and formal salute.

Otis Skinner squinted to get a more precise count of the American troops, headed north and west to Champlain.

As he scanned the horizon, Otis lost count of the bateaux and scows, filling his view. A single vessel, separating from the group, caught his attention. The raft appeared to head east, toward the customs house, behind which Otis hid. He watched as the small raft floated toward Windmill Point. He knew that raft, well. Otis waited until the splashing of an oar and the thud of wood against wood, announced the vessel's arrival. He removed his hat and took a quick peek. Charlie Wheeler stood just a few dozen yards away.

Skinner's mind raced through the options. Ambushing the girl within earshot of border guards would be too risky. The raft included no place to hide, and he possessed no raft or boat to follow her, when she left the dock. The sound of a door slamming told Otis that Charlie entered the building. He darted from tree and bush to a position as near the shoreline as possible. His plan, a bit daring, stood a good chance of working. He would wait until Charlie boarded the raft. She would be alone. He would spring from his hiding spot and rush the girl as soon as she slipped the cable.

Voices and the sound of boots crunching in the snow, forced Otis to his knees. He crouched behind a bush. Several of the revenuers, led by Charlie, moved small barrels and several crates to the raft. Charlie stacked the load several feet high and secured it with a length of rope. He saw the girl accept something from the older revenue agent. She thanked him and reached for the long oar. The agent slipped the rope which tethered the raft to its dock. The last officer disappeared behind the building. Charlie began to float away. Otis sprang forward.

"Charlie, we forget one," said a customs agent, running to the dock, with a small crate in his arms.

The sound of Otis, rushing through the snow, startled both Charlie and her agent friend. They swiveled in time to see Otis, as he slid to a stop. Charlie didn't recognize Otis, until he turned and ran. She knew his gait and overly large frame. The agent gave chase. Otis enjoyed a head start. Charlie, still on her raft, reversed course. The agent gave up his pursuit and the two reunited on the dock.

"Sorry. I never even saw his face," said the breathless agent.

"I didn't have to," said Charlie. "That was Otis Skinner," she announced.

"You know him?"

"Married my stepmother. Then he killed her. Got drunk and told me himself."

"He's the man on all the posters. They're all over town," said the officer.

Charlie nodded her head.

"I figured he'd stay north of the line. I guess I was wrong."

"You're the only thing between him and a hangman's noose. That's not a good place to be," said the border guard.

Charlie nodded.

"Yeah. I've been thinking about that. Been thinking about it, a lot. Maybe its best if I go away for a while," she said.

"Where?" he asked.

"I was thinking of a long ride on a big boat."

The border agent scratched his head.

Nathan, now aboard the *President* and below deck, inspected his new quarters.

He questioned how a surgeon might properly function in such a dank and dark environment. Nathan promised himself a conversation with the ship's head surgeon or McDonough himself. Changes would be necessary, he concluded.

As he turned toward the narrow ladder that led topside, an unknown force threw Nathan to the floor and shoved him into the far wall. The entire ship lurched to a halt and tilted to its starboard side. The sound of rocks as they scraped and splintered beams of wood, crashed in his ears. Even a landlubber like Nathan knew what that meant. Lieutenant McDonough's flagship, as yet untested in battle, ran aground.

He hurried to the deck, studying the horizon to ascertain their location. A number of sailors, most of them cursing and yelling, made no attempt to abandon ship. The *President*, wrecked by an outcropping of bedrock, lay motionless in the Bay of Plattsburgh.

The disabled ship lay less than two hundred yards from the docks.

When the initial confusion subsided, Nathan scrambled off the *President*, along with its crew.

After a short ride to shore, in a rescuer's bateaux, he trudged up the embankment in search of an officer. Nathan, uncertain as to where he might next be assigned, cursed his misfortune. As he wandered through the encampment, muttering to himself, Nathan caught sight of Dr. Beaumont, in the distance.

"Dr Beaumont. A moment please," Nathan shouted, waving

both arms and using cupped hands to magnify the sound of his voice.

Beaumont nodded and stood motionless as Nathan ran to his former boss.

"Dr. Coldwell, you have escaped with no apparent injuries," said Beaumont, as he studied the ship, its masts and hull exposed above the water.

"Yes, Dr. Beaumont. And I am unsure if and when Lieutenant McDonough's flag ship will be repaired," said Nathan, breathing heavily and hanging his head in disgust.

"I too, am essentially unemployed. Camp Saranac is bereft of soldiers. All but the most seriously ill are now in route to a place called Sackett's Harbor," he announced. "And many of the sick have been moved to Burlington, which I'm told has been significantly expanded."

"I should like to visit Burlington. I began my education and training there, under Dr. Pomerleau," said Nathan.

"I leave this afternoon for an overnight excursion. You are welcome to join me," said Beaumont. "Shall we meet at the docks, say about two this afternoon?"

"I'll be there," said Nathan, a grateful smile, covering his face.

Charlie delivered her load of cargo from the customs station at Windmill Point across the lake to Rouse's point, without incident.

As spring turned to summer, she made frequent runs for the revenuers. They preferred to spend their time chasing suspected smugglers. The neighboring communities supplied a steady stream of contraband. When May turned into June, America's declaration of war became one- year-old. Coincidentally, the reality of armed conflict dropped like a sledgehammer on residents of the North

Country.

As Charlie's raft drifted into the dockage at Rouse's point, she carefully maneuvered between two, large, military vessels. The *Growler* and the *Eagle*, American sloops of war, lay anchored just offshore. Both ships appeared to be taking on dozens of soldiers. A steady parade of bateaux ferried the men from shore to ship.

"What's going on?" Charlie asked one of the dockhands.

"I'm not sure," said the man.

He explained to Charlie that most of the army in Plattsburgh and significant portions of the infantry in Burlington, traveled to positions in western New York State.

"Them soldiers getting on the sloops, are Herrick's men," said the laborer.

He pointed in the direction of the sloops.

"If they leave, we're on our own."

The dock hand referred to Lieutenant Oliver Herrick. He and his forty-man company from Maine, arrived weeks ago. Their mission, to protect the border villages of Champlain and Rouse's point, appeared to have been abandoned. Today the men would cross the line.

"Well, the British have been on the lake quite a bit lately," said Charlie. "I've been harassed more than once."

"I think Smith is going after them", said the man, referring to Lieutenant Sidney Smith, commander of the two-boat flotilla.

When fully loaded, the American ships disappeared over the horizon and sailed north of the international boundary line. Charlie double checked the ropes that tethered her raft to the dock.

"I think I'll stay a while," she said, as the dock worker unloaded the cargo.

Charlie barely finished her breakfast when a light breeze from the north delivered the results of Lieutenant Smith's foray across the line. For several hours, the clear sound of exploding cannon and musket fire echoed through the village. Charlie, joined by dozens of others, waited quietly at the Rouse's point shoreline, for the American sloops to return.

They waited in vain.

The American ships did not return to Rouse's point.

The locals gathered in small groups, their anxious conversations solemn and hushed. Everyone assumed the worst. Charlie pushed off the dock, shocked and saddened. Two boatloads of American patriots suddenly became victims of war. The men she observed as they boarded the ships in Rouse's point were now either dead, wounded, or imprisoned. Every one of them. She thought of the horrors they faced and the suffering they must have endured. And she thought of their families back home. Wives, who might never again see their husbands, children who might never again see their father. Her stomach churned. Charlie's thoughts of joining the navy, also returned. But this time, she considered the possibility of enlisting. Not because she wanted to leave her miserable life behind but because she wanted to serve. To help. To do what she could, in the face of an oppressive, invading force.

The sights and sounds of men lost in battle dominated her thoughts as she rowed to Vermont. She used a hand and a sleeve to stop the tears. Charlie plunged her oar into the lake like a hunter's spear. The girl paddled furiously, ignoring the pain in her lungs. As the vessel glided through the water, her stomach burned with anger. She rowed even faster and when the muscles in her arms screamed with pain, she screamed back. A bitter, guttural, low-pitched howl that echoed on the quiet lake.

She slowed as she approached the Vermont shoreline. A motion in the weeds, caught her eye. She jerked to attention and verified the location of her musket. With a few deft movements of her extra-long oar, the raft silently floated toward the long weeds. The sound of wet wood pushing against the lake's fauna drove her prey into the open. A boy, her age or less, stood in two feet of water, and watched as she approached.

He wore no hat, with only his rough-cut, jet-black hair, to protect him from the sun. The boy focused on Charlie, with unblinking, brown eyes, his brown skin covered in scratches. He showed no fear of his unexpected visitor, standing with his legs apart and arms folded. His only weapon appeared to be an unyielding gaze. Charlie let the raft drift to a stop, reached for her weapon and raised it to eye level.

"If you're a British spy or an American smuggler, I'm not in the mood to be neighborly," she barked.

"I am an aide to Lieutenant Thomas McDonough, Commander of the American Navy, at Plattsburgh," said the young man, his voice respectful but strong.

"You're younger than I am. Is McDonough recruiting children?"

"I'll be seventeen in December."

Charlie blinked her surprise and lowered the weapon. She too, would turn seventeen, but in August. This kid didn't appear to be a threat. If anything, he looked exhausted. She wanted to know where he had been and where he was going. The boy interrupted her thoughts.

"I saw you at the docks in Rouse's point. You're a local," he observed.

Charlie ignored the boy's observation and announced a conclusion of her own.

"I heard the cannon fire, north of the line. But you saw it, didn't you?"

Charlie's inquiry sounded more like an accusation. The boy exhaled loudly and closed his eyes for a moment. When he opened them, he focused on Charlie and spoke in a murmur.

"We lost both of the sloops. The soldiers that survived are now prisoners of the British. I must report to the lieutenant, as soon as possible."

"How did you escape?" she asked, raising her musket, once again.

"I stole, I mean, I requisitioned a canoe. Stayed in the weeds and bushes. Followed our men into Canada. Missed most of the battle because I was too far behind the sloops. But I saw both ships when they sank. Lieutenant McDonough doesn't know yet. Can you help me?"

Although suspicious, Charlie found the boy's story, convincing.

"If you help with the rowing, we can reach the bay, late this afternoon," said Charlie, swapping her musket for an oar.

The boy splashed through the water, climbed on board the raft, and shivered an introduction.

"Kai Bellamy."

"Charlie Wheeler. There's a couple of blankets in the trunk. You best warm up," she answered.

As they glided south, her passenger related more bad news. McDonough's flagship, the *President*, ran aground in Plattsburgh Bay, just days ago. The vessel suffered significant damage.

Charlie concentrated on her rowing. Her passenger continued.

"Do you realize what this means?" he asked.

Charlie furrowed her eyebrows but kept rowing.

"The British now control Lake Champlain," he said.

Charlie, mostly ignorant of the geopolitical forces that surrounded the lake, chose that moment to rest.

"Seems to me they been doing a pretty good job of that already," she said.

Kai shrugged.

"Well, it just got a lot easier," he said.

"Your turn," said Charlie, handing the boy her oar and ending their discussion about the British.

As the duo rounded Chazy landing, another rafter, passing by, recognized Charlie and called out.

"Charlie! You must be doing good. Got yourself a boy, I see," said the man.

"Charlie blushed red and scowled at her competitor.

"Sorry, Kai," she mumbled to the boy.

"I'm used to it," he said, shrugging it off.

Charlie commented.

"Doesn't it bother you? My papa used to say, we all bleed red."

"White girls are the worst," said Kai.

Charlie glanced at her chest.

"What do you mean?" she asked.

"Most of them won't be seen with a black boy. And I'm not even black. My mother was Jamaican," said Kai.

Charlie prided herself on treating everyone the same. She felt the need to defend herself.

She reached for the oar, instead.

When Charlie rowed, Kai used the time to study his new-found friend and savior.

Charlie Wheeler seemed nice enough, he thought. The kid could navigate and propel a raft, with skill. Despite his small frame, Charlie struck Kai as one who could handle himself, both on and off the water. It nagged him, however, that Charlie did not compliment Kai on his dangerous mission, north of the line.

Although he would soon deliver bad news to Lieutenant McDonough, few if any, aide-de-camps, served their commander with such bravery.

Kai reached instinctively for the smooth jackstones in his pocket. They reminded him of just how far he had come, in the years since childhood. He played the one-handed game, for hours, throwing the large pebble into the air and retrieving the remaining stones, one at a time. That's what children do when they are abandoned by their parents. That's what Kai did at a time in his life when he lived another life.

The fishing town of Stonington, Connecticut, where he grew up, generated an endless number of bad memories. His absentee father, his drunken mother, and the horrible circumstances of his departure from home, instantly came to mind. He dared not share the details of his life with anyone on board the *President*. A woman who earned her income from strange men did not shock most people. And a father who traveled the sea as a fisherman, for months at a time, was commonplace. But a twelve-year-old boy, who stabbed and killed his mother, even in a moment of passion, could never reveal his secret. Kai blinked and forced his mind back to the present.

"Why did those two sloops move north of the line, to begin with?" asked Charlie.

Kai disclosed a serious error by the Americans.

"Lieutenant McDonough instructed Smith to remain south of the boundary line. He chose not to. The river is too narrow at Isle aux Noix. Our sloops didn't stand a chance," said Kai.

"Well, I think they were chasing the British," said Charlie. "And Lord knows, the British have been chasing us," she added.

Kai didn't like to be contradicted. He frowned, picked up his oar, and resumed rowing.

After arriving at McDonough's temporary quarters, Kai instructed Charlie to wait outside.

He knocked softly and waited for McDonough's acknowledgement before entering. The lieutenant paced the floor behind his desk.

"Do you have word? Where are my sloops?"

Kai took a deep breath and began his report.

"Both the *Eagle* and the *Growler* have been lost to the British," said the boy.

McDonough bit hard on his lower lip. He fell into the chair and rearranged the items on his desk. The Lieutenant squared the stack of papers, replaced the quill pen in its holder, and pushed several rolled charts and maps, to one side. He brushed some imaginary dust from his jacket and placed both hands, face down, on the newly organized desktop.

"Tell me everything you know."

Kai described his trip to Rouse's point on Smith's ship, his several-night stay in the village, and the last-minute decision to "requisition" a canoe.

"I remained well behind the sloops. I hid the canoe and crawled on my belly to the site of the battle. The river is very narrow when you approach the island. Both ships came under heavy fire, cannon and musketry, on both shores. The *Eagle* sank first, after a cannonball hit her below the waterline." said Kai.

McDonough listened without comment. Kai added a few more details and then concluded.

"That's all I have to report, sir."

"You could have been killed or captured," McDonough observed.

"I was fortunate, sir."

"Surely, you did not return to the bay by canoe?" asked the Lieutenant.

"No sir. I received assistance from a young boy, with a raft. He waits outside," said Kai. "His name is Charlie."

"Show him in," said McDonough, rising to his feet.

Charlie, unfamiliar with the required amenities, acknowledged McDonough with a quick nod of her head.

"Sir."

"Thank you for your assistance, young man."

"You're welcome, sir."

An awkward silence followed. McDonough returned to his chair. Charlie's jumbled thoughts about her past, and her plans for the business, evaporated in McDonough's presence. There were more important things in this world than rafting, fishing, and Otis Skinner.

"Lieutenant McDonough?"

"Yes Charlie," said McDonough, a weak smile on his face.

"I understand you are in need of additional crew members."

McDonough sat upright.

"Yes. Of course. We are desperately looking for new recruits. How old are you and what experience do you have?"

"I'll be seventeen in August and I've been on the water ever since I can remember," said Charlie.

McDonough looked away.

"Perhaps one of our gun boats . . ." said the lieutenant, allowing his voice to trail off.

"And I have this, sir."

Charlie reached into a pocket and retrieved the letter of recommendation from Army Captain Edgerton. McDonough read the note and beamed in Charlie's direction. A large grin crossed his face.

"I received my warrant as a midshipman, when I was just sixteen," said McDonough. "Welcome aboard, Seaman Wheeler."

Charlie grinned. Kai flashed a huge smile, featuring two perfect rows of brilliant-white teeth.

"Charlie, you will serve with me, on my flagship. When I get one." said the commander. "Kai, please see to the details."

"Thank you, sir," said Charlie.

"Now if you will excuse me, there is much work to do," said McDonough, waving the two youngsters from his office.

Otis did not enjoy his new assignment at the British ship works in Isle aux Noix.

His work as a spy, short lived because of Harriet and Charlie, triggered a change in duties. Although damaged and sunk at the battle of Isle Aux Noix, British forces quickly recovered the *Eagle* and the *Growler*. After repairs, the Brits intended to re-launch them as the *Shannon* and the *Broke*. There were other shipbuilding projects, too. Skinner's skills as a carpenter, made Otis a useful employee.

But he felt no loyalty to the British. The thought that he might be a traitor to the American cause, never crossed his mind. Skinner spied on behalf of the British, simply because he needed the money. Nothing more, nothing less. Harriet's stash lasted no more than a few weeks, because booze, when purchased north of the line, cost a pretty penny. Thanks to the constable in Isle LaMotte, crossing the line into Vermont, or even New York, became too risky. Posters, now ubiquitous in the North Country, plus the bounty on his head, made his capture more likely. The man's drunken confession to Charlie Wheeler made Skinner's conviction, if captured, a near certainty.

Otis remained hopeful, however, that he might still travel south of the line. A rumor, circulating in the naval yard, suggested that a British sortie might soon be organized. As told to Otis, Lieutenant Colonel Murray planned an attack on American towns and villages, bordering Lake Champlain. Such a move would be the opportunity that Otis desired. These types of missions resulted in the seizure of goods, weapons, ammunition, livestock and assorted valuables. The individual soldiers, who participated in these attacks, were often allowed to take personal possession of non-military items. It could be a very lucrative mission.

If allowed to tag along, Otis could continue south and begin a new life.

After storing her raft, Kai invited Charlie to spend a few days at the encampment, before her enlistment became official.

"A seaman with no experience is called a boy. They receive eight dollars per month," he announced.

"Some boys are musicians, some are powder monkeys, but most are just deckhands. And they do whatever they are told to do," said Kai.

"What's a powder monkey?" asked Charlie.

"They run the canisters, filled with gun powder, from down below to the cannon crews, up top," said Kai.

"Well, I don't play an instrument," said Charlie.

"Being a powder monkey is a dangerous job," said Kai.

"Do I have a choice," she asked.

"You'll do what you're told," said Kai.

"Well, you work for the lieutenant. That's a good job. How did that happen?" asked Charlie.

Kai explained that when McDonough first traveled from

Middletown, Connecticut to Burlington, Vermont, he rented horses.

"I worked at the stable and he hired me to return the animals. It took us four days to get to Burlington," said Kai.

"Did you return the horses?" asked Charlie.

"Yes, of course. But I asked the lieutenant if I could join the Navy. He took a liking to me and here I am," said Kai, once again, flashing a perfect smile.

Kai stopped in front of a small tent.

"You can bunk with me," he announced, pulling the canvas door to one side.

Charlie stopped at the entrance and studied her new quarters. One canvas cot, a tiny table, and a single chair. The privacy she required would not be possible, thought Charlie. On the other hand, she was now one of the boys, surrounded by people who would no longer treat her like a girl.

"But first we eat," Kai announced, reaching under his cot for a haversack.

The teenage recruits munched on hardtack and dried pork, washing it down with a canteen of lake water. Kai did most of the talking, regaling the Navy's newest recruit with stories about Lieutenant McDonough.

"He gets angry but never loses his temper. He expects his orders to be followed but the men respect him," said Kai.

"When he first got here, the Army generals were slow to cooperate. But the lieutenant did just fine, even though he's younger than all of them," Kai said.

Kai grinned another one of his spectacular smiles, his admiration for McDonough obvious. Charlie recalled her late father. He too, could do no wrong. She wondered what he would say about her decision to fight the British.

"Getting dark. And I'm exhausted," said Kai.

He kicked off his boots and let his baggy trousers, drop to the hard-packed dirt floor. Kai's head disappeared as he struggled to remove his shirt. Charlie's eyes grew wide when the boy's nightshirt, very nearly came off with the outer garment, fully exposing the young man's private parts. Kai, oblivious to the girl's embarrassment, fell on to his cot and rolled himself into a blanket.

"Latrines are at the end of the foot path, just inside the tree line," said Kai, his eyes already closed.

When the girl returned, the sound of snoring filled the tent. She slipped out of her shoes, wrapped herself in one blanket, and stretched out on the remaining blanket.

Sleep came quickly.

The exertion of rowing a raft for several hours triggered a deep and restful sleep for Charlie Wheeler.

Charlie's host woke her up with a gentle kick to the girl's backside.

"Hey boy. Are you going to sleep till noon?" asked Kai.

Charlie opened one eye. She required a moment to recall where she spent the night and why.

"I'm stiff and sore from rowing your ass to Plattsburgh. You can show your gratitude by serving me breakfast in bed," said Charlie, a smirk crossing her face.

"I'll give you breakfast in bed," Kai yelled.

He grabbed his canteen and dumped some of its contents on Charlie's head and face. Charlie jumped to her feet.

"You're a dead man, sailor."

She shoved Kai onto his cot, straddled the boy, and attempted to pin his arms to the blanket. But Kai proved much stronger than her deceased, wrestling partner, Hank Wells. The young sailor used his muscular arms and a violent twist of his body to overpower Charlie. Now, he straddled Charlie, pinning her arms to the cot. Charlie winced and wriggled, but to no avail.

"You will surrender, boy, or you will die," said Kai, looking more menacing than Charlie expected.

Charlie whispered her response, forcing Kai to lean forward.

"Never."

She caught him by surprise. Charlie raised her knees, pulled the boy forward, and bucked Kai over her head into the canvas wall.

"What in tarnation is going on here?" asked a deep, male voice.

Charlie, perched on the side of the cot, eyeballed the intruder and frowned. Kai jumped to his feet.

"Excuse me, Bosun Sharp. I was instructing our new recruit on the best way to defend himself", said Kai.

Sharp rolled his eyes. His grimace melted into a smirk.

"Adele's worried about you. Were you really north of the line when they sunk the *Eagle?*"

"Yes sir. And they got the *Growler* too," said Kai, catching his breath.

"But tell your wife I'm fine. Charlie here, brought me back to the bay on his raft," Kai added.

"Jim Sharp," said the man, extending a friendly hand to Charlie.

"Charlie Wheeler, sir, and just so you know, *I* was doing the instructing."

Sharp chuckled. Kai frowned.

"What is a bosun?" asked Charlie.

"I'm a bosun's mate, actually," said Sharp.

He went on to explain his responsibility for the ship's masts, rigging, sails, anchors and cables.

"Bosun is just another word for boatswain," said Sharp.

"Couldn't I just call you, Mr. Sharp?" asked Charlie.

"Yes, Charlie, 'Mr. Sharp' is acceptable and allowed," said Sharp.

The trio agreed to join the bosun's wife for breakfast.

Mrs. Sharp, shorter than Charlie, appeared fit and trim. Her dirty-blond hair and cheerful countenance impressed Charlie, from the moment they met. They took an instant liking to each other, and Charlie felt comfortable in her presence.

Jim Sharp, anxious to relate the latest ship gossip, did not allow the women enough time for the usual amenities. Charlie and Kai learned from the bosun that repairs on the *President* were complete and that McDonough would soon take the flagship to Burlington.

"The lieutenant purchased two more sloops and some smaller vessels. They will be refitted in Burlington," Sharp reported.

"And I will be joining all of you, on the *President,*" Adele announced.

"A woman on board the lieutenant's flag ship? I'm surprised," said Kai, a knowing look crossing his face.

Sharp explained it to Charlie. Because her husband agreed to leave his position in the Army, Jim asked for and received permission to be accompanied by his wife.

"That's how desperate McDonough is for sailors," said Sharp.

"I'm guessing that's how Kai got his job," cracked Charlie.

Kai delivered a friendly tap to her shoulder, with his closed fist.

"These new recruits have no respect for their seniors."

When Nathan arrived at the Burlington Cantonment, accompanied by the Army's head surgeon, he did not recognize the place.

He counted more than a dozen, newly built structures on the premises, including a two-story, 20 x 300-foot hospital. The facility, with a capacity for 300 patients, also included a cellar and a front veranda. During their self-guided tour, Nathan and Beaumont learned that the hospital's ward master implemented a long list of rules, designed to ensure good hygiene. Chamber pots were cleaned at least three times a day. The straw in each bed was to be changed monthly. If the patient died, the straw was to be burned. Each patient had to be washed daily. Attendants, working for six dollars a month, also cooked for the patients and regularly cleaned and scrubbed the premises.

"I am now uncertain about my decision to serve on McDonough's flag ship," said Nathan.

"Dr. Mann runs a tight ship," said Beaumont, referring to the cantonment's senior doctor.

The balance of the doctors' visit involved a steady stream of new buildings, including barracks, warehouses, an armory and officers' quarters. When they approached the Burlington docks for their return trip to Plattsburgh, Nathan received a message.

"Lieutenant McDonough will be in Burlington within the week. Your orders are to report for duty on the *President*, when he arrives."

"Apparently, the *President* has been repaired," said Beaumont.

Dr. Beaumont offered to send Nathan's personal possessions plus the necessary medical supplies and equipment, in advance of McDonough's arrival.

"Good luck, my friend," said Beaumont.

"Thank you, Doctor Beaumont. Thank you for everything."

Charlie, swallowed hard, as she explored the dark and dingy quarters, below deck on the *President*.

A series of canvas hammocks, most of them cluttered with the meager belongings of sailors, left only tiny pathways in which a person might walk. A few chamber pots served as latrines. Their odor, combined with the smell of sweat and mildew, made the large, below deck chamber, a very smelly place. Charlie swallowed hard, as she recalled the luxury of her spacious raft, drifting in a sunlit breeze on the clear, blue waters of Lake Champlain.

"What do you think?" asked Kai.

Charlie rubbed her eyes, still adjusting to the dark.

"Not what I expected," she said, trying hard to hide her true feelings.

"There's an empty hammock near mine. I'll show you," said Kai.

After claiming the hammock with her haversack, the duo explored every nook and cranny on the ship.

"This is the most important room," said Kai, stopping in front of a metal-sheathed door, bolted shut and locked.

"What's in there?" asked Charlie.

"Cannon balls and gun powder. When we go to battle, the balls will be moved top side. You and the other boys will deliver canisters filled with powder to the gun crews. Lots of exercise, takes a strong pair of legs. You'll get to practice when the gun crews sight their guns and conduct their target practice.

Charlie, afraid to admit her reluctance, spoke quickly.

"I can do the job. Just watch me."

"I know, Charlie, I know," said Kai.

When the tour ended, Kai and Charlie occupied a few upside-down crates on the top deck. In time, their conversation turned personal.

"My mother died when I was born. Never knew her," Charlie said.

A NOVEL BY MARK BARIE

She then related the story of her father's untimely death and described her stepmother.

"She sounds awful," said Kai.

Charlie, unwilling to disclose Harriet's murder, just nodded her head.

"My father was a fisherman. That's how I got my name. He told me that Kai is another word for sea."

"What about your mother?" asked Charlie.

Kai scowled.

"I hated her. My father would be gone for months at a time. She spent all her money on rum. And when the money ran out, she invited her sailor friends to visit. They spent the night, if you know what I mean," said Kai.

Charlie avoided Kai's gaze, embarrassed that the boy would disclose such a thing. Kai continued.

"Mrs. Sharp seems nice enough. But in my opinion, most women can't be trusted. Remember that Charlie," said Kai.

Charlie could feel the pink heat covering her face.

"I'm sorry you feel that way, " she murmured.

Kai jumped to his feet.

"I just remembered. The lieutenant needs me at his meeting with the officers. I gotta go," he said.

"You have a meeting with the officers?" Charlie asked, her skepticism, obvious.

"Oh, I just serve the rum," said Kai, with a perfect smile.

Charlie waved him off. But Kai stepped forward and used one hand to mess up her short head of hair.

"I like you, Charlie. Welcome aboard."

As she watched Kai leave, Charlie could feel goosebumps on the back of her neck.

Charlie returned below to the hammock room, hoping for a moment alone, in which to relieve herself.

As she yanked on her nightshirt and dropped her drawers, Charlie recalled Kai, as he accidentally exposed himself. She reminded herself to be especially careful when dressing or retiring for the evening. When she lowered herself onto the chamber pot, a woman's voice shattered the girl's privacy.

"Does anyone know?"

Charlie catapulted to her feet when she saw Mrs. Sharp. The girl's arms flailed as she struggled to stuff the nightshirt into her baggy trousers.

"Mrs. Sharp, you startled me. I thought I was . . ."

Charlie's voice trailed off. Her stint in the Navy would be short lived, she concluded.

"Don't worry. It will be nice to have another woman on board," said Mrs. Sharp.

Charlie started breathing again. Her curiosity prompted a question.

"How did you know?"

Mrs. Sharp announced her observations.

"Most men don't sit when they pee. And without your jacket to cover your back, I can see the outline of the wrap you are using."

Charlie reached for her face.

"I need whiskers, I guess."

Mrs. Sharp continued with a smile.

"And most men are not as pretty as you are."

"Thank you, Mrs. Sharp. Please don't tell anyone."

"Your secret is safe with me," said Adele. "But I would like to know how and why."

Charlie climbed onto her canvas hammock.

"It's very long story, Mrs. Sharp."

"I'm listening," said the woman.

Charlie began with her tomboy childhood. She described her papa's death, the fatal accident that killed Hank, her stepparents, and the constant assumption that "Charlie" was a boy. She ended her tragic story with the demise of her good friend, Reuben Quimby.

"No one would do business with a girl. I didn't want to lose the business, so I became a boy. Full-time," she said.

Charlie looked for signs of approval in Mrs. Sharp's face. Mrs. Sharp blew the hair out of her face.

"That's quite a story, young lady."

"I should go home and be a boring, obedient girl, just like everyone wants me to be," said Charlie.

But the snarl on her face said otherwise.

"Is that what you want?"

Charlie jumped off the hammock, with a loud thud.

"No, that's the last thing I want. I want to be on the water. And I want to fight the British. I have no interest in frilly dresses or needlework or kitchen chores."

"Why didn't you stick with the rafting business?" asked Mrs. Sharp.

"The war. If it wasn't for the British, I'd still be moving goods north of the line. My papa would still be alive, and I could make a nice living," she said.

Mrs. Sharp signaled her understanding with a nod. Charlie leaned forward.

"Now, I have a question for you," Charlie said.

"Of course," said Mrs. Sharp.

"How well do you know Kai?" asked Charlie, recalling her

goosebumps.

Mrs. Sharp explained to Charlie that her husband and Kai enjoyed a particularly close relationship

"When he first arrived in Plattsburgh, Kai ran into trouble. Some of the men decided to run him off," said Mrs. Sharp.

"Why?" asked Charlie.

"Well, his skin is darker than most even though he's not black. Actually, his mother was Jamaican and his father, a big sea fisherman from Connecticut. About a half dozen of the men decided they would cut the boy down to size, him being McDonough's aide and all. Jim stepped in."

"What happened?" asked Charlie.

"Both Jim and Kai took their licks but the two of them gave worse than they got," said Mrs. Sharp, smiling as she said it.

"Did the lieutenant find out?" asked Charlie.

"No. And that's the way Kai wanted it. He's been grateful ever since. I think he spoke to McDonough about me joining my husband on the ship. But he won't admit it."

Charlie shook her head, in disbelief.

"Amazing," she added.

"I'm at the far end of this room. A bit more privacy. Why don't you take a hammock next to me?" said Mrs. Sharp.

"What do I tell Kai?"

"Don't worry about Kai. I'll talk to him."

Charlie scratched her head.

"I'm not sure why, Mrs. Sharp. But Kai makes me nervous," said Charlie.

"Trust me. He's a good boy," said Mrs. Sharp.

Mrs. Sharp accosted Kai as he approached the short ladder that

led to the topside hatch.

The boy, in a hurry, responded with a desperate tone in his voice.

"Mrs. Sharp, the lieutenant is expecting me, topside."

"This will take just a minute," she pleaded.

Kai frowned. He wanted to be on deck, when the *President* docked at Burlington.

"What is it?" he asked.

"I moved Charlie to a hammock, next to my own."

"That's fine, Mrs. Sharp. Now I really have to go."

"But there's something else I would like to discuss," said the woman.

Kai snapped at her.

"Not now, woman."

Mrs. Sharp, unaccustomed to such reactions from Kai, stared in disbelief.

With his flag ship fully restored, McDonough proudly sailed into Burlington Bay.

The *President's* escorts included two good-sized sloops. McDonough first laid eyes on the boats when their owners appeared at the customs checkpoint to register the vessels. Despite the owners' objections, the lieutenant seized both of them for the war effort. Two smaller sloops also accompanied McDonough's flotilla. Carpenters from New York would refit those boats, once the flotilla docked at Burlington. The carpenters and a crew of army laborers would also construct four new gun boats.

Charlie, looking sharp in her new uniform, remained hidden behind dozens of officers, sailors and boys, who outranked her in seniority. Her new uniform, white pants and a blue jacket, did not include shoes, because boys and inexperienced sailors did not wear them. But Charlie owned a pair and wore them with pride.

As she waited for McDonough and the senior crew to exit the ship, Charlie considered the events of her first days on board the *President*. She quickly discovered that an inexperienced sailor, or 'boy', as she was called, took orders from everybody. Some of the men barked their commands and made no secret of their disdain for novice sailors. Others, a bit more genteel in their approach, addressed Charlie by her name. Cargo, endless lengths of ropes, canvas sails, crates of food stuffs, garbage and a myriad of errands and messages, prevented Charlie from enjoying her trip to Burlington on a glorious mid-May afternoon. Her new job with the navy would not be boring, she thought.

By the time she received permission to go ashore, the welcoming delegation and the ship's officers, disappeared from view. She wandered aimlessly around the cantonment. One particularly large building came into view. The sign said hospital and she entered for a closer inspection. Row after row of canvas cots, some of them with patients, filled the structure. A network of pathways separated the beds and allowed for staff to access each patient. A far corner of the room served as an operating theater. It featured two large, high-top tables plus shelves and walls adorned with a variety of medicines and medical implements.

"May I help you, sailor?"

The male voice triggered a quick pivot. Charlie's eyes grew wide, and she grinned.

"I'm not sick, if that's what you're asking," said Charlie, standing a few yards from Dr. Nathan Coldwell.

Nathan blanched.

"Charlie. Oh, my goodness. I didn't expect to see you, here.

"I enlisted in the navy. I'm on McDonough's flagship, the

President, she announced.

Nathan took a sharp breath, his eyes wide open. His voice trembled.

"You're serving on the *President?* In what capacity, may I ask."

"I'm a powder monkey," said Charlie, adding a detailed explanation of what powder monkeys do and chirping away about the duties and responsibilities of boys.

Nathan, unsmiling and swallowing repeatedly, did not react. Charlie noticed.

"Are you not feeling well, Nathan?"

Nathan snapped to attention and executed a salute. When Charlie heard a slight commotion behind her, she turned and immediately mimicked Nathan.

"Sir," they said in unison, acknowledging Lieutenant Thomas McDonough's unexpected appearance.

Several officers accompanied their commander. Kai, bringing up the rear, oozed with pride. When Charlie and Nathan came into the lieutenant's view, McDonough displayed his near perfect memory.

"Dr. Coldwell, Charlie, thank you both for agreeing to serve on my flagship," he said.

"An honor, sir," said Nathan. Charlie jerked her head in recognition.

McDonough and his entourage moved on. Charlie turned to Nathan. The girl's eyes sparkled, and a grin covered her face.

"We are serving on the same ship, Nathan. A stroke of good fortune, don't you think?"

Nathan shoved his nose in the air.

"It seems unlikely that we will see much of each other, Mister Wheeler."

Charlie frowned.

"You can call me Charlie, Nathan. I don't mind," she said, her voice wavering with uncertainty.

"I believe the proper greeting is "Seaman Wheeler or Mister Wheeler. And you may address me as Dr. Coldwell," said Nathan, his voice betraying no emotion.

Charlie's jaw dropped. She liked Nathan, a lot. But the man confused the girl. Friendly when he wanted to be, but arrogant and aloof at other times. Typical, she groused to herself. Nathan turned to leave.

"I must excuse myself, Mister Wheeler. Good day.

Chapter Nine

TENSIONS

Otis jumped to his feet as the British officer entered the wooden hut.

"I am Lieutenant Colonel John Murray of the 100th Regiment of Foot," said the man.

Otis extended his hand but the lieutenant colonel ignored the gesture. The officer inspected the American's disheveled appearance, from head to toe. Otis lowered his outstretched arm. He stood, trying hard to quell the anger rising in his chest.

"You are an American. Is that correct?" asked Murray.

"Yes sir."

"But you work for the British."

"Yes sir."

"Why?"

"Well, sir, I needed the money and I . . ."

The lieutenant colonel waved his hand as if shooing a mosquito.

"My sergeant tells me you know the lake, south of the line, quite well. Isle LaMotte, Chazy, Plattsburgh, and so on. Is that true?"

"Yes sir."

"And how did you come to be so knowledgeable?" asked the officer.

"I've been on the lake since I was a kid. Rafting mostly. I can tell you whatever you want to know," said Otis.

"You will draw a map. A detailed map," said Murray.

Otis reached his snapping point. He did not enlist in the British Army, and he certainly did not expect to be treated like an enlistee.

"I ain't drawing you no map," Otis growled.

Murray pivoted and glared at Otis. He reached for the chinstrap which held his top hat-shaped head covering. Murray placed it on the desk, using a sleeve to burnish the gold seal on the front. The officer's unblinking eyes locked onto Skinner's face. Murray made a show of removing the white gloves which covered his perfectly manicured hands. He tossed the gloves on his desk and tucked his red, waist-length jacket more securely into the red sash around his waist. Otis watched as the officer stepped around the desk and shoved his face forward. He spoke in a whisper.

"You will do what you are told Mr. . . ."

The officer's voice trailed off. He swallowed hard and a red blush covered his cheeks. Otis realized that Murray forgot the name of his American spy. Otis took a half-step forward. They stood eyeball to eyeball. A scowl covered the American's face. Otis used a thick finger to poke the officer's chest.

"Skinner. Otis Skinner. And if you want my help, Lieutenant Colonel Murray, I sail with the regiment," Otis growled. "I don't do maps."

Murray scoffed and returned to his chair behind the desk.

Otis turned his back, headed for the door. The British officer decided to back off.

"Very well, Mr. Skinner. You will sail with me. But I warn you.

If your information is either inaccurate or limited in its usefulness, I will have you shot."

Otis stood in the doorway. His head swiveled.

"And if my information is good?" asked Otis.

"You will be well-compensated," said Murray.

Otis cracked a big, toothy smile.

Charlie fumed.

She no longer wanted to see, much less talk to, Nathan Coldwell. The small pile of cargo at her feet belonged to him, however. She went below-deck to get Coldwell's instructions.

"Dr. Coldwell. You've got some crates dockside. They just arrived from Plattsburgh. Do you want them down here?" asked Charlie.

Nathan, by himself in the operating theatre, nodded his approval.

"Yes, please. Need some help?"

"No, sir," said Charlie, a coldness in her voice.

She exited the operating theater before Nathan could react. As she contemplated the crates, cases, and satchels, a familiar voice offered to assist.

"I think we can do this in one trip," said Jim Sharp.

"I don't mind, Mr. Sharp. But thank you for offering," said Charlie.

Sharp ignored Charlie's protest.

"I'll take the heavy crates," said Sharp, stacking one on the other.

Charlie stacked the remaining cargo and followed Sharp as he boarded the *President*. As the duo navigated the ramp, Charlie wondered why Sharp came to her rescue. This menial task belonged to inexperienced seamen, like Charlie. A bosun's mate did not engage in such activities.

"Can you take it from here?" Sharp asked.

"Yes, Mr. Sharp, and thank you very much for your help."

"Never hurts to be a gentleman," said Sharp, as he climbed through the hatch.

Charlie scratched her head. "I feel like a girl," she muttered.

She surprised Nathan with the volume of supplies and equipment from Plattsburgh.

"Oh my. I think Dr. Beaumont packed everything," said Nathan.

Nathan did most of the talking, directing Charlie to place certain items in specific places while he did the same. After moving several of the small items to a nearby table, Charlie pivoted to retrieve one last wooden box. She didn't know that Nathan, just a moment earlier, pushed the crate closer to her feet. Charlie tripped over the box and, but for Nathan's quick response, would have fallen on her face.

Nathan caught the girl in his arms and for a few seconds, the couple stood face-to-face. Charlie, unaccustomed to a young man's embrace, saw nothing but Nathan's light blue eyes. Nathan took a sharp breath, released his grip, and jerked backwards. He blushed his apology.

"Excuse me, Mr. Wheeler, that was my fault," he said, blinking his eyes and wetting his lips.

Charlie spoke slowly, as if in a daze.

"No. I should look where I'm going," she whispered.

An awkward silence enveloped the room. Beads of sweat appeared on Nathan's forehead. Charlie's heart pounded. She caught his eyes. They both looked away.

"I have to go now," said Charlie, but her feet remained in place and she spoke as if needing the surgeon's permission to leave.

Nathan stepped aside.

"Yes, of course. And thank you for the help, Mr. Wheeler."

Their eyes met, once again. The jumble of thoughts in Charlie's head confused the girl. She couldn't decide if Nathan attracted her or aggravated her.

Charlie rushed to the exit.

When the sergeant yelled, "again", Charlie groaned.

Her chest heaved and every muscle in her body screamed in pain. For what seemed the one hundredth time, Charlie and the other powder monkeys ran from their respective cannon crews to the powder magazine below. The diminutive girl returned to her cannon crew, well before the others.

"Now listen carefully to me, boys," said the sergeant.

When the young sailors gathered round the sergeant, he explained the concept of a "bucket brigade."

"If we come up short of powder monkeys, you will form a "bucket brigade" with the monkeys you got. That way, your running will be kept to a minimum and the cannon crews will still be supplied with powder."

Charlie didn't understand.

"Why? Do some of the boys leave their post?" she asked.

The sergeant smirked.

"Yeah. I suppose you could say that."

A number of the senior men, working a nearby cannon, shook with laughter.

"Sergeant, you will treat the boys as I treat you. With respect."

Lieutenant McDonough's sudden appearance on the deck of the *President,* triggered a series of salutes. No one dared smile, much less laugh. McDonough turned to Charlie.

"Your task is an important one, Mr. Wheeler. It is also very dangerous. Everyone on this ship is at risk. When the enemy attacks, it makes no distinction between the old and the young. Do you understand what I'm telling you, boy?"

"Yes sir," said Charlie.

McDonough turned to the sergeant.

"With your permission, I would like Seaman Wheeler to join me on a tour of the ship works," said McDonough.

"Yes sir. Our training practice is finished," said the sergeant.

Charlie's eyes opened wide as she quick-stepped in line, just behind the lieutenant.

"Good afternoon, Charlie."

The voice came from behind. Charlie acknowledged the greeting from Kai, with a quick glance. During the tour, McDonough did most of the talking. He repeatedly inquired of the carpenters about their progress and the ships' expected completion dates. The fifty-ton *Rising Sun*, formally a merchant ship, would soon become the *Preble*. The refitting would take several more weeks. When finalized, the war sloop would carry nine guns and move with much greater speed. A slightly smaller sloop, renamed the *Montgomery*, would carry six guns. It too, would take its place in McDonough's growing flotilla. McDonough, anxious for the work to be completed, urged the men on and turned to leave.

"Walk with me, Charlie," he ordered.

Charlie hustled to his side.

"Yes sir."

"I trust that you are pleased with your accommodations on board the *President*," said McDonough.

Charlie hesitated. She noticed a twinkle in McDonough's eyes. It revealed the lieutenant's dry sense of humor. Charlie, responded in kind.

"Yes sir. A powder monkey's dream," said Charlie, flashing a quick grin.

McDonough nodded and smiled. Moments later, he grew serious.

"Learn your job well, Charlie. Your very life depends on it," said McDonough.

"Yes sir. And thank you, sir."

The lieutenant turned to Kai.

"Kai, I want you to keep an eye on our boy, Charlie. He's a good man," said McDonough.

"Yes sir," said Kai, glancing at Charlie.

Kai waited until the Lieutenant disappeared from view.

"You seem to have become the lieutenant's favorite," said Kai, a serious look in his eyes.

"He treats everyone with respect," said Charlie. "I like that."

"You will be treated like all of the other boys on board the *President,*" said Kai, unsmiling.

Charlie recognized condescension when she saw it.

"My sergeant said he is in charge of the gun crew. I take orders from him. And if I'm not mistaken, Kai, you take orders from the lieutenant."

Charlie stepped closer as if to emphasize her observation.

Kai blinked first and the two separated without a word.

Kai vented his frustrations to Jim Sharp, as the older man rested in his hammock

"We were friends at first, now he thinks he's better than the rest of us. All because the lieutenant took a liking to him."

Sharp acknowledged the boy's complaint with a quick nod.

"And this is all my fault," said Kai. "I hitched a ride on Charlie's silly, little raft."

Kai fumed as he paced the narrow aisle between hammocks.

"Charlie's a hard worker, smart, and strong-willed. Sounds a lot like you, Kai," said Sharp.

"But he confuses me. One minute, I want to take him under my wing and be his mentor. The next moment, he acts like he knows it all and I want to throw him overboard," Kai complained.

"There's a reason for that," said Sharp, a knowing look on his face.

"What do you mean?" asked Kai.

Sharp climbed out of the hammock and scanned the entire chamber. His eyes darted everywhere. He lowered his voice to a whisper.

"Mrs. Sharp moved Charlie next to her hammock, to give the kid some privacy," said Sharp.

"See. That's what I mean. Everyone treats Charlie like he's special or something," Kai whined.

Sharp stepped closer to the boy.

"Charlie needed more privacy because Charlie is a female."

Kai stood perfectly straight. His eyes turned to slits.

"A girl?" he asked.

"Yes, Kai. A real girl. And if you breathe a word of this to anyone, Mrs. Sharp will kill the both of us. And the lieutenant, won't be too happy, either," said Sharp.

Kai fell backwards on to a nearby hammock, a frown on his face.

"I don't trust women," he grumbled. "Most of them are whores or idiots or both."

"Did you inform my wife of your feelings in that regard?" asked Sharp, a sarcastic tone in his voice.

"I wasn't talking about her," said Kai.

Sharp's eyes rolled to the back of his head.

"I'll be sure and let her know," said Sharp.

Kai climbed out of the hammock. He reached for the large jack stone in his pocket and squeezed as hard as he could. He started to leave, forgetting to say goodbye to his friend. Sharp cocked his head.

"Kai?"

Kai kept walking.

Otis, fascinated by the sheer size of the British invasion force, sat by himself, in the stern of Lieutenant Colonel Murray's vessel.

The flotilla, led by the *Shannon* and the *Broke*, (formally, the American sloops, *Eagle* and *Growler*) also included three gunboats, forty bateaux and more than 1000 men. Their mission, to destroy public property, military stores and American vessels, did not include the destruction of private property. At least, according to their orders.

On July 29, 1813, the waters of Lake Champlain, sparkled in the sun. The massive flotilla sailed south and crossed the international boundary line, at Rouse's point. The raiding party stopped first at Windmill Point in Alburgh, Vermont. Otis quickly proved his worth. He spotted a local physician, Dr. James Wood, observing the flotilla from a small boat in the tall weeds. After intense questioning, Wood revealed that he messaged American troops in both Plattsburgh and Burlington. The British took the physician as prisoner and kept a careful watch on the lake's eastern horizon.

Soon, the flotilla anchored off the Chazy shoreline. Murray issued a proclamation. Individual citizens and private property would not be molested. Locals, instructed to remain in their homes, offered no resistance. Nevertheless, British troops seized a small, privately owned schooner.

The raiding party arrived at Plattsburgh Bay, the next morning. They anchored in the Saranac River and destroyed an arsenal, a store house and a block house. Absent any opposition, Otis then led the British to Pike's Cantonment. Not one hut escaped the British torches. The entire camp, previously abandoned by the Americans, burned to the ground. Despite Murray's proclamation, the British troops then looted several homes and carried away large quantities of booty. They also seized an American sloop, the *Burlington Packet*, which they used to store and transport the spoils of war.

The British then decided to split their invasion force in two. The *Shannon* and the *Broke,* along with a gun boat, traveled south to Burlington. On their way, they seized eight more merchant vessels, ranging in size from ten to sixty tons. McDonough's practice, of refitting merchant ships for use in war, would, henceforth, be severely curtailed.

The remaining gun boats and dozens of bateaux, traveled north to Chazy landing. They burned the store belonging to Matthew Saxe and then returned to Isle LaMotte. Once in Vermont, the situation deteriorated. Otis confiscated a horse for Colonel Murray, enabling the officer to ride ahead. Otis hesitated, however, when a number of younger soldiers forcibly entered a Swanton farmhouse. He heard the screams of a young woman and ran to investigate. The dark-skinned women, no more than fifteen years old, emerged from a back room, her face bruised and dress torn. Otis glared at the British soldiers but left the building, in silence. At another farmhouse, he intervened when an older woman, surrounded by British regulars, struggled to fend off her attackers.

"That's enough," said Otis, shoving one of the men through the open door.

The other men seized whiskey, pork, boxes of soap and candles, plus clothing and calf skins. Otis suddenly lost his appetite for the rewards of war. He never thought of himself as a saint. But the cruelty of the British soldiers left him disgusted. They acted like animals, out of control. And he would not be a party to rape. When the troops began their muddy trek back to the waiting boats, Otis deliberately fell behind.

Just before dusk, he slipped, unseen, into the woods.

Charlie's day began with the memory of her encounter with Nathan.

For as long as she could remember, Charlie merely tolerated boys and men. Her father remained an exception to that rule, because, well, he was her father. Reuben Quimby gave her the respect she required and deserved. Hank, too, did not fit the mold because he was more like a brother. Nathan Coldwell, by contrast, broke all the rules. Despite his occasional arrogance and his tendency to view women with a barely disguised disdain, the man intrigued her. She sensed a strong independence in Nathan and a tremendous intellectual capacity. Underneath the man's cold exterior, she saw a kind and gentle soul. She wanted to know him better. But her secret and his attitude got in the way.

"You're looking more and more like a sailor, every day," said Kai.

Charlie jumped from her hammock to the floor. She assumed she was alone.

"Were you looking for me?"

"Well, the lieutenant did say to keep an eye on you," said Kai, sporting a larger than usual grin on his face.

168

Charlie cocked her head and squinted.

"What happened to treating me like every other boy on board?"

Kai stepped forward. He spoke softly.

"I've decided that you're different from all the rest," said Kai.

Charlie checked her appearance. She then peered into Kai's face for any sign that he might know her secret. She saw nothing obvious.

"Why am I different," she asked.

"Well, the lieutenant took a liking to you and I guess, I do too," said Kai.

Charlie could feel the goosebumps on her arms.

"I try to get along with everyone, Kai. Now if you don't mind, I really have to be topside.

Kai blocked her way. A serious look covered his face.

"Charlie, I found a boarding house just outside the camp. They serve a good fish dinner. You will be my guest, of course," said Kai.

Charlie thought it more of a directive than an invitation. She responded almost immediately.

"Thank you. I just came down for a quick change of clothes and then it's back to the cannon crew," said Charlie.

Kai bit his lower lip.

"I understand."

"Gotta go," she said, brushing by her would-be suitor.

Kai watched as she disappeared.

"You're just like all the rest," he growled.

Kai checked in with Nathan on his way to the topside hatch.

"How's the surgeon's mate, this morning?" he asked.

"Fine, thank you for asking," Nathan replied.

Kai's mind raced. His real purpose in the surgery had nothing to do with Nathan's well-being.

"I'm in the mood for a fish dinner, tonight. You would be my guest. Any interest?"

"Yes. As a matter fact, I am interested," said Nathan.

Hours later, the two young men chatted aimlessly as they negotiated the Burlington Cantonment and reached their destination. Kai wanted to know if Nathan also knew of Charlie's secret. He wondered how he might bring the girl into their conversation. Surprisingly, Nathan broached the subject first.

"Kai, what do you think of Charlie?"

Startled, Kai resorted to the obvious answer.

"Hard-working boy, confident, young, but lots of potential," he said, acting as if Charlie were his junior by ten years.

Nathan, absentmindedly folded and unfolded his cloth napkin.

"Yes, I suppose."

Kai ran through a mental checklist. Brown boy versus white boy. Limited schooling versus a degree in medicine. Skipper's mate versus surgeon's mate. The conclusion became obvious. If the two of them competed for the girl's attention, Kai would lose. He decided to embarrass the doctor into a confession.

"Are you taken with the boy?" asked Kai

Nathan's head snapped to attention. His ear lobes flushed a dark pink and his eyes grew wide. He sat perfectly upright in the chair, motionless and barely breathing. His stone-cold glare lasted only a moment and then he exploded.

"Your question is vulgar and inappropriate," Mr. Bellamy.

Nathan removed the napkin from the table, crushing it into a tiny ball, and throwing it onto his untouched food.

"I am not a sodomite," added Nathan, whispering and growling his response at the same time.

Kai quickly reversed himself.

"Please accept my apology, Dr. Coldwell. I did not mean to offend you," he said, secretly pleased that his inquiry triggered the hoped-for response.

"Certainly, there are matters, other than the boy, which we are able to discuss," said Nathan, reaching for the napkin and slowly folding it into a perfect rectangle.

Kai closed his eyes and bowed his head.

"Yes, my friend. I agree. And once again, I apologize for having offended you."

By outward appearances, Kai looked penitent. In his heart, the boy celebrated.

The sound of church bells echoed through the city of Burlington.

The loud warning announced the arrival of British forces. Murray stationed his flotilla just outside of the bay. The men on the *President,* ordered to their battle stations, scurried in every direction. Sailors caught below deck, scampered up the ladder. Several of the men appeared in various stages of undress, unable to complete the task and still be at their assigned posts in a timely manner. When Charlie got to the deck and reached her gun crew, she could see Lieutenant McDonough, spyglass in hand, at the bow of the ship.

For a few moments, the ship and its crew stood in an eerie cloud of silence. McDonough, with no more than a nod of his head, signaled to the gun crews. In a series of thunderous explosions, the ship's artillery spit long tongues of fire and dozens of cannonballs. The gun carriages catapulted backward, for half the width of the deck. Sailors used ropes to return the cannon to their positions, firing again and again. The *President* lurched and trembled with each blast. The land battery on the bluff roared in unison with its marine counterparts. The combined cannonade peppered the lake with a deadly scattering of geysers that neither ship nor man would dare to challenge.

The powder monkeys on board the *President* scrambled like mice in a panic. Charlie focused exclusively on the retrieval and return of powder cartridges from the below-deck magazine to the on-deck cannon crew. An older man, whom she recognized, but did not know by name, reduced her travel time by almost half. He grabbed her powder-filled canisters, whenever Charlie's head poked through the hatch.

In less than forty minutes, the canon fire ceased. The shots from British artillery fell short of their target. McDonough's cannonade met with similar results. Still, he complimented the artillery crews on their otherwise accurate aim.

"Your fire was in line but their ships were out of range," he said.

"Will we pursue them?" asked a voice in the rear.

"No. That is exactly what they want us to do. But our fleet is not yet ready," said McDonough.

McDonough brought the spy glass to eye level, one more time. "Soon, we shall have command of the entire lake."

After abandoning his British superiors, Otis Skinner thought it best to leave northern Vermont.

From Swanton, he traveled by foot to Burlington, utilizing unguarded barns, chicken coops, one smokehouse, and his considerable skills with a knife. The city of Burlington, dominated by the army's large presence and McDonough's navy, prompted Otis to visit the cantonment. More accurately, he visited the many taverns that surrounded the sprawling camp.

At a number of establishments, he overheard conversations about Murray's raid and the massive cannon duel, which resulted in neither damage nor casualties. He also heard, for the first time, the fleet commander's new title. 'Commodore.' The title, only vaguely familiar to Skinner, came to McDonough as a result of a recent promotion. The new rank triggered a great deal of confusion by a number of men, who continued to address their commanding officer as lieutenant. And everywhere he went, Otis heard grumbling about a severe shortage of sailors and soldiers. The navy crews complained of exhaustion and overwork. The regular army units did the same.

Otis, severely compromised by the steady consumption of alcohol, thought he should at least make inquiries. His enlistment would generate some badly needed cash and he could always abandon the American military, in the same way he abandoned the British. Looking dirty and disheveled, his whiskers and hair now long and unkept, he approached a table. The half-dozen Army enlistees celebrated their last night in Burlington.

"Is McDonough really looking for men?" asked Otis.

A number of the soldiers could not hide their derision.

"You need a bath, mister. Now go away," said one of the recruits.

The soldiers laughed hard. Otis didn't. He grabbed the mouthy private by the lapels of his uniform and pulled the young man bodily from his chair. Otis sat the soldier on the table. Tankards and tableware flew in every direction. Otis held his victim in place with a large hand around the man's neck. With his right hand, he flashed his long, hunting knife and snarled.

"I'm tired. I'm hungry. And I'm in no mood for smart talk."

One of the soldiers rose to his feet. An older colleague yanked on the man's arm and spoke quickly.

"We don't want any trouble, mister," pulling his mate back into the chair.

The poor soldier, still in Skinner's grip and blue in the face, struggled to breathe. Otis pushed hard and his victim fell backward. The man, now laying on the table, choked and wheezed.

"Now, I'm gonna ask you men one more time. Where do I go to sign up?" asked Otis.

Several of the men spoke simultaneously. But when the chatter stopped, Otis knew where he had to go. As he left the tavern, the drunken giant argued with himself about the idea of enlisting. On the one hand, he needed to earn some money and his country needed the help. On the other hand, he could easily be identified and end up in jail.

Despite his inebriated state, or perhaps because of it, Otis abandoned his mental debate, and concentrated on his destination.

Charlie, with a rare moment to herself, lay in her hammock, staring at the ceiling.

Her seventeenth birthday came and went without notice or celebration. Although rarely by herself, she often felt alone and lost. Her last encounter with Nathan Coldwell did not put an end to her daydreams about the young doctor. Her head ached just thinking about it.

"Why aren't you on deck, enjoying this sunny Sunday?" asked Kai.

Charlie jumped off the hammock and quickly checked her appearance, as she stood in the tiny space between Kai and her bed.

"You have a way of sneaking up on people, Kai. Is that done deliberately?" she asked.

The young man's eyebrows jumped to the top of his forehead

as he grinned.

"Sometimes," said Kai.

The hairs went up on the back of Charlie's neck. She watched Kai's every move.

"I've seen that look before. I had a large tomcat in our barn, back home. He looked that way whenever he caught a bird," said Charlie.

Kai glared.

"You have a sharp tongue, today."

He took a step forward. Charlie retreated, pushing her hammock on its side and to the wall.

"What are you doing?" she asked.

Kai spoke in a voice choked with lust. He leaned in, his face just inches from hers.

"We never finished our wrestling match," he said.

Charlie didn't wait for Kai to act on his wish. She hooked a foot behind the young man's leg and pushed hard. His butt hit the floor with a thud. The red-faced boy scrambled to his feet,

"What's the matter? I'm not good enough for you?" he growled.

"Kai, take a walk."

The voice belonged to Mrs. Sharp. The boy-man stood in place. The woman stood at Charlie's side.

"Leave us. Now," she said.

Kai stormed down the aisle way.

Charlie searched Mrs. Sharp's eyes. The girl's unblinking stare prompted the woman to fidget and squirm. Charlie assumed the worst.

"You told him, didn't you?"

Mrs. Sharp shook her head violently and reached for the girl. Charlie stepped back, shaking her head in disbelief. She repeated her accusation.

"You told him."

"No Charlie, I didn't say a word to Kai. I didn't tell anyone. I . . ."

The woman's voice disappeared into the stale air of the bottom deck. The color drained from her face. She used a hand to smother a groan.

"Oh Charlie. I'm so sorry," she whispered.

The girl stiffened and stared in disbelief. Mrs. Sharp searched Charlie's eyes.

"Charlie, there are no secrets between a woman and her husband. You'll understand that when you get older," Mrs. Sharp explained.

Charlie poked Mrs. Sharp in the chest with her finger.

"I understand perfectly. You told your husband and he told Kai,"

Mrs. Sharp hid her face with both hands. She started to cry.

"Yes," she sobbed.

"Why is my wife crying?" asked Mr. Sharp, announcing his presence with a question and embracing his wife.

Charlie's eyes flashed like lightening.

"What did you tell Kai?" she asked.

Mr. Sharp turned to his wife. His face reddened. He coughed to clear his throat.

"I don't remember telling Kai, anything."

His wife broke their embrace and raised her voice.

"You promised me, Jim. You promised me."

Mr. Sharp retreated to a nearby wall. He lowered his eyes, unwilling to face either of the women.

"I'm sorry, Charlie," he murmured.

"Why?" asked Charlie. "Why did you tell him?"

"Because you were driving him crazy," said Mr. Sharp. "He didn't know why he was so attracted to a boy," said Sharp.

"You must talk to Kai. Immediately," said Mrs. Sharp.

"I will. I promise," he said.

Charlie pushed past the couple and ran from the chamber.

Otis Skinner's frustration grew as he walked from building to building at the Burlington Cantonment.

Most of the 11th Regiment moved to Plattsburgh, during the previous week. No one seemed to know where he should go to enlist. The instructions he received at the tavern, proved worthless.

"May I help you?" asked the officer.

Otis blocked the noon-day sun as he stood in the soldier's doorway.

"Been looking to sign up, for more than an hour now. Can you help me?"

The officer grinned, jumped from his desk chair, and extended a hand.

"Second Lieutenant Bernard Ketchum," said the soldier

Otis looked up and decided on his new name.

"Otis Rafter," he said. "Nice to meet you, Lieutenant."

"You've come to the right place. Captain Scoville's entire company is made up of volunteers, said the officer.

"Infantry?" asked Otis.

"No, sir. Rifle Corps. Can you shoot?"

"Not with this," said Otis, flashing his hunting knife.

"We will get you a rifle, Mr. Rafter. I promise," said the lieutenant.

"Have a seat, sir."

Otis fell into the nearest chair.

"Are you headed to Plattsburgh too? Seems like everyone else is," said Otis.

"Yes, sir. And I will get you processed as soon as possible. Excuse me please."

The officer went to the open door and shouted.

"Sergeant Gates, I need you over here, now," said Ketchum.

Otis turned in his seat. Sergeant Gates, a man in his late twenties, appeared at the doorway, listening to the lieutenant's instructions, and locking eyes with Otis.

"Gates, are you listening to me?" asked the lieutenant.

"Yes, sir, I must retrieve two sign-up sheets at Captain Scoville's quarters," he said.

"Yes, Gates. Now get moving."

Gates waited until Otis turned his back to the doorway.

"I'll be right back," he said, but motioned frantically for the senior officer to follow him.

The lieutenant shook his head and grimaced. The sergeant hurried from the cabin and waited for his lieutenant, a dozen yards away.

"Lieutenant, I know that man," said Gates.

"Good. He's going to volunteer with the rifle company," said Ketchum.

His face is plastered all over Grand Isle. Wanted for murder. They say he killed his wife," said Gates, whispering but breathing heavy.

"Are you sure?"

"I grew up in Vermont, just north of Swanton," said Gates.

The two men quickly located rifles and several fellow soldiers.

Otis Skinner, with a half dozen long rifles pointed at him, surrendered without incident.

Sunday at the Burlington Cantonment allowed both soldiers and sailors several hours of leisure time.

Charlie no longer wished to spend time with either Kai or Nathan. She decided, instead, to tag along with a half-dozen members of the artillery crew. Unlike most of the men, Charlie did not worry about the money required for shore excursions. Although frugal with her funds, the lease of the Wheeler farm at Isle LaMotte left her with a healthy monthly income, in addition to her military wages. The proceeds, held for safekeeping by Alburgh's only attorney, needed to be accessed by Charlie, on the rarest of occasions.

A visit to one of Burlington's many taverns reminded Charlie of her first experience with hard liquor. At Otis Skinner's behest, she and her friend, Hank, got silly. And then they got sick. Her drinking friends, busy consuming large quantities of the stuff, took no notice as Charlie nursed a single drink for more than an hour.

After a few hours passed, the tipsy crew, now bereft of funds, started their trek back to the *President*. Several hundred yards from the cantonment's gate, a lone mule, tied to a hitching post, proved too great a temptation for the festive sailors. The first crewmember, after announcing to the audience his years of experience with farm animals, mounted the donkey. He did not remain on the beast of burden for very long. The stubborn animal tossed the unwanted passenger into the gutter. After a series of unsuccessful attempts by various members of the crew, it fell to Charlie to "tame the beast". With a handful of mane and two short, but muscular legs, Charlie managed to stay on until the donkey grew tired of bucking. She triumphantly rode the jackass, bareback, into camp Burlington. Unfortunately, the noisy adulation of her inebriated friends came to an abrupt halt. The mule's owner, with a navy officer in tow, accosted Charlie and her colleagues.

Lieutenant Peter Gamble made his presence known. The mule's owner, spitting and sputtering, related his tale of woe.

"And which of you is responsible for this ungentlemanly behavior and reckless conduct?" Gamble asked.

Charlie, the only sober sailor in the bunch, responded immediately.

"It was my idea, sir. It was my first ride on a jack ass," Charlie lied.

Except for an occasional hiccup, Charlie's colleagues stood in silence.

Gamble, startled by Charlie's youthful appearance, shook his head in disgust. He glanced at the owner.

"Has your animal been mistreated?" he asked.

"It matters not if my animal was harmed. These men stole it, and they should be punished," the old man demanded.

Gamble turned to Charlie.

"You will lose your rum rations for a month and your food rations for two days," he barked. "Is that understood, boy?"

"Yes sir," Charlie said, snapping a sharp salute.

The lieutenant marched away. The owner wore a victorious sneer as he stomped past the men, leading his tired donkey. The sailors waited for both Gamble and the owner to disappear from view.

"Charlie, you are a sailor's best friend," said one of the men, as they gathered around the girl, slapping her on the back, and pumping her hand.

On the way back to the ship, they carried Charlie on their shoulders and promised her all of the food rations she could eat.

A stern lecture from Jim Sharp triggered Kai's violent temper.

He paced the narrow pathway that separated two rows of hammocks. Kai's face glowed red and a vicious snarl hid his perfect smile. He turned abruptly and shoved a finger into Sharp's chest.

"I take orders from the commodore, not you," said Kai.

"And do you think the commodore would approve of your actions?"

Kai turned his index finger on himself.

"The commodore listens to me. That's the only reason your wife is on board this ship," said Kai.

Sharp stepped forward and shoved Kai against the bulkhead.

"If you so much as touch Charlie, I'll kill you with my bare hands," said Sharp, pinning Kai to the wall.

"Are you threatening a member of the commodore's staff, Bosun Sharp?" asked Kai.

Sharp rearranged Kai's disheveled shirt and brushed imaginary dust from the front of Kai's blue jacket.

"Now, now, Mr. Bellamy. Whatever are you talking about?" asked Sharp.

Sharp smiled and took several steps backward. Kai, a confused look on his face, took a few hesitant steps toward the exit. He kept a safe distance between himself and the bosun's mate. Sharp waited until Kai approached one of the low, overhead beams. In one smooth, noiseless, motion, he reached for the blade at his side. The hunting knife whistled past Kai's right ear. When Kai turned, the blade sank into the beam and vibrated. The low-pitched twang of metal as it penetrated wood, accomplished Sharp's purpose.

Kai ran from the chamber.

Charlie, doing her best to remove the mud and grime from the *President's* deck, looked up just long enough to recognize Kai. She returned to her scrubbing, with renewed vigor.

"What do you want?"

"Commodore McDonough wishes to speak with you, today. He is expecting you at noon," said Kai.

Before Charlie could inquire as to why the commodore wished to speak with her, Kai marched off. After her portion of the deck gleamed in the sun, she informed the sergeant of the commodore's request. Charlie waited for her salute to be returned and walked slowly to McDonough's quarters. The door was open. She knocked anyway.

"He has yet to arrive. You may stand over there," said Kai, pointing to the area in front of McDonough's desk.

Kai walked around and then behind Charlie, slamming the door shut, and locking it. Charlie twisted in place. She wagged an accusing finger at the boy. Her voice shook and she swiveled as Kai returned to the desk.

"I swear on my papa's grave, Kai. If you try anything at all, I will beat you like an old rug."

"You insult me, Charlie. I would never force myself on a young lady," he said, making himself comfortable in the commodore's chair. His eyes fixated on Charlie's loose-fitting shirt. With both elbows on the arm rests, he clasped his hands together using the steeple formed by his index fingers to support his chin. He peered over a pair of invisible spectacles and arched his eyebrows. A knowing smile crossed his lips. Charlie glanced at the door.

"Where is the commodore?" she asked.

"Oh, didn't I tell you? He was called away unexpectedly," Kai said. "I thought you and I could discuss your predicament," said Kai.

"I'm not the only woman on board this ship," said Charlie.

"The commodore is aware of Mrs. Sharp's presence on this ship and has approved of it. You, on the other hand, decieved the commodore. And for that you will be punished."

Charlie stepped forward, placing both hands on the desk and thrusting her chin forward.

"I do my job well. I am a respected member of the gun crew. And I will trust the commodore to make the correct decision," she said,

Kai slammed his fists on the desk.

"You're like all the rest. I'm not good enough for you. You think I'm dirty," said Kai.

An angry red darkened his face. Charlie's chest heaved but she did not back away. She spoke as a mother would to her child. With authority.

"You're not dirty, Kai, but your thoughts are filthy."

Kai ventured out from behind the desk. Once again, he wore the look of a satiated tom cat, thought Charlie. She backed away. Kai spoke in a soft voice.

"Charlie, Charlie, Charlie."

His voice dripped with condescension. He approached and whispered in her ear.

"Your secret is safe with me. Let's not quarrel when we can be such close friends, instead," he said.

Kai reached around her waist and pulled the girl closer. He pressed his lips against her forehead. Charlie stiffened but chose not to resist. She gazed into his eyes, a blank look on her face.

"Kai," she whispered.

He leaned in and pulled her hands to his lips, kissing one palm and then the other. Charlie shuddered. She forced her eyes shut and deliberately leaned forward. He did the same. For a brief instant, their lips touched. Charlie stopped breathing.

Her eyes flew open. Her lips twisted into a snarl. She grabbed both of Kai's shoulders and held him steady. When their eyes met, she jerked a knee into his groin, quickly and with great force. He yelled in agony and fell to the deck. Kai wretched from the excruciating pain. Charlie kicked hard at the body in front of her, hearing the crack of Kai's ribs as her boot made contact. As she stepped over the man, Charlie stomped on his face. Dark-red blood spurted from his nose. When she left the chamber, Charlie chose words that would hurt the boy more than his broken bones.

"Now you can tell everyone on board this ship, that a girl beat you up."

A week passed and no one confronted Charlie about her violent altercation with Kai.

She expected the commodore's intervention and a dishonorable discharge. The deafening silence triggered a near panic. She vented her frustrations and fears, by working continuously. Charlie outpaced several of the men assigned to a wall of heavy crates. When she stopped to catch her breath and wipe the sweat from her face, she noticed movement in the top row of wooden containers. Despite the lack of a cooling breeze, the boxes swayed wildly and appeared ready to fall. She dashed toward the nearest man, pushing hard to get him away from the deadly avalanche of containers. One of the sailor's legs got caught in the pile. Charlie emerged, unscathed. The man screamed in pain. Several of Charlie's colleagues came to the injured sailor's rescue.

Moments later, she stood in the doorway to Nathan Coldwell's operating theater.

"Dr. Coldwell. This man requires your attention."

Nathan's head jerked at the sound of Charlie's voice. The injured man stood on one leg, using two men as a crutch. The man's face, contorted with pain, prompted Nathan to approach.

"What happened?" he asked.

The victim spoke with difficulty.

"We were moving crates, loaded with foodstuffs. A wall of them, five high. They came crashing down. Not sure why. Charlie here pushed me out of the way. Could've been killed," he said, through clenched teeth.

"Let's get him on the table," said Nathan.

After a few screams of pain, the patient lay resting on the wooden slab. Nathan's examination did not take long.

"It's broken," he said. "Just above the ankle."

"It hurts like the dickens," said the injured man.

Nathan reached for the shelf behind him and retrieved a small jug.

"The pain will get worse. Drink this," he ordered.

"I'll need one of you to hold his upper leg. Sit on it if you have to," said Nathan.

The two sailors hesitated. Charlie hopped on the table. With her back to the injured man's face, she straddled the patient's legs. He groaned in pain. The injured man took a long draw from Nathan's jug. The surgeon studied the man's lower leg, focusing on it from different angles. He nodded to Charlie. She gripped the man's leg, just below the knee. Nathan yanked the sailor's foot, gave it a slight twist, and then pushed the broken limb in Charlie's direction. The patient screamed in agony.

"Looks good," said Nathan. "I'll put a splint on it and you should be fine, in a month or so."

The sailor, his face drained of color, mumbled.

"I don't feel fine."

His eyes fluttered shut as he lost consciousness.

Charlie watched, fascinated, as Nathan assembled and then attached a splint. Although impressed with the surgeon's work, she swallowed her compliment, still harboring a grudge for Nathan's previous behavior.

"He can rest here. I'll send for help when he's ready to be moved," said Nathan. "And thank you all for the help."

"You are welcome, Dr. Coldwell," said Charlie, unsmiling and executing a slight bow.

Nathan waited until she left the room. He scanned the doorway, reached for the jug, and took a large gulp.

In the days after the incident with the falling crates, Charlie enjoyed a new-found popularity.

The details of her donkey ride and the injured man's oft-told tale, about Charlie saving his life, spread quickly among the ship's crew. In a matter of days, everyone knew Charlie and Charlie seemed to know everyone. Although still nervous, she cautiously assumed that her secret identity would remain a secret. As she walked to the hatch, intending to deposit a heavy sack of flour in the below-deck storage room, offers of assistance came from every corner of the deck. Charlie used her free hand to waive her friends off and gingerly descended the ladder which brought her below.

The storeroom, pitch black, unless the locked door was open, housed supplies of all sorts and stood in the far corner, some distance from the hatch. As she dropped the sack on the floor and re-arranged some of the other cargo, Charlie heard the door slam shut. She couldn't see a thing.

"Hey, who shut the door?" she screamed.

It took a while before her eyes adjusted to the dark. Except for a long thin crack at the bottom of the door, the girl stood in total darkness. As Charlie walked slowly to the closed door, she heard the lock rattle shut. And then, the sound of retreating footsteps.

"Hey. I'm still in here," she yelled, pounding on the door with a closed fist.

The girl banged on the door, intermittently, for several hours. Charlie calculated that it could be days before someone discovered her. The storage room was accessed only when the ship was miles from its home port or when supplies needed replenishing. The room, almost full, might not be accessed for up to a week, she thought. Charlie positioned several sacks of flour or grain, she wasn't sure which, for a seat on which to get comfortable. She did not understand why even an inexperienced sailor, would shut and lock an open door. Normally, a person would first inquire as to whether the room was occupied.

A gentle stirring in the room, reminded Charlie that she would not spend the evening alone. Just last week, she killed several large rats, thinking her actions eliminated the rodents. Apparently not. She didn't know if such animals could see in the dark but they certainly knew how to get around in the dark.

Hours later, Charlie, tired of banging on the door, fell into a restless asleep. Still later, a sharp pain on the little finger of one hand, woke her with a start. She screamed. Charlie flung her long-tailed friend against the wall. The rat squealed. But she could hear the tiny footsteps as it scurried away. The slender crack between floor and door, told her she passed the entire evening in the storage room. When her stomach growled, she smiled at the irony. Trapped in a room filled with foodstuffs but unable to eat what she could not see. She considered what might be available and edible. As she puzzled over her dilemma, Charlie heard the sound of approaching footsteps. She lunged toward the crack and banged on the door with both fists. Charlie screamed until the footsteps, stopped. The lock rattled, but the door did not open.

"Charlie is that you?" said the man.

Charlie recognized the sound of Bosun Sharp's voice.

"Yes," she shouted. "Now get me out of here."

"Gotta get the key. I'll be right back," said Sharp.

Moments later, Charlie, famished and nursing a nasty bite, squinted her eyes, in the bright light of day.

"Mrs. Sharp had me looking for you half the night," he said.

Charlie explained the mystery that left her trapped in the storage room. Her head snapped to attention and she interrupted herself. A pair of legs descended the hatch ladder, stopped midway, and then disappeared through the hatch.

"Excuse me, Jim," she said, brushing past Sharp and skipping several rungs on the ladder as she sprinted up the hatch.

Despite the blinding sun, she caught a glimpse of a sailor as he ran away. The seaman, no taller than Charlie, wore his jet-black hair longer than most and sported a deep tan. He jogged behind a small mountain of cargo. She gave chase, thought she heard a door slam, but saw nothing. Except the door to Commodore McDonough's office. Charlie thought about the crates that almost killed her and the storeroom door that mysteriously slammed shut.

Goosebumps covered her arms as a picture of Kai, lying on the floor, bleeding, and groaning in pain, came to mind.

Charlie, at the door to McDonough's office, flinched when she first caught a glimpse of Kai.

"I wish to speak with the commodore," she said, her voice

wavering.

The young man's nose, misshapen and swollen, explained the half circles of violet mixed with dark pink, under each eye. Kai, his arms folded, looked beyond Charlie as if she wasn't there.

"State your business," he said.

Charlie gawked at the boy's blood shot eyes and required a moment to recover.

"I've been asked to testify at a murder trial in Isle LaMotte. I require a temporary leave from my duties," she said.

"Wait here," he snapped.

Charlie waited outside. She could hear male voices but could not decipher their spoken words.

"The commodore demands proof," Kai announced.

"I did not demand proof, Kai. I simply requested it," said McDonough, still at his desk but easily discerning Kai's raised voice.

Charlie surrendered the letter she received by special messenger. The missive, from her attorney friend in Isle LaMotte, recounted Constable Blanchard's search for his star witness. Apparently, Otis Skinner, forcibly returned by the army, would soon stand trial for the murder of Harriet Skinner. The letter described Charlie as an "ear witness" to the murder.

When Kai returned, he held the letter plus a hand-written authorization from McDonough. The commodore authorized five days of leave. Kai wore a snarl and his face flushed red.

"Your leave has been approved," he said, slamming the door shut before Charlie could respond.

Chapter Ten

THE TRIAL

Military maneuvers by the army and the navy, enabled Charlie's upcoming court appearance.

Army General Wade Hampton, preparing for a possible invasion of Canada, wanted to preposition his troops, in Chazy. British ships, making sporadic appearances at the north end of the lake, posed a risk to Hampton's army. He requested a naval escort from McDonough, and the commodore agreed. Coincidentally, McDonough's decision would place Charlie in Chazy, just a short boat ride from Isle LaMotte. The constant flow of bateaux, carrying troops and cargo between Chazy and Vermont, made Charlie's legal sojourn simple and without cost.

Days later, Charlie fidgeted in her chair at the Vermont state prosecutor's office. For the second time, she reiterated her earlier conversation with Constable Blanchard.

"But I didn't see Otis kill Harriet. He told me he did. Said it was an accident."

The prosecutor took copious notes. Charlie posed questions of her own.

"Will Otis be in the court room when I testify?" she asked.

The prosecutor explained the precise details of a criminal trial. A series of conflicting thoughts filled Charlie's head. Her real name was Charlotte. Otis knew she only pretended to be a boy. If she lied about that, would she be accused of lying about Otis? And she didn't want to be the one who sent Otis to the gallows.

"Charlie? Did you hear me?" asked the prosecutor, his eyes peering over a pair of wire spectacles.

Charlie faked her attention.

"Yes, sir. I understand."

"Very well then," said the man, "We start at nine, tomorrow morning."

Charlie nodded her head, the butterflies in her stomach now running amok. She walked the short distance to the same boarding house where Harriet met her untimely end. The hairs on the back of her neck reappeared. Goosebumps on her arms in the middle of a warm sunny day made her head swivel. Someone watched her. Maybe followed her. Silly girl, she thought.

Otis was in jail.

Kai lied to the midshipman in charge of the bateaux.

"Official business on behalf of the commodore," opened many doors and disarmed ordinarily suspicious seamen. The warm September day also explained why the young sailor carried, rather than wore, his Navy-issue jacket. The five-inch knife, secreted in its folds, lay on the boy's lap unseen.

Getting to the courthouse in Isle LaMotte proved less difficult than Kai originally thought. Curiosity about the proceedings attracted dozens of spectators. Kai located a spot in the rear of the temporary court room. Days earlier, it served as a granary. Kai immediately noticed the slender frame of a young sailor, in the front row of benches. Charlie, clad in full uniform, twisted in her seat, to survey the standing-room-only crowd. Kai looked down and away. He wanted his presence in the court room to be a surprise. A big surprise.

In moments, Constable Blanchard escorted the prisoner into the building. The iron manacles and chains on Otis Skinner's ankles scraped the wooden floor. A similar set of manacles bound Skinner's hands, in front of him. The judge, already seated, ordered the removal of the prisoner's leggings. Blanchard hesitated but did as he was instructed. Skinner sat on the Judge's right, Charlie on the left, allowing the accused and accuser to exchange anxious glances. As the prosecution made its opening remarks, Kai followed the wall and slowly worked his way to the front of the room. He took pains to remain hidden from Charlie's view.

The first witness to testify, the black servant woman at the boarding house, appeared visibly shaken. She trembled and her voice shook with emotion.

"You discovered Mrs. Skinner's body, early, on Tuesday morning. Is that correct?" asked the prosecutor.

"Ya sir, I did," said the servant.

"And did Mrs. Skinner greet any visitors during the previous day?" he asked.

"Ya sir. Mr. Otis cum a callin," she said.

The prosecutor required only a few more questions, to place Otis Skinner at the scene of the crime. When the judge told the black servant to step down, every eye in the room followed the nervous woman back to her seat. Kai used the break to step forward. He stood yards behind and to the right of Charlie.

Otis, glaring at the black girl, as she exited the chamber, noticed Kai. Kai raised his knife to a position behind his ear. Otis fixed his eyes on the blade and jumped to his feet. Charlie turned in Skinner's direction, visibly concerned with the large man's sudden movements. Kai snapped his arm. Otis sprang forward. Charlie, anticipating the large man's attack, jumped to a standing position. The blade glistened in the daylight as it flew toward Charlie's back. Otis crashed into Charlie. They landed on the prosecutor's table. Papers flew everywhere. Kai's knife hit with a thud. Otis groaned as the blade sunk deep into his side.

The courtroom erupted. The judge slammed his gavel and yelled for order. Four of the male jurors tackled Kai. Constable Blanchard tended to his prisoner. The spectators surged forward, desperate for a good view. Otis mumbled Charlie's name. Someone called for a doctor. Charlie stepped away. She caught a final glimpse of Otis, as he lay on the table, in a growing pool of blood. She continued to back away and the spectators gladly gave way. When her back pressed against the far wall, she slipped, unnoticed, through a side door.

Charlie ran all the way to the dock, at Isle LaMotte.

"You haven't seen Kai at all?"

Charlie, sitting and squirming on her hammock, did her best to answer Bosun Sharp's questions. She also lied.

"No sir, I haven't," she said.

Sharp shook his head.

"Well, I saw him a few days ago. He looked pretty bad, like someone beat him up. Two black eyes and a broken nose. Claims he fell down the hatch. Now, he's disappeared," said Sharp.

"I wish I could help you, Mr. Sharp," said Charlie.

"The commodore has everyone looking for him, you know," he said.

Charlie shrugged her shoulders.

"You'll let me know if you hear from him?"

"Yes sir," she said.

Charlie remained in her hammock for several hours. She didn't know what troubled her most. Kai, trying to kill her or Otis, trying to save her. And she wondered what happened in the aftermath of the court room attack. Did the trial of Otis Skinner continue? Did he even survive the knife attack? Kai did not return to the *President*. Was he in jail? Would he soon be on trial himself? The girl grew increasingly desperate to tell someone. She also needed some sensible advice.

Despite her reservations about Nathan Coldwell, she nursed a secret attraction to the young surgeon. She often considered the possibility that, despite his temperament, Nathan might be attracted to Charlie. She couldn't know for sure. For now, she needed his advice and counsel.

Charlie rolled out of her hammock and walked to Nathan's quarters.

Charlie stood in the surgeon's open doorway.

"Do you ever sleep?" she asked.

Nathan seemed less than thrilled with her presence.

"What do you want?" he asked, his voice a monotone.

Charlie grew quiet and fixed her gaze on a far wall.

"I'm not sure."

"Well, I'm busy. Now go away."

"Why do you hate me? she asked, temporarily forgetting the purpose of her visit.

Nathan took a deep breath, his mouth opened, as if preparing for an avalanche of angry words. But he stopped. He reached behind for a large jug. After several gulps, he slammed the jug on the operating table and yelled.

"I'm attracted to women. Not young men. Do you understand that Charlie Wheeler?"

Nathan belched and took another swig of rum. Charlie recalled Nathan's strict aversion to alcohol.

"I thought you were a strict Methodist."

"Go away," he growled.

"Maybe someother time," she mumbled.

When she walked away, Nathan flung the alcohol against the wall, sending ceramic shards and rum, in every direction.

"Dr. Coldwell. Are you in there?"

The man's harsh voice, accompanied by a loud banging on the door, woke Nathan from his drunken stupor.

"The commodore wishes to see you. Now," said the voice.

Nathan struggled to his feet. He did his best to correct the disheveled look of a man who'd spent most of the day drinking. He exhaled into an open hand and confirmed the overwhelming odor of rum. Nathan reminded himself to keep a respectable distance between himself and the commodore.

"Dr. Coldwell, I summoned you because the army is in need of a surgeon," said McDonough.

"With respect, sir. I volunteered with the navy. Your navy," said Nathan, a look of concern covering his face.

"I understand that, Nathan," said McDonough, rising to his feet and stepping out from behind the desk.

He placed a hand on each of Nathan's shoulders. Nathan closed his mouth, afraid to breathe.

"This is a temporary assignment. I give you, my word. And your brief assignment as an army surgeon would be good for your career in the navy," said McDonough.

Nathan examined his shoes. His mind raced. An *army* surgeon? The assignment did not please Nathan but it would separate him from Charlie. That was a good thing, he thought, hating himself for his twisted attraction to the boy.

"Your word is good enough for me, sir."

McDonough smiled in triumph and returned to the desk.

"Report to Captain Daly. He serves under General Hampton. You'll find him at the officers' tent.

"Thank you, sir," said Nathan, turning to leave.

"Nathan, before you leave. I seem to have lost my aide. Mr. Bellamy is nowhere to be found. I need a replacement. What is your professional opinion of his friend, Charlie?"

Nathan swallowed hard and bit his lower lip. He chose his words, carefully.

"Charlie is a hard worker, dedicated, and reliable, sir."

"I agree, said McDonough. Kai said the same thing before he decided to take his leave."

McDonough frowned. Nathan pretended to cough.

"Would you please summon Charlie, on my behalf?"

Nathan found Charlie, topside, cleaning one of the artillery pieces.

"The commodore wishes to see you. Immediately," he announced.

"Am I in trouble?" she asked.

Nathan's eyes were downcast. His head throbbed and he struggled to think clearly.

"No. I don't think so. He wants you to be his new aide. Asked me what I thought."

"What did you say?" she asked.

"The truth. You're a good worker." Nathan mumbled.

"Are you in trouble?" she asked.

"No. I've been temporarily assigned to Hampton's army. I report to Captain Daly, in the morning," said Nathan.

"Almost all of Hampton's troops are here in Chazy. The rumor is that they are headed north of the line. An attack force," said Charlie.

"And that's why he needs a surgeon," said Nathan.

Charlie turned to leave, took a few steps, and stopped.

"Please don't hate me, Nathan. I'm not what you think," said Charlie, before running off.

"Your new job is in addition to your duties as a powder monkey," said McDonough.

The commodore explained to Charlie that most of her work would be carrying messages to and from members of the ship's crew.

"I understand, sir. And I thank you for this opportunity," said Charlie.

"You may not thank me when we engage the enemy." McDonough said, referring to Charlie's war time duties.

"I will do my best, sir."

The commodore searched Charlie's face.

"You were friends with Kai, were you not?" asked McDonough.

The unexpected question startled Charlie. She cleared her

throat and wet her lips, giving her just enough time to compose a non-response.

"Yes, sir. We were," she said.

McDonough sat motionless in his chair and continued to focus on Charlie's rapidly blinking eyes.

"I have to trust my men," said McDonough. "Kai betrayed my trust."

Charlie avoided the commodore's gaze.

"You will have to earn my trust, Charlie. Do you understand?" asked McDonough.

"Yes, sir," said Charlie, panicking that the commodore knew more than he let on.

"Very well, then. Report to my quarters at sunup tomorrow."

Nathan's visit with Captain Daly, although brief and businesslike, triggered more questions than answers.

According to Daly, the troops would first march to the boundary line. The invading force would then separate into two brigades. Beyond that, Daly either refused to discuss or did not know, the enemy's precise location, its numbers or weaponry. Nathan's brief examination of the maps on Daly's worktable, bereft of detail, revealed little more. Although trained in medicine, Nathan knew enough about the confusion of war, to be concerned. Several thousand troops could easily become lost, victims of friendly fire or worse, massacred. Too many of his patients related the horrors of such battles while Nathan ministered to their wounds.

The stab wound to Otis Skinner's back and the subsequent loss of blood, left him unconscious and unable to participate in his own trial.

A discussion between the prosecutor and the judge took place a week later. The wheels of Isle LaMotte justice came to a sudden halt.

"Our most important witness has disappeared," said the prosecutor.

The lawyer explained to the judge that Charlie Wheeler, perhaps out of fear, could not be located. According to Constable Blanchard, the boy may have returned to McDonough's ship, but the flotilla's location was unknown.

"He could be anywhere," said the prosecutor.

"And where is the attorney for Mr. Skinner?" asked the judge.

"He's gone too. Didn't think he would get paid," said the prosecutor.

The judge did not require hours for his decision.

"Mr. Skinner claims this entire episode was unintentional. He merely defended himself when the late Mrs. Skinner attacked him with a hat pin. If no one else comes forward to testify against this man, the evidence against him is insufficient. In view of his heroic actions in my court room, I am inclined to release the prisoner," said the judge.

"Yes, your honor," said the prosecutor.

"Is the attacker still in custody?" asked the magistrate.

"Yes, sir."

"I must return to Burlington tomorrow. The navy can take care of their own. You are ordered to transport Mr. Bellamy as soon as arrangements can be made," ordered the judge.

Days later, Constable Blanchard gave Otis, not yet recovered but mending well, the news of his release.

"You're a very lucky man, Skinner."

Otis, pale and moving slowly, struggled to respond.

"Save your hangman's noose for someone else," Otis muttered.

"Why did you jump in front of that knife?" asked Blanchard.

"I've known that girl for years. She's hardheaded, but too young to die in a knife fight."

Blanchard leaned forward.

"You mean boy, don't you?"

The prisoner's face went blank.

"When do I get out of here?" he asked.

"Today, if you want," said Blanchard.

"Leave the door open," said Otis, reclining on the jailhouse bed and shutting his eyes.

Nathan struggled to get his supplies on board one of the many bateaux, leaving Cumberland Bay for Chazy.

He frowned at the pile of luggage, yet to be loaded. From a distance, Charlie waived in his direction and jogged to the shoreline.

"Nathan," she whispered breathlessly.

Charlie's short hair flew as she jerked her head in every direction and searched for witnesses. She stepped forward and spoke softly in the young man's ear.

"The fleet will stop at the line. The army is on its own after that," she said.

Nathan did not like that Charlie whispered in his ear.

"Why are you telling me this? I go where General Hampton and his troops go," he said.

She ignored his brusque manner.

"I'm worried about you. Please be careful," she said.

She extended a hand. He offered a limp-wristed response. Nathan chose not to return the young woman's affection, much less acknowledge her concern.

Charlie, stood motionless for a moment, swiped at her moist eyes, and then trudged up the hill.

When Otis left the two-cell jail in Isle LaMotte, a movement in the adjoining chamber caught his eye.

He stopped and grinned. Kai Bellamy jumped from the cot where he lay and slammed his body into the iron-barred door. His extended arms reached through the bars and flailed wildly. Otis stood just out of reach. The prisoner screamed.

"I'm going to kill you, Otis Skinner. I'm going to kill you, I swear."

"What's the matter boy? A little frustrated?" asked Otis, his grin now a broad smile.

Kai spit in Skinner's direction. The wad of spittle landed on the big man's chin. Otis used the sleeve of his jacket to erase the boy's anger. He reached inside the bar, wrapped one huge hand around the prisoner's neck, and pulled hard. When the inmate's nose crashed into the hard steel, the boy's broken nose broke again. The sleeve on Skinner's jacket slowly turned crimson red from the prisoner's injury. Kai struggled to breathe as Skinner pressed his oversized thumb into the boy's throat.

"Touch that girl again, and I'll wring your scrawny, little neck," Otis growled.

Otis waited until the boy's face turned a light shade of blue, and then released his grip.

Kai fell to floor, gasping for air, as blood pooled on the floor near his face.

Charlie stood in the stern of the *President.*

She watched as more than a hundred bateaux rowed behind the flagship, in route to Chazy. When McDonough's ship glided past the mouth of the Great Chazy River, General Hampton's army veered west and disappeared from the girl's view. The long, undulating snake, with several thousand men in its belly, traveled to the village of Champlain. They would arrive just as McDonough's fleet approached the international boundary line. McDonough temporarily anchored at Rouse's point.

Charlie grew queasy and her stomach churned. But she did not blame the stiff breeze or the sway of the ship underneath her feet. A dizzying stream of familiar images raced through her mind, leaving her weak and weepy. She saw her father, her friend, Hank, and then Reuben Quimby. All of them, deathly still in her arms. The visual stampede of death occurred once before. This one was different. On this occasion, Nathan made an appearance. He clutched at a gaping hole in his chest, blood oozing between his fingers. He appeared to be staring directly at her.

"Goodbye, Charlie," he whispered.

Charlie's daydream, a full-on nightmare, sent her running to the hatch.

Nathan, never too far from General Hampton's officers, bit his tongue and shook his head in disbelief.

Before all of the troops even crossed the line at Champlain, their march into Canada floundered to a stop. An initial detachment, with orders to march on Odelltown, lost their way and returned to the line. Several hundred of the local militia men suddenly decided their services were needed at home, to accomplish the annual fall harvest. They left without notice or permission.

A few days later, advance portions of Hampton's main force returned to the camp with more bad news. The streambeds and ponds in that area, although plentiful, contained no water. The dry summer season ruined the army's anticipated water supply. Hampton decided to move west and invade Canada, via the Chateauguay River. British forces, after receiving reports on Hampton's change of venue, responded by moving their forces, also.

But even that plan would be delayed. Hampton's colleague, General James Wilkinson, also in route to Montreal but via the St. Lawrence River, ordered Hampton to stop his attack. Wilkinson wanted Hampton to "settle in for the winter". Hampton refused to construct winter quarters. Instead, he delayed his forward march, for more than a week.

For days, Nathan and his colleagues fought nothing more than boredom and the cold winds of September.

McDonough's fleet patrolled Lake Champlain for the last half of September and well into October.

The British navy, realizing that the American fleet now sailed at full strength, chose not to challenge their American counterparts.

"A message for you, sir," said Charlie, handing the commodore a letter.

As Charlie exited, McDonough opened and read the letter.

"Charlie. Get back here," he barked.

Charlie groaned. Her intended lunch of hardtack and dried pork would have to wait. McDonough, wearing a very solemn look, peered over his reading spectacles and focused his unblinking eyes on Charlie.

"Charlie. This correspondence is from the constable in Isle

LaMotte. It is most disturbing," he said.

Charlie stood at attention, studying the hull wall, above and beyond the commodore's head. Her breath quickened and she bit hard on her lower lip. When she did not respond, McDonough broke the silence. He spoke softly, a hint of sadness in his voice.

"You lied to me, Charlie. You knew what happened to Kai all along," said McDonough.

Charlie's lips quivered. But still, she stood in silence. McDonough tossed the letter on his desk and scowled.

"Why did Kai want to kill you?"

Charlie closed her eyes and let her head droop. She took a deep breath.

"I refused his advances," she confessed.

McDonough jumped to his feet and leaned forward, with both hands firmly planted on his desk.

"Are you telling me that Kai preferred . . . ?"

McDonough's voice trailed off. Charlie did not mean to mislead the commodore. Apparently, Blanchard did not yet know Charlie's true identity. Without thinking, she compounded her lies with another one.

"Yes sir, he did."

McDonough exhaled loudly, his puffed cheeks announcing his disbelief. He fell back into his chair.

"Kai, a sodomite?"

Charlie knew what the word meant. She concluded that her secret remained a secret, whether the constable intended it that way, or not. Charlie, emboldened by her unexpected stroke of luck, acknowledged the commodore's conclusion.

"Yes, sir."

"The constable and the judge have ceded jurisdiction to the Navy. For his attack on you, there will be a court martial and a severe lashing. He will be discharged from the Navy," said McDonough.

Charlie's heart sank. A court martial. Witnesses. Testimony. A public spectacle. She spoke quickly.

"Sir. There is no reason to punish this man. I am in no danger. Just send him on his way. Please," she begged.

"You are a true Christian, Charlie. But this incident cannot be overlooked. Justice must be done," said McDonough.

"Yes, sir."

When the order to attack finally came, General Hampton's troops, cold, wet, and bored, welcomed the news.

The battle of Chateauguay did not go as expected. Nathan, with his medical supplies and equipment tucked safely in a wagon, stayed a mile behind the front lines. He quickly organized a makeshift hospital, in anticipation of the wounded. Within the day, forward parties reported resistance by a large contingent of Canadian soldiers. Wilkinson decided to split his forces. He directed 1500 men, led by Colonel Robert Purdy, to advance some fifteen miles on the east side of the Chateauguay River. Their mission, to 'emerge behind enemy lines and attack the Canadians from the rear', did not succeed. Lost and confused, they spent an entire night on the march and traveled only six miles. When they finally emerged from the swampy forest, they found themselves in front of the enemy's lines. They became easy targets and hastily retreated back into the swamp.

The remainder of Wilkinson's forces, 2500 men under the command of Brigadier General George Izard, attempted a frontal assault on the Canadian defenders. They soon witnessed the retreat of their bother soldiers and did likewise. Both commands suffered a great number of casualties.

Nathan's operating station, a small tent with several planks of roughhewn lumber piled on crates, would soon buzz with activity. Dozens of wounded and near dead filled and surrounded the hospital tent. Their stories and, in some cases, dying words, painted a horrible picture. Nathan watched as two men deposited yet another wounded soldier on the makeshift operating table. The man, still conscious, writhed in pain. He endured a musket ball lodged in the upper half of his right arm. The bloody mass of bone, muscle and tendon, could not be repaired. The enlisted man's only hope, an amputation just below the shoulder, triggered a telltale look on the surgeon's face. The wounded man understood.

"No, doc. I won't let you do it."

The patient struggled to a seated position. Nathan glanced at the two burly men who served as his orderlies. They used force and restrained the man with two long, leather straps. Nathan reached for a scalpel and his carpenter's saw. One of the orderlies offered the wounded man a cigar-shaped piece of wood.

"Bite down on this. It will ease the pain," Nathan lied.

The soldier sobbed, choking his objections. The sharp teeth of Nathan's saw cut through the bone in less than sixty seconds. His patient spit out the wooden anesthetic and screamed in pain, until he passed out. He lay deathly still as Nathan sutured the bloody wound.

"We're out of bandages," said one of the orderlies, staring at the patient's bloody stump.

"Use one of those," said Nathan, pointing to a blood-stained rag on the leg of a nearby patient.

"But he's dead," complained the orderly.

Nathan tossed the severed limb in a nearby barrel.

"Well, he won't be needing it anymore, will he?"

Nathan recognized his next patient. Captain Daly, wounded in the leg and arm, required assistance from two of the men. Daly spoke haltingly through clench teeth.

"We meet again, Dr. Coldwell," he said.

As the men laid their commanding officer on the table, Nathan's eyes scanned the captain's blood-soaked clothes. He cut a sleeve off the officer's shirt and a pants leg, from the man's trousers.

"I'm ruining your uniform," said Nathan.

"And that's all you get to cut, my friend. Just patch me up as best you can," said Daly.

"The ball appears to have gone clear through the arm. But your lower leg is shattered," said Nathan. "We have no choice," he added, offering the officer a shot of rum.

"Yes, you do," said Daly.

Nathan stared in the direction of his two-oversized orderlies. They knew the routine by heart. Daly saw them approach, leather straps in hand. The captain pulled a long, hunting knife from its leather sheath on his hip. He flashed the blade in Nathan's face.

"Don't make me cut that good-looking face of yours, Doc. I'm not in the mood," said Daly.

"Captain, I'm only doing what's best for you," said Nathan.

The two large orderlies stepped forward. Daly swung the blade. One of the orderlies yelled and jumped back.

"The bastard cut me," he screamed.

With his good arm, the captain grabbed Nathan, pulled him close and placed the blade on Nathan's neck.

"Now be a good doctor, and sew me up," he whispered.

Nathan motioned the orderlies to back away. He held his hands aloft, as if in surrender.

"We will do it your way, Captain."

"I want your word as a gentleman," said Daly.

"You have my word," said Nathan.

Daly relaxed his grip. Nathan reached for thread and needle. Daly noticed the surgeon's trembling hands.

"I think you need the rum more than I do, Doc."

Kai Bellamy could not be secured on board the *President* while awaiting his court-martial.

McDonough's flag ship did not include a brig for prisoners. The commodore requested that the accused be brought dockside, at Cumberland Bay. McDonough dispatched two sailors to install the prisoner in a makeshift jail. Word of the capture and court-martial of the commodore's former aide-de-camp spread like smallpox on the *President*.

Mrs. Sharp, below deck with her husband, blanched white when her husband announced the news.

"Why did you tell him, Jim. Why?"

"He almost killed her," said Jim.

"Yes, but none of this would've happened if you had only kept Charlie's secret to yourself. And now, the boy may hang," she said.

"I'm told he's likely to receive a severe lashing and a dishonorable discharge from the Navy," said Mr. Sharp.

"And what about Charlie? After the court-martial, the whole world will know that Charlie is a young woman. We may, all three of us, get kicked off the ship."

Jim Sharp, sitting on the edge of his hammock, cradled his bowed head with both hands.

"Let me think, woman. Just let me think," he growled.

Mrs. Sharp stomped off.

"I would like to visit the prisoner."

Jim Sharp knew the two sailors who stood guard over Kai. It made no difference.

"Sorry, Bosun Sharp, no visitors. The commodore's orders," said the taller of the two.

"Understood," said Sharp.

He inspected the building as he departed. No windows and one door, secured by a slab of lumber resting on long spikes of bent iron. The prisoner could not escape without assistance. Sharp calculated that only one of the guards actually stood post during the late evening hours. Each of them would take a four-hour shift, first to sleep and then to guard the prisoner.

Sharp decided that the guards needed a distraction.

Charlie studied the troops returning from the line.

Hampton retreated in the face of Canadian forces, far fewer than his own. The general's decision made him a laughing stock, in both the Army and the Navy. Charlie, thinking only of Nathan's health and welfare, scanned the long line of troops. A lone figure, walking in the dark, struggled with a crate and several large bags. She abandoned her reservations and raced down the ramp, which connected the *President's* top side to the main dock.

"Welcome back, Nathan,"

Nathan dropped his cargo on the dock and mumbled.

"I've got a few more bags on the boat. Lend me a hand, will you?" he asked.

A look of disappointment flashed across Charlie's face. She took solace from the fact that Nathan returned unharmed.

"You look exhausted," she observed, as the two of them split their load and trudged up the *President's* ramp.

"I am," he said, his voice flat and lips pursed in a straight line.

"The word is that Hampton's troops didn't do so well," said Charlie.

Nathan tossed some of his bags down the hatch, jerked his head in the direction of the crates, and waited for Charlie to hand them off.

"I'm just a surgeon, Charlie. Not a general," said Nathan.

Charlie, desperate to tell Nathan about Kai, swallowed her frustration. She jumped down the hatch and worked silently. They brought the medical supplies and instruments to Nathan's operating theater. At one point, when they stood within a yard of each other, she could smell the booze on Nathan's breath.

"The doctor's been drinking his own medicine," she grinned.

Nathan scowled. Charlie's face washed red.

"Thank you for the help, Mr. Wheeler. And now, I should like to be alone."

Charlie, insulted by Nathan's abrupt dismissal, abandoned her plan to explain the attack by Kai. The thought of revealing her true identity to Nathan, also disappeared. She turned to leave but stopped at the hatch, for one last glance at her doctor friend. Nathan, his back to Charlie, took a long swig from a jug of rum.

He crawled onto the operating table and closed his eyes.

A one-man hut, used to protect guards from the elements, lay empty, just yards from Kai Bellamy's temporary jail.

Jim Sharp lurked in the shadows with a pocket full of tinder and a small bundle of kindling. He approached the shed. After a few strikes of flint against metal, the tinder burst into flames. Using his boot, he pushed the flaming material into the hut's wooden sides and waited. When the conflagration burned brightly, Sharp yelled 'fire' and jogged to the rear of the storeroom jail. The Guard on duty yelled to his sleeping mate and the two of them ran to the burning hut. Jim Sharp removed the wooden beam and opened the door a crack.

"Kai?"

"Bosun Sharp? What are you doing?" asked Kai.

"No time to explain. Follow me."

They quietly shut the door and replaced the timber. The escapee and his rescuer ran into the woods. When both of the men could run no longer, Jim motioned Kai to a fallen oak.

"Sit," he ordered.

Kai, despondent after weeks of incarceration, offered no resistance.

"My wife and Charlie blame me for this mess," said Sharp, still breathing heavy.

Kai, as if unconcerned, played with his jackstones.

"My life in the Navy is over."

"You can leave. Go south and start a new life," said Sharp.

"Why are you doing this?" asked Kai.

"I'm doing it for Charlie. If there's no court-martial, her secret remains a secret," said the Bosun.

Kai glared at his rescuer.

"And if I refuse?" asked Kai.

Sharp stepped closer to Kai. He spoke in a monotone.

"You threatened to kill my wife and I had no choice but to kill you first."

"That's a lie."

Jim pulled the knife he carried on his waist.

"Lower your voice, you fool. And yes, it *is* a lie, but it's my word against yours. You lose," said Sharp.

Kai ran several fingers through his dirty hair and gnawed on his lower lip.

"That bitch asked for it," Kai muttered.

Sharp walked behind Kai. He placed a hand on top of the jet-black hair.

"Your choice, Mr. Bellamy. Run or die," said Sharp.

Kai climbed to his feet. Sharp leaned forward, his knife at the ready. Kai lifted his hands to chest level, palms facing out, signaling his unwillingness to fight.

"Must I thank you for your overwhelming kindness?" Kai snarled.

Sharp glared.

"Get out of here, boy. Now!"

Kai ran deep into the forest.

Nathan spent more and more of his time alone and drinking.

He no longer denied his physical and emotional attraction to Charlie. He dared not share his feelings with anyone, much less the girl. Sodomy and sodomites, damnable perversions in the Methodist community, were criminal and punishable by law. Participants in these "unspeakable sex acts" could be jailed, lose all of their property and suffer irreparable damage to their reputations. Nathan, feeling trapped and alone, regularly found solace at the bottom of a rum jug.

"I'm looking for Dr. Nathan Coldwell," said the voice.

Nathan struggled to his feet using the crude, operating table, to steady himself. His hair, dirty and unkept, also described his appearance. His shirt and trousers, wrinkled and stained with blood, smelled of stale rum. He tried unsuccessfully to smother a belch, before responding to his unexpected visitor.

"What is it you want?" asked Nathan, his speech slow and slurred.

The well-dressed visitor, refined and distinguished in his appearance, stepped back to avoid the overpowering stench of alcohol and body odor.

"The drinking of ardent spirits has become widespread, indeed," said the gentleman.

Nathan's head swayed but he intentionally rolled his eyes.

"And you are?"

"I am Dr. James Mann. And I apologize for the unexpected visit. I am in Plattsburgh, in route to Malone, to inspect our government's hospital facilities," said the visitor.

Nathan stood taller. He tucked in his shirt and tried, in vain, to hide the stains.

"Dr. Mann, I've heard of you and your good work in Burlington. But as you can see, there is no hospital on board the *President.* This so-called operating theater is the full extent of our medical facilities," said Nathan.

"If you suffer from a lack of patients, there are plenty of sick men here in Plattsburgh at the camp and elsewhere," said Mann, staring at the flask which lay on Nathan's operating table.

Nathan grabbed the container and tossed it in a heap of soiled bandages.

"I have been assigned to the *President.* My duties are here and here only."

Mann arched his eyebrows and nodded.

"I shall inform the commodore of the extent to which you are fulfilling your duties," said Mann.

The senior doctor executed a stiff bow.

"Good day, Dr. Coldwell."

Nathan focused on Dr. Mann's retreating outline. He retrieved the flask and used his tongue to search for one last drop.

Nathan's rum, and perhaps his luck, ran out.

"Bosun Sharp?"

Charlie, searching for Mrs. Sharp, discovered the woman's husband, instead. He sat on the floor, next to his hammock. Sharp, with his back to the wall, struggled to keep his head aloft. He jerked at the sound of Charlie's voice. He executed a sloppy salute, using the wrong hand.

"Charlie, my friend. How's my favorite powder monkey?"

Charlie dropped to her knees and sat on the backs of her legs, facing her friend. She leaned back when the strong smell of rum invaded her nostrils. She studied his bloodshot eyes.

"Mr. Sharp, you seem to have enjoyed more than your usual ration of rum."

Sharp smiled and giggled like a schoolgirl.

"How could you tell?" he asked.

Charlie rose to her feet, calculating that Sharp would soon sleep it off. She smiled her goodbye, turned to leave, but stopped short at the sound of footsteps.

"There you are. Both of you. Saves me the trouble of repeating myself," said Mrs. Sharp, her eyebrows furrowed and scolding Mr. Sharp with her eyes.

"Is something wrong, Mrs. Sharp?" asked Charlie.

Jim Sharp made an inebriated attempt at humor.

"Yes, Mrs. Sharp. I would like to know. Is something wrong?" he asked.

Once again, he slipped into a fit of senseless giggling.

Mrs. Sharp scowled. She turned to Charlie. She spoke slowly and softly.

"Kai Bellamy has escaped."

The girl fell backwards onto a hammock.

"How?" she asked.

Mrs. Sharp explained that Kai could not have escaped without help. There was a fire and the guards were distracted. The prisoner's absence was not discovered until the next morning.

"Unless he's re-captured, there'll be no court-martial," said Mrs. Sharp.

Charlie's eyes grew wide.

"I knew he was being held somewhere in the camp. But I didn't know where. I heard the commodore complaining about there being no brig on board the *President*," Charlie reported.

"A lot of the men are talking. But they think Kai is a deserter. Nothing more," said Mrs. Sharp.

Charlie and Mrs. Sharp exchanged long looks.

"I hope he gets away," said Mrs. Sharp.

"And doesn't come back," Charlie added.

Mrs. Sharp leaned over and embraced Charlie where she sat. She turned to Mr. Sharp and muttered as she left the room.

"You're disgusting."

Jim Sharp waited until his wife disappeared. He put a finger to his lips trying hard to focus on Charlie. He spoke in a whisper.

"It was me," he said.

"I don't understand," said Charlie.

"I gave him a choice. Live or die," said Sharp, jerking his head in the air and waving an arm as if it were a saber.

Charlie jumped to her feet and pulled on her hair with both hands.

"You helped the prisoner to escape? Are you mad?" she shouted.

Bosun Sharp hiccupped with a violent jerk of his head. The loud thud of his skull on the ship's hull, made him sober, but only for a moment.

"I did it for you, Charlie."

Charlie could hear the commodore's angry voice, as he addressed the Captain of the Guard.

"The prisoner did not escape by himself. I want the two guards questioned. And they will provide a full explanation, or I'll have both of them put to the lash in front of the entire crew. Dismissed," McDonough barked.

Charlie waited a moment, took a deep breath, and then knocked on the cabin door.

"Enter."

"Commodore McDonough, I wish to speak with you," said Charlie.

"You have no doubt heard the news," said McDonough.

"Yes, sir."

"You are to remain on the ship, unless escorted by one of the men. Is that understood, Charlie?" asked McDonough.

"Yes sir."

Charlie refused to move.

The commodore, unable to disguise his impatience, frowned at the young powder monkey. Charlie fidgeted in place.

"Is there something else?" asked McDonough.

Charlie swallowed hard. Her voice quivered.

"Yes, sir. There is something else. My real name is Charlotte Elizabeth Wheeler."

"I don't understand," said McDonough.

"Kai is not a sodomite. He is attracted to women. Even if that woman pretends to be a young man," said Charlie, her eyes moist.

McDonough blinked repeatedly. His face contorted.

"What exactly are you telling me, Charlie?"

"You have two women on board the *President*–Mrs. Sharp and

me," said Charlie, the relief in her voice, obvious.

The Commodore's jaw dropped. His eyes bulged. He took a deep breath, held it for a moment and then exhaled, loudly.

"You fooled me and everyone else on board the *President*. How did Kai discover your secret?" asked McDonough.

Charlie's mind race through the truth. She decided that the Sharps did not deserve to be punished. She alone, would take the blame for the entire affair.

"It's a long story, sir. But I am at fault, and I am the only one who should be punished," said Charlie, her voice now strong and resolute. Her eyes drilled into the commodore's face.

He blinked. Charlie continued.

"I expect the usual punishment and a dishonorable discharge," said Charlie.

McDonough rose from his chair, hands clasped behind his back. He turned and paced to the far end of the room and then back again.

"I will not put a woman to the lash," McDonough muttered.

Charlie studied the floor. McDonough pivoted in Charlie's direction and slammed his fist on the desk.

"And I need every man I can get, on this ship. Especially my cannon crews. Do you understand that Charlie?"

"Yes sir. We are shorthanded as it is," she said.

"Very well then. You will henceforth be assigned the work of two men. I will see to it myself. But I promise you, Charlie, if word of this . . ."

McDonough's voice trailed off as he struggled for the correct word.

"Situation, should get out, you'll be off the ship and out of the Navy. Is that understood?"

"Yes, sir," said Charlie.

"We are going into winter quarters in three weeks. You will remain on board or with me at all times," said McDonough.

"Yes, sir," said Charlie.

"Now tell the Captain of the Guard that I wish to see him again. Immediately."

Charlie scampered from the commodore's cabin.

"I spoke to Dr. Mann," said the commodore.

The unexpected voice at Nathan Coldwell's chamber interrupted the young doctor's drunken stupor. When he realized that Commodore McDonough stood in the doorway, Nathan jumped off the operating table. He made a half-hearted attempt to salute, but his unshaven appearance and filthy uniform, rendered the gesture meaningless.

"Commodore McDonough," said Nathan, clearing his throat and standing at attention.

McDonough studied the surgeon's slovenly appearance. He scanned Coldwell's operating theater. Soiled clothes and garbage lay on the floor. Nathan's instruments and medicines appeared disorganized and dirty. The room wreaked of alcohol. McDonough's voice, a low rumble, thundered in Nathan's ears.

"You will receive no rum rations for six months. After you clean and organize this room from top to bottom, you will make yourself available at the camp hospital. You will minister to the sick and wounded that are housed there. You will return to the *President* in the evenings and then only to sleep. Is that understood?"

"Yes, sir," said Nathan.

"Had I known of your preference for the spirits, I would not have accepted you as a member of my crew," said McDonough. "As it is, you are dangerously close to a dishonorable discharge. It is only my desperate need for recruits, that is prohibiting your immediate dismissal."

The commodore, a look of sadness covering his face, turned and exited the chamber. Nathan leaned against the wooden slab that served as his bed and operating table. His face blanched white.

His eyes squeezed shut as he leaned forward and threw up.

Chapter Eleven

ON THE RUN

Kai, cold, tired, and hungry, searched the burnt ruins of Pike's Cantonment.

He foraged for food and anything that might keep him warm. He refused to leave Plattsburgh or its environs. A deep-seated lust for revenge fueled his decision to stay hidden and simultaneously surveil the *President*. The comings and goings of its crew, one in particular, consumed him as much as his search for food and clothing. Jim Sharp be dammed. Despite his growling stomach, he bristled when the image of Charlie flashed in his mind. His failed search for warmth and sustenance made matters worse. He found nothing but ashes, burnt articles of clothing and an assorted supply of plates, bowls and baskets, most of them charred beyond use. Kai did discover and retain an old hunting knife, which he sharpened on a rock.

A dark, mostly starless evening allowed Kai to move with few restrictions. He could see the sentinels' fire as they stood guard near the *President's* gang plank. Occasionally, a sailor would return to the ship. Only a few men disembarked, it being too late in the evening for on-shore visits. An ox cart rolled to a noisy stop at the newly erected warehouse, near the docks. It's driver, working alone, moved crates from the cart to the warehouse door. Finding it locked, he stacked the goods against the storeroom's outer wall. When his cart was empty, he approached the sentinels. Kai could discern most of their conversation. The guards, with no key to the storeroom door, pointed to the *President* instead. When the ox cart driver disappeared from view, the sentinels returned to their post. Kai walked quickly to the storeroom, taking shelter in its shadows.

The crates, filled with a variety of food stuffs, made Kai's mouth water. He quickly stuffed his pockets and filled his buttoned-up jacket with handfuls of hard tack, dried pork strips, and other edible items. A quick glance in both directions allowed Kai to retreat to the woods, unnoticed. He chose a pine tree, with a large, raised root at its base, to relax.

He also enjoyed a perfect view of the gangplank which delivered people to and from the *President*.

Charlie wandered aimlessly on the deck of the *President*.

Ironically, her extreme fatigue prevented a restful sleep. Thoughts of Nathan, who treated her as if she were dead, competed with thoughts of Kai, who wanted her dead. And the commodore, she assumed, wanted all of them off his ship. Her dream of serving the Navy on Lake Champlain also lay in ruins, shattered by an unlikely conspiracy of people and events. Her days now stretched from sunup to sunset, a direct result of violating the commodore's trust and confidence. She rested her sore arms on the ship's rail. Days of running errands, moving cargo, cleaning artillery and practicing her role as a powder monkey left the girl exhausted. But a restful night's sleep, eluded her.

"You should be sleeping."

The voice at Charlie's back, belonged to Mrs. Sharp. The older woman squeezed the young girl's shoulders. She stood at Charlie's side, each of them studying the horizon. A series of docks, temporary shelters and storehouses stared back.

"Let's get off this boat and go for a long walk," said Mrs. Sharp.

"I can't do that, ma'am. commodore's orders," said Charlie.

"He's off the ship. And I'll be with you," she answered.

Charlie shook her head, her face a picture of gloom.

"Thank you, Mrs. Sharp. But I'm not going to disappoint the commodore again. You go ahead," said Charlie.

Charlie turned in the direction of the below-deck hatch.

"Try to get some sleep," said Mrs. Sharp.

Mrs. Sharp walked silently in and out of the shadows.

She gulped a lung full of cool crisp air and wondered to herself when the cold introduction to a Plattsburgh winter would commence. A quiet moment on a large boulder, her back to the forest, brought the dark waters of Lake Champlain into view. A grimace crossed her face when she thought of Charlie. The girl's entire life, filled with tragedy, grew worse when she became a part of the *President's* crew.

Mrs. Sharp's heartfelt sympathy disappeared when a cold hand suddenly pressed against her nose and mouth. She struggled to breathe. The unyielding hand spoke.

"Scream, and I'll slit your throat."

The sharp edge of a cold, metal blade pressed against her flesh. The hand yanked her backwards. She fell to the ground, unable to see her attacker. Her lungs screamed for air as the unyielding hand dragged her deeper into the woods. A single moan, almost inaudible, prompted her attacker to speak once again.

"Quiet, woman, or you will die," said the voice.

The hand loosened its grip. She took a series of short breaths. The sudden weight of a man, straddling her body made it difficult to breath. But the renewed flow of oxygen to her brain triggered the memory of her attacker's voice. She knew the man with the knife.

"Kai," she whispered.

Kai's face morphed into a mask of rage. He dropped the blade. His closed fist struck a glancing blow on the side of her face. He hit her again. Blood spurted from Mrs. Sharp's lacerated lip. A third blow, followed by a fourth and a fifth, sent the woman's eyelids into a flutter. The pupils of her eyes disappeared. The woman's mouth, now partially open, looked askew, confirmation that he broke her jaw. His arm grew tired and the sound of knuckles against flesh no longer echoed in the night air.

When Kai heard the sound of approaching boots, he lay flat on the body of his victim. He dared not move for fear of making a noise. The boots stopped. The men talked. The sound of their urine, splashing on the ground, prompted Kai to breath, once again. He waited until they finished. An unexpected moan rose from his victim's lips. One of the men heard the woman's cry.

"Who goes there?"

Kai jumped to his feet and sprinted into the deep forest.

Mrs. Sharp slipped in and out of consciousness as two sailors dragged and carried her up the *President's* gangplank.

The noise of several men as they struggled to deliver the woman to Dr. Coldwell stirred Charlie from her hammock.

"Another drunken sailor?" she asked.

One of the seamen, a somber look covering his face, answered.

"No, Charlie. Afraid not. It's the woman on board. I think her name is Sharp."

Charlie's knees buckled. She used both hands to smother a scream. Her face turned ashen.

"What happened?" Charlie asked.

"Someone attacked her. She's beat up. Real bad," said the sailor.

Charlie staggered to the nearest wall and took several deep breaths. She thought of the woman's husband. Jim Sharp would be held responsible for the attack on his wife, because he arranged for the predator to escape. Charlie also assumed a portion of the guilt. She refused Mrs. Sharp's request to accompany her on a walk. The attack may have been prevented, she thought. And Charlie's guilt did not end there. Her charade as a boy led to all of this. The entire mess could be laid at her feet. Charlie, overwhelmed with remorse, scrambled to Nathan's chamber. She stood at the doorway until Nathan looked up. Charlie searched his face for answers. Nathan brought a finger to his lips, checked on his patient, and tiptoed from the room.

"She has a broken jaw and a bad cut on the cheek that required stitches. She also has extensive bruising about the head and face," Nathan reported. "What in tarnation happened to that woman?"

"I don't know, Nathan. I don't know. I saw her on deck about an hour ago. She wanted to go for a walk. Invited me to join her. I said no. She must have gone by herself," said Charlie, choking back a sob.

Nathan, exhausted for a number of reasons, put his back to the wall and rested. His hands shook. His face looked pale and drawn.

"Are you sick or something?" she asked.

"No, Charlie. I am actually getting better," said Nathan, a slight blush on his face.

Charlie's eyebrows furrowed and then she remembered.

"Too much rum for too long of a time, is a bad thing, I'm guessing," said Charlie.

Nathan nodded. He bowed his head and suddenly looked up.

"Aren't we in the same brig?" he asked.

"I don't understand," said Charlie.

"The commodore has both of us doing double duty, does he not?"

"I thought you were his favorite," she remarked.

He answered with a question.

"I thought *you* were his favorite?"

"Not anymore," she said.

"What did you do to anger the Commodore?" he asked.

"I really don't want to say," she said.

"What did *you* do to anger the Commodore?" asked Charlie.

"I really don't want to say," he replied.

A tired but knowing grin crossed each of their faces.

The shared misery of the commodore's punishment allowed Charlie and Nathan to avoid the usual symptoms of their tumultuous relationship. They sat in silence, near the hatch, and focused on the stars that blanketed the opening. Charlie stole an occasional glance at Nathan, wondering if his feelings for her remained the same.

When she caught Nathan in a surreptitious glance, he turned away, a sad and forlorn look on his face.

Mrs. Sharp required weeks for her recovery.

During that time, McDonough moved his fleet into winter quarters. The trip from Plattsburgh to Otter Creek in Vergennes, Vermont, temporarily reduced the tensions on board the *President*. When she could speak, the woman identified Kai Bellamy as her attacker. Both Mr. Sharp and the commodore vowed to apprehend the savage monster.

McDonough tempered his frustration with Charlie, after learning of Kai's second attack. The commodore, necessarily preoccupied with the increasing threat of British forces at Isle aux Noix, could not afford to be distracted. By mid-February, he received authorization to build more ships. The Secretary of the Navy also urged McDonough to purchase an as yet incomplete steamship. The commodore brought Charlie with him on a tour of the boat works.

"What do you think, Charlie?" asked McDonough, pointing to the hull of an unfinished steamship.

Charlie, elated that her relationship with the commodore now approached normal, happily responded.

"Steamships break down a lot."

"And the spare parts are difficult to obtain," added McDonough.

"How long would it take the steamship company to finish it?" asked Charlie.

"Longer than the six or seven weeks we need to build a schooner," McDonough answered.

"Excuse me sir, but why are we even looking at this hull?" asked Charlie.

"Governor Tompkins has strongly recommended this purchase. I'm not sure why."

"With respect, Commodore, he won't be on-board when we next meet the enemy."

McDonough, in a rare display of emotion, allowed himself a soft chuckle.

"We can use the hull for a schooner, instead," McDonough concluded, his eyes on the docks.

Charlie, a few steps behind, focused on a nearby work crew.

Several of the laborers looked up. The commodore's colorful uniform and large bicorne hat attracted a great deal of attention. Charlie noticed one worker in particular. The man's massive frame, the way he swung a hammer and his deliberate stride, were all familiar to the girl. As if he could feel her eyes on his back, the man turned in Charlie's direction.

Charlie stood deathly still when Otis Skinner raised his hand and waved.

Jim Sharp paced the below-deck cabin which served as the crew's sleeping quarters.

Mrs. Sharp's empty cot brought his simmering anger to a boil. He repeatedly pounded on the hull wall with his closed fist, screaming in anger and pain. The rough-hewn wood, now stained with his blood, did not budge. Sharp fell to his knees with his head resting against the wall. His guilty sobs echoed in the large bed chamber.

"It's all my fault. It's all my fault," he cried.

For more than an hour, he lay on the floor, alternately whimpering in self-pity and screaming at the monster he freed. The man who nearly killed his wife. In time, Sharp's red-hot anger dried his tear-stained cheeks. He rose to his feet, searched furiously for the hunting knife he secreted in his bed roll, and flashed the blade at an imaginary enemy.

"Thanks to me, you are a free man. And thanks to me, you will soon be a dead man," Sharp growled.

As he stormed out of the room, Sharp shoved the knife into its protective sheath and fastened the weapon onto the waist of his trousers.

After Charlie completed her errands and assigned tasks, she approached the commodore.

"Sir. Is there anything else you require this evening" she asked.

"No, Charlie. You're dismissed," said McDonough.

The commodore's soft voice, no longer abrupt and brusque, prompted Charlie to ask the question which burned in her mind.

"Sir. Some members of the crew are going to shore tonight. I have been restricted to the ship for more than two weeks now. Permission to join my crew mates, sir."

McDonough looked up. He rearranged the correspondence on the desk, closed his eyes and hung his head.

"That predator is still out there, Charlie."

"I won't be alone, sir. You have my word."

McDonough caught her eyes with a stern look.

"It is what you don't say that has troubled me in the past,"

"Very well sir. I'm also hoping to visit the shipyard. The shipbuilders labor day and night on the construction of galleys, schooners, and sloops. I find it fascinating, sir," she said.

McDonough smiled his approval.

"A good sailor knows his ship, inside and out."

"Yes sir," said Charlie.

McDonough studied his young charge and returned to the unread correspondence.

"Permission granted."

"Thank you, sir. Thank you very much."

Charlie's artillery crew companions quickly discovered a nearby tavern. Just as quickly, they rejected Charlie's idea about an exploratory visit to the shipyard. She nursed her drink for a while and then excused herself, ostensibly to relieve herself. The men, well on the way to inebriation, ignored their popular crewmember as she left the tavern.

Her short walk to the construction site, bathed in the light of several dozen torches, eliminated any trace of fear in Charlie's mind. Even Kai Bellamy would not be so foolish as to attack a member of the crew, surrounded by burly shipbuilders and seasoned sailors. She recalled the halting wave from Otis as occurring at the far end of the drydocks. A half-dozen galleys, in various stages of completion, marked her way. A voice in the shadows spun Charlie in the opposite direction.

"Where is your friend, the commodore?"

The low rumble of Otis Skinner's voice sent a shiver up her back.

"Why aren't you in jail?" she asked.

"The state's attorney misplaced his star witness," said Otis, exposing a row of yellow teeth.

"Kai has escaped. He's still after me. He just attacked another woman on board the *President*. Hurt her something awful," she said.

"McDonough has two women on his ship? What in blazes is he thinking?" asked Otis, eyes wide with surprise.

"The crew knows only of one. I would be grateful if you kept that to yourself," said Charlie.

"Depends."

Charlie took a few steps forward. She could smell his bad breath. With both hands on her hips, she hissed her objection.

"It depends? If it wasn't for me your lying carcass would be in jail, right now."

"Not so loud," said Otis. "I would be grateful if you kept that to yourself," smiling at his repetition of Charlie's precise words. "Besides, you owe me."

"How do you figure?" asked Charlie.

"I saved your life."

The comment startled Charlie. She could not argue with the truth. Even when it fell out of Otis Skinner's mouth. She paused but her curiosity prompted a question.

"What is it you want?"

"Money. Enough to get me out of this place. Maybe Boston."

Charlie kicked an imaginary pebble on the ground. She studied the starlit sky, as if the heavens might inspire her thinking. She could feel a twinge of guilt in her gut.

"How much?"

"Fifty dollars," he said.

Charlie rolled her eyes.

"Are you insane?"

Otis winced.

"Sorry. How about twenty-five?"

"Deal," she said. "But I don't ever want to see you again, Otis Skinner."

"I promise. When do I get the money?"

"It'll take a while. Bank draft and all. I'll have it sent to me and then I'll send it to you."

"We'll be done here, come spring," said Otis.

"You'll get the money in plenty of time," Charlie announced.

Otis grinned in triumph.

"Always a pleasure doing business with you, Charlie."

"One more thing", she said, pulling the man closer with her index finger.

Skinner's smile disappeared. He scratched at his scraggly beard. His eyebrows now pointed to his scrunched-up nose.

"What?" he asked.

"I'm hoping you run into Kai Bellamy," she said.

"I'm not afraid of that toothy weasel," Otis growled.

Charlie looked around to verify their privacy.

"You have an opportunity to double your money."

"How?"

"Well, if confronted, I expect you to defend yourself against an attack. Vigorously. Do you understand what I'm telling you?" she asked.

"Don't worry about Kai," said Otis. "If I see him first, you will never see him again."

Charlie bowed her head in approval.

"I guess you do understand, Mr. Skinner."

Jim Sharp spent most of his evenings in Vergennes, searching the taverns, boarding houses, stables and barns.

His description of Kai, repeated dozens of times, prompted a series of negative responses. No one saw the boy-man with long, jet-black hair, brown skin and a brilliant smile. Sharp now questioned his earlier conclusion that Kai followed the fleet to Otter Creek. Jim walked slowly back to the ship, intent on visiting Mrs. Sharp, before he retired.

"How is she, doc?"

Nathan Coldwell glanced at his only patient, occupying a small cot at the far end of his operating theater.

"Her injuries are not life-threatening, Mr. Sharp, but it will take weeks more for her jaw to heal," said Nathan.

"May I speak with her?" asked Sharp.

"Of course," said Nathan, discreetly exiting the operating room. He remained within earshot, just beyond the open door.

The bosun's mate studied the woman's bruised and swollen features. A white-hot anger rose in his chest. Anger at the man who attacked his wife. And anger with himself, for having arranged the perpetrator's escape. Sharp fell to his knees, cupping her hand in both of his. She stirred at the sound of her husband's muffled sobs and squeezed the hands that held hers. The pained expression on her face conveyed the words she could not speak. Her husband, overcome with guilt, blurted his confession.

"It was me who arranged Kai's escape."

Her face froze. She yanked her hand away from his. A shocked glare covered her face.

"He promised to leave and I believed him," said Sharp, hoping his explanation would ease her mind.

Mrs. Sharp's eyes stabbed her husband's face. She groaned loudly through lips that could not open. Her head twisted in his direction as far as the pain would allow. He hung his head in shame. She turned back, refusing to look at the man she married.

Mr. Sharp rose to his feet. He shuffled to the exit and used a sleeve to wipe his tear-stained cheeks. Nathan overheard the man's confession. As Sharp approached, the doctor turned away, pretending to be preoccupied. Nathan returned to Mrs. Sharp. She lay there with her eyes open.

A steady stream of tears rolled down her cheeks.

Kai knew, from previous discussions, the precise location of the fleet's winter quarters.

His journey, from Plattsburgh to Otter Creek, proved less difficult than he imagined. Several days after the fleet's departure, an old man, pulling a rickety buckboard, offered Kai a ride. The geezer recently delivered a wagon load of deer skins to merchants in Plattsburgh. Kai offered the fellow his smooth and colorful jackstones, as payment. The old man's hunting stories, long and boring, made the journey even longer. Still, Kai thought it better than walking.

Days later, the young boy basked in the warm glow of a roaring fire. The old man grew colder. Kai retrieved the jackstones shortly after he slit the man's neck. But other than the temporary possession of his most prized possession, the dead man did nothing wrong. Jerimiah, as he called himself, could not have been more welcoming. The victim shared his food and invited Kai to spend the night. Jerimiah's one room cabin, located deep in the woods, made for an excellent hide-a-way. And it stood less than two miles south of Otter Creek.

Kai decided he should bury the evidence of his crime. The victim's staring eyes irritated the predator. But a burial would take time. Kai opted to cover the body with Jerimiah's tattered woolen blanket. The poor fellow, collateral damage as it were, would have to wait. Kai wiped his blade clean and returned the hunting knife to its leather sheath. He also liberated the hunting rifle which lay against the wall near the door. A search for powder and balls, yielded a worn leather pouch, with a little of both. He decided to explore his new surroundings. An enclave of trees and bushes would serve as his strategic hideaway. From there, Kai could observe soldiers and shipbuilders on the trail, going to and from the shipyard.

Otis, with more than twenty-five dollars in coins secreted on his person, rode the trail, south from Vergennes.

The old nag, given to him because the former owner could not afford a long winter's board, would not deliver Otis to Albany, anytime soon. Otis didn't care. As horse and rider plodded through the heavily wooded area, Otis smiled. The ease with which he converted Charlie's bank draft to coins, pleased him. And while he did not anticipate another encounter with Kai, he did not fear such a clash. He was certain he would be the victor.

The effects of a full breakfast made Skinner's eyelids heavy. The hypnotic regularity, of the horse's hooves on frozen ground, produced a sedative effect. His nodding head snapped to attention when the horse came to a sudden halt. Despite repeated blinking, the image of Kai did not go away. The young monster stood in the middle of the trail, with a long rifle pointed at the rider's chest. Kai's clothes, covered in dried mud and fresh blood, made him look and smell like a creature of the wilderness. He wore his trademark smile–two even rows of brilliant-white teeth.

"I did not expect to find you here, Mr. Skinner," said Kai.

Otis growled his dismay.

"Well. Isn't this just wonderful. I know a person who would pay handsomely to see you dead," said Otis.

"You're the dead man, Mr. Skinner."

The boy's smile vanished. He leveled his weapon and pulled the hammer back. Otis didn't wait for Kai to pull the trigger. He kicked the horse with force and let fly with a war hoop. Otis heard the explosion which echoed through the trees. A second later, he could feel a deep burning pain in his chest. A puff of smoke dissipated above Kai's head. Skinner's galloping horse twisted in midstride, away from the sharp report of Kai's musket. Otis flew off the animal, falling to the snow-covered ground with a muffled thud. He landed on his backside and could not get up. Kai approached. Blood flowed from Skinner's lips. His mouth opened to speak. He blew a few bubbles of blood. Kai grinned.

"Goodbye, Mr. Skinner."

Kai searched his victim's warm but lifeless body. He cheered loudly when he discovered the gold coins. Kai also liberated Skinner's wrap, a blanket roll, and the man's hunting knife, it being larger and sharper than the Kai's rusty blade. The lightly falling snow began to cover portions of Skinner's remains.

Kai rode back to the cabin, his tracks clearly visible.

Adele Sharp, still bedridden for most of each day, refused all visitors.

Nathan predicted that in a very short while his patient would be walking and feeling much better.

"Mr. Sharp has come to see you, every day. Sometimes twice a day," said Nathan, a gentle reminder to his patient that her husband cared deeply about her recovery.

"I do not wish to see Mr. Sharp," she said, turning her head to the wall.

"Mrs. Sharp, it is not my intention to interfere."

She cut him off.

"And yet, you persist, Dr. Coldwell. I am grateful for your care and concern. Truly I am. But my marriage is of no concern to you," she said, her arms folded and eyes flashing.

"Very well, Mrs. Sharp. Please excuse me, my presence is required topside," said Nathan.

Bosun Sharp waited quietly in the below-deck storeroom, with the door slightly ajar. He could observe the human traffic in and out of Nathan's operating chamber, without being seen. Sharp waited for a few minutes, after seeing the doctor climb the short ladder and disappear through the hatch. He tiptoed to the far corner of Nathan's chamber. Adele neither heard nor saw her unwanted visitor. When he stood next to her bedside, she instantly reacted.

"You will leave, immediately," she snapped, her speech still jumbled as a result of the broken jaw.

"I am your husband. Am I not allowed to speak with my wife?" he asked.

"You are my husband no longer," said Adele, cautiously probing her still swollen jaw and examining the remaining bruises about her neck and shoulders. "Look what you did."

"It was my fault, Adele. I trusted Kai to be a man of his word. He agreed to leave the area. I thought it best for everyone. I am truly sorry," he said, his eyes filling with tears.

"You were mistaken. Now, leave," she said.

"I *will* leave you," said Mr. Sharp. "And I will not return."

Bosun Sharp walked, trancelike, into the woods.

He wore no wrap to protect himself from the elements and carried a length of rope at his side. He took no notice of the quizzical looks from other sailors and passersby. And while several men recognized and greeted the popular bosun's mate, he ignored them. Sharp stared straight ahead, as if on an urgent mission.

"Mr. Sharp, how's the wife doing? Is she feeling better?" asked Charlie.

Charlie received no response from the man. The girl, although puzzled, could not afford to engage her friend in a long discussion. She possessed an urgent message from the commodore to one of the shipbuilding companies. After her delivery, she returned to the *President* and scanned the horizon for any sign of her friend. As several members of the ship's crew struggled to lift a platform of crates, using pulleys and ropes, she came to an abrupt halt. Ropes. Sharp carried a rope. And he didn't look right. Her eyes widened and she snapped her head in the direction of the forest. The girl ran as fast as she could, searching a confusing puzzle of footprints in the snow. One trail led to the deep woods.

"No … no … please no," she panted, following a trail of boot prints and simultaneously scanning the tree-filled horizon.

And then she saw him. Standing on a tree stump, his head just inches from a perfectly coiled noose. An overhanging branch of a nearby tree would be Mr. Sharp's executioner. He slipped the rope over his head. Charlie screamed. He slowly turned in her direction, a look of misery etched on his face. Sharp tightened the noose and then stepped off the stump.

The girl stretched every muscle in her body to reach her friend before it was too late. Several hundred yards gave Sharp too much time. She saw his unconscious body spasm and twitch from lack of oxygen. Charlie leapt onto the stump, wrapped one arm around her friend's waist, and pulled on the unyielding rope. She struggled in vain to loosen the noose. Charlie did not have the strength to lift the body with one hand and use her remaining hand to work the knot.

That's when she saw Jim's hunting knife. She yanked it from its sheath. Charlie slashed at the rope just above Sharp's head. It required several attempts. His lifeless body fell to the ground in a heap. She jumped to his side and pressed her ear to his chest. Charlie took a deep breath when she heard the faint sound of a heartbeat. Without a horse, much less a wagon, the girl could only sit on the cold ground and cradle the man's head in her lap. In time, his color returned, and the man's shallow breathing sounded almost normal.

An hour passed when the echo of men's voices reached her

ears. She yelled at the riders, even before they came into view. Two shipwrights, traveling in search of a good stand of lumber, recognized McDonough's aide. They required only a brief explanation before lifting Sharp to one of their mounts. The larger man, riding double with his patient, cradled Sharp between two strong arms. Charlie, sitting immediately behind the second man, hugged his waist, as the horses broke into a rough trot. She worried about sliding off the horse.

She worried more, about Jim Sharp.

Nathan looked up when he heard a commotion near the topside hatch.

Several men struggled with an unconscious man. The last set of legs to descend the short ladder belonged to Charlie. She ran ahead to brief the surgeon.

"It's Jim Sharp."

"What happened?" asked Nathan.

"He tried to hang himself. I'm not sure I got to him in time," she said.

They laid the still unconscious man on Nathan's operating table. As Nathan began his examination, he dismissed the shipwrights.

"Thank you, gentlemen. That will be all."

Charlie, too, turned to leave.

"Charlie. Wait."

She stopped at the door.

"How long before you got to him?" asked Nathan.

"It seemed like hours. I don't really know. Five, ten minutes. Maybe," she said.

"You saved his life," said Nathan, looking at Charlie.

"I've got to find Mrs. Sharp," said Charlie.

"She refuses to talk to him. Said she didn't want to see him again. I think his guilt and her rejection, sent him over the edge," said Nathan.

"This is all my fault," said Charlie.

"I don't understand."

"I've been pretending I'm a . . ."

A woman's voice interrupted the girl's confession.

"How is he?"

The voice belonged to Mrs. Sharp. Charlie twisted in place. Nathan stiffened. The woman glanced at the man on the table but did not approach.

"Word travels fast on this ship," said Mrs. Sharp.

She turned to Charlie.

"I suppose I should thank you," she added.

Charlie's lips curled in anger.

"I don't want your thanks, ma'am. And, in my opinion, your husband deserves a whole lot better than the likes of you."

Mrs. Sharp blanched. Nathan blushed a deep pink. Charlie stomped out of the room.

Nathan reported Sharp's attempted suicide to the commodore.

McDonough closed his eyes. He looked old and tired.

"Thank you, Doctor Coldwell."

"Sir," said Nathan, snapping a sharp salute and turning on one heel.

"Dr. Coldwell."

Nathan turned to face the commodore.

"I am told that you have made considerable progress. In your professional life and with your personal life."

"Yes, Commodore. I am doing my best."

"Very well, then. That is all, Dr. Coldwell."

Nathan returned to the operating chamber. Bosun Sharp remained unconscious. Mrs. Sharp stood at his bedside. Her eyes, red and swollen from crying searched the doctor's face for answers.

"When will he wake up?"

"That is a difficult question to answer," said Nathan. "It could be hours or it could be days. We know very little about the human brain and how it functions."

The woman wiped the tears from her eyes and turned back to her husband.

"I would like to remain here, if I may," she said.

"Certainly," said Nathan.

Charlie searched for the two shipwrights that rescued her and Jim Sharp.

They resumed their journey before the girl could thank them. Her frustration grew, when she learned that word of Jim Sharp's attempted suicide, spread to the ship's crew. She wanted to tell everyone, why Jim Sharp took the action that he did. But that would not be wise. Such an outburst would disclose the nature of the couple's disagreement. And it would condemn Jim Sharp. She fumed in silence, aimlessly pacing the deck and deliberately avoiding her fellow crew members. Nathan's voice interrupted her thoughts.

"Mrs. Sharp has chosen to remain with her husband," said Nathan.

Charlie took a few quick steps forward, thought better of it, and stopped.

"How is he doing?" she asked.

"Still unconscious," said Nathan.

"Is he likely to survive?"

"I don't know."

Before Charlie could react, a man's loud voice ended the conversation.

"We're back, folks. But you ain't gonna be much help to this fellow."

Charlie and Nathan stepped quickly to the gangplank. The same shipwrights, who delivered Bosun Sharp to Nathan's chamber, now pointed to their tethered horses. The larger mount carried a body, wrapped in a blanket, tied and slung over the horse's back. You could see a pair of oversized boots, protruding from the woolen shroud.

"He's been shot, I'm afraid. Cold and stiff when we found em," said one of the men.

"Who is it?" asked Charlie.

"He looks like that big guy, Skinner. He used to work in the yard," said the larger man.

Charlie ran down the gang plank. Nathan and the two shipwrights caught up to the girl as she fumbled through layers of gray blanket. Charlie's ashen face confirmed the dead man's identity. She took several steps back, turned away from the men, and fell to her knees. Charlie heaved the contents of her stomach. Nathan turned to the men.

"What happened?" he asked.

"We found him on the ground. A shot to the chest. One set of horse tracks leading into the woods," said one of the shipwrights.

Charlie rose to her feet, wiping her mouth with a sleeve.

"I've got to inform the commodore," she said.

"Our friend has returned," said Charlie.

The commodore jammed his writing quill into the inkwell. He glared at Charlie.

"I assume you interrupt me for good reason."

Charlie took no notice of McDonough's frustration. She stood in front of his desk, doing her best to hide her trembling hands.

"Otis Skinner was shot dead,' she blurted, her voice cracking.

"And why do I recall this man's name?"

Charlie reminded the commodore. She recounted how she knew the dead man as her stepfather and how Skinner's courtroom heroics saved her life. McDonough required only seconds to recognize the seriousness of the situation. His face grew solemn. He stood and studied the view from his cabin door.

"Mr. Bellamy appears intent on killing you and everyone associated with you," he said.

"I believe you are correct, Commodore. What are we going to do?" asked Charlie.

"We? You will do nothing. You will remain on board this ship at all times. Is that understood?"

"Yes, sir."

Summon the Captain of the Guard. I am ordering an immediate search party. This man is insane, and he must be apprehended as soon as possible."

Kai returned to his isolated hideaway, hardly able to contain himself after the successful confrontation with Otis.

His jubilation ended when the foul stench of the old man's body reached the murderer's nose. Kai dragged the geezer from the cabin using the victim's woolen blanket as a makeshift litter. After catching his breath, Kai pulled the body further into the woods. He retrieved an old hoe at the rear of the cabin and, with some effort, dug a shallow grave. As the old man's body rolled into the hole, face down, Kai thought about Skinner. His body too, should be hidden. The sudden sound of men's voices in the distance, forced Kai to move quickly. Kai retrieved his rifle and checked the girth on Skinner's old nag.

The two-time murderer disappeared into the forest.

"Fresh tracks but nobody's home," said one of the guards.

The Captain of the Guard, leading six-mounted soldiers, pivoted his horse in the direction of the tracks.

"We follow the tracks," he said.

One of the soldiers circled the cabin. He shouted his discovery.

"Captain, you may want to see this."

As the officer turned the corner, a freshly dug grave came in to view.

"My guess is another victim," said the captain.

The soldiers, ordered to exhume the body, struggled with the overpowering stench. When the victim's head and upper torso could be seen, the cause of the old man's death became apparent.

"His throat's slit," said one of the diggers.

"Probably lived here by himself," said the captain. "Let's move, before this snow makes it impossible to track the bastard."

Kai Bellamy, once again, evaded the authorities.

A think blanket of wet snow hid the evidence of his escape route. The uniformed men, no longer in pursuit of the fugitive, returned to the shipyard. Charlie received their report and transmitted the news to McDonough. The commodore admonished her, once again, to remain on the ship at all times.

Mr. Sharp remained unconscious for days. Charlie carefully chose her visiting hours, so as not to encounter the man's wife. An early morning sojourn to Nathan's surgery triggered a panic attack.

"Where is he?" she asked, pointing to Sharp's empty cot.

"He's fine," said Nathan. "Opened his eyes late last night and asked for something to drink."

"So, you just let him go?" asked Charlie, hands on her hips, and leaning forward.

"He's with his wife," said Nathan. "And lucky to be alive," he added.

Charlie pouted, unable to process the conflict raging in her head. Although still angry with Adele Sharp, she rejoiced at the news of her friend's recovery. When she looked up, Charlie caught Nathan in a stare.

"I thought you would be pleased," he said.

"Oh. I am," said Charlie, speaking loudly so as to disguise the girl's frustration.

She focused on the empty cot. Nathan came out from behind his operating table, leaning on the heavy-wooden slab, with his arms folded. He scratched his head.

"We're not arguing anymore, have you noticed?

Charlie flashed a genuine smile in the doctor's direction.

"Yes, I noticed. And I like it a lot better," said Charlie.

Nathan grinned. Charlie fought the urge to hug her male friend. Perhaps it was the fear of another attack by Kai or the good news about Sharp. Either way she suddenly wanted to tell Nathan her secret.

"Nathan. There's something I want you to know," she said.

Nathan stepped forward. Charlie swallowed hard and fidgeted with the buttons on her uniform.

"Yes," he said, waiting expectantly.

"He's all tired out from our walk."

Charlie turned as Jim and Adele Sharp walked through the door. The woman gently guided her patient back to his cot. Jim did not immediately acknowledge Charlie. He waited until he was seated and about ready to recline.

"Charlie. I owe you a drink," he murmured.

"You don't owe me a thing," and Charlie.

"We are both very grateful," said Mrs. Sharp, a distinctively penitent look on her face. "And I owe you an apology, Charlie. You have been a good and loyal friend to my husband and to me. My actions were unchristian and uncalled for. Please forgive me, my friend."

Charlie abandoned any thought of disclosing her secret to Nathan.

"I'm just glad that the two of you are back together," said Charlie. "I best be going now," she said.

Chapter Twelve

PREPARATIONS

Like the greenery of Vermont, now covered by layers of snow and ice, Kai Bellamy disappeared from view.

Despite dozens of wanted posters, each with a rough sketch of the perpetrator's face, none of the locals came forward. Commodore McDonough could do nothing and suffered from problems of his own. The British, according to McDonough's spies, recently began construction of the largest ship ever to sail the lake. With the necessary blessings of his Navy Secretary, the commodore moved forward with an ambitious plan. He would construct at least one large warship plus a series of smaller fighting vessels. (Row galleys) As February of 1814 made its bone-chilling appearance, the race for supremacy on the lake began.

And a vicious predator remained on the loose.

Kai rode his exhausted nag into the farm community of Shelburne, Vermont, just a few miles south of Burlington.

Normally, a four-day trip on horseback, Kai's journey required the better part of two weeks. He refused to travel by day. He emerged from the backwoods, suffering from the freezing cold and a lack of food. Despite his stash of stolen coins, the man's only nourishment, for the past twelve days, consisted of handfuls of frozen snow, scattered nuts, and berries.

The fugitive wore his hat pulled low over the front of his face. He occasionally looked up, in search of a place to eat. A boarding house, at the south end of town, offered a bed for the night plus meals. He took a chair in the furthest corner of the dining area, his back to the wall. The proprietor offered chicken and biscuits or venison stew. Kai requested both, saying little and keeping his head down. When he could eat no more, Kai exercised his mind. He mentally rehashed his plans for Charlie, the Sharps, and, if possible, the commodore too. Burlington would put him in close proximity to Plattsburgh.

Kai fully expected the American fleet to return to the bay, as soon as the ice went out on the lake.

"You're not going to like this," said Charlie, handing Nathan a signed letter from the commodore.

Army General Wilkinson announced his intentions to disrupt "illicit intercourse" between the British and local residents. By mid-March, Wilkinson moved the bulk of his men, some 4000 troops, to Champlain, in anticipation of a conflict. In response, the British government reinforced their positions at LaColle Mills, Isle aux Noix and Chambly. McDonough's missive, painfully brief, brought a deep shade of red to Nathan's face. A clash of significant size would soon take place. McDonough, still in winter quarters, refused to join Wilkinson's attack. He would supply medical personal, however, the need for which could be significant. Once again, Nathan's services would be required. He threw the commodore's orders high into the air. As the paper sailed to the floor, tacking left and right, Nathan slammed his fist on the operating table.

"I am a ship's surgeon. If I wanted to be with foot soldiers, I would have joined the Army," he bellowed.

Charlie reached for the paper at her feet and approached Nathan's operating table.

"You shouldn't be in any danger," she said, absentmindedly reaching for his hand.

The physical display of affection startled her angry friend. Nathan slowly pulled his hand back, his eyes drilling into the girl's face. Charlie, realizing her error, quickly stepped back.

"Those are your orders, Nathan," she said, wetting her lips after a deep breath.

Nathan's eyebrows furrowed. He cocked his head to one side. Charlie turned her back to him and walked, as if on thin ice, to the exit.

"Charlie?"

She stopped but refused to turn around, for fear that he might see her blushing face.

"What's wrong with me?" he asked.

Charlie twisted in his direction, startled by the question.

"I'm not sure what you mean," she said.

"You and me, Charlie."

She stopped breathing. Her eyes grew wide. Nathan's eyes, glassy from tears, locked onto hers. He swallowed hard, unable to go on. Charlie panicked. She wanted to say something. Anything. She blurted the first words that came to mind.

"It's not you, Nathan. It's me."

Nathan stared in silence.

Charlie ran from the room.

A last-minute council of war by Wilkinson, with all of his senior commanders, made it unanimous.

They would move to the line and attack the British at LaColle Mills. Nathan looked up when Wilkinson stepped to the front of the room.

"An officer will be posted . . . and will instantly put to death any man that goes back . . . this army must not give ground."

The young surgeon learned later that the general's motives had little to do with cowardice on the battlefield. Wilkinson's few friends in Washington reported that unless he produced a strategic victory, and soon, the general's military career would end. The Americans enjoyed a 2 to 1 advantage in troop strength. Their victory seemed likely.

Nathan anticipated a heavy number of casualties.

By late morning on the 30th of March, a portion of Wilkinson's troops encountered a picquet of British soldiers

The resistance occurred just north and west of their intended target; a two-story sawmill situated on the LaColle River. The Americans fell back and joined their counterparts, who traveled by road to the sawmill. The thick, stone-walled mill supplied the boat works at Isle aux Noix. As a result, it became a strategic objective for each of the warring parties. The British protected their post with one hundred eighty men and a cleared field, measuring one hundred fifty yards, in every direction from the mill. In anticipation of an American attack, they also installed barbed steel in all of the windows and doors. The building's eighteen-inch stone walls were reinforced with logs of the same thickness. Beyond the clearing, a series of felled logs, posed an insurmountable obstacle to attackers on horseback or with wheeled artillery. A number of the felled trees, sharpened and inserted into the ground at a steep angle, would inflict serious bodily harm to both man and beast. Three garrisoned block houses, nearby, added to the defenses of the mill, making the structure virtually impenetrable. Wilkinson would have to use the overwhelming numbers of his army to achieve victory.

Nathan ordered the erection of his medical tents very near Wilkinson's camp. The Americans' temporary headquarters lay immediately south of the cleared, killing field. When the battle commenced, Wilkinson employed his artillery pieces. After four hours of bombardment, the cannonade accomplished nothing. When the general made no move to press the attack, the British responded with a counterattack of their own. The result, a significant number of American casualties, created hours of frantic activity for Nathan and his medical colleagues.

A surprise launch of artillery by British gun boats caused a widespread panic among the American troops. The naval attack, too far down the river, did little damage. The psychological impact of the unexpected barrage on American soldiers, who faced execution if they abandoned their positions, could not be measured.

Dozens of wounded soldiers streamed into Nathan's crude hospital tent. He and another surgeon stacked amputated limbs into a pile several feet high. Near that mound of gruesome carnage, were the uncovered bodies of soldiers who succumbed to their wounds. When General Wilkinson, on his way to the woods to relieve himself, walked by, Nathan gave voice to his pent-up anger.

"This is not the bloodless victory you hoped for, is it general?" asked Nathan.

Wilkinson came to a sudden halt and spun around. He thrust a pointed finger in Nathan's direction, as if aiming a loaded musket. But it did not fire. Nathan, wearing an apron covered with blood and bone dust, did not flinch. The general went limp, his head drooped. He slowly turned away and continued his march to the hand-dug latrines.

The young surgeon resumed his post at the operating table.

"He quit," said Charlie.

"Who?" asked Nathan his voice still groggy after the days-long journey from LaColle to Otter Creek.

"I overheard the commodore. Wilkinson temporarily relinquished his command to General Macomb in Plattsburgh," said Charlie.

"The man was incompetent. He wasted the lives of too many good soldiers," said Nathan.

Charlie hoped to reveal her secret to Nathan, this morning. Her cheery news, a prelude to the big announcement, would set the mood.

"You'll be in new quarters, very soon," said Charlie, a mysterious smile crossing her face.

"Well, you're just full of good news this morning, aren't you," said Nathan, rising from his hammock.

Nathan, wearing nothing but his night shirt, turned his back to Charlie as he stripped off and reached for fresh clothing. Charlie swallowed hard as Nathan's white buttocks came into view. She turned her head to one side but her curiosity triggered one more glance. Nathan, oblivious to the girl's voyeurism, finished dressing as he pressed Charlie for more information.

"New quarters? What do you mean?"

"The commodore's new flag ship will be ready within a week," she reported.

"A new flagship?" questioned Nathan.

"The *Saratoga,*" said Charlie. "From tree to ship in less than forty days," she added, as if her other job was as a shipwright. "The *President* will be used as a transport," she said.

Nathan exploded. He marched in the girl's direction, his angry face, towering over hers.

"Why are you always down here and telling me these things?" he asked. "Don't you have something to do?"

Charlie, stunned by his outburst, blinked repeatedly. Her mouth opened to respond.

"Well?" he demanded.

Charlie's eyes teared up. She stepped away. Her downcast eyes dropped to the floor.

"I wanted to tell you something. Something important," she murmured.

"Well. Out with it," said Nathan, his voice rising.

"No one knows except the Sharps, the commodore, and Kai Bellamy," she said.

"Know what," he asked.

Charlie glanced down to verify that the wrap which bound her breasts into nearly invisible bumps, remained in place. Nathan threw his hands into the air.

"Charlie Wheeler, you are wasting my time. Do you hear me?" he barked.

"I'm sorry, Nathan, but I can explain."

"Out of my way."

As Nathan marched passed, a single tear rolled down Charlie's cheek.

The large meal Kai had consumed the night before conspired with the arduous journey.

The predator slept soundly for ten hours. Now, wide awake and alert, his anger with Charlie and her friends reappeared. He paced his rented second-floor bed chamber, windowless and smelling of stale cigar smoke. As he fumed, a variety of evil plans raced through his head. All of them ended with the demise of Charlie Wheeler. She would never spurn him again, he vowed. Kai stood at the old mirror which hung over the rickety dresser. A dust-covered bowl and pitcher, laced with cracks, matched the almost useless mirror. The mirror distorted and twisted Kai's smiling face. The commodore's aide-de-camp resembled a hideous monster more than a midshipman in the American Navy. Surprisingly, the image inspired the boy. He grinned widely and reached for the hunting knife at his side.

As long strands of jet-black hair fell into the porcelain basin, the predator howled with laughter.

"This just arrived, Commodore McDonough," Charlie announced.

She placed the letter on McDonough's desk, already strewn with maps, charts, papers and inkwells. She remained at attention, recalling McDonough's long-standing habit of responding to correspondence, almost immediately. Usually, he ordered the commodore's "boy" to summon an officer or deliver his hastily written response. On this morning, McDonough looked up. He removed his reading spectacles and tossed them on the desk. His normally solemn countenance disappeared. An angry look of steely resolve forced Charlie's gaze to the floor.

"Summon every officer in the fleet to our mess room and do it immediately. I will be there within the hour."

Less than fifteen minutes later, McDonough walked into the mess room. A scrum of uniformed officers saluted their commander. The room grew quiet. McDonough's second-in-command, Lieutenant Stephen Cassin, stepped away from the head of the table, motioning to the commodore as he did so. Charlie tiptoed to the door. McDonough noticed.

"Charlie. Stay," McDonough ordered.

She stood, motionless, just inside the exit.

McDonough's soft voice filled the room like a storm cloud.

"Gentlemen, I have received, not one, but two credible warnings that our winter quarters will soon be under attack."

A murmur rippled through the chamber. McDonough made a slight wave of his hand, and the room went silent once again.

"I shall read to you what our loyal friend, Customs Collector, Mr. Sailly, has written.

>*"A part of the British flotilla has been at Rouse's point since a few days ... We are apprehensive that they will pay us a visit in a few days and send us some of their heavy balls unless they choose to go first to the mouth of Otter Creek and block you up."*

McDonough announced his response. A heavy battery would be constructed at the mouth of the creek. A total of seven 12-pound cannon, on naval carriages, would be installed. He designated Lieutenant Cassin to work with the army and place up to fifty sailors and soldiers, to defend the ship works.

Fort Cassin, as it was called, required only days for its construction.

Days after that, McDonough's newest brig, the *Saratoga,* splashed into Otter Creek.

"Where are the guns? There's no rigging. It doesn't even have sails," exclaimed Charlie.

McDonough looked more like a father indulging his obstinate child than a commodore, as he patiently waited for Charlie's questions to end. He spoke softly.

"Charlie, those items have yet to arrive. It will carry twenty-six guns, ranging in size from 24 to 42-pounders. And the Almighty willing, we will be under sail and back to the bay in Plattsburgh, by the middle of May."

"But the ice goes out in early May. The British could be at our front door, before we are ready," she replied, wildly gesticulating with waving arms.

"Your concerns are noted, Midshipman Wheeler."

Charlie's hands dropped to her side. She took a step backwards, as if the commodore insulted her. The girl's mouth opened to speak but Charlie's tongue, usually wagging, stuck to the dry roof of her mouth. Charlie's unexpected promotion to midshipman came with a caveat.

"A midshipmen is considered to be in training at all times, Charlie. You are not an officer. Is that clear?" asked the commodore.

Charlie, still in shock that she had been promoted, responded with no more than a nod of her head.

"Now, if it meets with your approval, Midshipmen Wheeler, we shall continue our tour," said McDonough, a slight smile crossing his face.

When the duo slipped below deck, the sound of approaching footsteps could be heard.

"Dr. Coldwell. I trust your new quarters are satisfactory?" asked McDonough.

"Yes, sir. Most satisfactory," said Nathan.

McDonough's demeanor grew solemn.

"You will soon share the new, operating theater with a colleague," McDonough announced. "I have given orders for Dr. John Briggs, of the 33rd regiment, to be surgeon onboard the *Saratoga*. He will be your senior," said McDonough.

Nathan's eyes grew wide. He glanced to the floor and then back to McDonough. He nodded his head.

"Sir."

Charlie stood behind the commodore. Still stinging from Nathan's recent outburst, she refused to even look at the surgeon. McDonough, intent on finishing his tour, brushed past Nathan.

Charlie followed.

British Captain Daniel Pring stood at the helm of the *Linett*.

The brig, recently constructed at Isle Aux Noix, carried twenty guns and led a flotilla of six additional sloops plus ten row galleys. Like McDonough, Pring also suffered from a lack of experienced sailors. And he too, recruited Army soldiers, racing against time to train and test them, before clashing with the Americans. Today, however, Pring dismissed those worries. The large, dark-skinned officer, a fourteen-year veteran of the Royal Navy, crossed the boundary line on the morning of May 9. He intended to destroy the American fleet even before it left Otter Creek. His objective, McDonough's flotilla, lay moored or in dry dock at Vergennes. Whether Pring succeeded or failed in his mission, would be secondary, however. He also needed to know the precise size, number, and offensive capability of McDonough's fleet. This information could make the difference between victory and defeat on Lake Champlain.

"Seize it," Pring barked.

Pring pointed to a small schooner at Windmill Point. The vessel required a handful of Pring's men, for its removal. And no one, south of the line, dared to challenge the British invaders. The seized vessel prompted a series of messages. Both Army General Izard and Commodore McDonough received a warning. Izard immediately dispatched additional troops to Vergennes. McDonough installed the Vermont militiamen in the woods on both sides of the creek. He also alerted his gun crews.

Pring ordered the seizure of several more waterborne vessels before he reached Otter Creek. Two unfortunate Americans, caught and threatened by the heavily armed armada, revealed the vital intelligence Pring desired. The British officer now knew about the *Saratoga*, the soon-to-be launched *Ticonderoga*, and the balance of McDonough's ambitious ship building program. But Pring, not satisfied with the results of his interrogation, decided to confront McDonough's fleet at Otter Creek.

"We will destroy the American fleet before it enters the Lake," announced the lieutenant.

He ordered his sailors to prepare for battle. Pring sailed to within two and a half miles of the American shoreline. His heavy artillery opened fire on the American defensive positions, hoping to storm the patriot forces. The British attack did not go unanswered.

"They were expecting us," Pring yelled, as a thunderous volley from the Americans turned the water into a boiling cauldron of foam.

Pring's spyglass also revealed the presence of American militia on both sides of Otter Creek. He persisted. The Americans continued their stubborn response. After two hours of maneuvering, neither side inflicting any significant damage, Pring gave the order to withdraw. Lieutenant Cassin's hastily constructed fort performed as expected.

The precise size and capabilities of the American fleet, however, would prompt the British to return.

"The commodore would like a casualty report as soon as possible," Charlie said.

Nathan Coldwell, pleased that Pring's invasion produced only two modest casualties, noticed Charlie favoring her left arm.

"What's wrong with you?" he asked.

Charlie's voice showed no emotion.

I slipped and fell, topside. Patch of ice, I guess."

Nathan walked to her side of his operating table.

Take off your shirt," he ordered.

"No. I'm fine. And the commodore wants that casualty report, immediately," she said.

"No deaths, two wounded, only slightly. Both men are able to resume their duties," Nathan snapped.

"Can you raise your hand above your head?" he asked.

"No," she whispered, her eyes glued to the floor.

He reached for her shoulder and squeezed. She screamed in pain.

"Nathan, you're killing me."

"Your arm has popped out. I can shove the upper arm bone back into its socket. It will be sore for a while, but the pain will stop. Eventually, you will have full mobility.

"Now remove your shirt," he said.

Charlie, wincing from the pain, stared at Nathan. She took notice of the open door.

"Shut the door," she ordered.

Nathan's eyebrows arched.

"Why?"

"Please," she asked, her voice trembling from the pain and the fear.

Nathan did as she asked and stood with his back to the door.

Charlie, her head bowed, unbuttoned the baggy shirt, starting at her waist. She removed the shirt and tossed it on the operating table. The band of white material, wrapped tightly against her chest, came into view. Nathan snarled.

"You've been hurt. And who in tarnation wrapped you up in that silly bandage?" he asked.

Charlie caught his eyes. Her lips quivered. She refused to cry.

"I did. And it's not a bandage," she said.

Nathan scratched his head and blinked.

"Charlie, I'm confused. Why are you wearing that thing?"

"My real name is Charlotte Elizabeth Wheeler. I've been pretending to be a boy since I was twelve years old," she said, her voice a bit stronger.

Nathan tried to step back. The door stopped him. He gawked at Charlie and his jaw dropped.

"You're a girl?"

"I'm a seventeen-year-old woman, Dr. Coldwell. Now would you please fix my arm?" she asked.

Nathan stepped forward. His hands shook. He gingerly reached for Charlie's dislocated arm.

"Look the other way, please."

Charlie screamed as Nathan executed a smooth yank followed by a slight push. He stepped away from the girl. Charlie turned white. Her knees buckled. He caught her in his arms, his hands around her exposed torso.

He pulled her to a standing position. She stepped back, reached for her shirt, and hurriedly dressed. Her cheeks burned. He turned his head.

"I apologize for hurting you, Charlie. There was no other way."

"It's feeling better, already."

Nathan's eyes darted from the floor to Charlie and then back again. He wore a sheepish grin.

"You're a woman," he repeated.

Charlie managed a weak smile.

"Yes. I know," she said.

"Does the commodore know?" he asked.

"Yes, as do the Sharps."

"Anyone else?"

"Kai Bellamy."

Nathan took a step forward.

"Charlie, you're in danger."

Charlie rolled her eyes.

"I'm aware of that, Nathan."

She walked to the door. Nathan ran after her, reaching for her good shoulder.

"Charlie."

She refused to turn but stood motionless, wondering if he could see the red heat which burned her cheeks.

"Yes, Nathan?" she whispered.

"I am so very much relieved that you are a woman," said Nathan.

Still unwilling to show her face, the girl chuckled.

"Well, it's not as if I had a choice," she said.

Kai used a straight razor to finish his haircut.

Now completely bald, and with the strategic use of blacking, he no longer recognized himself. The fugitive resembled an older, black man. He made a mental note, however, not to smile. A perfect row of brilliant-white teeth did not comport with the image he desired. His goal, to become a mostly quiet man of color, would allow him to go unrecognized in Plattsburgh. Kai tested the disguise when he settled his account with the proprietor.

"I'ze gonna pay for the room at the top of da stairs," said Kai.

The old man behind the counter looked suspiciously at Kai but quickly announced the amount due.

"That'll be two bucks for the room and one dollar for the meals."

Kai deposited a pile of coins on the front desk.

"Ain't no good at ciphering," he announced.

The clerk counted four dollars and scraped the coins into his hands. Kai pretended not to notice the man's thievery. The proprietor glared at Kai.

"Why are you paying for a white man?" asked the owner. "And where did you get all that money?"

"I'z his niggah," said Kai.

"Well, you best leave. Your kind ain't welcome here," said the old man.

Kai scooped up the remaining coins and sauntered out of the boarding house. He calculated that a feigned limp would add to his new character.

His ride to the water's edge in South Burlington, required only a few hours. He found an out-of-the-way spot, tethered his stolen horse, and settled in for a long wait. His planned trip to Plattsburgh required passage on some type of waterborne vessel. How and when the journey would be accomplished remained a mystery. After several hours, the solution to his problem floated into Shelburne Bay.

The vessel, known as a horse ferry, featured two mules walking on a large turntable below deck. The turntable controlled the paddle wheel and propelled the boat. Kai heard about such contraptions but never saw one up close. He approached the operator and lied again about working for his master. He soon arranged passage to Essex New York, a small village, just south of Plattsburgh. Once there, a well-traveled road along the lake shore would deliver Kai to Plattsburgh, in less than a day.

As expected, Commodore McDonough and his entire fleet departed Otter Creek for Plattsburgh, in mid-May.

The commodore's arrival occurred later than preferred because of manpower shortages. Once again, army recruits by the dozen would serve on McDonough's ships. Most of them, untrained and totally inexperienced, required a great deal of supervision. Upon their arrival, McDonough's fleet spent much of their first week transporting troops and supplies from Burlington to Plattsburgh.

"I haven't seen you in days," said Nathan.

Charlie, resting on a crate, used the moment to catch her breath.

"I have moved more cargo in the last few days than I have in my entire life," she said, wiping her brow and gulping the liquid in her canteen.

"How's the arm," he asked.

"Better, but still a bit sore," she replied.

"Is that rum in your canteen?" he asked, a wide grin on his face.

"No sir. I donate my rations to the cannon crews. And I'm quite popular as a result," she said, using an innocent shrug to feign her unexpected surprise.

"You are a generous soul, Charlie Wheeler," said Nathan.

"Thank you, Dr. Coldwell."

She rose from the crate and scanned the upper deck.

"Looking for something?" he asked.

"Well, that next crate goes into the hold," said Charlie, pointing to a large container near-by.

"No way I can carry it myself."

"I'll help you," said Nathan.

Charlie did not resist.

After some maneuvering and a few loud grunts, the girl and the surgeon installed the wooden box into the below-deck storeroom. When Charlie turned to leave, she collided with Nathan, who unintentionally blocked her exit. They stood within inches of each other.

"Sorry," she said.

Charlie, breathing heavy from her effort, made no effort to move. Nathan reached for a lock of the girl's hair. It covered most of one eye. He gently pushed it to one side.

"Charlie, I . . ."

Nathan's voice trailed off.

"Yes, Nathan?" she said, instantly regretting the rapidity with which she responded.

Nathan attempted to speak his mind, once again.

"I just want to say that . . ."

Charlie decided to help him.

"Thank you for the help," she said.

Nathan wet his dry lips and pretended to inspect a large crate to his left.

Charlie reached for his chin. She gently forced Nathan to look at her. Charlie gulped and took a deep breath. Nathan leaned forward. She closed her eyes. He lightly pressed his lips on hers but just for an instant. He pulled back, as if doing something wrong. She smiled her approval. They embraced and the tension drained from Charlie's body.

The moment of their first kiss ended with a crash. A fat sailor stood in the doorway. The look on his face suggested that he witnessed the entire episode. The small-wooden crate he carried. crashed to the floor with a loud bang. The man, unknown to Charlie, but recognized by her, glared and shook his head.

"That ain't right," he muttered. "That ain't right."

He slammed the door behind him.

"Why must we go into Plattsburgh village, tomorrow?" asked Jim Sharp.

His wife frowned and with a fist on each hip, raised her voice.

"James Sharp. You promised me last week that we would walk to the village. There are shops, a large general store, and plenty to do and see. And we both have permission to leave," she said.

"I know what I said."

Mrs. Sharp stepped forward.

"What is it, Jim? What's bothering you?" she asked.

"Three soldiers will be executed in the village tomorrow. There will be large crowds and it's nothing you want to see," he said.

"I have no intention of witnessing an execution," she announced. "Can't we just avoid it?" she asked.

"I suppose. I just have this bad feeling, that's all," he muttered.

McDonough called for a meeting with his top officers.

He did it on short notice and appeared uncharacteristically anxious. The commodore tapped nervously on his desk as the men gathered around. It grew quiet when he rose to his feet.

"Gentlemen. Together you are responsible for every ship in my command. All of you have fresh recruits, many of them inexperienced soldiers from the army. We currently enjoy a decided advantage over the enemy. But if our supremacy is to continue, through the course of this war, we must all perform at the highest levels. And that is why I called you here today."

The commodore then explained that a very strict regimen of training would be implemented. Over the next two months, June and July, the men would be required to train, continuously. The exercises included the canon crews and those sailors required for the use of springs and ketch anchors. (The use of ketch anchors in conjunction with a series of ropes, enabled a ship to turn on its axis, without benefit of sails. Such a maneuver would allow the vessel to fire both its portside and starboard side artillery. This maneuver could be critical in the height of battle.)

"We will be perfect in the use of springs. Is that understood?" asked McDonough.

The commodore received a chorus of 'aye ayes' in response.

"Every day?" asked Nathan.

"Yes," said Charlie. "The commodore's orders," she added.

Charlie recounted McDonough's orders for both the line crews and the cannon crews.

"I've never seen him so concerned," said Charlie. "I'll be running up and down the hatch, all day."

"Well, there's literally nothing for a surgeon to do when his ship is not engaged," observed Nathan.

"I beg to differ, Dr. Coldwell."

Nathan swiveled in place, looking for the man who contradicted him.

"Dr. John Briggs," said the gentleman, extending his hand and nodding in Charlie's direction.

Charlie excused herself while Nathan inspected his new supervisor. Briggs, despite a receding fore line that reached halfway to the back of his scalp, wore his white sideburns and beard three to four inches long. His bushy eyebrows, with more than a hint of gray, partially obscured a pair of faded blue eyes. The red splotches on his long, thin nose and face, suggested an aversion to the sun.

"Dr. Briggs. I was expecting you," said Nathan. "It would be my pleasure to give you a tour of our operating theater."

Briggs dismissed the offer with a wave of his arm.

"I have accomplished that particular task, already," he said.

Nathan's eyebrows arched. He started to reply, but Briggs interrupted.

"Walk with me, Dr. Coldwell," said Briggs, pointing to the far end of the ship.

Briggs spent the next fifteen minutes interrogating his young charge. He questioned the extent to which Nathan was formally trained and educated. He asked about the precise nature of Nathan's past medical practice and the frequency with which Nathan served in battle. Dr. Briggs also quizzed Nathan on his knowledge of the latest methodologies, with respect to amputations and the treatment of disease. The senior doctor's habit of interrupting Nathan, irritated and unnerved the young surgeon.

"I am of the opinion, Dr. Coldwell, that both your education and experience are limited. But we are at war and your performance, satisfactory or not, will have to suffice," Dr. Briggs announced.

Nathan could feel the heat rise in his cheeks. He came to a halt, watching as Dr. Briggs continued several steps forward.

"Dr. Briggs, I can assure you that . . ."

Nathan never got to finish his sentence. The retreating Dr. Briggs spoke over his shoulder.

"Thank you, Dr. Coldwell. Our discussion has been most

illuminating."

Nathan spun on one heel and stormed off.

The horse ferry ride to Essex, New York, proved the effectiveness of Kai's disguise.

He encountered a series of suspicious stares from the male passengers and frightful looks from the women. The ferry's operator eventually directed him below deck with the animals. After several hours of watching the wheels on the turntable, Kai emerged top side. The contraption, safely docked in the village of Essex, did its job.

The journey on horse-back, from Essex to the village of Plattsburgh, would require an overnight stay. Three different boarding houses refused the "black" man's request for lodgings. In the end, Kai agreed to overnight in a barn. The proprietor of the boarding house charged him the same amount as if he were in a comfortable bed and staying for the morning meal. Kai delighted in the discriminatory treatment, convinced that he would go unrecognized when he rode into Plattsburgh.

The streets and walkways of the village overflowed with soldiers and civilians. Kai could barely navigate his way through the main road, continually giving way to white folks, soldiers, and sailors. He spied a black man, at the local livery, pushing a cart filled with horse manure.

"I ain't never seen so many white folk in one place," said Kai, trying his best to sound like an uneducated black man.

"Theyz gonna be an execution," said the livery worker.

"One of our own or one of them?" asked Kai.

"No suh. Three soldiers. Theyz deserters I think."

Kai trotted on, hoping to reach Cumberland Bay and

McDonough, well before dark.

A mounted soldier, moving at a gallop, used the extra length of his reins, to force Kai out of the way.

"Move it, boy," said the soldier.

Just months ago, such an incident would trigger a nasty confrontation. The aide-de-camp to Commodore McDonough demanded respect from his subordinates and his seniors. Instead, the pretend-black man waited until the angry corporal passed by, turned, and flashed a sparkling- white grin.

Kai forgot about his earlier admonition.

Jim Sharp, frustrated with his slow-moving wife, worried that he might be late for evening roll call on the *Saratoga*.

"Why are you staring?" he asked Adele.

"Did you see that?" she asked.

"Mrs. Sharp pointed at an army corporal galloping down the crowded street.

"Another corporal who thinks he's a general. What's to see?"

"He whipped that black man with his bridle," she replied.

"So?"

Mrs. Sharp explained.

"After he passed, the black man stopped, turned in his saddle, and smiled."

"Adele, we must hurry. Please?"

"I've seen that smile before, Jim. Perfect white teeth," she said, her voice shaking now.

"Adele. Why is this so important?"

"That dark-skinned man was no Negro. That was Kai Bellamy," said Mrs. Sharp, struggling to catch her breath.

"Don't be foolish," said her husband. He's long since left the area."

Mrs. Sharp trembled.

"Jim, I am certain of it. That was Kai. I know it, sure as rain. He's disguised himself."

Jim Sharp grimaced and blew a cloud of imaginary steam from his pursed lips.

"What would you have me do, woman?" he answered.

He grabbed his wife by the elbow and forced the woman to walk on.

"The commodore wishes to see the both of us. Now," Charlie announced.

Nathan scowled and shook his head in anger.

"The good Dr. Briggs has me organizing all of our supplies and medical instruments. And then I'm supposed to clean the entire operating theater," he complained.

"Nathan, the commodore looked especially serious," Charlie replied.

Nathan stopped what he was doing. The midshipmen and the assistant surgeon hurried through the hatch and quick-stepped to the commodore's office chamber.

"Shut the door, please." he directed, without returning their salute.

"Once again, I am loath to discharge even a single man on board this vessel, the shortage of men being that critical," said McDonough, his eyes flashing, first on Charlie and then on Nathan.

"Sir?" asked Nathan.

"On the other hand, I could have both of you court-martialed for sodomy and ruin your lives," he snapped, his voice rising.

Charlie's eyes closed. Her head drooped. She recovered and

turned to Nathan.

"Yesterday. In the storeroom. We were seen," she said softly.

Before Nathan could react, the commodore spoke again, this time a bit less forcefully.

"Yes. You were seen. And the site of two men, in a romantic embrace, is something which will not be tolerated on this ship."

"Yes sir," said Charlie.

Nathan blushed.

"I am very sorry, sir. It is entirely my fault."

McDonough ignored the apology.

"Midshipman Wheeler. I told you before. If word of your true identity should leak out, you will be immediately discharged from the Navy. And it will not be an honorable discharge. Is that understood?"

"Yes sir," said Charlie.

"And you, Dr. Coldwell. Is it possible that you could exercise some restraint?"

"Yes sir," said Nathan, now blushing a bright red.

"We have quite likely not heard the end of this," said McDonough.

"Dismissed."

Adele Sharp, still agitated by her vision of Kai, began to question her own eyes.

She shared the details of her close encounter with Charlie. Charlie reassured Mrs. Sharp that yesterday's fleeting glimpse of the man she saw in the village did not prove that Kai followed the flotilla to Plattsburgh. And even if he did, Kai would not dare to attack the woman, while she worked on the *Saratoga*.

"Charlie, would you come with me while I go to the store

house?" asked Mrs. Sharp.

The two women, perhaps because they were the only two women on board the *Saratoga*, decided to forgive and forget their previous confrontation. Once again, they relied on and confided in each other.

"His smile is hard to forget," said Charlie, guessing that Mrs. Sharp did not wish to leave the *Saratoga* without an escort.

"I'm sorry to bother you, Charlie. You must be exhausted."

Charlie squeezed Adele's hand, as they descended the gangplank that delivered them dockside.

"I am. But it's nothing compared to what you must be going through," said Charlie.

"He attacked you too, Charlie. Aren't you scared?" asked Mrs. Sharp.

Charlie thought for a moment.

"I'm not afraid of Kai, or any other man, for that matter."

She reconsidered her spontaneous bravado.

"Well, the commodore makes me nervous."

Charlie scanned the horizon with narrowing eyes, as if Kai was listening. In truth, she wondered if the acquisition of a sidearm or a knife, would be a good idea. As Mrs. Sharp went about her chores, Charlie's head swiveled in every direction. The shoreline, spotted with buildings, created a countless number of shadows. Kai could be anywhere. When Mrs. Sharp finished, Charlie sighed, her relief, obvious.

They returned to the *Saratoga* in less than an hour. The ladies agreed that their normally uncomfortable hammocks would not prevent some badly needed sleep. Charlie recounted her day with a detailed description of the cannon crews' efforts during marksmanship practice. Her endless trips to the gun powder room left her sore and tired. Mrs. Sharp observed that cleaning dozens of chamber pots had to be the worse job on earth. When the two women finally reached their respective hammocks, the older woman jerked to a stop. Adele blanched white. She used a hand to smother a scream. Adele backed away from her bed and shrieked hysterically. Dozens of sleeping sailors, came running.

"No, no. It can't be," she cried.

There, on each of their beds, lay a single, colorful stone. Each woman instantly recognized the smooth jackstones that Kai considered his most valuable possession. He played the one-handed game, usually by himself, throughout most of his horrible childhood. Charlie held Mrs. Sharp as tight as she could. The woman wailed like an animal caught in a trap. She trembled uncontrollably and crumbled to the floor, forcing Charlie down with her. Charlie cradled the woman's head in her arms, while studying the stones. There could be no doubt.

Kai Bellamy had returned.

Charlie hoped to inform the commodore about Kai, at the first opportunity.

McDonough struggled with other matters. Intelligence reports from trusted sources indicated a massive buildup of men and supplies in Montreal. Estimates of British troop strength now exceeded 14,000 men. By contrast, General Izard, the newly installed replacement for the disgraced General Wilkinson, commanded a mere 5500 regulars. A few hundred militia men, mostly inexperienced locals, rounded out the American army.

Additional reports, received in early June, indicated that the enemy recently began construction of a 32-gun vessel. It would be the largest ever to sail on Lake Champlain. McDonough immediately requested permission to fabricate another brig or schooner. But according to Secretary Jones, the funds required for yet another war ship, did not exist. Jones said no.

"I refuse to believe that we have been abandoned by the Lord Almighty. But His plan for the lot of us, remains a mystery to me," said McDonough.

Charlie, unsure if the commodore's solemn pronouncement required a response, said nothing. Instead, she informed the commodore that a visitor waited for him, just outside the door.

"His name is Mr. Adam Brown," she reported. "He says you were not expecting him," she added.

McDonough's head tilted to one side. His face and eyebrows became a question mark.

"I know Mr. Brown. Show him in. But you are to remain outside the door, in case I need you," he said.

Charlie sat outside for only minutes when she heard McDonough whoop with joy.

"Thank God Almighty," he shouted.

After a full hour of animated conversation, only a portion of which she could discern, Mr. Brown exited the commodore's chamber. Charlie ducked into see if McDonough required anything. She saw a different man behind the commodore's desk.

"Smile, Charlie. My prayers have been answered," said McDonough, grinning from ear to ear.

He reported that President Madison overruled Secretary Jones. McDonough's new vessel would be constructed by mid-August, at the latest.

"Now all we have to worry about is the damnable smuggling," said McDonough.

Chapter Thirteen

SURPRISE MOVES

Adele Sharp paced the floor near her hammock.

"I want to leave. Now," she said.

Jim Sharp sat on the floor, his back to the wall. The man's head jerked up.

"You want me to desert the Navy? Is that what you're saying?"

Mrs. Sharp stopped pacing and fell to her knees in front of the sergeant.

"Jim. He's going to kill us both. We have no choice," she cried.

Jim searched his wife's face.

"I would be willing to speak with the commodore," he said, holding her hands in his.

Adele pulled away and wrung her hands.

"Jim, he's not going to give you permission to desert the Navy. You said so, yourself. He's desperate for every man, and even women, he can get on board this ship."

"But I have to be straight with him," he replied.

Adele rose to her feet, arms folded. She glared down at her husband.

"Like when you released that animal from jail. Were you straight with the commodore then? Were you straight with me?"

Jim studied the floor, unable to look his wife in the eyes. She was right, he thought. None of this would be happening if he had left Kai where he belonged.

"I don't have a choice, do I?" he asked, his voice trembling.

"No, my dear husband. You do not."

"We will leave within the week. When I am next asked to go into the village, you will accompany me," he told her.

"And then what", she asked.

We will not return to the ship."

"You can't be serious," said Nathan.

Charlie did not anticipate Nathan's response to her news. She stepped forward, her flaming eyes drilling into Nathan's face.

"Why? Because I'm a woman? I'm too weak and too stupid to go on such a mission? Is that what you are saying, Nathan?"

Charlie volunteered for a special assignment. The commodore requested volunteers to go north of the line on a search and destroy mission. A number of large masts, thought to be for the enemy's largest war-vessel to date, needed to be located and destroyed.

Nathan could barely control his anger. He flung the carpenter saw he was cleaning, across the room. The wooden handle broke into pieces. The loud noise made Charlie jump. Nathan raised his voice.

"You will all be captured and very likely, hung. Do you understand me, Charlie? No. I will not allow it," he barked.

Charlie stepped back and continue her backward movement until she reached the doorway.

"You what?" she asked.

Nathan did not hesitate.

"I will not allow it," he said, slamming his closed fist on the operating table, for emphasis.

Charlie hissed her response.

"You can go to blazes, Nathan Coldwell."

She slowly walked to the shattered carpenter saw, retrieved the pieces, and carefully placed them on Nathan's operating table. Her eyes flashed with anger. She spoke firmly; her voice dripping with rage.

"A surgeon does not tell a midshipman what to do. And neither does a gentleman tell a grown woman what to do."

Nathan twitched but did not back down.

"When that woman is being foolish, a gentleman has a responsibility to correct her," he yelled.

"Foolish?" she asked.

Nathan leaned forward.

"Yes, Charlie Wheeler. Foolish."

Nathan did not see Charlie's moving hand. The blow caught him entirely by surprise. She slapped his face with such force that a handprint, outlined in hot pink, remained on his cheek. Nathan fell back. Speechless.

Charlie stomped out of the room.

Twenty-one-year-old midshipman, Joel Abbott, would lead the mission north of the line.

After McDonough addressed the small cabal of volunteers, he turned to Abbot.

"Are you ready to die for your country Mr. Abbot?"

"Certainly sir; that is what I came into the service for," he responded.

If caught, Abbot would surely be executed as a spy. On this evening, he wore the uniform of a British officer.

Charlie, along with a handful of other volunteers, did most of the rowing. Their small craft traveled at night, north across the line until they reached Isle aux Noix. The crew waited several hours for Abbott to locate the large-wooden masts. The growing consensus, that Abbot failed in his mission, turned into unbridled joy, when the soaked soldier reappeared. He struggled to breathe.

"I found them. Four spars, one of them big enough for a main mast on a very large frigate," he said.

Charlie knew what came next. She pulled her oar from the water and wrapped the paddle in some oil cloth. The other men followed suit. The crew, about to begin the most dangerous portion of their mission, silently rowed north. Abbot and his colleagues reached the extra-large timbers without incident. They towed the lumber to the broad lake, just south of the line, and cut the masts into pieces. When they returned to the main portion of McDonough's fleet, now anchored at Point au Roche, the men, including Charlie, were too exhausted to climb into the large ships. Each of them required the assistance of several other sailors.

She slept for most of the next day.

Charlie, still white-hot angry with Nathan Coldwell, avoided the ship's surgeon as much as possible.

Instead, she confessed her anger and frustrations to Adele. The older woman seemed sympathetic but showed clear signs of being distracted. After a long soliloquy on the nerve of a man telling any woman what she could and could not do, Charlie waited patiently for the woman's response. Mrs. Sharp, busy stuffing her husband's clothes into a haversack, barely acknowledged the girl.

"Yes dear, I understand," she said.

Charlie, growing increasingly impatient, pressed the matter.

"Do you think I did the right thing, Mrs. Sharp"?

"Did what dear?"

"Mrs. Sharp. You haven't heard a word I've said. Is there something wrong?"

Adele reached for a second haversack, hanging on the wall above her husband's hammock. She slowly placed the backpack on the bed and turned toward Charlie. They were face-to-face, Mrs. Sharp's gaze, solemn and unblinking.

"Charlie. Jim and I have decided to leave," she said.

"Leave? You mean Mr. Sharp has been transferred?" asked Charlie.

"Not exactly."

"It's Kai, isn't it? You're running away. That's it, isn't it?" asked Charlie, yanking the haversack from Mrs. Sharp's hands.

Mrs. Sharp, her eyes downcast, stood silent. Charlie reached for the older woman's shoulders, a hand on each of them.

"Do you understand what you are doing? Jim would be a deserter. We are at war. He could be executed," Charlie said, raising her voice.

Mrs. Sharp returned to the haversack, shoving the couple's limited wardrobe into the leather bag.

"Mrs. Sharp. Did you hear me?" asked Charlie.

The woman hesitated and then jerked her head in Charlie's direction.

"Is it your intention, Midshipman Wheeler, to inform the commodore?"

The girl winced. Adele's use of Charlie's formal title made it clear. The older woman's anger, fear and frustration left her no choice. Charlie did not agree but she understood. She reached for the last pile of clothing on Mrs. Sharp's hammock and handed it to her. A long, almost unbearable, silence enveloped the two women. Charlie spoke first.

"When?" the girl asked.

"Jim goes into town tomorrow. I will accompany him. We will not return," she said, her eyes swollen with tears.

Charlie reached into her pocket, retrieving most of her monthly pay. She shoved the coins into the haversack. Their eyes met.

"Good luck," said Charlie.

Mrs. Sharp, biting her lip, nodded her thanks.

"I want this delivered to the entire fleet, today," said the commodore.

Charlie, with just one communique in hand, would be required to visit each ship in the fleet. She would remain there until the commander of that vessel read McDonough's order. She would then move onto the next war vessel. It would be a long morning, thought Charlie.

By the time she finished her rounds, Charlie understood the substance of McDonough's orders. Reading the directive became unnecessary. The entire fleet would soon travel north to the line and anchor near Isle LaMotte. The decision by McDonough meant that an encounter with the enemy might soon occur. And while Charlie did not relish the thought of armed conflict, she looked forward to visiting her childhood home, once again. The old homestead, long since rented, triggered a rush of memories for Charlie, both good and bad. When she returned to McDonough's chamber, her mission complete, she faced an unexpected interrogation by the commodore.

"Bosun Sharp and his wife have gone missing," said McDonough.

"What, if anything, can you tell me about this?" he asked.

Charlie blew the hair out of her eyes and momentarily looked away. McDonough rolled his eyes.

"There are times, Charlie, when I feel that you are the captain of this fleet, and I am but a midshipman."

Charlie faced the commodore, feeling guilty and turning a slight shade of pink.

"Take a seat, Wheeler. You didn't do anything wrong," said McDonough, waving his hand toward a nearby chair.

"Or did you?"

"No sir, I did nothing wrong, but I think I know why they are missing."

Charlie recounted the incident in the village when Mrs. Sharp claimed to have seen Kai. She then described Mrs. Sharp's hysterical panic when they discovered the jackstones.

"He was on this ship? Kai Bellamy has returned?"

McDonough rose from his chair and began to pace, hands clasped behind his back and studying the floor.

"Yes sir. I'm afraid so," said Charlie.

McDonough twisted in Charlie's direction.

"I refuse to believe that Sergeant Sharp is a deserter," he said.

Charlie searched for the words that would defend, if not protect, her friend.

"Jim wears the uniform of a sailor. His wife does not," she said, her voice soft, her eyes, downcast.

"I think I understand what you are telling me."

Charlie sat in silence. The commodore did the same.

"Why are we moving all these supplies on board the *Saratoga?*" asked the burly sailor.

Charlie, pointed to a number of crates in and around the shoreline warehouse.

"Those too."

She then searched in every direction for earwitnesses.

"Well, the word is out, now," she responded. "The entire fleet is moving north to the line. We are supposed to anchor near Isle LaMotte," she said.

"Why," he asked.

"I don't really know," Charlie lied.

In fact, she overheard a number of conversations between the commodore and his officers. The continued proliferation of smuggling by Americans, made McDonough's intervention necessary. The consensus seemed to be that, but for the smugglers, the British would be unable to build new ships or even feed themselves. The commodore, his patience exhausted, decided to act. Charlie and the sailors continued their laborious task, well into the day. But the unseen eyes that observed their activity and overheard their discussion slowly made his way back to the village.

Kai Bellamy wanted to reach Isle LaMotte before the commodore.

The Sharps, now on the outskirts of Albany, stayed at a cheap hotel, near the Hudson.

The fatigue, or perhaps their decision to abandon the American fleet, triggered an ugly disagreement.

"This was your idea," yelled Jim, slamming his haversack on the floor.

Mrs. Sharp, curled up on the bed in a fetal position, turned her back to her husband. She sobbed loudly and refused to speak.

"Talk to me, woman, or I shall leave you this very moment," he yelled.

She suddenly twisted violently in bed and thrust an accusing finger in his direction.

"Very well. I will talk to you. If you had left that monster behind bars where he belonged, we wouldn't be here. As it is, I still carry the scars of your foolish ideas and unbelievable gullibility," she growled.

"Once again, you wish to live in the past. We agreed to move on with our lives, but you can't do it, can you? This entire episode is going to haunt us for the rest of your life."

Mrs. Sharp sobbed all the louder. Her screams led to a knock on the door.

"Mr. and Mrs. Sharp, we are getting complaints from our other guests," said the desk clerk, through the door.

Mr. Sharp reached for the knob and flung the door open.

"Don't worry, it's going to end right now," he said, retrieving his haversack.

"I'm going back to Plattsburgh where I belong."

Sharp marched out of the room. The desk clerk tiptoed into the room. He repeatedly used a hand to smooth his slicked back hair and beard.

Ma'am, are you going to Plattsburgh, also?

"No. I shall stay here."

"Do you require anything else, ma'am?"

Mrs. Sharp looked up, her tear-stained face, contorted in pain.

"No sir," she said.

Charlie cursed the darkness as she hopped down the hatch and turned toward the large chamber filled with hammocks.

Ironically, the glow of light from under Nathan's closed door, made it less difficult for the exhausted midshipman. As she slow-walked into the chamber, her pathway suddenly lit up.

"Are you still angry with me?"

The voice belonged to Nathan. His outstretched arm held a candle, in its copper holder.

"I'm sore and tired Nathan. Unless you think I am unable to navigate the short trip to my hammock, I intend to go to sleep," she replied.

But she did not move forward. Nathan approached.

"Congratulations. I understand that your mission across the line was most successful," he said.

Charlie paused.

"Thank you, but . . ."

Nathan interrupted.

Charlie jabbed a finger into his chest, her anger rising.

"I am speaking, Dr. Coldwell," she said,

Nathan bit his lip.

Charlie could not remember the last time she experienced such profound anger. Her words came freely, and she spoke with a conviction that occurs only when mind, heart and soul speak as one. The young woman that confronted Nathan Coldwell, no longer resembled the Charlie of the past. The proper use of the English language, taught to her by Reuben Quimby, flowed from her tongue like never before. The death and tragedy in her life, reminded her that who you love could never be as precious as love of self. Beginning today, Charlie Elizabeth Wheeler would no longer doubt her wisdom, her common sense, or her rights and freedoms as an adult woman.

"I thought you were different, Nathan Coldwell. I really did. But you're not. You're just like so many of the other men in my life who think females are stupid. That women can't be trusted to take care of themselves. And that a woman's only purpose in life is to look pretty and do what they are told."

Her angry voice filled the room. Nathan's head drooped. Charlie continued.

"Well, no more, Dr. Coldwell. If you want an obedient servant who has neither the intelligence nor the courage to question you, get yourself a hunting dog."

Charlie stepped forward, blew out Nathan's candle, and disappeared in the darkness.

With his fleet anchored just off the shores of Isle LaMotte, McDonough immediately ordered a series of soundings.

Measurement of the lake's depth at various points, would determine the fleet's precise position at the time of battle. McDonough also ordered his remaining row galleys to patrol the lake, in search of smugglers.

"Sir, permission to join the gunboats patrolling the waters, south of the line," asked Charlie, as she stood in the doorway to the commodore's quarters.

"Why do you want to join the galleys? I don't understand," asked McDonough.

"Midshipman Abbott assembled the same crew that accompanied him across the line," said Charlie.

"I see. A reunion of sorts."

"Yes, sir."

"And he requested you?" asked McDonough.

"Yes, sir, but I was told to get your blessing first."

"You have my approval, Charlie. But remember, confronting a smuggler is also a very dangerous mission."

Charlie nodded her understanding. But she, more than most,

understood the dangers of smuggling on Lake Champlain.

The row galley, captained by Joel Abbot, left the Vermont shore early the next morning.

Row galleys, also known as gun boats, could be as long as seventy-five feet and fifteen feet wide. Although some included a small sail, most were propelled by men with oars, up to forty of them. Each row galley came with one, possibly two, small, artillery pieces and, depending on the number of oarsmen, could move with great speed. They also navigated with no difficulty, in waters as shallow as two feet.

Charlie looked forward to the adventure but soured on the trip when she first boarded the vessel. In the back of the gunboat, sat the overweight man who interrupted the romantic moment with Nathan. And judging from the snarly look he gave her, Charlie did not expect the seaman to be quiet, much less discreet. It would be a long day, she thought.

Several vessels, heading north on the lake, prompted the row galley to pull alongside and inspect the occupants' cargo. Most of the rafts carried food stuffs and limited amounts of pot ash. One raft transported lumber. Although the others were turned away with a warning, the smuggler carrying lumber, received an escort to the customs building at Windmill Point.

As the row galley negotiated the choppy waters, a long raft appeared on the horizon. Abbot made good use of his spyglass. The occupant carried no cargo.

"A black man alone on a raft," said Abbot, repeatedly eyeing the vessel with his spyglass.

Charlie strained to see what Abbot described. She recognized the man's form, his silhouette, and the way he moved. She jumped to her feet.

"Mr. Abbot, I know that man," she shouted.

"Do you like black men too?" growled the chubby sailor.

But Charlie did not respond to the voice behind her. Her eyes focused on the raft. The angry sailor persisted.

"I saw him hugging the ship's doctor," he yelled.

Charlie screamed at the top of her lungs.

"I know that man. He's wanted for murder and for assaulting a woman. And he's a deserter. That's Kai Bellamy. He's changed his appearance, but I'm sure of it. After him. Now," she ordered.

She spoke with authority and no one thought to question her directive. Kai's raft, using the channel's northerly flow, enjoyed a sizeable head start. The fugitive from justice rowed like his life depended on it. And it did. The row galley, despite its compliment of twenty muscular sailors, paddled in vain. The race did not take long. Kai easily reached the boundary line, while the galley trailed several hundred yards behind. Abbot ordered the men to stop rowing. Charlie slammed her oar on the bench.

Kai turned and deliberately flashed his trademark smile.

When Charlie disembarked from the row galley, she made it a point to accompany Joel Abbot.

"Thank you, Mr. Abbot, for at least giving chase."

Abbot nodded but stopped and put his hand on Charlie's shoulder.

"What is Mcfeely talking about?" he asked.

"Who is Mcfeely? asked Charlie.

"The big guy in the back of the row galley. You don't know him?"

"No sir. Was he with us when we crossed the line?" asked Charlie.

"No. I needed two more men to round out the crew today. Mcfeely volunteered," said Abbot.

"I've seen him once or twice before. But I have no idea what he's talking about," Charlie lied.

Abbot shrugged his shoulders.

"None of my concern," he said, and walked on.

When Kai crossed the line, the Richelieu River narrowed.

Within minutes, he found himself surrounded by three British patrols, two gunboats, and three more men on a raft.

"Where are you going, boy?" asked a British corporal.

"I am a deserter from the American Navy and I wish to speak with your commanding officer," said Kai, standing erect and furiously wiping the blacking from his face.

The corporal watched, as Kai licked his fingers and rubbed the exposed skin, with only marginal success.

"You trying to be a white man?" asked the corporal.

"I was the aid-de-camp to Commodore McDonough. I have critical intelligence that would be of great value to the British military. I demand to speak with your superiors, immediately," Kai said, wagging a finger at the corporal.

The corporal bowed low and then turned to his crew.

"Did you hear that, men? The slave boy demands to see our superiors," said the corporal, a sneer on his face.

The soldiers laughed. When the British officer jerked his head toward Kai, several of the men jumped on board Kai's raft. They rushed Kai before the deserter could retrieve the knife, strapped to his waist. The men grabbed Kai by the arms and flung him into the water.

"Take the raft," said the corporal.

Kai choked on several mouthfuls of water and yelled at the departing patrol.

"You ignorant fools. I am Kai Bellamy, Commodore McDonough's personal aide."

The British soldiers said nothing and disappeared over the horizon. Kai slapped at the water and kicked his legs until he reached the shoreline.

It would be a long walk to Rouse's point, most of it, through a swamp.

In the weeks following his arrival at Isle LaMotte, Commodore McDonough cemented his relationship with the businessman who supplied food for the fleet.

The commodore dined at the home of Caleb Hill and regularly visited Hill's tavern. On one occasion, Caleb Hill seemed particularly upset and raised his voice while speaking to the commodore.

"With respect, Commodore, if you are unable to control your men, I am left with no alternative but to have then arrested."

McDonough's eyes closed. He bowed his head, and raised his hands, palms facing Hill.

"My friend, listen to me, please. These marauding sailors, even if under my command, must be caught in the act," said McDonough. "Otherwise, there is nothing I can do."

Charlie recalled snippets of previous conversations when Hill described the vandalism, thievery and disturbances, caused by American sailors. The cabal, four to five men, came onto the island in the late hours of the evening. They stole chickens, raided households, and generally took whatever they wanted. They often told their victims that the U.S. Navy was entitled to "requisition" such items. Hill, his patience exhausted, announced a new strategy.

"I will confront these men, myself. And I trust, Commodore McDonough, that you will discipline them accordingly."

"You have my word, Mr. Hill."

After a long day at the general store, followed by a busy evening at his tavern, Caleb Hill crawled into bed.

As he lay there, contemplating tomorrow's chores, he heard a noise in the kitchen. He and his son, Arthur, arrived in the front room at the same time.

"We are English soldiers and you will tell us everything you know about McDonough's fleet, said a sailor, brandishing a sword.

Several of the men, armed with pistols, glared at Caleb Hill and his son. No one wore a British uniform. Caleb recognized the men. The very same vandals plundered his neighbor's home, just last week. Those thieves managed to escape, but not before they were seen. Caleb reached for his musket. Two of the sailors pointed their flintlock pistols. A third sailor reached for his sword. Caleb's son stepped forward, unarmed. The swordsman sliced at the young man's face. Arthur moaned and cupped his cheek. Blood spurted between his fingers and dripped to the floor. One of the pistols, clicked harmlessly. The cold, wet weather rendered the gunpowder useless. The second pistol did not suffer from the same problem. Caleb Hill took a ball in the chest. The explosion sent him crashing into the wall. He fell to the floor, his eyes wide open in a blank stare. Caleb Hill died instantly.

When the American sailors realized the extent of their carnage, they panicked. As they ran back to their ship, a breathless voice in the dark, complained to their ringleader.

"Why'd you go and shoot him?"

"Shut up, Mcfeely, or I'll shoot you next."

Several weeks later, Charlie escorted Caleb Hill's son, Arthur, into the commodore's office chamber.

The son, recently promoted to his late father's rank, as captain of the local Vermont Militia, stood in front of McDonough's desk.

"Captain Hill, please accept my apologies and deepest condolences on the loss of your father," said the commodore.

Hill executed a formal bow. McDonough motioned to a nearby chair and immediately proceeded to the business at hand.

"We have identified and captured all five sailors, Captain Hill. They will be court-martialed and punished."

"Forgive me, commodore, but punishing the perpetrators will not make my family whole," said Hill.

"I am unsure as to your meaning," McDonough replied.

"You moved your entire fleet to Chazy Landing the day after my father was killed. You now source your foodstuffs, elsewhere. Am I to assume that my family is being punished for the tragedy they have suffered?" asked Hill.

"Captain Hill, I position my fleet to maximize its effectiveness, when under attack. Our soundings in Blanchard Bay revealed deficiencies which could not be overcome," said McDonough. "The move to Chazy landing had nothing to do with your father's tragic murder," said McDonough, firm but polite.

"I have no choice but to accept your word as an officer and a gentleman," said Hill.

Hill studied the commodore. McDonough did not flinch. A long silence ensued. Charlie fidgeted in her chair at the far end of the room. McDonough rose to his feet.

"Thank you, Captain Hill."

The commodore, hands clasped behind his back, looked down at his guest.

Captain Hill rose to his feet and glared at the commodore through eyes that mimicked slits.

"Commodore."

Charlie rushed to open the door as Hill marched out.

"Did you hear the news?"

Nathan's happy voice stopped Charlie, as she climbed the topside ladder. She refused to turn around but stopped in mid-step.

"What is it you want, Nathan. I have a great deal of work to do today."

Nathan tugged at her elbow. She stepped backward, pivoted, and glared when Nathan came into view.

"That fellow who saw us in the storeroom—Mcfeely. He's one of the sailors facing court martial, said Nathan, an excited smile on his face.

"I know that," said Charlie, her voice a monotone.

The smile on Nathan's face flattened into a straight line.

"Charlie, for how long will this childish behavior continue?"

Charlie bit her lower lip and squeezed both hands into fists. She stepped forward, her eyes slicing into Nathan's face. Nathan stepped back.

"I am not a child, Nathan Coldwell."

Charlie stopped and scanned their surroundings. Her barely audible voice did not disguise the girl's anger.

"I am a grown woman and you would do well to remember that fact."

Nathan studied the ceiling.

"Did you hear me, Nathan?"

"Yes ma'am," he said, his voice soft and tentative.

"Very well, then," said Charlie, turning to the ladder and disappearing from view.

"You are requested to join us at table, this evening."

Charlie beamed her gratitude. The commodore's invitation to join him and his officers at a formal dinner came as a surprise. She learned that McDonough would host two, young men, recent graduates of Yale, as a favor to one of the commodore's Burlington friends. It promised to be a delightful affair. The ship's officers would be in full regalia and the menu far superior to a midshipman's daily fare.

Joseph Dulles and his classmate, James Potter, could barely hide their excitement when they first boarded the *Saratoga,* late that afternoon. As their escort until dinner, Charlie's task was to keep the guests occupied and entertained. At one point, she suggested that the young men observe the crew as it furled and unfurled the sails. The ship's crew did this so as to dry the canvas. The exercise also demonstrated the precise teamwork required of experienced sailors. With nothing more than a series of hand signals, the deck suddenly grew noisy. Dozens of men scurried in every direction. They pulled on ropes, climbed mastheads, and worked as one, to accomplish their task. A few more hand signals, and every two-masted brig in the fleet, replicated the *Saratoga's* maneuver. The sight of an entire flotilla engaged in such maneuvers, proved nothing short of spectacular When the exercise ended, the ship took on an almost ghostly silence.

Their mouths still agape, Charlie pointed to the ship's railing.

"Let me introduce you to Commodore McDonough," she said.

The entire crew stood at attention and saluted their leader.

After a moment, McDonough approached his visitors. As they entered the dining area, there too, every man in the room, stood and saluted. The two guests were seated at the center of the table, opposite Charlie. Commodore McDonough, at the head of the table, gently motioned with his raised hand. Immediately, the room grew silent. Charlie pretended to cough and used her eyes to warn the two guests. Bowed heads meant that grace would soon be given.

Charlie failed to notice one of the attendees until the main course arrived. Nathan Coldwell sat at the far end of the table, enjoying an animated conversation with Dr. Briggs. The distance between her and Nathan, along with the menu of roast pig, fried fish, dessert with blackberries and Port wine, made it easy to ignore the man she once called a friend.

After dinner, Charlie assumed her usual perch on a stack of crates in the bow of the ship. She studied the shimmering reflection of a full moon on Lake Champlain. Although no one on board knew of the milestone, Charlie celebrated her eighteenth birthday, just a week earlier. Tonight's feast was a celebration of that event, she thought. The girl contemplated her new life in the navy, grateful for the kind-hearted men in her life, like her father, Reuben Quimby, and the commodore. She winced when images of Otis and Jim Sharp floated through her thoughts. She scowled angrily when the perfect smile of Kai Bellamy flashed in her mind. And when Nathan's look of arrogant condescension reappeared, Charlie fought to maintain her composure.

"I thought I'd find you here."

Charlie dabbed at her eyes and twisted to see the man who interrupted her time alone.

"Dr. Coldwell," she said, unsmiling.

"Did you enjoy your dinner?" he asked.

"Yes, very much so," she answered, turning her back on the man.

Nathan shifted from one foot to the other. The awkward silence seemed to make him fidget all the more. Charlie spoke first, still talking to the open lake.

"You came all the way out here to ask me if I enjoyed my dinner?"

Nathan took a deep breath.

"No, Charlie. I wanted to speak with you."

"I have no interest in listening to another one of your condescending lectures," she said, pleased that her anger had such a positive effect on her language skills.

Nathan approached the crate and stood in front of her. He stood in silence until she looked up.

"For some time, now, I have refrained from the consumption of alcohol. And I am much the better for it. And while I can easily tolerate the absence of rum, I am not at all sure that I can tolerate your absence."

Charlie turned away to hide her startled face. Nathan continued.

"My words of the past have offended you. And rightfully so. I wish to formally apologize and beg your forgiveness," said Nathan, running fingers through his hair and biting his lip.

Charlie refused to look at him. She doubted Nathan's sincerity and remained angry with him, heartfelt apology or not. A snide comment about the stubbornness of men rose in her throat but she swallowed the words. She persisted in her silence. Nathan's head drooped. He turned to leave. For some reason, she did not want their conversation to end that way.

"I'm still angry with you, Mr. Coldwell."

Nathan stood motionless.

"I know. I'm angry with myself," he said.

"I don't understand."

Nathan looked for anyone within earshot.

"Charlie, you are unlike any woman that I have ever met in the past."

"Is that supposed to be a compliment?" asked Charlie, still suspicious of the doctor's sincerity.

"Yes. It is the highest compliment I can give you."

He went onto explain that for all of his adult life, women were treated as no more than the accessories of life, by their husbands, their adult sons, their friends and their acquaintances. Nathan's voice trembled with emotion.

"I learned by their example, Charlie. But I learned all of the wrong things."

Charlie's heart pounded in her chest.

"I make no excuses but I am entitled to an explanation. I was never taught to treat a woman as my equal. And then you came along. When you were a boy, I loathed you because I was attracted to you. When you revealed your true identity, I no longer loathed you. I was afraid of you," he said.

Charlie challenged him again.

"Because I am your equal?

"No, Charlie."

The girl frowned.

"Because you are better than my equal," said Nathan.

Charlie rose to her feet. She couldn't believe what she just heard. Nathan went on.

"You are so smart, Charlie, and I don't mean book smart. My brain is filled with the stuff of medical journals. But I know a fraction of what you know, about a man's heart and soul. You are kind and generous and loving. Even to underserving men like me," Nathan said, his voice soft, his eyes moist with tears. "And you are the bravest woman I know," he added, biting his lower lip as several tears escaped and ran down his cheeks.

Charlie trembled. Her voice choked with emotion. She used the sleeve of her fine, blue jacket and wiped at the tears that streaked both cheeks.

"You have accomplished the impossible, Dr. Coldwell. I am without words," she said.

"I'm not finished," he answered, his voice stronger and more determined.

She panicked, thinking that his next words might erase all of those perfect words.

"My heart is full, Nathan Coldwell. You need say nothing more."

"But I must," he said.

"What is it?"

"I love you, Charlotte Wheeler."

Mrs. Sharp refused to leave the boarding house.

Several days later, when her husband did not return to the room, she went in search of him. Adele did not believe that Jim Sharp would abandon his wife in a strange city. The Albany streets overflowed with pedestrians, riders on horseback, and wagons, loaded with cargo. The noise and bustle aggravated and flustered Mrs. Sharp. She missed the quiet beauty that characterized the village of Plattsburgh.

Her first stop, at the General Store, yielded nothing. The proprietor did not recall seeing a man that fit Jim Sharp's description. Mrs. Sharp left for her next destination, the local livery. She and her husband used a ferry plus a crude two-horse stage, to reach Albany. Jim Sharp may have returned to Plattsburgh in the same way but he more than likely leased a horse. When she walked further down the street, she noticed a black man following her. He wore a straw hat and a dusty brown jacket. Mrs. Sharp refused to take another step, staring at the negro as he approached. The man flashed a big smile and tipped his hat. Mrs. Sharp screamed. The black man turned and looked. No one walked behind him. He turned back to Mrs. Sharp, a quizzical look on his face. Her screams grew louder. She jumped off the boardwalk and into the street. People on both sides of the road stopped and stared. Mrs. Sharp didn't see the fast-moving, horse-drawn wagon. The dark-skinned man with the straw hat tried to warn her. Several women screamed. They looked away as the horse's hooves landed their blows. One of the wagon wheels crushed her chest. The crumpled heap lay motionless in the mud. The driver pulled his animals to a halt. The black man with the hat came running, as did several other witnesses.

"Do you know her?" asked someone.

"No," said the man, his hat in one hand, as he gingerly examined the injured woman.

"She's dead," he said.

"I know you, don't I?" asked one of the witnesses.

The dark-skinned man answered.

"My name is Andrew Cockburn. I help Mr. Brumfield at his general store.

Cockburn removed his jacket and covered the body.

"I'll get the sheriff."

Kai reached Rouse's point, as the sun set, on the day of his encounter with British patrols.

He wandered the streets of Rouse's point for most of the next day. An army crew, busy at the docks, inspired a plan to reach Plattsburgh.

"I wuz hopin ta inlist in da ahmy," said Kai, utilizing his best uneducated black man's accent.

The handful of soldiers, loading a row galley, looked at each other and grinned.

"We got a bunch of blackies, digging trenches near the bay," said an older soldier.

"I sho could use a ride," said Kai.

One of the men objected.

"Now just hold on a minute, we ain't no passenger ferry," he complained to the senior man.

The older soldier shook his head and turned to Kai.

"Help us load the rest of the crates," he said. "And you can sit over there," he added, pointing to the bow of the boat.

Kai forced a smile.

"Yes, suh. Thank you, suh."

McDonough moved his flotilla from Chazy to Cumberland head, in early September.

When the *Saratoga* approached its mooring, Charlie noticed a new vessel in the water. Commodore McDonough returned the salute of an officer, standing on the new brig's deck.

"She's a fine brig, don't you think, Charlie?" he said, never taking his eyes off the new ship.

"Yes sir. Looks brand spanking new," she said.

"It is," he replied. "And I shall call her the *Eagle,*" said McDonough.

He explained the *Eagle's* recent and very rapid construction to Charlie. The commodore used words she never heard of much less understood. He also confessed his serious concern about manpower shortages.

"We will soon have the machinery of war but lack the manpower with which to operate it."

The commodore's dissertation ended when a young sailor interrupted. The boy carried a message.

"For you, Commodore."

McDonough opened the note immediately. The color drained from his face. He shook his head slowly from side to side. Charlie caught his eyes.

"Something wrong, sir?" she asked.

"The enemy launched their newest ship of war two days ago," he announced. "Twice as many guns and a third larger than the *Eagle*."

When Kai reached his destination, dozens of black men came into view.

They dug a deep trench and piled the dirt, rocks, and debris into a berm on one side of the ditch.

"You there. Grab a shovel. And why ain't you in uniform?"

The burly sergeant stood at least a foot taller than Kai. Not waiting for a response, he shoved the young man toward a newly started trench.

"You don't understand. I have not yet enlisted," said Kai, slipping back into a refined use of the English language.

The sergeant backhanded Kai with enough force to send the young man falling backwards into the trench.

"I said get to work, you black bastard, or I'll shoot you dead where you stand." barked the sergeant.

Kai wiped the blood from his lip and reached for a shovel.

Jim Sharp spent the better part of a week, on the trail to Plattsburgh.

He cringed when he thought of Mrs. Sharp, alone in her room at the Albany boarding house. The guilt which plagued him, however, would not be eliminated by remaining in Albany. In his mind, deserting one's spouse paled in significance when compared to deserting the United States Navy. His eyes moistened when he thought of the commodore, who never objected to bringing a woman on board. Sharp dreaded his anticipated meeting with McDonough.

Sharp entered the village proper with great difficulty. The street, clogged with civilians, could hardly be navigated. The people led horses and wagons loaded with personal possessions. The masses headed south, in search of safety. Several of the evacuees warned Sharp as he rode against the tidal wave of humanity.

"You're headed the wrong way, Mister. The British have crossed the line. They'll be here in a few days," said one old man.

Sharp continued on his way. More than 100 homes dotted the landscape in the village of Plattsburgh. Stores, shops and a handful of hotels, made the village a pleasant place in which to live. But not today. Almost all of its 3000 residents decided to abandon their homes. What Jim Sharp saw most, in the streets of Plattsburgh, could best be described as fear. Unbridled, frenzied fear.

No one stopped him or even made an inquiry, as the former bosun boarded the *Saratoga* and approached McDonough's chamber. Soldiers and sailors scurried on the deck like rats on a sinking ship.

"Excuse me, sir, I would like to meet with the commodore," said Sharp.

He should have recognized Charlie, even with her back turned, but the purpose of his visit, proved too powerful a distraction. Charlie spun around. She rushed forward and hugged her old friend.

"Jim."

"Is the commodore in?" asked Sharp.

"No," said Charlie. "But I expect him very soon. He went on shore to a meeting, with General Macomb, I believe."

Sharp stood there in silence, scanning the entire deck. A man returning to his childhood home, after decades away, felt the same way, he thought.

"Mrs. Sharp?" asked Charlie.

The deserter studied the deck and slowly shook his head.

"She's in Albany," he mumbled.

Charlie smoothed her uniform.

"Do you think he'll take me back?" asked Sharp.

"The commodore is desperate," said Charlie. "We are short of men on all the brigs and the row galleys too."

Sharp recalled that McDonough was a devout Episcopalian. Perhaps the commodore would grant the deserter some measure of leniency and forgiveness.

"Bosun Sharp."

Jim and Charlie snapped to attention. The commodore, approaching from behind, caught both of them by surprise. McDonough inspected his absentee bosun, as if seeing Sharp for the first time. He spoke in even tones.

"You are no longer a Bosun's Mate. You are henceforth a first-year seaman. You will no longer be allowed the privilege of a wife on board this ship. You will report to the *Allen*, today. Is that understood, Seaman Sharp?"

McDonough elongated both syllables in the word, 'seaman' to

ensure that Sharp understood the reduction in rank. Sharp blinked, uncertain if he should be pleased or apologetic.

"Aye, sir."

But McDonough continued, his eyes flashing.

"And if we survive this war, Mr. Sharp, I will see to it that you are punished for your desertion."

"You are dismissed," said McDonough, as he marched into his chamber.

Charlie walked with Sharp to the gangplank.

"Did you come through the village?" she asked.

"Yes. It's a sad and terrible sight to behold."

Charlie repeated what she heard in McDonough's countless meetings with naval staff and army officers.

"The British have crossed the line and are in Champlain as we speak. There are reports that much of the British Navy is now at anchor in the lower Richelieu. They are within hours of Plattsburgh."

"May the good Lord protect us all," whispered Sharp.

"One more thing," said Charlie.

"What?"

The British invaded Washington last week. The Executive Mansion, the White House?"

"Yes. What of it?"

"Burned to the ground."

Jim bit his lip and walked slowly to the shoreline.

After practicing with the crew of the *Allen*, rowing, navigating and firing its two artillery pieces, Jim spent most of his spare time alone in his tent. He missed the *Saratoga*, the camaraderie of the crew and the companionship of his wife. He thought often of

Adele, wondering if she continued to see Kai Bellamy under every bed and around every street corner. He tried to shake such thoughts from his head because they also made him angry and bitter.

"Jim Sharp?"

The voice belonged to an enlisted man, caring a small stack of letters. Jim did not bother to rise from his cot.

"Yeah. What do you want?" he asked. The man stepped forward, handing Sharp an envelope.

The letter, addressed simply to 'Jim Sharp, Plattsburgh', did not reveal the sender. Only after opening the missive did Sharp discover its origin. The Albany County sheriff tracked Sharp to Plattsburgh after talking to the hotel clerk. When he finished reading the note, Jim crushed the paper into a tight ball and flung it at the canvas wall. He sat on the edge of the bed with his head in his hands.

And he wept.

Chapter Fourteen

THE BATTLE OF PLATTSBURGH

"We move into the bay, tomorrow."

McDonough's pronouncement came during an officers' meeting. Despite her years of experience on the lake, Charlie listened with fascination. The naval officers discussed where and how their confrontation with the British Navy would take place. McDonough calculated that the shifting currents in Plattsburgh Bay would confuse and impede the enemy's ships

The commodore's plan, to draw the enemy into the bay, would also eliminate the advantage of British artillery. Intelligence sources reported that British guns could reach distances much greater than the American artillery pieces. And finally, the narrowness of the bay would limit the maneuverability of the much larger British vessels. McDonough would entice the British by positioning his fleet one hundred yards offshore. The flotilla would be just out of range of the enemy's land-based artillery.

"This just arrived," said Charlie, handing the commodore a handwritten note from the army, as the meeting adjourned.

After reading the missive, he folded the paper, taking care to utilize the same creases. But it wasn't the paper that consumed his thinking, thought Charlie. She recognized that deadly serious look of concern.

"Commodore?" asked Charlie.

He looked north, over the choppy waters of Lake Champlain.

"The British now occupy Isle LaMotte. We must prepare for battle, Midshipmen Wheeler,"

"Your assistance is requested to aid in the evacuation of the sick and make preparations on the island," said the orderly.

Nathan listened as the soldier explained that General Macomb decided to evacuate the sick and injured soldiers. They would be moved from Plattsburgh Bay to Crab Island. The much-anticipated battle of Plattsburgh would soon commence.

How many men?" asked Nathan.

"A little more than 700, sir."

Before Nathan could react, Dr. Briggs appeared in the doorway.

"You have received the news, Dr. Coldwell?"

"Yes, Dr. Briggs."

"The commodore approved the army's request but we must return to the ship within forty-eight hours," Briggs announced.

Nathan followed Briggs, topside, to the gangplank. He caught a glance of Charlie as she exited McDonough's quarters. Nathan told Briggs he would catch up. The young couple paused in their duties, an entire deck between them. Their eyes locked. Both of them stood motionless, as if seeing each other for the last time. Nathan wanted to wave, but a sign of cheer at a time of fear, seemed inappropriate. They would soon be in battle. They might be injured or worse. Nathan, less likely to be hurt or killed, thought only of Charlie. She would be topside, in the midst of endless cannon fire. He might never see her again.

Charlie acknowledged Nathan with a quick nod. But Nathan's angst did not evaporate. Neither did the tears in his eyes, despite the stiff breeze. He wanted to tell her, just one more time, how much he loved her. But that would not be possible. Not then. Not there. And suddenly, it occurred to him. Charlie wanted love but she demanded respect. Respect from the people in her life, male or female, but especially from the men in her life. Nathan pushed the sadness in his heart to the back of his mind. He stood as tall and straight as he possibly could. He slowly raised his right hand, fingers and thumb in the required position, holding the salute for several long seconds. He didn't expect Charlie to formally acknowledge the salute. He prayed that she understood his gesture.

For one brief moment, the girl maintained her composure. Seconds later, Charlie's tear-stained face twisted into a distorted smile. Her shoulders heaved and her head drooped.

She wept with joy.

Kai, fuming about his circumstances, leaned into the shovel.

Forts Brown, Moreau, and Scott appeared unworthy of their designation as forts. In fact, they would be very effective when the land battle commenced. Their walls consisted of trenches surrounded with dirt berms, as high as the trenches were deep. Piles of felled trees, sharpened to a point, and placed at steep angles in the ground, reinforced the dirt walls. The walls surrounded hundreds of soldiers plus eight to twelve artillery pieces, in each bastion.

"You ain't no black man. Youz just pretendin," said the large, dark soldier next to Kai in the trench.

Kai's accuser wore no shirt. His chest and arms rippled with muscles. Kai said nothing and resumed his backbreaking labor.

"Ize talkin to you, white boy," said the oversized brute.

In his previous life, Kai commanded the respect of such men. The memory of those days triggered an angry and foolish reaction in the boy. Both of his hands slid to the top of his farm implement. He stood to his full height and swung hard in the direction of his accuser. The forged blade of his shovel missed its mark. Instead, the seasoned soldier blocked the blow with his own spade. Kai stared in disbelief, dumbfounded by the man's raw strength. The boy tried to duck when he saw the man's shovel rise in the air. The blade struck Kai in the head.

The black man's angry face would be the last image in Kai's mind, before he fell, unconscious.

Many of the men in the *Allen*, knew Jim Sharp.

They deferred to their new mate, often calling Sharp by his previous title. The gunboat's commander, Sailing Master William Robbins, positioned Sharp in the bow of the boat. He expected Sharp to assist with navigation. Although humbled by his new assignment, Sharp anticipated that the *Allen* and McDonough's remaining gunboats, approximately ten, would inflict great damage on the British fleet. Although British ships did not yet approach the bay at Plattsburgh, the enemy's land forces marched well within range of McDonough's row galleys.

"We have orders to engage the enemy," said Robbins. "Prepare to get underway."

Nathan seemed to be every place at once.

Several trips to and from Crab Island, all the while assisting the seriously ill, left him exhausted and out of breath.

"You've got another one," said Briggs, pointing to a litter.

The crude litters, made with the canvas of leftover sails, featured the bloodstains and grime from previous battles. But they performed as needed. Nathan trudged to the patient's side.

"He's still bleeding. What happened to him?"

No one answered Nathan's inquiry. The injured man's face, covered with blood, could hardly be seen. A large gash near the man's hairline, oozed dark-red blood at an alarming rate. Nathan reached for a much-used, bloodstained rag, left behind by an ambulatory patient. He pressed the material on the man's wound and tied the compress in place, with a leather strap. The strap, donated without objection by a nearby corpse, performed as expected.

"He goes to Crab Island," said Nathan, pointing to the litter but getting the attention of a nearby private.

Crab Island now featured makeshift hospitals, to shelter the sick and injured. Although the two, large tents accomplished nothing more than protection from the elements, the patients and their caregivers did not complain. The canvas structures would also serve as operating theaters, should additional casualties of war be delivered to the island. Ambulatory patients, instructed to assist the doctors, learned of an additional assignment.

Ensconced on the island's shoreline, and somewhat hidden in the underbrush, lay two 6-pounder artillery pieces.

When the *Allen* and its sister galleys, rowed within range, they commenced firing on British land troops.

The enemy, now at Dead Creek, (Scomotion Creek), just north of the village, found themselves under heavy fire. Musket fire from the village and artillery fire from the lake inflicted significant damage to British ranks. The rainstorm of musket fire and grape shot forced the British to fall back, but not for long. The enemy, making good use of their own artillery and vast numbers, set their sights on land targets but also on McDonough's gun boats.

Sailing Master Robbins barked a series of orders, to ensure that both of his artillery pieces repeatedly fired at the British. All of the row galleys, now under heavy fire from the onshore batteries, did the same. No one noticed that the commodore's flagship posted signal flags, ordering the galleys back to the main fleet. Jim Sharp, aware of the killed and wounded on several other galleys, did notice a gig (a small rowboat) headed in their direction. Sharp pointed.

"Mr. Robbins, look."

The gig belonged to the *Saratoga*.

"It's Duncan," said Robbins, "and he's shot up pretty bad."

In fact, Silas Duncan took a direct hit from a British cannonball. His right shoulder, including the bones and muscles, disappeared. Bleeding profusely and barely able to row his boat, Duncan delivered the commodore's message.

"The commodore says you are to return to your positions, with the fleet. Immediately."

The *Allen*, as the first boat in the line of row galleys, passed the message along. Jim Sharp didn't wait for Robbins' actual command. The former bosun steered and rowed in the direction of the *Saratoga*. Volley after volley, from British land-based cannon, splashed in the water on both sides of the gunboat. It took more than ten minutes for the row galleys to travel beyond the range of British guns.

On September 7th, McDonough ordered his ships, currently in the bay, to anchor in a straight line.

Their formation, from slightly southwest to the northeast, positioned the *Eagle,* north most, followed by the *Saratoga,* the *Ticonderoga* and the *Preble.* The row galleys would take positions between the shoreline and the larger American ships.

"Your new recruits are prisoners?"

Commodore McDonough could not hide his shock. He learned from the Commander of the *Eagle,* First Lieutenant Joseph Smith, that forty new recruits recently joined the lieutenant's crew. Smith explained that Army General Macomb refused to release to the navy any more men from his understaffed regiments. He invited Smith to visit the local jail. Smith "liberated" forty of the prisoners, all ex-army soldiers. The men, previously assigned to digging trenches, welcomed their new assignment. After a bath, a shave, and a haircut, the men were released from their manacles and issued clean uniforms. They were now sailors. McDonough shook the lieutenant's hand.

"And their training?" he asked.

"All day, every day," said Smith.

The good news lightened McDonough's heavy heart. As he surveyed the mile-long string of American war vessels, in Plattsburgh Bay, he contemplated the horrible battle which lay ahead. No one would be spared from the terrible sights and sounds of war. Water-borne vessels, designed to rain death and destruction on their opponents, did not discriminate between young and old, male and female or the evil and the righteous. No one could guarantee their survival.

Everyone would look death in the face.

Charlie spotted the red ensign of old England, flying high atop the *Confiance,* even before the British flotilla rounded the Cumberland peninsula.

When the commodore realized that the battle would soon commence, he removed his hat, fell to his knees and bowed in prayer. The crew did the same. Charlie heard the commodore as he beseeched the Lord to *"take the cause into thine own hand and judge between us and our enemies."* Charlie squeezed her eyes shut and asked her papa to put in a good word with the Lord Almighty.

Charlie clutched the commodore's spy glass while he conferred with the ship's lieutenant. She observed several hundred people gathered on the western shore of Cumberland Head. Spectators, she concluded, and her stomach churned. McDonough reached for the spyglass and Charlie assumed her post, near the hatch. Her access to the below-deck powder magazine, would be quick and easy. She practiced the entire exercise, cannister in hand, at least a hundred times. Charlie did it in her sleep. Literally. The canister she held, would be the first shot fired in the battle of Plattsburgh. That honor would go to the commodore.

"There," shouted McDonough.

More than 800 sets of eyes, from a variety of American war vessels, studied the *Confiance,* as the largest ship on Lake Champlain, led the British armada to McDonough's flotilla. The one hundred forty-seven-foot vessel, carrying thirty-seven guns, experienced some difficulty in traversing the bay, just as McDonough predicted. The sporadic winds and baffling currents made its short journey to the *Saratoga* painstakingly slow. The large brig arrived with several escorts.

The first British vessel to sail within range of the American fleet, the *Linnet,* passed the *Saratoga,* intent on sailing further north. On her way by, she leveled a thunderous broadside. Most of her fusillade fell short, and the Saratoga suffered only minor damage. One small projectile, after whistling over Charlie's head, struck the corner of the *Saratoga's* hanging chicken coop. The wooden cage fell to the deck and shattered. Its occupant, a large rooster, began to crow and wildly flap its wings. The angry bird eventually discovered a perch in one of the ship's masts. No one suffered an injury. Everyone laughed uproariously, interpreting the incident as a good omen.

After the *Linnet,* came the *Confiance.* The large frigate, still struggling to reach its desired position, sailed within range of the commodore's favorite artillery piece. He nodded to Charlie. She handed her canister to the crew chief. The cartridge, once loaded, required a number of sharp thrusts with a ramming rod. A large cannonball, followed by a piece of wadding, completed the combination. The gun, some six feet from its port, then had to be run up against the hull wall. A 24-pounder, on its carriage, weighed 6000 pounds. The gun crew performed this task with ropes and muscle power. After installation of the firing apparatus, the captain of the gun crew, in this case, the commodore, took careful aim. Charlie said her second prayer of the morning.

"Fire."

The white cloud of dirty smoke obscured Charlie's view and burned in her eyes. She blinked and rubbed them until her vision returned. Charlie could see a portion of the damage caused by the skipper's first salvo. A cannon ball of that size could slice through several feet of hard wood. McDonough's aim, deadly accurate, raked the deck of the *Confiance* and destroyed its wheel. Large wooden splinters, flying in every direction, killed and wounded a number of British sailors.

When the roar of McDonough's salvo sounded, the balance of the American fleet fired their artillery. The enemy roared its response. Billowing clouds of smoke appeared everywhere. Until their view became obstructed, the spectators on shore looked on in awe, mesmerized by the sights and sounds of war. The deafening thunder of artillery shook the ground they stood on. Both fleets, now fully engaged, created a constant, ear-shattering series of explosions. The waters of Lake Champlain erupted with violent geysers and churned to a deadly boil. Charlie dared not linger. She scrambled to the powder magazine and retrieved another canister. Several other boys did the same.

She froze in place, below deck, when the *Saratoga* suddenly rocked. The entire ship shuddered. Charlie trembled. Between the explosions, she could hear the sound of men screaming, some in agony, all in fear. When she returned from her second run, more than three dozen sailors lay on the deck. Some motionless and some writhing in pain. Several of the men, mutilated and disfigured beyond recognition, could not hope to survive their wounds. The human body did not fare well in a collision with flying shards of wood. Cast iron cannonballs, pelting the deck like hailstones in a winter storm, systematically severed limbs and heads. One sailor, a victim of a direct hit, lay in two pieces, his body sliced in half.

"Where is he?" Charlie yelled, when she could not locate the commodore.

No one heard her screams. The thunderous sound of cannon fire ringing in her ears made communication, impossible. A small group of sailors, near McDonough's cannon, caught her attention. A midshipman, between explosions, tried to explain. A damaged, spanker boom (the thick mast used for a sail) struck McDonough on the back. He lay unconscious. Several men carried the injured commodore to the hatch. McDonough suddenly regained consciousness.

"No. Bring me back," he ordered.

The commodore rose and returned to his post.

Dr. Briggs and Nathan, surrounded by injured sailors below deck, yelled to be heard over the noise of artillery.

They worked furiously, prompted by the shrieks of at least a dozen men, in agony.

"Take this one next," said Briggs, pointing to a seaman with both limbs severed at the knee.

Nathan jumped to the task, working frantically to stop the bleeding. His tourniquets proved too little, too late. The man groaned no more. Nathan motioned to an orderly, who moved the body to a far end of the room. Brigg's patient, a man with large-wooden splinters in his legs and hips, screamed in agony. The senior surgeon, overwhelmed with the task of removing the projectiles and simultaneously restraining the patient, yelled to Nathan.

"Need some help, here."

But Nathan, in the midst of an amputation, could not leave his operating table. A bosun's mate, delivered below deck with a number of smaller splinters in his body, hobbled to Dr. Briggs' table.

"I'll hold him," he said, laying over the patient's stomach and using his weight to immobilize the badly wounded sailor.

At times, Charlie welcomed a trip to the hatch; the scene, top side, too horrible to watch.

At least three of her fellow powder monkeys lay dead or dying. A "bucket brigade" for the canisters would soon be necessary. Another sailor, his abdomen sliced open by a flying shard of wood, dropped to his knees, fully conscious. He worked furiously to retrieve his bowels from the blood covered deck. Charlie saw several of the man's organs. Two of the crewmembers, judging the man to be just minutes from death, dragged him to the rail and heaved him overboard. Charlie returned to the hatch but not before throwing up.

When she next appeared, topside, Charlie discovered that all of the gun crews abandoned their posts. A fire on deck required everyone's assistance. The enemy's use of "hotshot" (cannonballs heated in a furnace before firing) doubled the damage inflicted by their artillery. The red-hot cannon balls, either smashed the vessel into splinters or started a fire, or both. Charlie, a canister of powder in her hand, stayed well away from the conflagration.

When the commodore emerged from the gang of firefighters, he pointed to his favorite artillery piece and Charlie followed. The enemy's cannon fire, almost constant for the past ninety minutes, appeared to slow. But it did not end. Their next blast struck a sailor in the head. The decapitated mass of bone, brains, and blood struck the commodore squarely in the chest. The grisly projectile hit McDonough with such force that he flew clear across the deck. Momentarily stunned, he scrambled to his feet, brushed the bloody mess from his jacket and returned to his cannon.

Charlie noticed a sharp reduction in the number of *Saratoga's* broadsides. In fact, all but one of the ship's artillery pieces, no longer functioned. McDonough noticed it first. As if reading her mind, McDonough shouted a series of orders. A half-dozen sailors ran in several directions. They retrieved some of the anchors and released others. They also pulled on a series of ropes. As if by magic, the ship slowly began to turn on its own axis. An entire side of McDonough's flag ship, with fourteen, unfired artillery pieces, now faced the *Confiance*. McDonough's previously implemented plan to install "springs" (anchors and lines on both ends of the ship) worked flawlessly. Even before the *Saratoga* completed its winding maneuver, a number of its cannon crews took aim at the *Confiance*. The enemy ship attempted a similar ploy but failed miserably. After a series of devastating cannonades, the *Confiance* struck its colors. The British surrender prompted the remainder of their fleet, to do the same. The British row galleys, however, chose to make a run for it.

When the commodore turned to acknowledge the shouts and cheers of his crew, his jubilation came to a sudden end. His eyes plunged to the deck. There, laying on the blood-covered surface, with a two-foot shard of wood in her chest, lay midshipman Charlie Wheeler. He motioned to several of the men, and they carried Charlie to the hatch.

"Put him over there," shouted Briggs, pointing to Charlie's lifeless body as he finished severing a man's leg.

Nathan, focused on the gaping hole in a man's abdomen, stuffed the stomach cavity with a blood-soaked rag.

"There's nothing more, I can do."

He pointed to a stack of bodies in the far end of the operating chamber and the orderlies took his patient away.

"And I need more sand," said Nathan, slipping and sliding in a greasy pool of blood.

One of the men responded.

"I'll get you some more sand, but can you take him next? It's Charlie."

Nathan's face lost its color. He closed his eyes in prayer, but only for seconds, using a nearby bandage to wipe his surgical table.

"Yes, over here, quickly," said Nathan.

Dr. Briggs, close enough to observe, offered the junior surgeon some advice.

"Very near the clavicle and it's on the right side. Nothing there to damage," said Briggs.

"Yes, Doctor Briggs. He's very fortunate," said Nathan, surprised that he remembered Charlie's "proper" pronoun.

Nathan sliced at her shirt and then her night shirt, with great care. He took pains to leave the white wrap around her chest, unexposed.

"This is going to leave a big hole," he muttered, as he tenderly poked and prodded where wood sliced into flesh.

"Yank it as quickly as you are able. And be prepared to stuff the hole with rags," said Briggs.

Nathan wrapped both hands around the projectile and yanked. The large splinter came free. A loud sucking noise triggered Nathan's gag reflex. He flung the bloody piece of wood to the floor. Nathan reached for the same rag he used to clean the table and pressed hard on Charlie's upper chest. He stitched the wound as best he could and breathed a sigh of relief when the wound stopped oozing blood.

"The commodore wants both of you, topside, now," said a sailor, breathless from his trip to the hold.

Nathan used a strap of cloth to keep the bloody plug, in place. He tied the last knot when Briggs shouted.

"Let's go, doctor. The commodore wants us."

Nathan abandoned Charlie, still unconscious on the table.

McDonough ordered Briggs and Nathan, exhausted and covered in blood, to assist with the evacuation of the wounded.

The two surgeons would go to Crab Island, and remain there, until no longer needed. The row galleys would be used to transport the wounded. No distinction would be made between British and American sailors. All would be given aid and comfort.

Crab Island, human entrails and bodies now washing up on its shores, encapsulated the aftermath of war. Dozens of wounded sailors, some in red, some in blue, came to the island in gunboats and on canvas litters. Jim Sharp, greeted by a red-coated British sentry pacing between the tents, stared in disbelief, but continued his lifesaving duties.

Inside the tent, British doctors worked alongside their American counterparts. The medical teams, desperate to save as many British and American lives as possible, refused to rest. The evidence of more than three dozen amputations and life-threatening wounds could be seen everywhere. A grisly carpet of human entrails, severed body parts, and mutilated corpses covered the ground in each tent. The shrieks of men, undergoing amputation, accompanied the agonizing groans of those who waited for their suffering to end. One way or the other.

Nathan, obsessed with Charlie's injury, forced himself to focus on the endless parade of wounded men, brought to his operating table. Many of his patients would succumb from their wounds, he thought. Charlie may too. The dead, carried on crude litters to a burial ground just south of the tents, went to their final resting place, without pomp or circumstance. At least 100 bodies, some rolled up in blankets, some with clothes only, lay face down in the long trenches. British and American soldiers who just hours ago, fought to the death, now lay side-by-side in eternal peace.

When Sharp passed through the hospital tent, with yet another mutilated sailor, he came to an abrupt halt. The sailor on the opposite end of the litter yelled at him.

"Why are you stopping, Sharp?"

Jim, spellbound by the wounded man on a nearby cot, did not

respond. The unconscious patient he studied, wore a bandage around most of his head. The man's face, despite blotches of what looked like black boot polish, appeared tanned but not dark. He wore a leather sheath at his side, but it contained no hunting knife. And the patient's hair was dark, black and long. Sharp placed his litter on the floor, for a closer look. He reached for the unconscious man's mouth and examined the patient's teeth. Two perfect rows of brilliant white, confirmed the unconscious man's identity. Jim's partner in the litter brigade, grew impatient.

"Come on Sharp."

The former midshipman's eyes drilled into the unconscious man's head. He struggled to control his anger and clenched his fists. Sharp paused. With great deliberation, he reached for the injured man's face, touching the back of his hand to the man's cheek. Although warm to the touch, Sharp did not flinch. After covering the bandaged head with the patient's blanket, Sharp turned to his partner.

"He's dead. We'll take him to the trenches on the way back."

The sailor, unquestioning, followed Sharp to the operating theater and then back to the "dead" man's cot. As they loaded the body onto their litter-turned-bier, Sharp's partner volunteered an observation.

"He's still warm," said the sailor. "Must've died just a little while ago."

"Yup," said Sharp.

They placed the body in the trench, face down and feet pointed east. The two men took a break, Sharp leaning against a tree, his partner off in the bushes, relieving himself. Sharp maintained his vigil until the digging crew made their appearance. Within minutes, Kai Bellamy, alive but unconscious, lay under several feet of dirt, rocks, and debris. Sharp walked away, cursing under his breath.

"I hope you wake up, you bastard."

A delegation of British officers arrived on the *Saratoga* to make their surrender official.

McDonough circled in place, looking for his trusted aide. He cringed, convinced that Charlie did not survive her wounds. Despite his grief, McDonough recalled that, even in war, the vanquished must be shown the utmost of respect. As is custom, British officers, removed their swords from their scabbards. McDonough let his hand rise high into the air.

"Gentlemen, your gallant conduct makes you worthy to wear your weapons. Return them to their scabbards," said the commodore.

When the formal ceremony of surrender ended, McDonough sat at his desk and penned a short note to Secretary of the Navy, William Jones.

"The Almighty has been pleased to grant us a signal victory on Lake Champlain in the capture of one frigate, one brig, and two sloops of war."

A waiting sailor rushed the note to a messenger.

A day and a half later, Nathan returned to the *Saratoga*.

Despite his exhaustion, Nathan climbed the gangplank, intent on seeing Charlie. The ship, not yet cleaned of the blood and gore which characterized the battle of Plattsburgh, did not resemble the war vessel of just two days ago. The greasy deck, still covered with flowing blood, made walking on its slippery surface impossible. Even the barefoot members of the crew, survivors trying to clean the ship, experienced difficulty when walking. Body parts and human entrails covered large portions of the surface.

Nathan slipped and fell twice on his way to the hatch. Once below, he hurried to the operating room. Charlie was gone. Not believing that she could walk out of there, much less climb the ladder through the hatch, he examined every motionless body. They were all cold and none of them even resembled Charlie. His mind raced. He did not see her on the island. She must be somewhere on the ship.

He returned topside, his head swiveling in every direction, as he searched for the wounded woman. Discouraged and fatigued beyond anything he had ever experienced, Nathan collapsed to the deck, his back to a fallen mast. For the first time since the battle, he studied the *Saratoga*. Not a single mast could support even the tiniest of sails. The ship's lower rigging looked like rags, hung out to dry on a series of broken broom handles. The hull itself, contained so many holes from cannon fire, he could not count them. Nathan shook his head in disbelief. His eyes moistened when he realized that Charlie's favorite hiding place, a large stack of crates at one end of the ship, no longer existed, blown to bits by enemy fire.

"She took a tremendous beating."

Despite his exhaustion, Nathan jumped to his feet and spun in the direction of her voice.

Charlie, her hair still streaked with blood and a homemade sling holding the right arm close to her body, looked weak and pale. But she wore a big smile. He searched their surroundings, painfully aware of McDonough's previous admonition. She stepped forward. He did the same.

"I don't care anymore," said Nathan, rushing forward.

He placed his hands on either side of Charlie's blood, streaked face. Tears rolled down their cheeks. He struggled to speak but his voice, choked with emotion, refused to cooperate.

"I thought you were . . ."

He couldn't finish the sentence. Charlie, touched by his concern, put her arms around the doctor and squeezed.

"I'm one of the lucky ones, Nathan. We lost almost fifty men. Even more, wounded."

Nathan closed his eyes.

"Thank God, you're safe."

"Not sure who the surgeon was who patched me up, but he did a pretty good job," she said, stepping back, with a huge grin on her face.

Nathan, laughing as he did so, used his sleeves to wipe the blood from her cheeks but only made it worse. Charlie, always stuffed with the latest intelligence, did not disappoint.

"The British army is also in retreat," she reported. "It's over."

"I heard," said Nathan, reaching for the girl's good hand. "You need to rest, Charlie."

"I've been discharged from the Navy," she said.

"The commodore?" Nathan asked, his jubilant face turning serious.

"Honorably discharged, and at my request."

"Where will you go? What will you do?" he asked.

"I still have a cabin and some land in Isle LaMotte."

Nathan's eyes locked on to hers.

"I have always wanted a medical practice in the country."

Charlie laughed through her tears.

"We could always use another doctor in Vermont."

"Yes, but I want to be *your* doctor," he said, using both hands to grasp her free hand.

Charlie's face lit up. Her lips quivered. Her body shook with anticipation. Nathan continued with his proposal.

"I too will soon be discharged, Charlotte Elizabeth Wheeler. Will you wait for me?" he asked.

"Forever, Dr. Coldwell. Forever."

CPSIA information can be obtained
at www.ICGtesting.com
Printed in the USA
BVHW080051180122
626430BV00001B/21

9 781954 396180